Y.

The Year of the Woman

a&b

The Year of the Woman

JONATHAN GASH

First edition published in Great Britain in 2004 by
Allison & Busby Limited
Bon Marché Centre
241-251 Ferndale Road
London SW9 8BJ

http://www.allisonandbusby.com

10 9 8 7 6 5 4 3 2 1

ISBN 0 7490 8316 6

Printed and bound in Ebbw, Wales by
Creative Print and Design.

Dedication

To the Chinese god Wei Dto, who protects authors'
manuscripts from destruction, this book is
humbly dedicated.

Appreciation

To Mr M.Y. So and Mr Francis Sham,
instructors in Cantonese at the Language School,
Hong Kong University, during my years in the then
Crown Colony of Hong Kong, for their teaching, and to Mr
W.I. McLachlan.

Thanks: Susan.

KwayFay hated losing sleep, but what can you say to the ghost of a grandmother she'd never even met?

"Please, Grandmother," KwayFay whimpered. "I'm sleepy."

"Because I am ghost," said Ghost Grandmother, always sarcasm, "you complain, lazy girl! Lessons won't kill you. Learning Chinese traditions didn't kill me!" Ghost screeched with merriment then, immediately serious, asked, "Did you learn the Calendar of Festivals?"

Last night had been hell with hardly a wink of sleep. Ghost had made KwayFay go over lists of dates, ancestors KwayFay couldn't believe. So many gods, and all of them trouble. Except you had to believe. Ghost Grandmother said so.

"Yes, Grandmother." KwayFay had dozed chanting them to herself in case the old harridan came during the next night. As the crone indeed had, wasting KwayFay's precious sleep.

"You found them interesting, dozy girl?"

"Yes, Grandmother."

Ghost was actually more than Grandmother. She had lived north of Canton City on the great Pearl River, where the sailing junks were too many even for the Emperor himself to count. But KwayFay knew that ghosts went unquestioned, so could get away with – even without – any explanation, very like MaiLing. MaiLing lay on her back with the impossible HC Ho, her revolting boss, atop her even during noon rest when the others in the office could hear his final squawk. Highly embarrassing.

Ghost Grandmother first appeared when KwayFay became twelve, simply suddenly there in the night with the blithe announcement that KwayFay must *never* let her hair be touched on certain days of the month.

"Why, Grandmother?" KwayFay had bleated in alarm, knowing Ghost instantly.

"Calamity follows carelessness!" Ghost Grandmother snapped. That was her first rule, watch who touches your hair at wrong times of the month.

"Don't stupid girls know even *that* nowadays?" Ghost

demanded scathingly. "Now the Emperor is almost fully grown to manhood, all China must learn these things. Modern girls are lazy! It wasn't like that when I was child!" Ghost Grandmother went on about it while KwayFay desperately tried to sleep.

KwayFay immediately knew Ghost was none other than Great-Great-Great-Great (plus possibly even -Great-Great) - Grandmother herself, who had washed clothes in the court of the Provincial Governor of Kwantung Province in the Celestial Empire, a man of many flags. Ever since, Ghost had come, sometimes every night in a single week, rousing KwayFay to learn traditions and festivals of incredible pointlessness and ceremonies of mind-bending dross.

"You like my teaching, lazy girl?" Ghost asked slyly.

"Yes, Grandmother!"

"Lying bitch," the ghost said, the insult making KwayFay gasp in affront. "You thought *maa-maa deiy,* wretched girl! You thought, 'Not so much', that's what! Remember I am ghost and can see thoughts. Now tell me." Ghost thought a moment, humming to herself as she chose, for contrary to what folk assumed, spirits hated silence. "Tell me," Ghost continued, having chosen, "the wedding ceremony of the Chicken Bride Marriage."

"Please, *Ah Poh,*" KwayFay moaned, tears coming even in her doze. Never *Ah Ma,* for that would denote that the ghost was on KwayFay's father's ancestoral side instead of her mother's. Ghosts were lethally particular. Use the wrong mode of address, you'd be for it. She felt like weeping at Ghost Grandmother's theft of her precious sleep.

The ghost settled down to listen. "When given task by Grandmother, Chinese etiquette requires you express gratitude, KwayFay."

"Thank you profoundly, Grandmother," KwayFay said, miserable with Cantonese politeness, wondering how much sleep she had left before she must rise to work. "*Do jeh,*" she repeated, thank you for something given, like stealing a night's sleep was a gift.

She lay on her side on her truckle bed in her hovel, the only sounds those of the South China Sea shushing on the stones in

Sandy Bay and the sighing of the night wind in the bauhinia trees along Mount Davis Road. She did not open her eyes. Why should she, to see nothing?

Each night the mountain side cooled with dramatic swiftness, the wafer thin walls of her squatter shack shaking in the breeze that came swooping off the sea a hundred climbed paces below. All around, similar hovels stuck like crustaceans to the bare mountain's granite and laterite surface, the lantana bushes rustling as the deep blue velvet of night rolled overhead and turned westward to hide before dawn burned up from the ultramarine rim of the South China Sea.

Ghost said contentedly, "Begin!"

"The wedding of a bride when bridegroom is far away," KwayFay said through a thin veil of sleep, "is special."

"Why!" Ghost asked sharply in her cracked old voice.

"Another man standing proxy for husband-to-be confuses Chinese gods. So a living cock stands in for the bridegroom. That is why it is called Chicken Bride Marriage."

"And?"

"First, the bride is carried to the home of her new mother-in-law, in the red chair of marriage."

Ghost sighed. KwayFay thought, Oh, please *please* don't reminisce or I'll get no sleep at all. But Grandmother Ghost was already into nostalgia.

"I saw this often near Shun The. Do you know Shun The? It was so pretty! Girls nowadays have no idea!"

"Then," KwayFay interrupted, trying to get on, "as the bride is set down by her bearers in the courtyard, a living cockerel is cast across the chair!"

KwayFay found herself giggling at the silly image, but humour is dangerous in the presence of a ghost, even if she is your own ancestral grandmother. Ghosts could take umbrage, and then what?

"The relative who catches the cock gets eight-fold luck!"

"It *is* exciting," Grandmother said as if contradicted. "Now tell me: Is it a true marriage?"

"It is a true marriage, Grandmother. All wedding arrangements must be made as if the bridegroom was actually there, and not away in Meihgwok, America, seeking gold for his clan."

"Bad girl!" Ghost cried. "I hate those new names! America is Gau GamSan, the Old Gold Mountain Country. That is how we speak of America, sloppy girl! Remember, New Gold Mountain Country, Australia, has not yet been discovered! Thoughtless girl!"

"I sorry, Grandmother. I am so sleepy I can't concentrate."

"Lazy girl!" The pause did not last. Ghost resumed slyly, "Tell me. If the bridegroom dies before wedding, what then?"

"Then no chicken is required, Grandmother."

"Explain!"

"The bridegroom being dead, his stone tablet takes his place."

"You are not bad," Ghost Grandmother said reluctantly. She hated KwayFay doing well. "And then?"

"Then immediately the stone tablet ritual must follow. The stone tablet is married, instead of dead son."

"Correct! The wedding now?"

KwayFay stifled her anger, for even ghosts grew tired. They tricked you into doing wrong so they could get the upper hand and impose silly penalties. Look at the Wall-Building Ghost, on Mount Davis Road near the Lee Yuen Garden Centre. What a creature *that* was! Malice from start to finish.

"Does Grandmother not mean the betrothal ceremony?" KwayFay asked innocently. "For that comes first, even if both bridegroom and bride are deceased."

"Mind manners, rude girl!" Ghost was annoyed at being caught out.

"In that case the betrothal ceremony must be enacted exactly," KwayFay mumbled through her doze. "The dead bride-to-be is exhumed, and the coffin carried to the dead bridegroom's cemetery."

"Which cemetery?" Ghost Grandmother started to sulk because KwayFay was so good tonight. KwayFay felt proud.

"The cemetery belonging to his ancestral clan, Grandmother!"

"Yes." Ghost stifled a yawn, KwayFay's strategy working. "Did

I ever tell you, lazy granddaughter, that I once did all the arrangements – including food! – for sixteen such weddings? It was in the village of Yan Ling – in Kwantung, of course, by the bend in the river where little Ah Dee drowned on Dragon Boat Festival, before the Emperor Chien Lung ascended the Throne. Substitute children can be bought from that village when a husband's seed is too weak to form babies in his bride's belly."

"And they're so expensive!" KwayFay prompted, knowing the rest of this nonsense, hurrying the ghost along so she could sleep.

"Criminally expensive!" Grandmother tutted and grumbled. "So much dearer buying children from Yan Ling than Toi Shan; the journey's easier though, and you don't need to hire a mule. Children cost the earth nowadays. Don't you find that? And half of them turn out scoundrels. It's all gone downhill. I honestly think the Emperor should be told. Don't you?"

"Yes, Grandmother," KwayFay said, wondering if the sky was now pale over the Lamma Channel. Little sleep time left, the night fast slipping away. "You've already told me all about the puppy."

"That was a terrible business." Ghost drowsily pulled herself together. "A life must be given for a life. That is Chinese etiquette. Barbarians like your English do not know this, being ignorant. A puppydog, or even a cat, must be handed over with the correct purchase money – you can't cheat! – when buying a child from its clan. One thief – Hoi P'ing district, of course; I blame the Governor of Kwantung Province for putting that mad cousin of his in charge, a lunatic who counts butterflies – tried to give me a puppy so sick from worms it died during the feast! Can you believe it?"

"Such treachery!" KwayFay murmured. The ghost would be asleep soon.

Ghost got her words in. "There was trouble about that, I can tell you!"

With relief, KwayFay heard Ghost Grandmother snore. She slept.

***

The sound of traffic woke her, with televisions and umpteen radios in nearby squatter shacks creating an inordinate squalling din. She pulled aside the slab of corrugated tin that formed the seaward wall of her one-roomed shack and glanced out of the ragged hole that was her window.

Hong Kong's mass of squatter huts, cardboard packing cases, ropes, and old tea chests, was crammed on the steep hillside like so many barnacles, hundreds in the early morning sunshine amid the morning smoke. Below she heard the sickening blare of horns. Headaches weren't all ghosts, though many were.

Ships were already grappling in the harbour, American warships in the Lamma Channel blaring out their silly messages to nobody. *Now hear this!* they bawled, as if anybody cared. Distantly she heard the sound of firecrackers, the Flower Girls down Wanchai and Causeway Bay already celebrating the arrival of yet more visiting ships filled with drunken men careless with dollars. She got her laptop computer, still not stolen, from under her truckle, grunting at its impossible weight, and slung it over her back as she prepared to go to the toilet. One day, she might have electricity, if she earned enough money to fund the theft of wires that would enable her to charge her laptop's battery during the night. Perhaps, one day!

Mercifully, her water can was still partly full. She had covered it with plastic against flies and robbers, lodging her shoes on top. She always tied a string from her shoes to her thumbs, against night-stealing thieves. She looked down to the road. A queue had already formed at the water standpipe. She had to hurry.

Carrying her computer and her only towel, she hurried down to wash, preparing herself for the horrid day to come.

Chapter Two

KwayFay's dream was to take her time going to work. Hopeless, considering the frantic journey.

Her choice was frankly shaming: Mount Davis Road, the long uphill walk to the helter-skelter bus. It ran downhill through Sai Ying Pun, past the university where students wore thick glasses and wouldn't take their examinations on any day they saw a stout individual – "fail-low" sounding uncomfortably close to the Cantonese for "fat man." (And, she thought acidly, *they* were the Crown Colony's *intellectuals?*) Or, those swaying clanking tombs of wreckage that were trams past the teeming godowns to Central District.

It was a choice of degradations.

Consider them:

The walk along Mount Davis Road (where the Wall-Building Ghost plotted to get you at its mercy, creepiest ghost ever) eventually took you by the little garden centre overlooking the coal merchants that clung to the cliff face over Sandy Bay. You passed the steep Cape Mansions and St Clare's Girls' School. KwayFay had longed to study there (in fact anywhere), but, being only a street child among scavengers, had worked from the age of six as a water carrier. She paid a clever rich schoolgirl "roof-top money" to teach her after hours. The girl who took KwayFay's precious three Hong Kong dollars said education was claptrap. KwayFay heard three incomprehensible lessons, then used the money she stole for food instead.

Or she could catch the 6B bus that idled at Felix Villas waiting for the downhill sprint through Kennedy Town market, thence along the waterfront to the hopeless tangle of Des Voeux Road and yet more clanging trams as far as Princes Building. Destination! There, the slogging misery of her computer travail waited, ready for her to clerk its mad imaginings called Investments and National Currencies.

The other route was even crazier, a long slow walk to Pok Fu Lam, catching the bus by the Chinese Christian Cemetery for the swirl down Pokfulam Road among the madly angled schools (why so many there? and most of them Christian, God help Hong Kong). Then the crazy chase below the Mologai, that sinister district of evil memory that didn't need ghosts to become wicked.

Very well, Ghost Grandmother, KwayFay reminded herself to say, in case the ghost demanded to know what she'd been thinking on the way to work: *The Mologai is Hong Kong Island district of lepers and whores, of Triads and Hongs and other secret societies, thieves galore who crowd each other to death and worse. There!*

KwayFay worked at the Brilliant Miracle Success Investment Company. The office stood on the sixth floor because the owner HC Ho and his hopeless gambling-addicted wife who called herself Linda, English fashion, could not afford the lucky eighth. Eight of anything was lucky. The sixth floor was dire, which was the reason the Brilliant Miracle Success Investment Company was gunge. KwayFay smouldered with rage about it. She didn't dare tell Grandmother Ghost because she'd never let her forget she worked as a slave to incompetents, men of no name, *mo meng*, chief duckegg being Business Head, the proprietor HC Ho.

KwayFay alighted from the lift, lip curling in disdain. What was the good of working for a Business Head, that all-important *See-Tau* who owned and hired and fired and, on occasions, mauled, yet who was too thick to really go after money and make the firm boom? The air conditioning was functioning, with its coughing and whirring, thank heavens.

Used to her cramped tin shack, the office cool was luxury after the impossible heat of the morning journey into Central. She reached her alcove – HC called it a pod, thinking the word trendy, which showed him up for a fool.

She set up her own laptop – no telling anyone what that instrument had cost her, and no thinking it either in case Ghost Grandmother got wind of *that* little purchase. Mr HC Ho and his eagle-eyed wife *Tai-Tai* Linda Ho and the rest would know she arrived, by some miracle always on time. She went to the Ladies and there had a decent wash. The luxury of endless water, from a tap where she didn't have to pay some eagle-eyed wart with a knife! Hoodlums collected money for a Triad, bragging with tattoos and smoking English cigarettes to show they had connections.

In a loo cubicle she dressed in the work outfit she always carried with her. Two layers of plastic wrappers, then a plastic shopping bag and, next to the clothes against the all-seeping humidity of Hong Kong, her one cotton towel. Different shoes, a decent *saam*, not too revealing because of the swine HC Ho. She bagged her rubbishy travelling clothes and emerged looking quite like a beautiful butterfly, though not too proud because some ghosts had thousand-league eyes, including one she didn't care to name because it made her shiver.

And stepped into the direct gaze of *See-Tau* himself, waiting outside the Ladies checking how long she'd been in the toilet. He did that.

"*Jo san*, HC. Good morning."

"Morning, KwayFay. I want you for a minute."

"If it's about the American Denver-Blorkence prospects, they're done. I only need to format them out."

She had finished them on her laptop. Her one perk was charging her battery in the office, though only when HC was at his noonday grope in the store cupboard with MaiLing or some other girl wanting a favour. Otherwise he would make her pay for the electricity, HC being a right pirana. She lied that she bribed the local Mount Davis Triad's fixer for one light bulb and a yard of flex in her shack. In the way of some lies (but only some) it wasn't altogether true, though it stopped him charging her a dollar a minute like he had fined KT Man, a Hong Kong University economics graduate too mean to buy new shoe laces. Instead, KT inked office string and tied his shoes like that.

"Good, right."

HC's spectacles were bottle thick, his balding head shining with sweaty anxiety, damp spreading from armpits into his waistcoat. She followed him to his office, embarrassed by her plastic shopping bag. Shame never lacked fame; she was so obviously a clerk from the squatter areas, the plastic shopping bags her hall-mark.

He sat wringing his hands, looking out into Des Voeux Road and Statue Square. He seemed desperate for help. She chose to make him sweat all the more.

"If it's about centralising those South-East Asian Tracker Funds, HC, I kept the data."

"KwayFay. That personality profile. Remember?"

"A while back? Yes, *See-Tau*."

"That clothing shambles in Sheung Wan?"

KwayFay nodded. She hadn't been invited to seat herself, even though she suddenly knew this would be a big moment. She stared at this liquidising oaf and felt a glow. With a fortune in cosmetics and clothes she'd conquer the world, the whole globe being for ever western. Why else did those unspeakable Japanese girls, always on TV, pay surgeons to do away with their eye folds so they'd look American, at a cost of four thousand US dollars for the two eyes? They took advantage, and were to be despised, spending money like water. She refused to feel that twinge of envy.

"*A!*" she said, suddenly remembering. "I apologise, HC. How is he getting on?"

She was conscious of two other clerks walking past at a slow stroll. She could see them through the door glass, working out what HC had her in for. Promotion and sacking was always in the air. HC had twelve employees in the company, making fourteen to be paid from the trickle of money that came from selling guesses about investments. Firms ought to know better than buy HC's blunders. He was driven by his wife Linda's need to gamble in Causeway Bay, a right *do-toh,* gambler. She would gamble her last catty of rice.

"It's been a disaster, KwayFay."

HC crumpled. KwayFay watched him sag.

"No!" she gasped, as if overcome by the fool's plight, whatever it might be.

"True." He swivelled in his chair. He spent all his time staring wistfully at great motors that stormed eastwards to Wanchai and

Causeway Bay. She knew why, as did *Tai-Tai* Linda with her gimlet eyes and pinched gambler's mouth. "I have to pay money because of it, KwayFay."

This was serious, she thought with a thrill. HC *never* paid money. Risk made her pleasure exquisite, except it was the risk of losing her job. Sex was nothing to the excitement of seeing her boss in anguish. At least, not the sex she'd had so far, which wasn't much.

"Remember the profile you did for me?"

"I remember." She had mostly forgotten, but who could admit such a thing? She remained standing, her plastic bag now a definite weight. Her fingers would make a slow start today. They often got cramp after an hour's clicking and tapping. It wouldn't happen if she could afford better food. "I should have done better, HC," she said in pretended shame, her way of goading him to more revelations.

"No, KwayFay." Tears shone in his eyes at the thought of lost money. "I should have listened to you."

She decided on more self-abasement, show him what he'd missed by not taking her advice. "I ought to have made a better summary."

HC swivelled some more. He couldn't even make up his mind which way to do that, right or left, and him the *See-Tau*. She watched him with contempt, on her face a sorrowing smile. Showing compassion was woman's work, *ge*!

"Remember what I said when you told me?"

"You are so kind, HC." She wondered whether to make her eyes go all misty, like that favoured English actress did in that desert film with such superb effect, the ugly conniving bitch. Or would it be over the top?

"You said he was a scoundrel. I should have listened."

"I hope I did not presume," she said meekly. She'd recently read a Jane Austen book, interminable dull phrases stodging up endless pages, where they never cut to the chase but waffled on with hardly a mention of money in the entire book. One or two of the yawnsome authoress's catch-phrases actually caught. KwayFay always found herself trying them out.

"No, KwayFay. I am frankly impressed."

She murmured, eyes downcast but still tempted by misty, "*Yao sam*." You have heart. That was a laugh. Praise idiots, listen to the wise, as ghosts always said. Good Cantonese advice.

"You saw my dilemma, KwayFay."

Now she remembered. She had power! She thought it over.

The problem that odd day had been a datum default, something KwayFay took personally because data records were her province. She had shrieked down the phone at the Philippines office, causing much laughter among colleagues who had overheard with their bat ears. As humble keeper-of-information clerk, KwayFay still smarted over it.

"All very well laughing like fools," she'd told her friend Alice Seng bitterly when it was all over, "but they criticise me when the share prices go crazy and there's no projection on a stock."

"Sorry." Alice was still laughing over their *heung pin* tea. "Your face! You looked like you could kill her!"

"I could, easily," KwayFay said bitterly. The fuss died down.

She did not mind talking of death as much as other Cantonese. She never told people she talked to Ghost Grandmother. They would think her mad. She'd get sacked, and have to go back to scavenging along Hong Kong's waterfronts and thieving, as she'd done ever since being a little no-family girl running wild.

She now knew over thirty rituals, thanks to Ghost Grandmother, each painstakingly learned by heart over restless nights. The more she learned the less scared she became, which was truly odd because as a little girl she'd been timidity itself, the butt of all the other Cockroach Children's ribald jeering.

That day was when HC had entered her pod, polishing his spectacles and sweating, asking for KwayFay to come to the reserve office. It was a place for storing records, old computer systems and notes about employees. It was also a place for HC's clumsy fondles, given half a chance.

In there, though, on that strange day there had been no funny business, just a frightened bleat for her advice. It had astonished KwayFay.

"You clerk all our data, KwayFay. You store systems."

"Yes, HC." What else would a lowly data storage clerk do? She did not know many men who were also cretins, for all men did something vigorously weird, that being the way of the male gender. She gazed at HC almost with admiration for being a world-record fool.

"Even when the others throw data out?"

This was the office joke. "Yes, HC. I store all."

Had she done wrong? More importantly, were English tax officials in Government breathing down his neck? Was he hoping past data was crumbled, and no facts left for Government accountants to pick over?

"Keeping records is good!"

She bridled. If he was about to start joking like the others . . .

"Is it some American system, the one you use?"

She went guarded, in case she'd inadvertently blamed some shifty friend of his or, worse, some gambling lady friend who went to Happy Valley Races with his sow of a wife.

"I have those also. And Chinese." She laughed apologetically, as most locals did at things ancestral, so hopelessly dud in this modern world, putting her hand over her mouth to cover her teeth. "Old Chinese systems. *Ho gau.*"

He cleared his throat. Puzzled, she watched him for clues.

"Do your records say what decisions to make?"

"Yes, HC," KwayFay said firmly, sealing her fate. What else could she say? "Some are extremely reliable," she added, hedging a little in case he doubted her value.

"Are they!" His gleaming head nodded eagerly. She felt a new strength, giving him the answers he wanted. "Old Chinese give definite yes or no?"

"Indeed, HC!"

"What sort of questions, KwayFay?"

"Put in a definite question, it answers."

"Good, good." Still he remained abstracted. "KwayFay, this person I'm thinking of. Some people say employ him. Others say don't."

"Is it important?"

"Of course it's important, stupid girl!" he'd shrilled, then collected himself and tried to smile. It was a gruesome gern. "Yes. Very."

"Shall I ask one of the modern data systems, HC?"

She rattled off the three names of the American personal selection programmes, then gave him South African and two English. At each, HC grimaced and explained. He'd used those. Each was dazzlingly efficient but only left you with the guesswork you started with.

"There is only one other," KwayFay said, getting the drift at last. "Ancient Chinese. It takes," she added in a fit of inventiveness, "twice as long as modern western ones. I installed it at my own expense on my laptop computer."

"It's in your computer?"

KwayFay did the embarrassed laugh she was good at. "Encrypted, of course." Would HC offer to pay extra?

"Could you use it, test this person for me?"

"Yes." She readied herself. "Please do not tell me his name or anything personal about him. Old Chinese system requires no guesses, just describe. Nothing else."

In the crummy store room, he spoke about some relative. She listened as haltingly he'd described a young man.

She asked about the possible candidate's forehead, breadth of skull, his eyes, shape of his mouth, ears, anything at all, much of it invented nonsense, until her head was spinning. Drying up, she coined desperate questions she hoped would sound mystical, like was his face sometimes very different depending on his moods? Did he prefer different colours? She asked if this mysterious applicant had a lucky number, and other suchlike drivel. She lost track and found herself asking questions she'd already put. The young man was maybe in his close family. Nothing could be worse than next-of-kin trouble. She'd heard that, though secretly she longed for kin of her own. Such trouble must be wonderful. Why did people not know their plights were lovely?

An hour later she was allowed to work in solitude. Even urgent work was cleared away.

The office respected her for it. Clearly HC was on some

investment fiddle. Maybe, the entire office thought hopefully, some new tax dodge would bring in a bonus for all! Her friends admired her. Alice thought KwayFay was going to get a salary rise.

At the console on that odd day, KwayFay dozed. Ghost Grandmother had come into her head out of the blue and told her how to learn to trust people.

"The Water Mirror is very ancient. Of course Cantonese, for all other provinces of China are second-rate. Canton Water Mirror is best."

"Yes, Grandmother," KwayFay had muttered inwardly on that fateful afternoon.

"Ancient Water Mirror teaches," Ghost went on, her shrill voice making KwayFay's head ring, "fourteen types of human beings exist. Therefore it is true. You learned how to use water mirror, lazy girl?"

"Yes, Grandmother. Fill bronze Kwantung bowl with water to knuckles. Rub wet fingers round rim. Water piles up in a great cone in centre, like a candle. Ask question of the balancing water. Look in water mirror, see answer."

"Good. Some people are obvious: Ox, Deer, Crane, Dragon, Tiger, all those people are easy. It is in the person's features. I've always liked the Chi Lin, because he borrows strength both from Crane and Dragon, and becomes at least Deputy Assistant Provincial Governor, with many banners."

"Which is worst, *Ah Poh*?" KwayFay murmured in her office doze.

"You have three," Ghost Grandmother said, pleased at being asked. "Snake persons are untrustworthy. The Eagle also; has ferocious temper. *Lu Ssu*, the bird person, even worse, for it has feminine features and walks too lightly for a man. Who can trust such a person? Only another *Lu Ssu*!"

"I'm unsure, Grandmother, never having divined a person before for my *bosi*."

"Bad girl," Grandmother whispered, because other workers were trying to walk near KwayFay, inquisitive to know what she was up to, dozing and mumbling when she ought to be slogging to save the firm income tax they could divide up among themselves. Her screen was covered with meaningless numbers. KwayFay always made them up, as a precaution whenever she felt a drowse coming on. "No borrowed English words when speaking to Grandmother. Say *See-Tau* or *Louhbaan*, proprietor, as Chinese speaker should."

"Sorry, Grandmother. Which shall I tell him?"

"Snake," said Ghost with a cackle.

Snake! Untrustworthy snake, for a promotion?

At the end of the hour, HC fetched her into his office, closing the door on everybody.

"Well, KwayFay? Do I employ him?"

"I have answer," KwayFay said carefully, searching his face. "I consulted ancient Chinese system. It says he is untrustworthy. Do not employ him."

HC wrung his hands.

And now he came saying it had all gone wrong. KwayFay's heart sang.

"You see, KwayFay," HC said, swivelling helplessly in his chair, "the man is my wife's cousin."

"I understand, HC," KwayFay said, merciless with her warm convivial smile.

"My wife's elder brother wanted him to be a buyer above Sheung Wan. You know Ladder Street?"

The Mologai, KwayFay thought with apprehension. "You mean by the Man Mo Temple?"

HC actually winced. "He made mistakes. I incur payment."

"I am sorry, HC." She wasn't. He'd gone against her advice.

"I didn't heed what you said, KwayFay." He looked up at her with sheep's eyes. "I should have listened to you. You were right. The carpet emporium is bankrupt. I must pay."

Fear chilled her. She was afraid to ask the only question that now mattered. He spoke on in a low moan.

"My backers made me confess I had had the right advice but disregarded it."

Wiping his forehead with a handkerchief, he stared out at the traffic lights, moving his head every time they changed.

"They want your advice, KwayFay."

"Who?" she asked blankly. Advice for what?

"I explained how correct you were, and how you arrived at the correct answer."

"Who?" She was now badly frightened.

"Who knows how to use an ancient Chinese system nowadays, with things as they are in Hong Kong? Nobody, except phoney necromancers and tourist hackers in the Lantern Market by the Macao ferry."

"I can't," she wailed. It was true. The People's Republic of China was going to send armies to govern Hong Kong. The Handover would take place when Great Britain's Treaty ended. Ghosts, spirits, Chinese traditions, were so much mumbo-jumbo. That was China's decree. You would get the death penalty, or ridiculed into starvation.

"You can, KwayFay." He'd gone quite pale. "Or the firm goes down. I haven't enough to repay them. They were the backers of all my wife's elder brother's textile firms."

"*Tai-Tai* Ho's firms?" KwayFay said blankly. "Just for cloth?"

"It's more than – " He stopped shouting and forced out, quieter, "It's much more. And it's not cloth. Don't you understand?"

"No, HC."

"Think," he commanded harshly, checking his watch. He was always doing that because his motor was parked in a time zone in Ice House Street. He kept getting fined, every morning the same policeman. That's what came of pretending he was a high-flying stock broker in Ice House Street's stock exchange, when any idiot could follow the Hang Seng Index. Why not use the City Hall and pay the legit parking fee? Because he was a chiseller, that's why.

"To repay your debts, HC?" she asked, putting it as it was. Evasion was a rat in the rice.

"To keep our jobs, KwayFay," he said harshly. "I had to tell them you can prophesy."

"Me? Who?"

"Stop saying that!"

"O!" she said, meaning that she suddenly saw clearly, though she was shaking.

"Yes." He felt in his pockets for another handkerchief but finally had to use his sleeve, his nape and face running with sweat. It was disgusting. Even squatter children never did that. She had only resorted to wiping herself in that way when a Cockroach Child. Even Christian nuns in their impossible thick garb only ever used a folded handkerchief to dab at their upper lip. "Yes, KwayFay. They want you to advise."

"I can't, HC!"

"You have to, KwayFay. It is like from an Emperor." He faced her, would have cried real tears if he'd any body fluids left in him after so much melting into his crumpled stained suit, great Business Head that he was. "Guide them right. Understand?"

She nodded, throat too dry for speech.

"If you tell them wrong," he went on, "they will think I've taken some bribe. Or they'll assume I'm being vengeful, wanting them to make the wrong decision. They would . . . they would come for me. And for you!" He added the last with a kind of pathetic hope, we're in this together, the way she imagined, so wistfully, that children spoke to each other when teachers brought them to the front of the playground for punishment. She used to watch the English children, her face pressed to the wire mesh, at the school playground in Glenealy Infant School, wishing she was one.

KwayFay wondered if she could borrow enough to escape to Taiwan, except that would be hopeless, for where on earth was there beyond reach of the Triads? Nowhere.

Nothing but misery today. She wondered for a moment who the defaulting ex-employee was, for she had never seen HC's wife's cousin, the fool who put them all in this terrible quandary. She shelved the question. He no longer mattered. That was Hong Kong's way with failures.

She left HC's office, put a brave face on in front of everybody and resumed work in her pod while all the others gave her sly looks, signalling each other, guessing good or bad, lucky or unlucky.

She said nothing, not even to Alice Seng, wondering when the bad men would come to ask their questions that she had to guess right.

Chapter Three

To a street urchin terror had been avoidable. Now it was back. The more she thought the worse her plight seemed. She was sure HC Ho meant the Triads. Her boss was shaking with fear when she left the office buildings for her noon break. London's Stock Exchange was barely alive at this hour, Japan as usual screaming alarms, its Nikkei Index on the wobble and KT in Statistics vomiting in the men's room from panic, complaining he'd eaten something raw the night before.

KT imitated Elvis Presley at the Club in Easy Street with some Wuhan tart called Grace, kidding himself he was a high flyer. With KT, every gripe was "something in the food." Yesterday it was *ngaw-paa*, the beefsteak; today it would be *gow-haa*, the fat crab they flew to Kai Tak from Australia. Yet KT never even ate, depending for sustenance on *bey-jao*. Any old beer would do. He loved San Miguel, in the hopes that alcoholic elation would carry him to success. He'd been told "Drink more!" by a necromancer down the Lantern Market where his father sold sandals to tourists at twelve times the Hong Kong price. Quite honest, all office staff agreed, because twelve was the fabled magical Number Eight plus half that again, which only proved how fair extortion could be, when properly defined.

She used to like KT, once had almost let him work into her on a date in a shabby cinema in Kowloon, then a near-erotic maul on some staircase – but that was when she was new to the firm. She'd been astonished the way he reached ecstasy groping her breasts. She remembered thinking, What on earth's he doing *that* for? What was this breast business all about? Until then she'd thought breasts of no account, simply there like the Peak District or the Motorola sign reflected in the Kowloon side torpid waters of Hong Kong harbour.

No, definitely no more KT. And no more submitting when HC did his heavy-breathing grope. She'd once had a share from one of Alice's cousins – that was the way she thought of sex, a share of something for brief gain – and was amazed to find her palm filled with a creamy ejaculation in a cinema (re-run of *The Sound of Music* in Wanchai, the gazebo scene where Captain von Trapp kisses Maria). She'd used her handkerchiefs on that occasion, no less than ten cents for two down Port Stanley market, scandalous. The gruesome incident taught her to take two tissues in future, in case. For her, kissing was a problem. Anything oral she found far too laborious. Maybe you needed a bedroom behind a locked door, a building of high rent (not in Happy Valley, either) to carry kissing off? She knew from the blue films off Nathan Road – she'd seen seven; might she go for a lucky eighth, learn something? – what they did, but how did one lead into it? She didn't trust virginity. You were dispossessed when you asked gods for things. You were no bargainer if you hadn't been broken in. You started off cheap. A virgin, you were a no-sale person. Virginity was a nuisance, like an unwanted blemish, a sort of mole eyelid that was an irritant when you blinked, so best got rid of. She hadn't, though she'd tried twice.

She went to sit in Statue Square, boldly racing to a stone edge and hating the Philippino women who got in her way, thousands of them chattering like colourful starlings. The People's Republic of China would soon make them all go home and good riddance . . . but only maybe. KwayFay liked differences. Except this new problem was a serious difference, a risk. Had she been talked into it by Ghost Grandmother? She couldn't remember.

It felt bad. Like when she'd realised with terrible finality that she, alone of everybody in Hong Kong, had no ancestors. Some Cockroach Children, skulking tribes of street scavengers, actually knew their own names, ages, parents even. She was so envious.

Alone, she watched people emerge from offices. They risked life and limb to cross the road as Tram No. 70 to Shaukeiwan intimidated hordes of pedestrians with its ting-tinging and growling clamour. It was a scene made for barbarism, as befitted a British Crown Colony established back in the 1840s by scruffy sailors wading ashore in Repulse Bay. Yet it was brilliant, for Hong Kong owed nothing yet owed everything, and also owned nothing yet owned everything. Why else could America, that

omnipotent giant, come cap-in-hand, begging this dot of a place
to restrict its manufactures because the USA suffered? Hong
Kong laughed a lot at things like that.

She was hungry. Already her hour was eroded by silly
thoughts. She allowed herself six Hong Kong dollars a day for
food, nearly a whole American dollar! She'd brought a plastic
bottle of water, having filled it in the office. No costly Coca Cola
for KwayFay, despite her need.

The hot rice street vendor was a scarecrow. He moved swiftly
on his bicycle with the elastic bounce of the coolie under loads
slung on a bamboo yoke. She admired his knack, pedalling baskets of hot food on poles, among dense traffic.

She queued, third in line, her stomach churning unpleasantly at
the aroma from his steaming baskets.

Today, he had the ubiquitous *jap-seuy*, the equivalent of the
English bubble-and-squeak. Tempting, but money was always a
problem.

She asked for plain boiled rice in a foil box. It would do. She
carried her own chopsticks, and ate the food leaning against the
end post in Statue Square, her place having been stolen by numer-
ous Philippino women. Not wanting to be shamed, surreptitiously she brought out a piece of foil and unfolded it, placing her
secret strip of boiled green vegetable on the rice, to make a lunch
she could be respectably seen with.

Then she noticed the man.

He was standing smoking a cigarette at the corner as if waiting
for someone. Taxis dashed, wheels shrilled, trams clanked, pedestrians rushed, but the shrivelled man looked steadily in her direction. Face of a walnut, clothes of a star, watches to die for glittering on each wrist, stones of higher reflectivity than diamond
showing he was at least partly phoney yet composite, in the way
of shopping malls financed by different companies without a
common theme. He was calm, absurdly so. Oddly, people
avoided him. Usually, Kennedy Town to Quarry Bay, you were
hard put to walk a step without being nudged, elbowed, shoved,
impeded. Not this man. He stood in ominous serenity, as if the
populace conspired to leave him alone.

Perhaps they felt an emanation of threat? She noticed a young clerk bump into him and immediately withdraw with nodded acceptance. Obeisance? The man drew on his cigarette. The ash stayed intact! He wore sunglasses that made hollows of his eyes. He wore a hat, almost unique except for tourists off some cruise ship at the Ocean Terminal.

He looked at her, still as a stork. Waiting for her to finish her meal, perhaps? Were Triad threat-men so polite?

KwayFay drank from her bottle, replaced the cap, slipped it into her bag and wrapped her chopsticks away. The foil container she always took back to the office, making sure it was seen, as defiant proof that she'd eaten a meal more expensive than any hawk-eyed observer might assume. It showed them that she was doing quite well for herself, thank you. Even if she had no man, she could eat like the rest. She moved off, deciding not to see the spy, and was almost in the building when he touched her elbow.

"Come, *Siu-Jeh*." He said Little Sister as though she were a shop assistant and he about to buy something. "I give you a lift."

"Me?"

"The taxi can only wait so long." He was so calm. How did people be calm?

"*See-Tau* is expecting me at work."

"We expect you more."

"I might get the sack."

"Impossible." So calm, that "impossible". Others would know this man represented others who were calmer still.

For a moment she stood in the rescuing bliss of air-conditioning, then reluctantly went back into the street. She felt little desperation, just her familiar sense of loss. A taxi was parked and held up a tram, several bicycles, a column of motors. All waited with unusual serenity, so weird. For her? No, for this calm man.

He extinguished his cigarette. She settled in the worn leather seat. He sat away from her and didn't need to tell the driver the destination. They drove to the Vehicular Ferry.

"You take me to *Gao Lung,* across to Kowloon?" she asked timidly, wanting friends – had she any, for events on this scale? – or anybody to see her, take the taxi's number, stop the ferry because of a *dai-fung*, typhoon, coming across the South China Sea.

He said nothing. Was being calm boring? She envied him his tranquillity. Perhaps it was all show, just as a woman, dressed for an occasion and looking serene, might feel her heart thumping as her reception neared.

They crossed the harbour and in Kowloon took a series of turns. She tried seeing where the detours led: hateful Jordan Road itself, where she had stolen food so often when six, seven, eight years of age. Then Nathan Road with drifters looking for girlie bars that would charge them $800 for entry and another $1,000 for a girlie to sit with and drink the coloured waters, to report back home that they'd had a good time.

Tsim Sha Tsui, with its charging pedestrians and streams of motors and buses, shops glittering like one giant elongated crystal, seemed to be the destination. The taxi turned in behind Chungking Mansions, the cramped tourist ghetto of which the whole world knew, at 30, Nathan Road, dormitories with cockroach-infested landings stacked off malodorous stairwells. The streets grew more louring, shoddier. Twice the taxi ignored one-way signs, oncoming vehicles meekly backing away. The man twice took out a cigarette and each time put the smoke away unlit. The taxi driver never once checked the rear-view mirror, another first.

"Here, Little Sister."

She alighted. The narrow street was new to her. Had they re-crossed Nathan Road, to finish up near the Bird Market? Or near the huge tented Jade Market, where she might be able to get an apple, some orange juice? She felt quite dizzy.

The man didn't pay the taxi. It drove away with a screech of tyres as if yelping at its liberation.

He led into a hallway. Two grubby vendors shifted their cardboard panels of Rolex and Swatch lookalikes, eyes downcast as the man walked past. He made a gesture to a small bicycle, move it, and a hawker dragged it outside. KwayFay edged past up the stairs. The man was fidgety now, clicking worry beads and humming under his breath. He was afraid. KwayFay knew fear.

Cockroaches scuttled. The place stank.

A door opened on the second landing. Two men were seated in a pleasant room. A troubling aroma of antiseptic made her eyes water.

"Sit down."

There was only one chair. KwayFay placed herself in it, clutching her handbag with its chopsticks, empty foil, her dollars for tomorrow's street meal.

The two men were so different. One was a transparent threat-man, tense, young and full of aggression. The other was hugely fat, middle-aged, his features shiny with a constant beaming grin she instantly distrusted. He hugged a black ledger. They wore western suits. The bulbous man had appalling teeth, all corrugations and brown stubs, and wheezed as he spoke.

"I am Ah Min. Have you heard the name?"

"No, *Sin-Sang*."

"Do you know why you're here?"

"*Mh ho yisi*." She truly had no idea. HC's garbled explanation had told her nothing, but was this anything to do with HC?

"Ghosts? I know nothing about ghosts."

Except of course for Ghost Grandmother, and that was beyond human conversation. The mad thought crossed her mind that some Triad man might be a relative who shared her nocturnal lessons with long-dead Grandmother. Like listening in on a broadcast? Yet this older man looked vaguely Shanghainese, as did many from the east side of Central District on Hong Kong. "Little Shanghai", the indigenous Cantonese called that place of sandwiched families and horizontal forests of washing projecting on bamboo poles from windows. She had no Shangainese relatives. Who had? she thought nastily. No Cantonese would admit to it anyway.

"But you guess – " the younger man began angrily, only to pale in terror as the other lifted a hand. Silence was prolonged. The senior almost looked at him but didn't turn his head.

The younger man mumbled an apology, using the *pay-yan* term for himself to show humility.

"Profound apologies, Min *Sin-Sang*."

The boss waited to some satisfying count on an inner scale of horror, then addressed KwayFay. Both men kept glancing at a vast wall mirror to their left as if at an invisible observer.

"Can you kill?"

KwayFay felt her cheeks go grey and could not speak.

"Let me be clear. Can you predict death?"

"No, *See-Tau*."

"You told HC of a man who would be late."

"Late?" KwayFay bleated in panic. Had she? Who? She'd thought she was here because of someone in a carpet warehouse.

"For Happy Valley, the horse races. HC went to meet a friend. They were to gamble. You told HC that you'd taken a message from his friend who was going to be late."

"I did?" She struggled back over the office's chaotic entanglements. To her relief something came to mind.

"Ah, yes, First Born. I remember."

It had been three months before. She had been working through a London broker's instructions about a Tokyo transfer through Sydney, Australia, when she had come on suddenly, her menses as ever taking her by surprise. She'd made a run for the loo. HC interrupted her flight with some diatribe – if this man rings take a message, if that person calls say I'm out, HC's usual nonsense.

She remembered telling HC a lie, swiftly invented.

"Somebody rang just now, said he'll be late."

And made it just in time, leaving HC flummoxed. When she finally emerged he had left the office, to her relief.

That hadn't quite been the end of it. He called her in next morning, a strange look on his face. Sweating, every split second adjusting the air-conditioning, doing his irritating finger-snapping ritual and jumping when the phone went. He grilled her about her made-up message for almost an hour. It was weird. During the session some new Englishman, an arrival so recent his face was still not sun-scarlet, dropped in from an investment company beyond the Hang Seng Bank, and had gone away baffled by HC's stutteringly inept answers. As he left, he'd given KwayFay a look that spoke volumes: And this Colony is a preeminent trader with blokes like your Business Head?

Several times during that puzzling interview, the distressed HC had gone over the phoney message. Distraught, she'd had to stick to her lie, agreeing that, no, it might not have been HC's friend phoning himself. No, she'd never seen his friend. To keep the lie consistent – essential for lies – she stayed definite. No, the man gave no name. With so many people in and out bringing orders, requests, checking on Unit Trust sales halfway across the world, London brokers forever on the phone, investment urgency across International Time Zones, how on earth could she pick out one memory among so many?

In the end HC let her go, but he'd made mistake after mistake all week. Twice he'd hidden from unexpected visitors, scared out of his wits. He'd done exactly the same once, when the US dollar exchange rate changed. KT vomited all that week because the American Federal Reserve suddenly did a policy switch. It could be counted normal office behaviour.

Except now this man's questions about her lie.

He was waiting.

"I needed to go to the bathroom," she explained, embarrassed. "HC stopped me. I was hurrying." The man gestured, get to it. She babbled on, "I hadn't time to stand and talk. I invented that somebody had phoned, said they would be late."

"Who?"

"I told HC a man."

She tried to quilt up a truth to fit the occasion, so the man would let her go. She narrated through HC's interrogation. Ah Min listened. He must have had the features of a cherub when young, like babies on those terrible Christian Christmas cards printed in Taipei, so much drossy colour, so little fact.

"How did HC seem?"

"He was afraid, First Born."

She embellished this a little, making much of HC's edginess, how he'd been unable to sell a single thing to the Englishman from the finance company up Des Voeux Road. The younger man facing her recovered his composure, filled out and lost some toxins.

Ah Min said something she didn't quite catch. The young man ingratiated himself by laughing too much at the remark, nodding and saying, "Yes, yes!" too many times.

"Do you know why HC was afraid?"

"No, *See-Tau*."

Clever; KwayFay saw the manoeuvre almost as the man spoke. He must already know exactly what questions HC had asked her that morning. It was the knight's move in chess. You tally up rectitude, answer by slow answer. How many stock-investment truths did one frank lie relate to? It was the vital question in commerce. She'd created a computer scheme for it once, and been terribly disappointed to learn later some man long since dead had done it much earlier in England before computers were even invented.

She waited. Here it came.

"Did he not tell you?"

"No, *See-Tau*."

"If you can not kill and cannot predict death, Little Sister, then how did you know that a man would be late for a meeting you did not know about?" He leant forward from the sofa, his shoes squeaking as they bent with his feet. She realised how troubled he was. And, in turn, she.

"I do not know, First Born. I made the message up. I had to go to the toilet urgently."

"Why did you make up *that* message?"

"I do not know. HC mentioned a message, so I said whatever came into my head." She looked from one face to the other. They were full of scepticism, the younger man's hooded eyes disbelieving.

"And when you came out of the Ladies, HC had gone. Where to?"

"I do not know. The races? He once owned something at Happy Valley, somebody told me a share in a horse." She knew never to volunteer information, but fright made her garrulous. "HC's wife bets on horses."

"Which?" The younger man clarified impatiently, "That day. Which race?"

"I don't know!" KwayFay cried desperately.

Ah Min gestured for silence.

"You made up a lie?"

Over and over the same thing, their glances at the big wall-mirror more frequent still.

"Why lie? Why not the truth? Why didn't you say you needed the toilet?"

"People don't say that."

"But they do. In films, cinemas, offices and factories all over Hong Kong. It's normal."

"I just lied. I don't know. I'm sorry if I did wrong. I needed – "

"Tell me about choosing employees."

This time KwayFay knew exactly and told him everything, how HC had come to believe in her silly old Chinese guessing scheme.

He listened attentively and this time the younger man had the sense not to interrupt. She didn't like men's eyes to be so intent that their gaze never wandered to her legs or her shape. The one called Ah Min was inert to gender. To such a man, events were only affects. Which meant she was in the presence of craziness, like zany old Cantonese films without consequence. She was among madnesses, not knowing where one ended and the next began. Her head swam. She began to feel ill.

She told of every guess she had ever made to do with investments, employees. Scraping the barrel, she explained schemes she'd coined for HC to ruminate over, suppositions she'd told him as truths, half-truths, near-untruths, fibs to which she'd felt briefly partial and fables she'd dredged up from sheer imagination simply to get her boss HC out of the way while she got on.

"Get on with what?"

"Work, *Sin-Sang*."

"What work?"

"London brokers are terrible people, First Born. They give you no time to do what they've rung about. They all use the same words."

"What words?" They quivered with excitement.

"Like when you say the Hang Seng hasn't come in yet because

of GMT and the USA time zones. They say *Work round that*, as if we can do it before everybody else. It's an office joke. We say to each other, *Don't shunt it*, okay? And we laugh."

She paused. They didn't know humour, despite the fat man's constant beam. Without gender, without humour. Maybe they knew more about guesses that came right – or went wrong – than anybody in Hong Kong? She felt stifled.

"Do you speak to ghosts?" Ah Min asked.

"Me? No! Of course not!" She saw it was a trick, to condemn her. She would die because of this interview, when Communist China came in at the Handover and the English left.

"How do you know what lies to tell?"

"I don't. I just say anything so things are straighter."

"Straighter?"

"Children pretend fairy stories, don't they? And superstitious folk go up to Amah Rock or burn a red candle in doorways. The usual."

"Do you?" they both asked together. The younger man looked abashed for intruding.

"No. Well," she embellished quickly because of her fear, "you know the gods. All the time. Anything, about anything."

"You do? About anything?"

"Of course. Everybody does, but pretends they don't."

She was conscious of a rap on her soul, almost a blow that shifted her in her seat. She looked round. Nobody. Yet she distinctly felt a buffet and her momentary recoil was seen by the two men opposite. She rubbed her arm. It hurt. Static electricity, she'd heard, did that.

"No," she corrected, retrieving her handbag. She had dropped it. "I'm sorry. I was wrong to say that." The taipan, for such Ah Min surely was, nodded to forgive. "I know traditions. Perhaps most," she added daringly.

"Most what?"

"Old customs, from the Middle Kingdom, in the Celestial Empire. It is my hobby."

"How?"

"I learn them, though I am not a good student." She added

that, in case it was Ghost Grandmother who had clouted her.

"Who from?" He leant forward, squeak, creak, knees a-shine. "Hong Kong is changing. Superstition is gone. Traditions have died. Apart from the *dai-hok,* the university. And they know nothing; I sent to ask them."

"My grandmother." She winced for another clout, but none came.

They showed keen interest, the taipan looking with meaning at the other man, who readied himself to spring away on a mission.

"Where is she?"

"She is dead, and I am very sorry." That proved safe. "She was very clever, and knows everything."

Knew? Does know? KwayFay became flustered by tenses. Ghost Grandmother had struck her several times before now, of course, that being what grandmothers did to granddaughters. Everybody knew that. But she had never before hit her in open company and the taipan had definitely noticed something. Once, when KwayFay had failed in obedience, Grandmother had beat her unmercifully, leaving KwayFay weeping until dawn. It had been for such a small thing. Grandmother had taken umbrage when KwayFay, completely done for after a harrowing day of kaleidoscopic exchange rates and computer glitches, had fallen asleep while Grandmother was teaching her the list of primary festivals. KwayFay had smarted across her shoulders and legs where Ghost had whacked her. In the morning she had woken with sunken eyes and a skin like a rattan mat. All because she had sleepily mumbled that the Double Ninth day of celebration was *Chunq-gao* instead of what Grandmother wanted to hear, *Chunq-yeurng.*

"Knew," she completed lamely. The huge fat man's beaming face unnerved her. "Her cleverness is forever in my mind."

It was getting harder. The younger man was impatient to be off killing somebody or extracting Hong Kong's famed squeeze from shopkeepers and hawkers down Nathan Road, anywhere near a ferry. *Where water, there water!* Cantonese folk muttered the old saying gleefully, the slang word for money being water, that passed through the fingers however carefully you tried to retain it.

"You go to the temples?" the taipan asked, frowning.

"Yes," KwayFay said firmly. She didn't go regularly, only when she'd made mistakes at work and didn't want them found until she could get in on Monday.

"Will it work for me too?"

She stared. What a question this was! A man could do anything, being male. Females couldn't, of course, being female. And a taipan could do anything without squaring it with anyone, for he was the business shark.

"Would what?"

Ah Min was in difficulties. He gestured dismissal, and the other left with a painstaking lack of noise. Why did he sulk so? Men were a problem, but their business was beyond her, very like HC's incomprehensible deals that never came off. Not like women, who were enemies to each other whatever their degree of kindred. Sure, you laughed with Apple Woman on Mount Davis because she was Hakka, of the Guest Family People who did all manual labour around the Colony, but that was only because Apple Woman insisted on shoving her wheeled barrow up and down hills when she was secretly rich. She was female so you had to watch her, laugh as long as you like.

"If somebody wanted somebody prayed to." He paused. "For. About. Would that work?"

"By me?" And to his nod she said defiantly, "Yes. In Hell." She used the English word for the Hereafter – Heaven, Purgatory, Limbo, those places being more or less synonymous. Ghost Grandmother had lengthy explanations for that, all as tiresome as each other.

"Good." He seemed reassured. "If I had to choose among several people, could you do it? Or tell if somebody was to be trusted?"

She was unsure what he was asking.

"Like you did before, in HC's shop?"

Shop? HC would fire any employee who spoke so derogatorily about his wonky business. She regarded the man with new admiration. One who cared so little about others deserved respect.

"I will try, if you say." She knew her place.

"What do you need?"

Guesses needed nothing. Guessing was simple. You suddenly opted for something that came into your mind, or you didn't. Then you, what, asked Ghost Grandmother if the guess was right or not? She forgot how it had worked that time. A random flick of her pen? Her head ached. What if she'd annoyed Ghost and Ghost deliberately told her wrong? But Ghost was her only relative, so on KwayFay's side.

"I have to ask." The best she could do.

He became almost reverential, nodding that he understood her status in relation to the Powers Out There. She began to hope that she would get back to work safe.

"How long does it take?"

He was asking *her*? In a world where China and Great Britain were doing a deal honouring the Treaty of Nanking and the later Peking Conventions? This strong man, whose motors streaked unimpeded through Tsim Sha Tsui, where even police motorcyclists braked to avoid delaying a taxi he'd hired? To that wisp of hope, she felt something slyly add itself. Was it a little dose of authority? She'd never experienced genuine power. It was fascinating.

"I never know."

"Can you tell me what happens?" he asked humbly.

"I am sorry." She tried to work out a formula to tell him no. "I wait until I am told."

Told? She wondered why she'd said that. Nobody ever *told* her what to guess when HC came bumbling in with his stupid questions about what to buy, who to send to Singapore, if so-and-so was to be trusted. She simply . . . well, guessed, often in a temper, more usually laughingly picking somebody who'd make most trouble for the odious creep. It was luck. Anybody could be lucky. She often wondered if HC bribed some god or other to stay flukey. He'd be bound to do it on the cheap, though, and that would irritate them. You didn't short-change gods. No, HC was just lucky and asked her the right questions.

"Do you gamble, Little Sister?"

"No, First Born."

"That is good. I would have to . . . find someone else."

She swallowed, tried to look dependable and no gambler.

"Little Sister, we want you to make choices for us. Some people who are not yet in Hong Kong. I want to know which ones."

"Which what?"

"We shall send for you." Ah Min glanced at the mirror and paused. "You will decide which, among several girls. And if a man."

"What girls for?" she bleated. "And if a man what?"

"That is all."

"How long do I have?"

Ah Min's beam did not change, but his eyes narrowed and she instantly realised her blunder. Wouldn't ghosts and gods know instantly? Didn't they fly, like the magic Goddess Tin Hau, over oceans to deflect typhoons away from Hong Kong and send them instead to damage Japan?

"You ask me what?" he said with quiet intensity.

"Who is the one who must come for the answer?" she said with quick invention. "What if an imposter asks for the answers instead of you?"

His brow cleared. She was safe. "We shall send. You tell us directly."

"Thank you." She said, on a whim, "Can I come in a black motor, please?"

"*Yat-ding*, certainly. Anything else?"

He asked it politely, quite as if he'd provided her with afternoon tea, English style, in the Gloucester Tea Rooms over in Central.

"Thank you, no."

He made a signal and the door opened instantly. A strange man slowly entered, one of great age wearing the traditional long black habit she only knew from old photographs. He was skeletal, his parchment skin a varnished integument. His skull was hairless, his features cleft by deep lines and his hands clawed into uselessness. The taipan leapt up, on guard. KwayFay also rose, not knowing what to do. Authority flowed from this old man, yet if he was so thin, attired so anciently, surely he must be some sort of prisoner? She warmed to him immediately.

"Why black?" the old gentleman whispered. She stared at him, nonplussed. "The motor car. You wanted black."

"I do not know, sir." Her power had flown. She had just been stupid. Her reply was in English. He nodded as if at some implied rebuke.

"You *guessed* it?"

"Yes, First Born."

"Do you know all the old festivals, Little Sister?"

"Imperfectly, sir. I am still learning."

He sighed. "I find that sad," he announced in his whispery voice.

"First Born," she asked, her voice tremulous at the risk she was taking by asking. "Which choice must I make first, and which second?" She felt the whole world go silent.

"Do it, Little Sister. Please."

He inclined his head. It was over. She did not know how to curtsey or bow properly. She did neither.

The annoyed young man was waiting on the soiled landing. He let her out into the street and simply left her there to make her own way back to HC's office. It took her the best part of an hour.

Defiantly she didn't take a taxi, though the time she wasted crossing the harbour on the Star Ferry would make the whole day impossible. She would be lucky to finish half of her work. Tomorrow would be hellishly full of blame.

HC was waiting, pacing, when she finally walked up from the Star Concourse past the three dozing rickshaws, no tourists eager to photograph the idlers today and serve them right. Her boss saw her return but said nothing. He was useless for the rest of the afternoon, and never even came to ask what had happened.

She kept wondering about the age of the ancient man. He had spoken with "high-nose" quality, used ancient traditional suffixes fast going out of use in ordinary speech. He would have got along fine with Ghost Grandmother. Poor, poor old man, though. Once in authority, now a mere *foki*, or a prisoner. If he was their old relative, they ought to see he was properly fed, instead of keeping him so thin. Usually, old grandfathers in Hong Kong looked after grandbabies, but probably Triads didn't have many. They probably made him work in the kitchen, poor old thing. She'd liked him.

Trying to catch up, she set to work. Eighteen waiting calls, several from London's sleepless brokers screaming where the hell, what the hell. None of her friends had done a single thing to help her, not even Lee Sik-King, who doted on her and could normally be counted on to do a hand's turn. He merely used his university degree – B.Econ. (Hons) – skills to ease his own passage today, thank you very much. She smouldered, quickly settling down in the three hours remaining.

Just let Lee S-K come grovelling with his postgraduate smile, hoping for her to submit to yet another pointless maul while he shed into her Kleenex in his cousin's near-derelict 10hp Standard car. Just let him, that's all. She'd draw him on long enough to get him to pay for a meal, then leave him standing. She almost giggled at the pun but had no time for fun, gave her computer her code word and rushed in.

Old Man went to sit in his high room. His six lieutenants stood waiting. He sipped almond juice. KwayFay was the name of a Chinese dancer, married a Ming emperor.

"Let her live," he said finally. "She must make choices, then I decide. And Ah Min?"

"Yes, master?"

"Ask doctors if she is mad."

"Yes, master. Which doctors?"

"The right ones."

Ah Min flinched, and retreated clutching his ledger, still frantic, still beaming.

The lieutenants dispersed. Old Man sighed. His problems seemed insurmountable today.

Chapter Four

That evening she avoided Mount Davis Road's Wall-Building ghost by accepting a lift from Alice's brother WC Seng. He was married and drove a small Volkswagen that roared even when not moving. It stank of petrol and had no springs to speak of. He chewed flavoured cachous and claimed an extra income but even Alice didn't know where from.

He drove her down Belchers Street so she could stop and buy two-day rice, cheap because it was old. He never stopped talking. KwayFay knew he fancied her. Several times he'd asked her out. She refused.

"I like Pok Fu Lam," he rabbited on during the drive. "Except Bonham Road past the university's a pig. And those Middle School kids! Never still. They should be taught traffic. My friend's kids go to Chiu Sheung Middle School. You know how much the fees are? Go on, guess."

"I know," KwayFay answered, because she looked everything up about money. As a Cockroach Child she used to sit outside the air vents trying to overhear lessons.

He laughed without pause, a waft of scented cachou unfortunately coinciding with her inhalation. She turned away, her rice on her lap.

"Is there anything you don't know?" he laughed.

He thought he had a gay, cavalier laugh, caught from some sword-and-staircase movie. He never went to Cantonese pictures, thinking them dated.

"Yes."

"There is? What?"

"HC's friend was delayed at the races. Nobody talked of it in the office, but they all knew why." She sighed, to prompt him. "I'm so slow on the uptake."

"I know." He turned to avoid a hawker pedalling his impossibly laden bicycle then had to wait while the market traffic disgorged up Smithfield. "They all park down Smithfield," Seng laughed bitterly. "If I tried that, I'd get police stickers all over my windscreen. They bribe to get away with it."

"I wish I did," KwayFay sighed, shifting her catty of rice on her lap in a way she knew to be alluring.

"HC's friend died."

"Died how?"

Seng laughed his abandoned laugh. "Doesn't matter if you're dead, right?"

Another line from some Yankee film. She looked at him, her eyes as hooded as a Chinese girl could make them. She practised this endlessly, once bribing a hateful friend along Robinson Road to hire an old black-and-white American video for an evening so she could see Gloria Swanson hood her eyes at a man to vamp him. It worked, but only for Gloria Swanson.

"You know everything," she said, unsmiling.

"Traffic accident!" Seng laughed sincerely this time, as was customary in Hong Kong at any disaster.

Her heart constricted. "Really dead? It must have been in the papers and I missed it," she said.

She never bought a newspaper. She had a natty little radio powered by two Duracell batteries. She'd been so proud of her plastic radio, having bought it from a street hawker – haggling for two days – until she discovered that it came given free with subscriptions of *Time*. Teachers' common rooms sold them to *fokis* down Connaught Road.

Sometimes she left it on all night, very low volume, to deter marauders who robbed shacks in the dark hours. Squatters were reluctant to raise the alarm and attract attention to their illicit presence among the mountain nullahs.

"He was run over in Mong Kok, Kowloon side." Seng hawked up phlegm and sniffed. Scented cachous never stopped his constant bubbling litany. It made her feel ill. He told her that he'd installed air-conditioning in his motor but it wasn't true. Why did men boast about things obviously unattained? A woman never would. "A lorry backed over him from Argyle Street. Seen the traffic there? Worse than Hong Kong side."

"Here will do," KwayFay said, sooner than she should have.

"Are you sure?" he asked, startled. "Walk uphill, from here?"

"Yes, I'm sure." She started to open the door so he had to pull in by the bus stop. Behind, the curving road overlooking the Sulphur Channel was already dark. "My friend will be waiting at the flower stall."

There was no friend. The flower stall shack showed a bare electric bulb, opaque plastic covering signifying it had closed.

"Look, KwayFay," he laughed. "How about I drive you to Jardine's Lookout, maybe a meal at the Peak one day? Just us, eh?"

"I'll think about it." She hesitated. That would not be enough of a rejection for this persistent goono for whom she'd hooded her eyes, giving him the free benefit of so much study. "I'm busy lately. Good night."

He racked the window up and drove off with a cheery wave. She heard his roguish laugh even over the guttural roar of the engine, and with relief started up the slope – Victoria Road was so steep, climbing out of town. She needed to think.

No doubts now: her boss's friend had been killed. Okay, she told herself grimly, accidents happened. But HC's fear had all but paralysed him. After the news, he'd crumpled. Had this friend been involved in some financial scheme that displeased the Hongs, the great Triads who ruled where even police could not go?

The important question was, had HC delivered KwayFay to the Triads in part payment for something she didn't yet know? Or had he remembered one of her offhand excuses and represented it as a magical recommendation?

It was evil. She almost stopped walking at the terrible thought. The heat was sapping, making rivulets of sweat down her back and sticking her collar to her hair. HC had made her responsible for his fiddles. She had no illusions about the man. He would see a way out and take it, congratulating himself on a brilliant escape even though it landed her in trouble.

She would make fewer offhand remarks in future, then he'd have no way out. Serve him right. Her immediate hope was to save herself. She could drop HC in it later, find a way. How many pardons did Triads give before making some lorry reverse over you in Sham Shui Po? She'd once seen a lorry crash in Nelson

Street, not far from Argyle, and a woman had been knocked unconscious against a parked motor, to bleed profusely while throngs had assembled to chat admiringly at the carnage. It gave her nightmares for months.

Mount Davis Path was steeper than Victoria Road. She had to take her time, her thighs aching and shoes beginning to hurt. The rice proved a problem, causing her to walk aslant. She stumbled in runnels as the path wound up in impossible turns. When she finally reached her hut she saw her water had been stolen, the can completely dry. Someone must have taken it as soon as she'd gone to work. Two bare-bottom urchins were playing *chai-mui*, the children's guessing game, played with the fingers opened or held up. How often she had played like that!

"No cat walked in today," she sighed, "so no luck." A cat straying into your home brought luck. If only.

Wearily she replaced her shoes with the worn sandals that she'd left carefully by the god at her door, the red cord tied to the god's base to prevent theft. She suspected Ah Fee, a woman who worked in the Chinese Legation houses on Mount Davis, very grand dwellings so old that they were made by the first English who'd come on their warships before anybody could remember. Ah Fee was a thief, despite having three sons who worked in the godowns and imported opium. So why was their mother a scivvy and a thief, dwelling in a squatter shack on a hillside? A family thing, she thought with sorrow, something she would never know.

KwayFay got her can and carried it to the stand pipe, a hundred yards down the path she'd just climbed. Luckily the queue was only fifteen people, mostly ancient grandfathers and little children, each with a tin or a plastic bucket, waiting in turn to get water from the one tap. People hardly talked, except mentioning the likelihood of a *dai-fung*, a typhoon from the Philippines. She found her laptop burdensome, slung forever over her shoulder. And her plastic shopping bag of clothes she had to carry as well, because in the dusk any one could steal and be away up among the shacks or down to Kennedy Town before she even saw him go, or maybe reach Heung-Gong-Jai, that "Little Hong Kong" the world tourists knew as Aberdeen Harbour.

She struggled back up the slope, lifted aside the tin sheet and went inside. She took out her radio and set it there, struck a match and lit her oil lamp, almost in tears at its suspiciously light weight. Sly fingers had leeched out half her paraffin while she'd been at work. Third time in four days. She wondered whether to see Safe Oil Man, who came past Victoria Road. They said he was Hakka really, though he spoke like a native Hong Kong Cantonese. He supplied oil to save you having to carry it home from Kennedy Town. It cost extra but his oil never got stolen, because he paid squeeze to Triad knives. They knew who stole what, and took revenge.

It was a question of payment, as in life. Could she afford extra to Safe Oil Man? If she didn't pay, it would mean forever hauling heavy cans of paraffin oil up from Kennedy Town. They didn't like people carrying great tins on the buses. The 5B drivers wouldn't allow her, especially the ones marked Felix Villas. Another dilemma, when she already had too many to cope with.

She got her pan from its twisted wire just above the house god. The god's battery was failing, depending for reflected red light upon a crumpled piece of tinsel. She wanted a real red lamp with its electric light showing true devotion, so rendering all her belongings sacrosanct, but who could afford that? Ah Fee could, for one, KwayFay thought bitterly. She dropped enough two-day rice in the pan for her evening meal.

The way you cooked it, as everybody except non-Chinese knew, was to pour out the rice. Wash it four times until the white stopped coming out, then give it a quick final rinse. Put in just enough new water to reach the second joint of your finger. Heat it on your dismally slow lamp's tepid flame. Taste the rice grains between your incisors. When soft, it is cooked. Simple! Yet even in Hong Kong people got it wrong and served hard rice. Unbelievable. Ghost Grandmother was always on about it.

She took down her chopsticks from their string on the shack roof, and brought out a twist of green cabbage and a sliver of fish (one Hong Kong dollar extra on the price) and placed it on a level stone above the rice pan in a piece of foil the fish man had thrown in free, though tomorrow he would charge for both. He did this day and day about.

The rice water she would use as a drink later, and then be set for the evening. She would think her way through the impossible hazards HC had placed her in. It would then be time for bed and sleep.

To pick the best of girls . . . for what? Who? She must simply guess two answers, and be right. Was it to do with money? Bets on an English horse race, that drove the young Hong Kong men crazy with dreams of wealth so they stared at TV screens in Causeway Bay all night long? She was so tired. Hers was not much of a life.

Dully she sat in her shack and watched the rice pan. Her mind was empty except for wraiths, each as amorphous as mists that faded from the East Lamma Channel before the dawn sun became hot. She was so tired. She thought of Seng, Alice's brother. He might possibly lend her some money to escape to Taiwan. Except the Triads knew everything. They would stop her at the airport. She could go down to the Taiwan ship and try to slip aboard, but the Taipei authorities recorded everyone from Hong Kong, being in the grip of the Kuomintang. You might be a suspicious right-wing political Koumintang character, or communist from China mainland.

Her chopsticks were easily cleaned of ghekko dust. She did this in a little hot water from the rice dipped out on her spoon, and felt her food. Ready.

Wearily she ate, wondering what to do. Barely ten o'clock yet she decided to go to bed. It would not do to be late tomorrow, with this problem hanging over her head. She needed to see what HC was going to do, ask, reveal, beg. Her ghekko chuckled and scurried up the shack wall.

It didn't remind her of Seng, because he did nothing useful. At least the ghekko caught flies.

"Wake up, lazy girl!"

"I am awake, Grandmother."

"Awake?" Ghost Grandmother shrieked in her grating voice.

"They hear you snoring in Hay Ling Chau?"

KwayFay shivered, trying to pull up her one blanket over her at the sudden mention of the Isle of Happy Healing, so beloved now of western tourists. They didn't know the place was the colony's original leper island, shunned even by the Japanese during the War, though its festivals had now returned, to please tourists for money.

"Tonight, snoring girl, I am restful." Silence, then accusingly, "Your water stolen today!"

"Yes, Grandmother."

"No cat walked to your door today, then!"

"I said that to myself when I realised," KwayFay said miserably.

"Or a hen sat on your roof. That brings bad luck."

"What must I tell you tonight, Grandmother?" Get it over with, and sleep.

"Why do you go in the *cheh*, the car of that fool man?"

Which KwayFay thought a bit much, for Alice's brother after all found KwayFay very desirable. Better not argue.

"I do not like to come down Mount Davis Road, Grandmother."

"Why not?"

KwayFay was sure Ghost Grandmother was laughing. She didn't dare become petulant.

Now she truly was laughing. KwayFay could hear her wheezing.

"The Wall-Building Ghost is there."

"Old Cantonese name, as is proper?"

To the scathing rebuke KwayFay muttered, "*Kuei Tang Chiang*, Grandmother, but – this one doesn't build only at night. It's there at dusk, sometimes even in broad daylight!"

KwayFay heard Ghost's sharp intake of breath. "How sly! That is unfair and cunning! You did well to see that trick."

"Thank you, Grandmother." KwayFay thought proudly, see? Grandmothers don't know everything.

"Tell me how you escape, timid girl."

KwayFay carefully marshalled her thoughts, because ghosts

have fantastic hearing, among other things.

"When walking along a road, you know a Wall-Building Ghost is suddenly with you. Usually," she added pointedly, "at night, but not always."

"How?" Ghost Grandmother cried, serious now.

"The suspicion that he is there means that he is, Grandmother."

"True! It is the only time he plays fair."

"You must stop. Sit right down. Even if he has only just begun building his wall round you, you must stay absolutely motionless. Even if," she couldn't resist needling Ghost Grandmother, "it is dark."

"That will do, bad girl!"

"He will then realise that you have seen his trickery, and leave from boredom."

"Good! What then?"

"Put your face in your hands for a count of your lucky number. The ghost and its wall, will be gone. You are free!"

"Excellent! And the danger of the Wall-Building Ghost?"

"He may build the wall so it grows taller than you."

"And then?"

"Then he lives inside with you for ever. You may choose to do a thing – go to the pictures, eat, make love, change your job – but you will never know if he is controlling you."

"For how long?" Ghost Grandmother cooed sweetly. It was a trick.

"For life, Grandmother."

"That is true," Ghost said, losing interest because KwayFay was right to the last detail. "Do you know anybody who has fallen prey to Wall-Builder? I never did."

"Yes, Grandmother. A policeman. He wears red collar tags to show he is fluent in English, and white gloves, in the point-duty pagoda at Queens Road West – you know where it goes up to Belchers Road? – who is in a wall made by Wall-Building Ghost. The policeman knows, which is why he is so sad."

"*Waaaiii!* Any more?"

"One of the teachers in Tsuen Wan, Grandmother."

"So Wall-Building Ghost has snared a teacher, has he?" Ghost chuckled, coughed once and came to. "I like that! You do well, Granddaughter."

"Thank you, Grandmother."

"Next, learn the Bun Festival of Cheung Chau, the Moon Festival, New Year customs, and the God of Wealth."

"All those?" KwayFay wailed.

"All," Ghost Grandmother said firmly. "How else will you learn, lazy girl?"

"Please, Grandmother!" KwayFay called, suddenly not wanting the lesson to end, for she was in trouble. "Can I ask about choosing?"

"The Water Mirror is for choosing. Have you forgotten so soon?"

"No! No!"

"Then what?"

KwayFay knew Ghost was just prolonging her agony from devilment.

"I am in serious trouble."

"What have you done, bad girl?"

"I am compelled to make choices for powerful men."

"What choice?" Ghost asked with relish, for ghosts love choices even though they didn't often get to do the choosing.

"Among girls, and one yes-no for a man."

"How many? Apples, lemons, pears? What?"

"The men did not say."

"Then there is only one course, KwayFay. You must ask."

"Ask what? Who?"

"Ask questions, and pay no heed to any of the answers. You will then say right choice. You understand?"

"No, Grandmother," KwayFay bleated.

Ghost Grandmother had gone, and KwayFay slept.

When she woke it was already daylight. She had to scurry to find her clothes and go to the toilet – a hole in the ground, like in mainland China, the refuse dribbling down into a night-soil pit that stank. She had enough water to wash with, and this time made it go all over, armpits, breasts, waist, crutch and finally feet, before dressing in her go-to-work clothes. She had got nothing ready for the morning like a stupid girl, and she felt worn out. She thought of doing her make-up at the 5B bus stop but instead managed a hasty patch job. She started to pull her piece of corrugated iron across the gap, then paused.

She noticed something strange.

Beside the door was the fragment of mirror she always kept by her ramshackle bed. It was near her Kitchen God and was tilted as if placed there for her to notice. She was careful about glass, for a cut meant you might be late and suffer one of HC's punitive fines. Last time she'd been really late – no fault of her own; a Typhoon Signal Three hoisted at Little Green Island stemming traffic in Kennedy Town – he'd fined her half a day's wage. She'd had to give Chao from Ice House Street, who was no more than a messenger, a maul the following Monday so he would pay her squeeze to the Shack Money Collectors who came of a Wednesday and buy her rice parcel for the first three weekdays. If she hadn't groped Chao the Odious she'd not have eaten, and might have had her shack disappeared or sold when she got home that Monday. Life was that precarious.

The chip of mirror was no more than an inch oblong. It was her standby piece.

Picking it up, she paused to think. She hadn't yet been out of the shack. She hadn't moved from where she'd performed her ablutions. She had not seen anybody make to enter. People had rushed past, heading downhill from other squatter shacks. Any variation in morning noises alerted her instantly.

Therefore?

Therefore *somebody had been inside*. During the night, he must have been watching her. She felt numb with shock and rather sick. Queasy, like a bad meal from Szechuan or, much worse, from too-oily Shanghai.

She stepped outside and looked about. Nothing extraordinary. She looked back inside to check again. Nothing odd. Then, amazingly, she saw a watch, large as life, its second hand going on in jerks. A watch? There, on the earth floor.

What kind of robber enters, then leaves a donation? A ghost?

She thought wildly, surely Ghost Grandmother would have had something to say about *that*? She wondered suddenly: Had he listened? Did she in fact speak her conversations with Ghost Grandmother aloud, or just think them? There was no way of knowing if the intruder heard her.

Did Ghost Grandmother simply scan thoughts as KwayFay formed them inside her head, speech being superfluous?

She was badly frightened. She picked up the watch. It said Rolex, a fame-name denoting enormous cost. Fakes were available in Kowloon from hawkers and street men. Anywhere down Carnarvon Road they'd sell you lookalikes, ten dollars Hong Kong one piece. It might in fact be a cheap replica. She examined it, realised the time suddenly, caught up her things and fled down the ankle-breaking path to the main road below and caught the bus.

The watch went in her bag. She'd been awake over an hour and not done a stroke so far. Ghost Grandmother had told her absolutely nothing that might help. Ask questions then paying no heed at all? What sort of advice was that? She cautioned herself and erased that critical thought. Ghost might be listening in. No wonder she was in a mess.

Things changed when she got to work.

HC's wife's cousin, David YeePak Huang, was in charge. He insisted on being called Mister David by the twelve *fokis* he – repeat he alone – employed. He hired, he fired. In the Giant Super Designer Emperor Carpet Emporium Co.'s confines in Tit Hong Lane, off Jubilee Street, Mr David's word was law. He set the prices, planned MegaGalactic Super Sales (SPECIAL DISCOUNTS A SPECIALITY), and ruled.

And he did one other small thing. Late Thursdays, he filched nineteen per cent – never more, never less – of the gross for himself. The tenth he was supposed to use paying off his cousin Linda's husband's debts to some loan shark from Mong Kok were overdue because of this, but what was a manager for?

He was a shopsoiled man, stout for his relatively young age, only twenty-seven but with definite prospects now he had the money thing licked. He already had his eye on an apartment in the Mid Levels, halfway up the Peak beyond earshot of those noisy little brats at the English children's school in Glenealy. He would rent it to gullible tourists and make more even than the money he stole from the carpet centre.

These financial affairs had to be handled firmly, not allowed to slide into inactivity. Money brought responsibilities, and that meant doing something, as opposed to idling along in neutral like HC, his cousin Linda's fool of a husband. A Jaguar motor wasn't built to remain still, right? Leave it to HC the entire syndicate would run into the sand in a twelvemonth.

And Linda was no better. A penny gambler. Fine, she took herself off to Macao now and again. Who didn't? There, she gambled about the same as his own weekly income, which wasn't much. She also borrowed a little more now and again from Mong Kok money lenders, but they were no big deal. He, Mr David, could handle them. These people needed putting in their place. He was master of the Emporium, and guarantor of the cash they lent Linda for her horse-racing flutters down Happy Valley and the new track at Sha-Tin Heights. Borrow a dollar you *owed* the lender. Borrow a million you *owned* the lender!

Let them never forget that.

He'd actually said that to the money collector: "Don't ever forget that." He'd said it straight out last week when the man came. Mr David was astonished it was so much. He demanded a written statement of all Linda's transactions.

"You mean for the whole twenty-three months?" the man had asked, so calm.

"Every cent." Mr David lit a cigar, Cuban of course, none of your Yuhan dross, which were probably nothing only banana leaves.

"In writing?"

"Written down." Mr David had fixed the money collector with an eagle eye.

"You joking?" Calm? The guy was soporific! He knew he was face-to-face with a real business mogul.

"No joke. Write it down. I don't trust this sudden jump in the debt. Get it?"

It came out like an American gangster: *Geddit?* The money collector had actually paled, like one of those children you now saw about South-East Asia, cross between a negroidal person – American Forces, doubtless from Vietnam days – and an ethnic Chinese from the China coast, say Malaysia, Singapore, or somewhere in the Philippines. Local Hong Kong people called them "green children" because of their peculiar colour. White teachers believed such offspring were specially gifted in painting, drawing, and textiles. Nonsense people, the English. He often quoted the Chinese saying: "Three thousand years ago, what was England?"

Idle today, he went to the door of the Emporium and spat into the gutter. Odd that so few customers had come today. The staff seemed on edge. Maybe his imperious manner had made them all apprehensive? But was a manager to befriend every labourer who moved a broom?

He noticed two young men, both in suits and wearing dark sunglasses, standing looking into his picture window at the Afghan and Tientsin carpets. New this month. Exploited children wove them, but so what, if profit was the result? Labour earned money, and so the world spun.

"Can I help you?" he asked.

"You Mr David YeePak Huang, the manager?"

David glanced back into the interior of his Emporium. None of his staff was about. He felt suddenly uncomfortable. These did not resemble customers wanting carpets.

"Yes."

They rushed him, pinning him against the door. One took out a knife, piercing David's jacket so he actually felt the sharp point.

"Get a taxi," the knife man said. The other flagged down a yellow cab just crossing the end of Tit Hong Lane, heading along Jubilee Street by Central Market. It came with a bumping rush, its wheels spattering discarded offal from the gutter. A tourist lady shrieked as the wet chilled her legs and stained her skirt.

The two youths bundled David into the cab. It bumped away.

"Y'see that?" the American tourist cried.

Other tourists took up the call, demanding what was the police number in Hong Kong for God's sakes, why wasn't it 911 like in New York and struggling with their tourist booklets.

"It'll be under China Town," one suggested. "Where's China Town?"

"See that? He had a goddam knife!"

One entered the Emporium and shouted, "Hello? Anybody here? Only, somebody's just been kidnapped . . ."

There was no answer. The place was vacated. The police were there within minutes, but too late.

Chapter Five

Work began slowly, Alice smiling across and the others not quite knowing how to say *jo-san*, good morning, without looking harassed. It was KwayFay's nature to suspect that everybody knew the worst of her, including the terrible knowledge that she was so poor. This made her furtive.

For an hour she laboured at impossible new currencies. Some neophyte nation (inevitably another Indian Ocean titch sandbank with the acreage of Stonecutters Island but without even that miserable snake-infected mound's elevation) had invented an independent currency, hoping their grubby bits of paper would rival the Almighty American Dollar, so providing free wealth for a camilla of seedy officials. HC of course was in a lather, whimpering that his information clerk KwayFay was useless.

Cheapskate, that was HC. He came in doing his wriggle that told of unbelievable compromise on his part, and beckoned her. She took fifteen minutes leaving her pod to follow the incompetent cheat.

Here it came, she thought. He was going to shunt her somewhere for a week then sack her by a notice pinned to the office notice-board. Come Monday, he'd strut and tell how he'd finished KwayFay for idling, or some other contrived myth, and feel important.

She already had clues. One was her friend's sudden check on her greeting, usually "Okay! In a minute!" Alice Seng merely said, "In a minute!"

Omitting the okay.

Uk-kay meant home. Said quickly in Cantonese it sounded a little like "Okay!", that everyone knew derived from Gold Coast's "*Waw kyehh*!" (while being polite to the Yanks who pretended it was their own because they had the Almighty Dollar). Homophones were an endless source of mirth in Hong Kong, but also of peril. What greater risk than mentioning home, when redundancies were whispered in the early morning tea break, gatherings that KwayFay could never afford to join?

"KwayFay! Sit down."

Churlish to decline, but she was already sticky from the heat. No wonder western peoples had so much energy on arrival in the Colony. Only later did they develop the economical gait, the listlessness for which their women were famed when, sapped of vitality, they knew sunshine for the skin-ageing malignancy it truly was. She sat on the plastic chair, determined not to cry when he gave her the sailor's elbow.

HC smiled, sweat on his brow.

"KwayFay, you have a rise! Not," he put in at speed, "permanent, for your wages already bleed me to the bone."

He brought out a red envelope with gold lettering and passed it across his desk. His smile was that of the hopeful courtier, puzzling and dangerous. She left it lying there. What, did he want her to pinch her left sleeve in the fingers of her right hand and move her hands up and down, as she'd seen old women do in Cheung Chau? For what? She suspected this was a cruel joke, dismissal couched in pretence.

The last of the Manchu Emperors was so learned that Republicans published his divine poems anonymously, in shame at having no poets of their own. Ghost Grandmother called Republicans deceiving scoundrels, with worse and much coarser invective on a bad night, even speaking badly of the great Doctor Sun Yat Sen, the First Republican, who surely must be only round the corner from wherever Ghost Grandmother lived now, across the Heavenly Bridge. Well, KwayFay would make HC, chief deceiving scoundrel, say it outright, not hide behind tricks so banal they wouldn't deceive a Hainanese.

"I don't understand." She didn't know if she spoke the words or merely thought them. She sat still.

"It's a present, KwayFay! Money!"

More sweat, with a real distress now? Traffic roared, shouts rising from below. Some motor had stolen space from another. Trams pinged and crashed, accelerating in that slow musical crescendo that ended in a whine as they took the curve to the Pacific Place shopping mall.

"Why?" she asked, conscious of incongruity.

He stared. There was no why in money. It was simply there,

like weather and politics.

He shoved the red envelope forward in small jerks, as a fledgling bird made hesitant starts on the edge of its nest. One-handed, she noted with scorn. What a boor! You passed even the smallest gift with *two* hands, proper Cantonese style, not one. Sloven; she worked for a sloven. The shame of it! Ghost Grandmother would go on about him tonight. She'd say, "What a tortoise! Forgetting the Eight Laws of Politeness! What is he, a Japanese?" and cackle at her offensive wit. Little sleep tonight, then. KwayFay hated him.

"Is it rebate?" Definitely her own voice now and without a quaver.

"Rebate?" His smile became a ghastly rictus.

Over time, HC imposed fines on the staff. She was especially at risk. Smarting over some domestic reversal with Linda his gambling-mad wife, he'd say, "KwayFay! You are bated five per cent! Work faster, understand? More encouragement for clients to invest!"

And one-twentieth of her wage would be missing. Or one-tenth, on a bad day. Mostly for his wife's gambling, or sheer spite caused by poor trading figures. She understood. His theft was therapy, as a doctor gave tranquillisers to see a patient through some horror. At her expense, of course. She and her friend Alice never discussed this except by nudges and looks.

"Rebate?"

HC tried to make it an imperious demand, but failed. Astonished, KwayFay recognised supplication, like the expression he wore when attempting a maul. She might have felt compassion but detestation proved more satisfying.

"Of the fines."

"The fines!"

He attempted a laugh. It strengthened her. She felt as if she had burned joss sticks at the little Tai Wong Temple on Ap Lei Chau island where the god Hung Shing was worshipped; or, more aptly, pausing for a discreet mental worship when she passed by 22, Tin Hau Temple Road, where, decades ago there once stood the Fung Sin Ku Temple. Uplifted, perhaps. A temple, however poor, had a right to memory just as if it were a person. Ignore that kind of responsibility and you would find yourself in trouble. Righteousness overcame ignorance at every level. Perhaps she might tell Ghost Grandmother that tonight, it being quite clever, able to boast a little, at the thought. But was it clever to refuse money?

"Yes, the fines."

"Who takes notice of those!" he boomed. "Flea bites, KwayFay! A captain has his hand on the tiller, so a boss has to control his business by discipline!"

She rose slowly. The heat had stuck her bottom to the chair. How slovenly to skim office spending on proper chairs! Those Triad men had the grace to think ahead in this; why not a businessman?

"I must get back to work."

Sack me for that, she thought with belligerence. The red and gold envelope seemed to wince: *I am money, left ignored?*

"KwayFay. Please."

"I have problems," she invented, to escape. "Bounty Cook Island Republic. The Hang Seng Bank will refuse to set a currency exchange rate at three o'clock."

"Will they?" he shrieked in a frantic gusher of sweat. She observed him with open contempt. "For sure?"

She was surprised. She'd simply assumed that's what would happen. The Hang Seng gave the cheapest rates of exchange for tourist money, as everybody knew except tourists. Why would a sound bank do otherwise with a dud currency?

"Sure." Let him do what he would with her guesses. Today was awry, things in it beyond her control.

"Then we mustn't touch it!" he gasped out, clutching his chest.

"I've already refused it twice."

No thought that she might have guessed wrong. What if Australia or some place, New Zealand even, maybe Fiji if things went disastrously wrong, decided to support the new money for political reasons?

"Tell all the other staff."

"No, First Born." And explained, cold, "You docked my salary last month for doing that."

"No!" He wiped his brow, looking about as if for escaped logic. "Yes! No, KwayFay! I'll see to it!"

His bravado, truculence in the face of adversity, such as a brave man might feel, was as convincing as a cardboard cut-out.

She marched out, pleased. She walked down the corridor, reached her pod and sat. She closed her eyes for a second. The office still felt the same; her screen still glowed, saving its pixels by a writhing coloured shape. Yet she felt as if she'd suddenly been promoted. The money she'd left on HC's desk would serve as a reproach. He would be devastated. Let him give it to his grasping failed-gambler wife. (As fail she would, KwayFay felt with delight, in the third race this afternoon at Happy Valley when her miserable beast, straining every nerve under the wild flogging from its Australian jockey in scarlet and white, yellow starred cap, would come in a sorry fifth.) Serve the bitch right.

"All well?" Alice put her head round. "What were you saying about some horse?"

Oh, dear. "Just thinking aloud. Has anybody cited that new money?"

"The Indian Ocean thing? They say America will, before Ice House closes this afternoon." Alice paused. "Did you hear YeePak's missing?"

KwayFay looked up. "HC's cousin?"

"Him." Alice's whisper intensified. "HC was full of him a month back. Remember, the Carpet Emporium?"

KwayFay went cold. The office was quiet, people looking her way. Did they know she once advised HC against hiring him?

"Since last night. The police came round."

"Some woman, is it?" KwayFay tapped the computer mouse but she felt sickened. People didn't disappear. If a man vanished over some woman, all Hong Kong knew within minutes exactly where and why.

She tapped in another refusal for Bounty Cook Island Republic's new currency. Whatever office rumour said, no thank you, get lost. Guides, all hedging like crazy, were shoaling in from Central Office, but let them whistle. She'd given her delirious guess, HC could fight it out and set his own rate if he was stupid enough. He'd maybe make another fortune for his wife to squander.

What respect could she feel for an oaf who hadn't even the decency to put a small god in there? The CID, head of Hong Kong police, had a diminutive shrine to Kuan Kung, the Ruling Essence of Heaven and Earth, with a red votive light burning before it. The practice originated in Yaumati Police Station long ago, but so? It explained why Hong Kong police were so successful. Obeisance now and again pleased a god, especially one feeling neglected for lack of attention. Stood to reason. Meanwhile, HC feared the derision of chance clients.

She rejected three other client demands for quotations on the new currency, sweetly ablating their e-mails. Let HC joke all he wanted. He would probably sack her at the day's end anyway. Maybe the gaunt elderly man, Old Man, who strangely felt such concern even about her asking, on a whim, for a black motor car, had felt like this when those Triad threat-men had taken him prisoner? Poor, poor thing.

She didn't trust hope. It was a myth, being without numbers, unlike money.

"You know the place above Kennedy Town?" Old Man said. He was smoking. He only allowed this in special circumstances, as now.

"Many places there, master."

The young suited was guarded. Old Man stood watching as the killers cut away the bound man's kneecaps and dropped them into the dish. The floor was well sanded with cement mixed well in, according to old traditions. Lime would be sprinkled on the sand-blood mess afterwards, making everything decent.

The victim had done screaming, given up. His mouth was stuffed with rags, and small bamboo shoots stuffed up his nostrils, green so they would bend into his throat to provide an airway. He could not choke while the pain was inflicted.

"You must know it. Broad steps go up, those small shops all the way up." Old Man waited.

"Green Lotus Terrace!" the suited threat-man said with relief. "The stair steps are Precious Dragon Terrace. Trees along the wall, with a school?"

"That's it." Old Man nodded at the torturers' quick glance. They resumed cutting wide flaps from the victim's abdominal wall and bent it over his scrotum. The man screwed his eyes tight shut in agony, stayed silent. "Why is it not on Government lists?"

"The temple belongs to the Guild of Builders and Contractors, First Born."

"I thought so. Whom do they pay?"

The suited man grew uncomfortable, found wanting. "Not known."

"Look into them."

Mister David, the victim, slumped, his eyes protuberances of horror. The two killers waited for instructions, facing each other awaiting new orders, quick or slow. Old Man dusted his long black garb and smiled at his assistant.

"You are unhappy at my remark?"

"No, First Born. Whatever you decide."

The gaunt man did not smile. "You are wiser than your years." He turned to the victim and inspected his plight with detachment. He said in a quiet voice, "You caused me a deal of trouble, and took my valuable time. You now know what you ought to have known long ago."

A terrified hope lit the victim's countenance. He tried to focus, but it proved too much.

"You should not have stolen my money."

He moved slowly to the door and paused.

"Another half hour," he told the killers. "Then end it."

"Yes, First Born."

Old Man sighed and left. Two suited threat-men waited outside with his limousine. He stepped into it, pleased by the air conditioning. There was none indoors in that dreadful place, an omission he would have to rectify. He felt quite worn out. Soon it would be time for wine and a little grilled salmon, with possibly a few large Sydney Harbour oysters flown in daily by Cathay Pacific and Quantas.

He worried about his ancestors. No wonder he had been so furious with HC's disrespectful cousin. Disrespect was a cancer. No escaping its effects. The taint wasn't merely a stain; it was contagion setting up malignancies of its own. Now, he felt, that balance was righted. HC would realise. Terror would spread manners, and the criminal world would sail on.

But what to do about ancestors? He had made his minions interrogate that girl while he'd watched behind his two-way glass. He had actually shied away from asking that girl's advice. KwayFay had been so frightened she might have said anything, and what good was that? Later, he might summon the fortitude to ask outright, and see what she said. You did not disturb the spirits with impunity.

Her advice had better be sound, trustworthy, and correct. In short, worthy of his ancestors. He would not like to become annoyed twice in one month. It took it out of him so.

Oysters, he needed those big Australian oysters.

That afternoon, all the Australian jockey's efforts failed to get his mount to the line. He finished a disappointing fifth. He heard the abuse as he went through to the weighing room. The aggro was the usual punters' suspicion that he'd been bribed. Punters everywhere had the same thoughts: if you won, jealous losers knew you'd bribed the rest to trail on the run-in. Lose or win, you were at risk among Hong Kong's gamblers.

Coming from the weighing room, the jockey found his next seven races cancelled. He would lose a fortune in race fees. He swore under his breath as he changed.

In the car, he found a parcel under his steering wheel. It was adorned with a gold-edged red ribbon. Inside he found a fortune, twice what he would have made had he won all his cancelled races. He had only been in Hong Kong four months, but already he knew when to speak out and when to drive home silently to Chai Wan as if nothing had happened. He did not smile, until he closed the door on his fourth-floor apartment in Cheung Lee Street. It was the only time he'd arrived home not cursing the bastard-awful one-way traffic system.

HC's wife Linda was furious. She had shouted the same allegations among the abusive punters. She lost five out of her six wagers, the paltry winner an odds-on filly hardly paying enough to bother with. She considered the numbers: *five*, out of *six*. Were numbers trying to tell her something? Perhaps that she ought really to try her hand at blackjack, or even go back to roulette on the second floating casino in Macao? The problem was enough money. If HC wasn't so wretched a provider she'd have enough money to work a proper gambling system.

Worse, she just knew that her favourite friend KwanChoi Wah, who'd recently adopted the lucky western name Betty, had won again. She'd doubled her stake, bringing odds of 11-8 against and making it by a neck. If HC wasn't spineless he'd have his friends (were *any* left?) creep in at midnight and slash the hamstrings of the horses that had lost his wife serious money. She knew two wives whose husbands had exacted that revenge for their loving wives. The priceless thoroughbreds had suffered, serve them right. What was the alternative, she seethed, *reward* failure?

"Madam." A Eurasian man was standing nearby. He raised his panama. A young, pleasant man, not one of your race-course louts without tie or jacket.

"Yes?" she said uncertainly.

"May I stand nearby, while I select my next bet? I can see you will bring a gentleman superb luck!" He sighed. "I need it badly!"

His Cantonese was perfect. She gave a sideways glance to see if her friend KwanChoi, the successful Betty, was watching. The newcomer's manners were impeccable, his clothes expensive, his hands manicured. He wore a diamond tiepin. His shoes looked English handmade. How could a man so rich need luck? HC's wife wondered if he had crossed some fortune god today, and decided she ought to keep her distance.

"My luck has not been good today," she confessed.

She had an alexandrite stone – English sailors favoured them to prevent drowning, and of course it worked, for weren't they born for the sea? Would her luck be offended because her own cheap blue topaz stone wasn't costly enough?

Worry about that later, after this charming man had gone.

"Impossible! Beauty brings its own good fortune!"

He must be ten years younger than she. She was flattered. Betty KwanChoi was looking back from the winnings window.

He stood closer to mark his card.

He touched his hat to her in thanks and headed for the bet window. She felt slightly breathless. Perhaps he was a good omen? From the way he held his pen it couldn't have been farther down the call-over than second, third at the lowest.

"Who on earth . . .?" KwanChoi asked, returning.

"Hello, Betty. Nobody you need know!"

"Come on, Linda. Is he local? New? What's his name?"

"What do you fancy for the next?" she asked innocently.

Linda had already decided to put everything she had left on the second down, hoping it was the same horse on which the handsome young man had probably placed his.

And lost it all. The animal came second-last. Betty, the bitch, crowing, got another place, third, paying 9-5. The end of a miserable day.

All the way home she blamed HC. See what happened when you didn't have enough money to gamble properly! You lost time after time. A few dollars here, a few there, pinching and scraping for the next hundred to put on an each-way, was betting like some worried little housewife.

It was shaming. HC kept her short of decent gambling money.

And all the time KwanChoi Wah, Betty, the smarmy winner with her genuine branded clothes and accessories, crowed and collected her winnings. You had to lay out money in gambling to win. Every gambler knew that. It was common sense.

This was the tenth consecutive time she had been to the races and lost. All down to HC, too damned mean to see the obvious. Lay decent money *out* to bring decent money in. She needed enough money to win handsomely.

The young man had been so courteous. She'd glimpsed him, not letting him see her looking of course, at the winners' window to collect a sickeningly large wad of notes.

He must have laid a *sizeable* bet. He had *won*.

She had placed *trivial* money. She had *lost*.

There was only one way out of her unspeakable shame. She would take it.

She must borrow enough to construct an infallible scheme. Then let her best friend Betty smirk, the bitch. Linda would be triumphant.

Bet enough money, gambling became a certainty. You had the thrill of winning without the dismay of losing. She began to plan: Get more money, for the one great gambling coup of her life.

Chapter Six

KwayFay was followed home. She alighted from the Kennedy Town tram, changing direction until she came to the street players. She watched the marionette Chinese opera, smiling in spite of her fears. The Flag Cloth Opera! The story always gripped her. How many times had she seen it here? She saw the poor little girl from Kashgar, played with a silly (so wrong!) Shanghainese accent of unbelievable shrillness, move with slow jerks across the marionette stage being abducted by the great Western-China General.

She cried out with the street audience standing amid the traffic, as the girl, Siang Fei, Fragrant Consort to the Emperor, was taken to Peking there to languish alone. Emperor Chien Lung was entranced. KwayFay found herself applauding with delight at the wickedness of the Imperial Palace concubines, hating this new rival's exquisite beauty. They were defeated by Siang Fei's innocence. Unaware how time was passing, KwayFay wept as the girl, newly promoted to Fragrant Consort, ascended the Dragon Bed.

Desperately wanting to see the end, KwayFay glanced at somebody's watch. Almost eight o'clock! No wonder darkness was on the sea, lights stringing out in the bay like so many stars, the junks now puttering with only three lights showing. She might as well find some street stall and have a bowl of hot rice, perhaps with green vegetables. She could make a drink of tea before bed in her squatter shack, and then it would be dawn and the start of another day at HC's wilting firm. Amazingly, he still had not sacked her. What on earth was in his mind?

She walked slowly away, her calves aching from so long a day, saddened by the story she had just left. The crowd would all be in tears as the lovely Siang Fei stabbed herself. Marionetteers always used a knife of hugely disproportionate size, its blade glittering with aluminium dust. As a little girl she had climbed this very thoroughfare, Water Street, and gone through the narrow lane into Second Street to see the same puppet displays! Were they the same people running the little theatre? You never saw.

Like life.

Once, thrilled, she had been allowed to sprinkle the precious silver powder onto the wooden knife! She angrily brushed her tears away.

There was a food stall at the junction with Third Street. She bought a bowl (four HK dollars, a fortune) and seated herself on a trestle stool, eating with a swift shovelling action in the gathering darkness, the mad cars streaming past towards Sheung Wan in a crazy dash down the one-way system.

For a moment, as the bare rice settled in her stomach and her hunger melted, she wondered why she had stopped off here, then remembered.

He had not been the same man following her. Not that calm stranger with such a sure tread. The new man was stout, wore trainer shoes boys ran about in to bother pedestrians. Youths pretended they were great runners who had paid the right bribe to Olympic judges at the next Games.

The new man smoked long cigarettes and wore a hat like a gangster. She was frightened, but the stall was crowded with night people. Cars were still about, but the buses were fewer now and the sea below darker. Had she been foolish to choose this way home?

She walked to Bonham Road and waited for a bus but none came. She had no money to pay a taxi, though two passed her and beeped their insolent horns, just as if she was a *sai-yan*, a westerner, maybe English from the University.

The man suddenly was there in front of her. Nobody was about. A car roared past. For one insane moment she wondered if the motor might be Alice's brother Seng who fancied her. It swished by.

He held a knife, so small it almost could have been amusing in other circumstances.

"Handbag," he said.

"I have nothing," she said, which was true.

Then she remembered the Rolex watch, that had appeared so mysteriously in her shack, and felt her rice meal try to force itself back up her throat. Bile rose. She had declared her own death, for street thieves hated to be lied to. He would kill her.

"Give me red, or I take red!"

It was the street thief's standard line, red or red. Red hundred dollar notes, or you forfeited your red blood.

"*Hung hung*. Red red!"

He grinned, two gold teeth large and protuberant.

KwayFay's heart failed. This demand of street robbers was unknown thirty years go, but now was the most feared confrontation. If you had none of the red $100 Hong Kong note, you would die.

And she had lied to him. Double bad luck.

Humbly she held out her handbag. He took it.

"I am sorry," she said with humility. "I forgot. There is a new watch inside. My friend's gift."

Where was her friend now that she was about to die? Her unknown admirer, disturber of mirrors and leaver of priceless watches, why did he not save her like an American comic-book hero?

Desperately she wondered whether to run across the road in front of some passing car. No use. The motorist would assume she was getting rid of some chasing ghost and swerve angrily. It was so common, the gambit of children who, imagining some pursuing spirit, would dash across swift traffic, narrowly escaping with their lives. The ghost, distracted from its prey, would then chase the motor car, and bring bad luck to the motorist instead, for ghosts travelled in straight lines.

"What friend?"

The thief rummaged in her handbag. She watched dully. He exclaimed and brought out the watch. A car went by, students shouting rude comments at the sight of a couple standing talking.

"I do not know."

"You Queen's woman?" he asked.

That was the old English euphemism for prostitute. European women, though mostly American, over a hundred years before inhabited the area between Graham Street, Wellington Street and Hollywood Road, selling sexual favours for money.

"No. I am office worker."

"Why does a stranger give you expensive watch?"

"I do not know."

"How did he give it you?"

"He left it in my home."

"This watch is genuine." He grinned at her. "Friend pay well! Good climb volcano, *ne*?" Climb volcano was Hong Kong's euphemism among the older generations for sex.

"It must have been during the night. I saw nothing."

"What else did he give?"

"I woke, and it was there. I was afraid. I might have been accused of theft."

"You speak truth?"

She was about to reply when she noticed the strangest thing. The man shook slightly, as a dog emerging from water shook away moisture. A prominent bulge appeared in his abdomen. He looked down in vague surprise. KwayFay imagined a friend having tapped him on the shoulder.

Blood seeped onto his clothes, almost black in the falling dusk, him standing with that stupid grin. Then blood spurted, narrowly missing her as she stood watching the weird performance.

Two young men stepped round him, one muttering in annoyance as he almost stepped into the blood. They watched the man crumple and fall, and stooped to retrieve the watch.

"You okay, *Siu-Jeh*?"

"Thank you," she said politely, staring at them.

The speaker kicked the thief. "Die, you pig."

"He'll end soon," the other said, rubbing the watch with an unfolded handkerchief before politely offering it to KwayFay.

"That's not the fucking point," the kicker said. "It was my knife."

The dying thief groaned and gave a great exhalation. They beckoned KwayFay and began strolling up the road. They paused, looking back.

"Come on, Little Sister. We don't want the police asking questions, do we?"

"But he is . . ."

What exactly was he? Dying? Dead, with a knife projecting?

She saw it in the gloaming, in the fallen man's spine. Somehow it had been thrust with enormous power through his shoulders, down and forwards so its point came out from his abdomen. And she had seen it all with remote detachment, thinking it a pat from a friend.

"We must telephone for an ambulance," she said faintly.

"I will, soon," one said, chuckling.

She felt suddenly dizzy, and was relieved the two men did not let her fall. They took her arm with extraordinary gentleness.

"Jesus!" one said with feeling. "Don't let her go. If Business Head finds she's marked, we'll get more than a couple of scratches."

"I know, I know!"

She did not recall getting into a car, only finding herself somehow in a Chrysler, the sort becoming so fashionable among young tearaways. It was all leather and walnut dashboarding. She saw the two men clearly and, aware of the appalling risk that glimpse might bring, put her face in her hands to hide their features.

They laughed.

"Not necessary, Little Sister! We saved your life, remember?"

So they had. These two had saved her and restored the watch to her. She wanted to disclaim responsibility for the thief, the encounter, being late, having in her possession a watch she knew nothing about.

"Please," she begged, still concealing her face as the car's acceleration forced her into the plush seat. "I will say nothing."

"We know that now, Little Sister," they assured her. "You did good there."

He spoke in fluent English. Did good? That was what footballers cried to each other, TV trendiness.

"I did?" One was looking back at her from the front passenger seat, the other driving.

"You said nothing," the passenger said, nodding. "Good! You saw us plant the watch – incidentally a gift from our boss – during the night, yet you said nothing."

"I did not see you."

The driver laughed. "Your eyes were open. You watched us."

"I did not see a thing." It was the truth.

"Keep it up, Little Sister! Our boss will be very pleased."

"Even when threatened with death by Ah Tseng, you refused to admit you saw who brought you the gift. So brave."

"I . . ."

She decided to say nothing more. Truth might condemn her, when ignorance seemed to be saving her life.

"Yes?"

"I am grateful that you rescued me."

"It's our job, Little Sister."

They spent time laughing, talking in some crooks' dialect she failed to follow. She noticed with a shock that they were taking her down Mount Davis Road, past Cape Mansions and St Clare's Girls' School and Felix Villas. She was deposited at the path to the squatter shacks.

Politely the man opened the rear door.

"How did you know his name?" she could not help asking, still frightened.

"Ah Tseng?" The man hawked up phlegm and spat expertly down wind. "Chiselling bastard owed. Gambling, see?"

"Gambling's fine," the driver said from his window. "Losing isn't."

They chuckled as if at the wittiest saying.

KwayFay could not believe that, a short while since, she had been standing in the small streets by the harbourside watching the marionette Flag Cloth Opera. She stood waiting for them to tell her what to do, badly wanting to ask how they came to follow the assassin.

"Little Sister," the driver said soberly. "Check your clothes for blood. If you need new clothes, there is money. Buy."

"I cannot be late tomorrow!" she wailed, fear of normal events returning.

The man returned to the car and got in, slamming the door.

"I don't fucking believe this," he told his friend.

"It's orders."

"Listen, Little Sister," the driver said reasonably. "It will not matter if you are late as long as you get rid of any stains. Understand?"

"Yes," she said, though she wanted to say no.

"Get going," the other commanded. "I can hear police sirens in Pok Fu Lam."

She too could hear the distant wah-wah. The car pulled from the kerb and she was left looking at its dwindling tail lights. She turned and began to climb the narrow steep path, her ankles folding from weariness.

The squatter shacks showed oil-lantern lights, except hers was in darkness. She approached it slowly, realising she had left no water in her tin. She felt delirious, and almost laughed, with so expensive a watch in her handbag. The silly amusement almost turned to weeping as she entered, fumbling with the wire. Her key was still in place.

"KwayFay?"

She screeched and almost fell from fright, but it was only Li ChangShih, an elderly lady who lived by hawking in Kennedy Town market. She sold fish, to keep her brother in the leper colony on Hay Ling Chau, sometimes running errands and carrying messages among the squatters. She had a narwhal tusk and kept it by her door god to ward off predators. She had only three teeth, she was proud of telling KwayFay, but they were perfect. She had a cousin, a policeman who was imprisoned for obtaining money squeeze which he had declined to share with his superiors.

"Ah Li!" KwayFay said, relieved.

"I stayed until you came," the old lady said.

"Good. Thank you, *Tai-Tai*."

It was polite to address her as married, for once she had been Chang until she was wed. Her husband lived in the Walled City, where police were ignored.

"I am to tell you nobody has been inside your house."

"Thank you, *Tai-Tai*." KwayFay paused, then asked the question she knew was doomed to fail for want of answer. "Who told you to do that?"

"I do not know."

"Did they not speak to you?"

"Nobody has spoken to me today."

Mrs Li knew everything, including how much the Apple Seller Lady was worth in Tai Kok Tsui, in Kowloon side.

"Thank you, Mrs Li."

KwayFay heard the old lady clop up the rough path. She sat in darkness and let tears fall, hearing the occasional child outside shouting, stones clattering. The children were playing the Cockroach Game, chanting, shrieking with laughter. KwayFay told herself that one day she too would laugh, but now look at her; lost, not knowing who was a friend, who would let her live.

Days, not too long ago, when she had almost cried herself to sleep from loneliness, now seemed like paradise, where all the gods were friendly and she could sleep. Solitude outdid fear, best of all when terror roamed the street where she ought to be able to walk, come and go.

The watch was inaudible. She fumbled for her handbag, opened the clasp and took the watch out. It illuminated in the darkness. It had a smaller hand, presumably Greenwich Mean Time, so essential in Hong Kong's financial houses.

Then she felt a wad in her handbag. It felt thick and convincing. A dense wad of used notes. She felt something else. A lighter, cigarette lighter? Something she had never possessed in her life, except once when, aged nine, she stole one from a café table in Hung Hom. It was heavy. She struck the lid with a thumb and yelped at the sudden flame. It was adjustable. Gas? It stayed on. She placed it carefully on the floor beside her trestle cot, awed by its dazzle.

The note wad was in her other hand. She unclipped the silver pin. They were mostly red, high denomination, a bundle any thief would kill for.

Therefore the thief had been told to kill and rob her. As a test of her veracity? The two men had wanted reassurance that she would not disclose anything. Yet she honestly had seen nothing of them before.

Her reply to them had been truthful. They believed she was standing by them, loyally determined to reveal nothing to that wayward street thief. They implied their *bosi* would be pleased.

They'd said she had money for clothes. This must be it.

Was this another test? Tears flowed faster. How to survive a test, when one didn't even know why it was being set? And how to answer unknown questions?

She undressed thinking of Mrs Li, who had patiently sat guard on her shack. All Hong Kong was conspiring. KwayFay simply could not comprehend. She placed the bag with her laptop inside under her pillow and slipped under the single sheet.

Instantly she fell asleep, praying Ghost Grandmother would leave her alone tonight.

Chapter Seven

"Welcome, sir."

Ah Min hated walking more than a few paces. The doctor had the sense to use a Queen Mary Hospital consulting room, ground floor, but this put the Triad lieutenant at a disadvantage. He had to traverse the two corridors, and was wheezing when he entered. The doctor's instruments and screens chilled him. It shouldn't have been in some charnel house.

He sat uninvited and remained silent, beaming while his breathing stabilised. The doctor fussed.

Dr Choy was a prattler in pin-stripes. The senior neurologist in the Medical Faculty at the *Dai-Hok*, university, was only marginal value to the Triad, hardly worth a retainer. Ah Min watched the man make quips, rearrange papers on his desk. Ah Min had overcome all adversities in life, and risen to be the treasurer of the Triad, the feared "Society of Three Harmonies". It had been a hard road, progress marked by deaths and violence. Now, smarting with outrage, he was sent to obey the Triad master's instruction to consult this dealer in calamities. Illnesses were for the weak. A doctor's existence must surely be contaminated by ailment? He regarded the man with contempt. The neurologist was anglicised Cantonese, a human being in which two degradations combined. Voluntary indoctrination, but at what sacrifice?

"You listened to the tapes," Ah Min said.

"Yes, sir."

"Has she a madness?"

Dr Choy sat, tipping his fingers. Tapes of KwayFay's ramblings lay on his desk.

"One is of her sleep-talking, I take it? Two from her work place?

The man had been told that. Ah Min had not come to be patronised.

"She talks," Choy added quickly, "to somebody. There are faint squeaks." Ah Min waited, scorn in his beam. "Perhaps – "

Perhaps, possibly, maybe. They were serf words. "Is she mad?"

"There are three possibilities." Choy gathered himself as if about to spring, crouching forward in his swivel chair. "She is tricking herself – common among hysterics. Or simply dreaming. Or imagining someone she once knew and does not consciously recall."

"Are these madness?"

"Not in the medical sense, no."

"Which of the three is it?"

"I cannot tell from tape talk."

"Which?" Ah Min's beam hardened. "Tell me. One."

Dr Choy swallowed. "Perhaps the last, sir?"

"No perhaps."

"The last," Choy said. He might be safest with that.

Ah Min rose and left without a word. Western medicine was contemptible.

Linda Ho had a flaming row with her husband, the one she had planned with such pleasurable anticipation.

HC dismissed the two serving amahs when he finished his evening meal, and sat with the TV turned off as if waiting for some axe to fall, uncommunicative.

"No name!" she shrieked, pointing at him as he sat there like a stuffed fool. She no longer cared if the servants heard. "*Mo meng.*"

"Not now," he said.

To her it sounded like begging. He hadn't even the strength to fight back and put her in her place. A worm of a man. HC would never have charmed at the race track, not like the suave gambler who'd won such a vast amount of money. That man was a winner.

And look what she'd got, a fool.

"Not now?" she screamed. "You make me look a fool at the racecourse! My friend flaunted her winnings. I'm made to look a *foki*, a serf, a peasant. Am I a Hakka woman from the street diggings? You are too mean to provide me with enough money to place a decent bet!"

"He was killed," HC said listlessly.

"You never listen!" she wailed, flinging cushions. "You don't care!"

"They killed him."

"Don't think I haven't been tempted to . . ."

His words finally struck and she faltered, standing there breathing heavily. She was a dumpy woman, unable to create that devastating look of affluence so necessary to a Hong Kong woman. All her friends said that behind her back. With sufficient money she could . . .

"Killed?"

"Your cousin David, YeePak Huang."

"Killed?" she repeated. Something was wrong with the words he was saying.

Cousin David, manager of their carpet warehouse? He couldn't be dead.

"They killed him. The phone call."

"During supper?" There had been a call earlier.

"The police said it was in Wanchai."

"Who?" she asked stupidly. An accident, surely nothing more sinister than that. Not David, so young, vibrant, certain to make something of himself.

"Your cousin."

She sank slowly to the sofa, holding a cushion, her next missile.

"A tram? A motor car?"

"Murdered." HC did not turn. He talked into space. She remembered now; he had eaten his meal like an automaton.

"Was there a ransom demand?" Now it bit, the terrible calamity this worm of a husband should have prevented.

Ransom was Hong Kong's tactic, to abduct a person and demand ransom equal to a third of his wealth. Businessmen were the prime targets. The police were frantic about it, but ransom was the Colony's way.

"Yes. One thousand dollars."

"*One . . .?*"

A breathtaking insult. Nothing! It also meant that David was already dead or in his last bout of torture when the ransom demand was announced. That too was the Colony's code of insult, to abduct then send in a ludicrously paltry demand. It was always a great source of amusement to Hong Kong. People would walk along laughing, crooking a little finger to show derision, the other hand covering the mouth as they laughed. The same tactic – abduct, demand, return on payment – had been exported with great success to the Philippines and elsewhere abroad.

"Things frighten me."

"What things?" Her voice rose, quickly quietened because this the amahs should not hear.

"There's a girl in the office. KwayFay. She knows spirit talk."

"She *what*?"

Linda stood, the better to glare down at him, wanting to assault him, this idiot telling her such fantastically unacceptable things. Did he not know that the days of Hong Kong as a Crown Colony were to end soon, by treaty, and that The People's Republic did not allow such thoughts? Spirits, ghosts, necromancing, were not ideologically correct. They were political treachery. There couldn't be such a girl. Pretend, yes. Real, impossible!

"I never should have given him the job," HC said dully.

"He was a good man, with a sound business sense! My sister – "

"I knew he'd screw up. I asked the girl if I should."

Back to her crescendo: "I told you to appoint him. So you check with some trollop?"

"I wanted to do right. No!" he almost shouted. "I didn't! I wanted to do what was safe!"

"Safe? You talk *safe*?" She saw an amah about to enter and kicked the door on her. "You ask some bitch should you do what I tell you?"

HC passed his hands wearily over his brow, wishing that he had never abandoned cigarettes. He was down to one surreptitious smoke a day, his incompetent staff his only colluders.

"The point is – "

"The point is you listen to a harlot instead of me!"

She almost launched herself at him, but the amahs would only hear. Then the news would be all over Hong Kong. Newspapers, English and Chinese alike, had stringers reporting salacious filth every midnight to their sleazy offices in Causeway Bay.

"You were wrong. KwayFay was right. They killed David because he would not deliver payment on your gambling."

"They . . .?" She managed to repeat the terrible news, making it authentic. "Who are *they*?"

"Some Triad, some Hong, who knows? They hold your – our, my – loans."

HC explained, choosing words carefully and speaking slower than he had ever done. He felt desperate to pursue his investment schemes. They had seemed so orderly until now.

"I tried to pay off your gambling debts to the Mong Kok lender. He phoned today. He will lend no more money. David stole the repay money. The lender has sold your debts."

"Sell debts?" she squeaked, never having heard of the manoeuvre. Cousin David went out of her mind, because this was important. This was gambling.

"It is common. Factoring, sharing, split indebtedness, commission halving, the usual."

She drew back to appraise him, never having seen him like this. Helpless, yes. Defeated, certainly. But sure of these strange words, suddenly revealing that he knew things she had thought beyond him?

"You did not pay my borrowings off, like always?" She felt enraged. "What sort of a husband lets his wife's debts be bought and sold like cheap street linen?"

"A husband with debts."

HC admitted it with sorrow. Saying it like that made it suddenly highest priority for action. He thought of KwayFay.

"You too have debts?" she yelled.

The nerve of it! *He* had debts, when she was in hell?

"Investments have done poorly. The London FTSE index and the Nikkei a month ago were off. The Dow Jones – "

"Why you talk of these things?" she howled, in tears.

"I hated giving your cousin the Emporium. I asked KwayFay. She said don't. You kept on saying give him the managership, he would do brilliantly. So I did."

"They killed him?"

Linda thought in shock how furious her sister would be.

Monica had always wanted to get back at HC and Linda, ever since Linda's father died and his money was shared with a little bias, but whose fault was that? Advantage existed to be taken, *ne*? You saw a good bet and went for it, or you were a fool. Just like life.

"I told David to pay a tenth of the gross to the Mong Kok lender. They have weekly collectors. Paying interest only buys time."

"A *tenth* a *week*?" Linda screamed.

She immediately thought of her untried gambling scheme, perhaps a roll-up with twists on the side, three races, just perfect as long as the odds could be guaranteed more than 13-8. Or, she worked out with her mouth watering, there might have been enough to bribe some jockeys to obey a gambler's inspired guess. She could have raked in an absolute fortune! Instead, HC had been paying out her money to that stoat of a money lender! Typical of HC, one waste after another.

"We owe them more than the Emporium is worth."

"It is ours!"

"It *was*. Not now. When I began the firm, I used a collateral loan. They claim it. We still owe the whole sum, need to pay weekly interest."

"What did he do with the money? Where is it?"

"Falsified the accounts. For me. For them."

"This girl knew Cousin David?"

"No. She dreamed her answer. She does that."

"She *dreams*? And you listen to some tart's fucking dreams instead of me?"

"That's the trouble, Linda. I didn't listen to her. I did as *you* said." He glanced about the apartment as if tallying its worth. "She knew you would lose at Happy Valley. I heard her mutter. She described the jockey's colours, everything."

"She *knew* my bets . . .?"

"I tried to give her a gift of money, sort of back pay. She refused it. I heard her speaking to herself later before your horses had even run."

"Does she learn from the computer?" Linda knew nothing of

computers, but held them in awe. "She refused a gift of money?"

"She dreams."

HC sat looking out at the brilliance of Hong Kong harbour. It dejected him now. Only days ago it had seemed a lovely jewel filled with promise.

"Spirits are not understood these days. We shall soon be forbidden to observe all ancient customs in the new Hong Kong."

Linda thought hard. A girl who dreamed of horses losing could also dream the winner, *ne*? "You must not tell anyone."

"I have said nothing. She is always right. She decided about a new Pacific currency out of the blue. She decided one way, the banks predicted the other. She was right. The international banks were wrong."

"Then she sleeps with Triads," Linda concluded.

"No. She is poor, a girl of no family."

"You sure?" More than one girl had advanced her prospects by taking the route of a Flower Girl. It was a well-trodden path.

"She lives among squatter shacks."

"Would she help us?"

HC stared at his wife, astonished.

"She hates me," he said simply. "I abated her wage, to squeeze a little money for . . . debts."

"Wait!" Linda Ho said. "There is chance here! If this girl dreams horses that win . . ." There! It was out.

"No more horses," HC begged. "No more gambling."

His wife eyed him. No more gambling? Gambling was life!

"She was taken from work yesterday to some place. I saw from the window. The driver was one who called at the Emporium."

Linda exhaled slowly. "KwayFay is in with the lenders?"

"No. She has nothing. I have a few days to get payment. I must give them the Emporium and the retail outlets. No credit is left in my firm."

That enraged Linda. "Money is what an investment house is! What husband are you?"

"A husband living in a flat not his own, carrying debts not his own, working in a firm no longer his own."

Linda got up, shocked. He had never spoken this way. She

went to stand in the vast picture window.

Hong Kong was out there, lights shimmering on the sea, the harbour frantic with activity even at this late hour. HC's account was impossible. Had she not always brought him through? Wasn't she still capable?

"Always a no-name man," she said with detestation. "I shall think of a scheme."

"Maybe I could work off the balance. I have nothing else. At least I would not be killed."

The idea came to her with such a mental explosion it was like fireworks on the Double Tenth. She turned, smiling.

"Trust me. I know what to do!"

"I cannot even pay for David's funeral. Who gives credit for the assassinated cousin of a gambling wife?"

She took the description on the chin without rebuke, sure of herself, thrilled at the gamble she was about to take.

"Where does this KwayFay live?"

Chapter Eight

Today, KwayFay knew, was a day for being dispirited. It was not her fault, more that of Ghost Grandmother. She must have appeared to her during the night, yet not had the decency to leave memory of what she had imparted.

This spelled misery. Grandmother would come screeching questions that her granddaughter, idle girl, could not answer. KwayFay was in a sulk. How could she answer forgotten questions? It was unfair.

So she went to find out, in the Lantern Market where fortune tellers congregated.

She carefully checked the date: not the Twelfth Day of the Second Moon, famously the worst day for consulting fortune tellers. It wasn't, so she went.

The Lantern Market began at nine o'clock, not always an auspicious hour for everyone's luck, but she had no time to wait until the tenth hour which was her best. She decided to wander among the hissing paraffin lanterns before the Driving Licence sheds, near where the Macao Ferry arrived soon after eight-thirty, and not select a fortune teller until tennish. That would do.

Street hawkers were already laying out their wares on strips of rugs. Her favourites were the jade sellers. Mere pieces of cloth were laid upon the tarmac where, until dusk, cars parked and police strolled. Now, it was a world of glowing amber lights, crouching men and women hoping desperately to make a sale. Fruit, vegetables, but mostly toys, games, clothes, gems, jades excavated from burial chambers on the China mainland and illicitly brought in on junks descending the Pearl River, mostly unchecked by the Governor's water police.

And the fortune tellers.

Fortune tellers had a special place in Hong Kong Island's Lantern Market. The market was laid out in rows parallel with the harbour road. The best were always nearest the General Post Office. KwayFay let herself drift, as if only casually interested.

She paused by the blackbird. She liked to see the blackbird in action. An anxious man, probably a godown worker from his shabby attire and plastic sandals, approached the fortune teller who crouched by the side of his minah bird's cage smoking a cigarette, eyes wrinkled against the smoke. He shuffled a pile of warped cards, several of them so greasy they stuck together. Not much chance of those contributing to the God of Luck's selection then, KwayFay thought wrily.

As was polite, she listened closely. Other drifters came to join in the customer's haggling, the fortune teller's refusals, everyone chipping in to say if the fee was too little for a decent fortune. KwayFay did not contribute, for she might soon be a customer.

Finally, they settled on HK$ 100, not much but the night was young. The absence of customers was always death to fortune telling, for was it not proof that the spirits had deserted that particular mystic? Hawkers who wanted a particular pitch paid over 10,000 dollars for the right to place their rug down only a few yards further along the waterfront, fearing a bad *Fhung Seui*, the wind/water axis, could destroy chances of good trading.

She waited to see how the nervous customer's fortunes would pan out. A loud *"Waaaaah!"* of approval rose from the crowd clustered about the bird cage as the anxious labourer stooped and whispered his question to the bored creature. It eyed the customer balefully. Its trick was coming.

The fortune teller settled back on his haunches, then flipped open the cage door. The minah bird immediately hopped out, pecked through the pile of cards then selected one. It cast it to its master with a dismissive air and hopped back into its cage as if wanting to slam the door on the world. The crowd murmured appreciation.

Some tried to read over the fortune teller's shoulder. KwayFay knew many of the cards were covered with invented hieroglyphics, meaningless to all except the mystic, and often not even to him.

The necromancer read, murmuring to himself, but not for long since this was a mere hundred-dollar consultation and didn't deserve much of a show. He spat, and told the worried man that he was at serious risk of losing his job, that there was no way of staving off this disaster, but that in five months' time he would escape a serious chest illness. The woman he wanted would ignore him. He would lose several bets, including five he shared with his brother. He would never own a motor car or be rich. He would not buy a successful shop, and it was pointless hoping.

The crowd remained silent but imperceptibly began to withdraw, until the customer was crouching in a wide space all his own. Nobody wanted to stand near somebody cursed with bad luck. Spirits were well known for being sloppy enough to transfer their intentions to anyone situated nearby, forgetting their original victim. Even KwayFay, who knew that the man wasn't going to be as unlucky as all that – he would win a small lottery prize the week after next anyway – found herself stepping away. She waited a decent interval until the man left, the crowd showing him scant sympathy. Sympathy wasn't much use in Hong Kong, for wasn't misfortune the result of either failing to propitiate some deity, or in shunning duty? That it might be due to chance was also a possibility, but chance had a way of falling in with those sufficiently powerful to make it behave itself.

She moved to the sand writer. This mystic had a tray of warmed sand and a lantern to heat it, keeping it dry enough for ghost writing. Humidity was dreadful tonight, every stitch clinging and damp.

Most customers wanted to see a ghost actually write characters in the sand. The fortune teller simply did nothing. This was often rumoured, had been seen a million times, but in fact had never even been photographed. KwayFay herself had never seen it. Either customers could write their question, or have it written in the sand by the mystic for HK$ 100, who would then pore over his scrawl. There was little mystique, no trance or sign of the supernatural. It was a simple money transaction.

The best thing about Hong Kong's necromancers, KwayFay thought, was their cavalier disregard of the desire to please. Whether news was good or bad, auspicious or grim, they trotted out their information with abandon, coughing on their cigarette before moving on to the next customer. Death, wholesale business failure, loss of loved ones or family, ruinous fires or scholastic catastrophes, all were delivered with the same casual nonchalance to the applause of the crowd. Good fortune could never be guaranteed, not even by the payment of immense fees, sometimes up to HK$ 500. Smaller sums were a risk, for spirits were easily offended. They might take umbrage and see low fees as a mortal insult. Spirits loathed stinginess.

It was also a hazard for the necromancer himself, for ghosts hated a fortune teller who thought so little of the netherworld that he had the unmitigated nerve to charge a mere fifty dollars or even less. On rainy nights, with tourists the only clientele, many mystics faced the choice of going home penniless or risking giving offence to spirits by reducing their prices. KwayFay knew it wasn't worth it.

The Taoist man she sought sat apart on the kerb beneath two adjacent parking meters. He held a small wooden box. In it were minutely small slips of inscribed paper. He would select one randomly, or, for more money, allow a customer to choose one herself. He would consult the paper and deliver his verdict.

KwayFay considered, for he was alone. He was a small wizened man in the traditional long *cheong saam*, inevitably smoking a cigarette and wearing his skull cap, all black.

She checked the time, close on ten, and said good evening. He looked up.

"I am busy, *Siu-Jeh*," he said.

She could see he wasn't.

"Business Head," she said politely, "you do not want money?"

"Little Sister," he said, putting down his wooden box firmly, as good as telling her to go. "You have no need of my services."

"Thank you," she told him, heart pounding, and went her way.

Nobody noticed the brief exchange. Disturbed, she moved on along the line of vendors, and found herself inexplicably staring at a plastic sheet on which were several small arrangements of gears, chains from bicycles and wheels.

To calm her nerves she bought a small drink of fragrant jasmine tea from a stall vendor by the Star Ferry Concourse.

Saturday was tomorrow. HC had been moved to close the office, claiming it was a family holiday. They all knew this was frank deception, for he looked abysmally frightened. Alice said it was on account of some Singapore defaulters. Tony Hung, an ebullient graduate who'd managed to swim the Sum Chun River into Hong Kong, reckoned he knew everything that was bound to happen once the Crown Colony was handed back to the People's Republic of China, said HC's wife was finally going to make a killing on her new betting system and the whole firm would receive a bonus. Tony actually knew nothing. His degree in commerce statistics had been bought for him from a diploma mill in Carolina, USA, for US\$ 3,000, a loan from a maker of plastic flowers. He had it framed on the office wall.

KwayFay knew Tony would come to grief, but liked him. He was a spy for the People's Republic of China. Only a spy could give her that cold chill when the air-conditioning was off and sweat was running down the nape and her blouse was sticking to her back. She didn't bother with spies, so pretended to like Tony's crude jokes because a spy with influence was possibly more than a spy, *ne*?

She finished her jasmine tea, truly revolting, thanked the stall holder and went to catch the 5B bus. She would not go to have her fortune told again. They were a waste of time.

Chapter Nine

Old Man hated the smooth surfaces of Hong Kong's redesigned harbour, easily the most inelegant façade on earth. What was wrong with the greasy turmoil of the old waterfront (Kowloon side, of course) with its flotsam, the seething mess of rubbish the junks and sampans had to shove aside with their blunt prows? Now the harbour was clean he missed the floating layer of wood, orange peel, dead rats, decaying fruit, the endless bobbing plastic bags, the whole sorry slick of laahpsaap.

Hong Kong was sadly changing, all because the Emperor of China and England had signed some stupid treaty centuries ago. Can you imagine? He was furious. Did kings and emperors not think ahead? Could rulers not simply leave things as they were? He wanted to feel comfortable with life now he was old and felt things slipping away.

He smiled at the reminiscence.

That had *been* a waterfront! Before the mad English decided to make pretty walks where young lovers could admire the cross-harbour view of Hong Kong Island under globes of white electric light of an evening. Too many English, that was the trouble. Not a single governor Chinese. And, worse, what was coming would be disastrous to trade – well, *his* trade. These madmen had decided to obliterate the Walled City, that haven for crime and evil. Who could buy so glorious a place?

Now, it would become another housing estate full of dull folk who would pay him a single percent on his outlay. And yet more shops, paying less than four percent to his threat-men. He grieved. Three-point-seven percent return gross on six-figure investments, in English Sterling pounds, not a cent more. Heartbreaking. Redevelopment was filthy treachery.

And the threat-men! *Waaaaiii!*

You couldn't get good threat-men these days, not at any price, unless you trained them yourself. Who had time for that? Brainless, ignorant know-alls. He felt old and tired.

Look at the last two idiots. They all wanted to be admired, "respected" *bhoh-ngaw* tough guys, when they were about as terrifying as a nettle. He had taken on two youths – gold teeth at the age of seventeen, would you believe – both passed Hong Kong Middle School, both skilled knife throwers, tough, "tearaways" in English slang. They came highly recommended. He had entrusted them with kidnapping that dross David YeePak Huang, cousin to that HC moron whose wife gambled. They'd caught him in the Emporium. Then they'd done something outrageous.

They hailed a taxi.

Old Man moaned. These were the people he had to work with, infants who thought they were Hollywood gangsters. He had twenty-four motor cars on permanent stand-by. The fools called a taxi.

He accepted the glass of cold tea from an amah who laid it before him on the old rosewood table and retreated. He gazed after her. Not too bad, but did she have buck teeth? And did her hair grow the wrong way? These were terribly wrong in Chinese tradition. He had not slept with a woman for two weeks now, and that was bad for a man's skin and fingernails. He knew that much. But risks were everywhere in sex. What if he discovered some flaw while in the throes, such as a black hair on her chin? *Waaaiii!* He would never live it down. Despite the People's Republic of China, Hong Kong folk were still full of traditions, superstitions, dreams, omens, and the inescapable grief about luck, luck, luck.

He sighed, moved to his emperor chair and lowered himself carefully on its phoenix-embroidered cushions. It was his little joke, to have a coloured red and yellow phoenix writhing on the soft satin. That was the symbol of an empress, more correctly, but at least signified resurgence.

"Ready, Business Head?"

Nothing for it. Work, work, work. "Ready."

The mirror directly in front of the seated man was unveiled as a curtain hissed back. Lights in the ornate room dimmed. He was looking into a sitting room, set for an interview with a Formica covered table and two chairs. A sofa, side table, and two paintings of Ladder Street as got from any tourist stall, completed the furnishings.

A police lieutenant entered as if on cue, and Ah Min the Triad's principal negotiator followed, smiling.

Old Man had never seen Ah Min without that beaming smile. Rotund almost, quite like some old Shanghainese roué bent on pederasty or one of those oily meals of snake and onions, Ah Min was devoted utterly to money. Ah Min was a walking pope of money. Once, Old Man had seen Ah Min, walking in Nathan Road, suddenly cry out, holding his arms wide, shouting for all Hong Kong to stop.

And had picked up a cent from the pavement.

A single cent. One.

He'd pocketed it, and walked on beaming. Money and Ah Min were destined for each other. Money and Ah Min were lovers.

Another time, the ledger books had been a day slow coming. Old Man wanted them in his hands at ten o'clock on the due day, no variation. Eventually, fuming, he'd sent for them, punishing the principal messenger by a massive fine from anger. And Ah Min had arrived, waddling in with tears of humiliation streaming down his beaming fat face.

Without a word he had placed the top ledger before his master. He'd knelt, and would have kowtowed as before an emperor had Old Man not snapped for him to get on with it and say what had gone so calamitously wrong.

"Master," Ah Min had sobbed, resorting to English from shame, "there is discrepancy. I accept full responsibility, and will agree to any punishment you decide."

"Indeed," Old Man remembered saying in a cold voice, for that was undoubtedly true. "Who is guilty?"

"I am guilty, master."

"How much is missing?"

"Three cents, sir."

Three cents, namely nought point nought three of one Hong Kong dollar; current standing, one thousand cents to a Sterling pound? For this Ah Min sobbed uncontrollably. In one week Old Man's enterprises distributed over eight million American dollars in gate money, drops, payments. Such was Ah Min.

Old Man observed the police lieutenant seat himself first, as guest, Ah Min following suit. An amah brought in tea. The policeman did not drink, western barbarian that he was, and had the insolence to push the cup away with a let's-deal gesture that made Old Man suck in air. The effrontery of the coarse uneducated loon! Could these people have once ruled the world? It was beyond comprehension.

Ah Min kept beaming, as on the day he'd been mortified because somewhere among Old Man's seventeen million dollars, the Triad's income for the month, three Hong Kong cents had gone missing. There was no single American coin so paltry. That incident had shown Old Man Ah Min's excellence. At the time of that confession, Old Man had remained still, watched Ah Min kneeling there sobbing and beaming.

Finally, Old Man remembered having had the good sense to say, "This once, Ah Min, I forgive you. I allow you this crime for past friendship. I will not tolerate such error again. Go!"

Ah Min had waddled out backwards, carrying his ledgers, weeping and grinning. He had, all unbidden, paid a donation of twenty-four thousand dollars to the master that evening, this being three times eight, for twenty-four was Old Man's luckiest number. It could have been a simple twenty-four cents, but Ah Min multiplied the gift by a hundred thousand. Money was Ah Min's religion, his reason for being. No-one should make fun of religion, spirits being capricious beings, *ne*?

He watched Ah Min, his expert negotiator for money, confront the police lieutenant. The silly youths' carelessness during the kidnapping still smarted, but Ah Min would get something out of this.

"The incident is regrettable," Ah Min said in perfect English.

"Many tourists saw the incident."

"I understand." Ah Min beamed, spreading his hands wide to show his lack of duplicity.

"Broad daylight, after all."

"And so many people saw!" Ah Min added.

"Two youths, bundling a frightened man out of his carpet warehouse into a taxi, well, I mean to say . . ."

What an idiot language! the Triad master thought to himself, watching through the one-way glass. What did the inspector of police "mean to say"? If he meant to say something, why not say it? Yet these English had the whole world talking the same barbaric tongue, a babblement of inferences, hints, evasions, understatements. He thought with bitterness, give me Chinese any time, where the pun was the highest form of slick speech and was always hilarious, instead of this slithery tentative language. What a stroke of luck Americans had never learned nuance!

"True, true," Ah Min soothed, his beam intensifying. "Your hands were tied! I can see that."

Even then the moronic uniformed man did not recognise the implication, simply kept on nodding, waiting for his bribe.

"I've kept the incident under wraps, but sooner or later I'll have to move on it."

"That is natural, Inspector! Police procedure!"

"By the end of the day."

Ah Min seized the allusion. "All days must come to an end, is that not so?"

The inspector seemed uncomfortable, for his own days were soon to end. He would return to run a shoe shop for his cousin in Warminster, where his salary would plummet like a shot bird. In England, opportunities for graft and extortion were rare beyond a man's understanding. No lost cents in England's inflexible income tax laws.

Old Man watched the scenario. He shook his head; an impossible world to live in, where greed was detected, suppressed, hunted down. Changes, too many changes.

"And today's work is no exception, Inspector."

"Correct."

"I realise you must make a very awkward decision."

"I must follow procedure."

"Of course! Without deviation!"

"To allow any incident to pass without a proper resolution would damage my position."

"It would! Damage severely!"

"There is little I can honestly do."

"True!"

And Ah Min waited. The policeman waited. Old Man watched.

There was no greater intellectual thrill than seeing money enter an arena. Ah Min might bring money in like a carnival, with trumpets and banners, teams of cut-throats and maidens adorned for feasts. Or he might slip in money as no more than a shifty shadow edging onto sand, stepping daintily across blood-soaked ground. It was theatre, as in those puppet theatres that the lovely KwayFay paused to see down Central Street before surviving her test of a threatening assassin. Such theatre! How interesting this thought was, that Chinese theatre was the exact opposite of English theatre, the former so immediate and frank, the latter full of meanings impossible to excavate.

He dragged his attention back to the arena visible through the glass.

The inspector of police cleared his throat. Old Man's lip curled in contempt. Greed made whores. This man was revealing himself a whore.

"There might be something, though."

"Might there be?"

Ah Min had a degree in languages. Six of his tongues were Chinese vernaculars, with two English things and one the sort of French the Swiss spoke. See? Foreigners couldn't even get their own speech uncrossed. Ah Min's pretence of pidgin-speak was dropped. His beaming smile widened. He was enjoying this, now he had the upper hand over this man from Yinggwok, the "hero country" of barbarian England.

"I might be able to help you in some way."

"Might you?"

The hero almost went red, this fighter in the arena, now that money was about to enter. A slither, this time, watching Old Man guessed, money creeping along the walls before the tigers noticed and pounced.

"I could make things easier for you by losing the police records of the incident."

"Does that happen?" Ah Min asked innocently.

"Very rarely. A file goes missing, there is an investigation."

"Would that not be a terrible risk, Inspector?"

"It would. That's the point."

More waiting. Ah Min beamed, relishing the joust. The inspector hesitated, wanting Ah Min to mention payment.

The policeman sat forward on the edge of his chair, leaning his elbows on the table even though tea had already been poured. See? Barbarian.

"Er, the point being . . .?" Ah Min murmured, a frown with his grin this time.

"I would need some recompense for taking the risk. I want to be friendly, but it should be made worth while. You see that."

"I do, I do! Yet the incident was a small matter, was it not? Two youths, bundling some man into a taxi. They might have been on their way to a football match at Hong Kong Stadium!"

"Except the man was found dead. Mutilated."

"Do you think, Inspector, that the tourists could prove that the man they saw was the deceased person?"

The victim's face had been irreparably changed by knife work on Old Man's order. At least the idiots, the two new so-clever threat-men, had remembered to do that. He had to think of every little thing these days, not like when he was young. Standards had gone. Old Man blamed the mothers.

"I'm sure they could. The clothes were the same, and the taxi driver could confirm it too."

"The taxi driver," Ah Min said, deep in thought. Believe that, you'd believe a politician. Taxi drivers' memories were written on water.

"We already have his statement."

"In the file?"

"In the *same* file."

"The risk, though, to you would be great."

"For enough compensation I might take the risk. For the sake of friendship."

"How generous!" Now the frown gone. Money was in the arena!

"I would expect the money to match the risks I would be taking."

"Why shouldn't that be so?" Ah Min asked, hands out again.

Old Man could tell Ah Min was seeing himself exactly like a

character from ancient Chinese operas, perhaps KwayFay's favourite, the Flag Cloth Opera, where astonished nobles cast back their gigantic oval-cuff sleeves to show what was about to happen. He smiled. He missed Chinese opera, where the audience noise was so deafening from chattering that actors had difficulty hearing each other. It was totally lacking in reverence, as opera should be. More contrasts to be thought over, with the People's Republic of China loomed darkening the northern political sky.

"I would want it to be sufficient compensation."

"Indeed you would!"

The inspector's begging bowl was out now. Entering the arena as a combatant, powerful and questing, he was now a supplicant, begging the threatening beasts prowling out there for enough time to scrape up the coins thrown by his contemptuous employers.

"Perhaps sixteen thousand dollars, American?"

"And the purpose would be . . .?"

The Triad master sank back, replete. The game was over. He did not want to watch the conclusion, for endgames were inevitable. It was no longer a joust, nor even a negotiation. It was the sordid transaction of a boss paying off some minion. All serfs were beneath contempt. Why else were they serfs? They loved to grovel, thinking themselves lords. Had the mighty inspector of police shown some spirit, Old Man might have watched events unfold. Were the police inspector Chinese, he would have allowed the police report to go forward to trial, and settled on his "compensation" only when the case entered the Law Courts, Hong Kong side. Old Man might even have had himself driven to Statue Square to observe the final play of withdrawal and resolution, when witnesses appeared only to renege. He loved the expressions on all the defeated lawyers' faces.

Now? Now a Home Counties shoe-shop clerk whined for his pennies. Where was the entertainment in that?

He signalled and the lights came on. Where was finesse? Life was barren. And he now had the problem of placating his father.

That his parent had passed away more than forty years ago was irrelevant. Ancestors had to be addressed.

To whom could he turn? He thought of KwayFay. It would not be beneath his own dignity to go down Jordan Road and inspect the side alleys full of paper shops, ready for the ceremonial burning of their wares, for everyone still did this while denying they did anything of the kind. It was the Hong Kong way, to pretend conformity while doing the opposite. But would he be thought disrespectful if he was to go alone, or with uncomprehending henchmen? He could send that girl, whose skilled communications with the spirits and the hereafter seemed so sure.

He pondered, then signalled for attention, and in came the amah.

Speaking quietly, he couldn't help examining the amah's hair and teeth as she stooped to hear his whispered commands. His eyes were definitely going. His inspection was incomplete. He was too tired to tell her to move closer while he had a good look. This was becoming serious, this advancing age. He should decide on some lieutenant who would take over, but who? Who might fit the bill?

He heard two of his men approaching. They knocked. He told them to come in and stand by the door while he thought about the decision he had just made. The girl?

Yes. She would arrange the funeral ritual for his dead father.

Three hours later Old Man sent for Ah Min. He did not invite the Triad's treasurer to sit down.

"The past files, Ah Min. Still secure?"

"Certainly, master! In the storeroom, at the Brilliant Miracle Success Investment. The security system is updated – "

Old Man gestured for silence.

"They have been searched, as ordered? HC Ho has had all this time. He must be close to completion, yes?"

"His search must nearly be done, master."

"Check, and report."

Old Man watched Ah Min waddle out. Still the beaming face, but a trace of worry in there. It would not do for a precious advantage to be lost. The Triad needed one colossal coup to face the coming political changes. He thought again of KwayFay. Was she the one?

Chapter Ten

KwayFay sat on the edge of her truckle cot, wondering.

Work had been stupid all week, HC behaving stupidly. Nothing in the office had any sense.

What had he been thinking of, telling her to leave her work station, telling Larry Tan the illegal Canton immigrant to take over her lists when the poor hopeless youth couldn't even count.

HC even told her she should go through some old files, even those of customers long since moved to other, more salubrious, firms or even (the shame!) to bank investment counters, always hopeless except for the Hang Seng in Des Voeux Road Central, surely the most odious and repellent bank building.

On HC's orders she seated herself before the mounds of dusty files in the storeroom gloaming. The slightest move set her coughing, so much must from the fungus-ridden files. It was a hellhole, a punishment posting, as all the Yankee war films called dangerous work sites.

Her first three hours were torture. She actually went to knock on HC's door and ask what she was supposed to be doing in there. He'd lifted his haggard face with an effort. Maybe he had been weeping.

"Do?" he'd repeated. "I told you. Find the file."

"Which file? There are thousands."

"You will know."

She hesitated. "I *don't* know, HC."

"What do you want, KwayFay?"

"I want to know what work I should do in the storeroom, Business Head. Which old file must I examine?"

"Find it," he said dully, unseeing eyes looking beyond her. "It's there somewhere."

"What, HC?"

"How do I know? You're the one with the . . ."

With what? "You gave me no coding, no year, no sign."

He said, broken. "Go. Look."

So she'd returned to the gloom of the stacked cavern with its tiers of shelves reaching the ceiling, dust everywhere, coughing herself almost to sleep in her anxiety to find . . . what, exactly?

She began to sob at the hopeless task. The files went back a score of years. Each unit file contained hundreds of chits, each with a dozen chops – stamped franks of authenticity. These were from times before computers made the written word redundant.

The one chair in the room was unspeakable. She spent almost a whole hour trying to clean it, and finished up dragging it into the corridor and setting about it with the cleaning woman's spray polish. The others in the office ignored her, except for whispering about her inescapable bad luck, undoubtedly the prelude to an ignominious sacking.

Her erstwhile friend Claire Yip came by, swinging her hips, showy in her lace blouse. KwayFay was sure the bitch had had her breasts implanted at a private clinic, hence the inescapable billowing-sails front and canyon cleavage.

"Do the job properly, KwayFay," Claire said airily, swishing by for the tenth time, deliberately accentuating her narrow waist. "Impress the boss! You might keep your job."

"Thank you, Claire."

"Don't thank me, KwayFay. I would hate you to lose your wage."

And had gone on her way, to return a few minutes later, cooing, "Good! It's beginning to look usable! So soon!"

It did not matter. Claire would finish her life limping when the North Point tram caught her foot, as would happen next Double Fifth when, on her way to the Dragon Boat Festival that day, she would cross Queensway to collect her car at the Multi-Storey next to Chater Gardens. Serve her right. She would then lose her rich Taipei fiancé. Claire expected the world to come running to help. Check this space, KwayFay thought.

About eleven o'clock that morning she had come to, blinking at the bare globe of light. She must have dozed among the stacked files. No ghost talk. Stiff, she went out to drink from the water fountain in the main office, conscious the noise abated when she appeared as everyone glanced her way.

Charmian Sau the *foki*, the office servant, was the only one who spoke to her. Charmian had borrowed her western name from a song.

"You want anything, KwayFay?" she asked, as KwayFay turned to go back to staring with blank incomprehension at the stacks of old files.

"No, thank you, Charmian."

"Shall I bring you water later?"

Such a kindness, to accord status to a demoted girl. From clerk to storeroom was shameful. Or, KwayFay wondered with sudden venom, did the *foki* perhaps see in KwayFay some ally now lowered to her own level? KwayFay smiled, guessing the innocence of the cleaner.

"Thank you, Charmian."

She returned to her prison. Charmian was forty-two, and destined to lose every cent and stitch next year in her endless pursuit of fortune at the game of Mahjong in her dreadful flat in Lai Chi Kok. KwayFay wished Charmian a better life. Soon would come that terrible time for Cantonese women, when their sudden lovely shape would crumple. It resembled a paper bag losing all its air, to shrink into a wizened mass of wrinkles. It always happened, unless sufficient money was available and surgeons preserved an aging woman's beauty, as in America where everyone was a millionaire.

The room seemed to have grown smaller. She sat and stared at the stacked files. The bulb, disturbed by KwayFay's return, swung slightly. Shadows lengthened, retracted, lengthened.

She watched them. What was the point of reading any one of the folios? None. She would have no idea of the figures, the names of companies. They were all before her time. Didn't they cease some twenty years ago? Faded inked-in dates said so.

Not only that, how could she interpret the figures? They had different accountancy systems back then. Even HC would be hard put to find any sense in the columns and double-accountancy systems she'd only heard of. Times had changed.

The bulb swung. Shadows danced. She dozed.

***

"Sleeping, lazy girl? You think slumber find husband?"

"No, Grandmother! I am searching in these files, but do not know why, or what for."

"Always sleeping! You know what would have happened to me if my grandmother had caught me sleeping?"

"Yes, Grandmother. You would – "

"Don't interrupt Honoured Ancestor, rude girl!"

The voice quietened into a monologue KwayFay had heard a hundred times.

"I would have been sent out to feed the chickens of neighbours. Then ducks. And then animals in the Hakka peoples' little valleys, so they would mend our village path. Made to labour in exchange for a few road stones! The shame!"

"Yes, Grandmother."

"And you sit idle doing nothing!"

"Yes, Grandmother."

"Where was I up to in your education?"

"How to solve quarrels without screaming in the street, Grandmother."

"Did you learn it?"

"Yes, Grandmother," KwayFay said miserably, hoping for a chance to wake and get on with staring uselessly at the thousands of old files, to please HC so he might forget to sack her.

"Tell how, lazy girl?"

"A *Ma Chieh Ti*, a shrieking Curse-In-Street woman, tells family secrets and brings dishonour on family."

"Truly terrible!" sighed Ghost Grandmother. "I remember one woman, bad temper! We tried poison but she bribed a medium to warn her, so survived all we could do. She was third cousin of your great-aunt, father's side, nine generations before yours. Or ten? I forget. She still wears yellow jacket, thinks herself so grand! A bitch. Terrible to be street-shouting woman."

"I was coming to the breaking of combs, Grandmother."

"Get on, get on."

"Street-shouting woman breaks a comb in front of the other woman, to show friendship ends."

"She – the *Ah Pau* I was talking of – broke three combs against three different women in five days," said Grandmother, with admiration despite the shame. Prowess indeed. "She shrieked at them all for a week. Go on, the ritual?"

"Nobody must pick the comb up, or hatred of street-shouting woman is shifted to you."

"All the trouble, and none of the pleasure of hating!" sighed the ghost.

"The village's Earth God rules disputes," KwayFay went on, feeling she was sailing on some drifting river, serene and sleepy. "He needs to be placated with a square of paper – "

"What colour?" demanded Ghost Grandmother sharply.

"Yellow," KwayFay said smugly, remembering easily now with such clarity she could see the very features of the Great-Aunt's third cousin of nine generations gone. Or maybe ten. "Plus fine gifts of paper clothing, and the Five Demons tokens."

"Good, good! She was a terrible bitch," Ghost said contentedly, "but I quite took to her."

"Firecrackers, best got from Gao Lung, the city of the Nine Dragons, namely Kowloon, by where the Walled City stands."

"Don't buy from that evil man in Cameron Road," Grandmother warned. "He short changes everybody. He cheated my daughter."

"Yes, Grandmother. And fresh eggs, to the lucky number, are then broken before the shrine of the Earth God. It must be brick, not wood, with a pointed stone in the middle for fertility."

Ghost Grandmother giggled, a weird high pitch that made KwayFay shudder. Some ghosts could laugh kindly; a pity Grandmother's laugh was so horrid.

"No good settling arguments if women end up barren, *ne*?"

"You are so right, Grandmother," KwayFay said, hoping praise would make her go away. "Firecrackers are put in the teapot, with the Five Demon emblems also, as the yellow paper is waggled above. Then the firecrackers are lit. The explosions defeat the enemy woman."

"You learned well for a change, lazy girl."

"Thank you, Grandmother."

There was a small silence, then, "I tell you a trick. After all, you are my granddaughter, and have learned well – for once."

KwayFay smarted. For once? She did really well every single time Grandmother came with her silly pointless questions and ridiculous stories. Wisely she said none of this.

"Thank you, Grandmother."

"If you argue with Street-Shouting Woman, girl, even if you have settled the quarrel, here is trick to cause her endless grief."

"But the quarrel is mended, Grandmother. The ritual has healed it, *ne*?"

"Yes, silly girl," the ghost said patiently. "But is it not pleasurable to cause a rival woman distress, even if you have become friends?"

KwayFay said nothing.

"Your enemy woman will do the same to you, so you do it first, d'you hear?"

Into KwayFay's silence Ghost Grandmother whispered, "Listen carefully, KwayFay. Here is how to trick your enemy Street-Shouting Woman. Bribe her family to tell you the Eight Characters of her birth time. Write them down. Then write on the same paper a prayer for trouble to come to her – I used to like blindness and belly pains a lot, used them quite often – and throw the paper into an urn where human bones are buried."

"What will happen, Grandmother?"

"She will suffer from yellow jaundice within the week, or go mad. Everybody knows this, but modern people forget, being ignorant like you."

"Did you do it, Grandmother?" she asked in awe.

"Of course! I did it once to a woman who hated me because I was very beautiful and her husband smiled at me when I went to the Feast of the White Tiger, who was general in the Yin Dynasty – you won't remember him – at the start of the Second Moon. It was to prevent argument, that being the best day for it. Her husband smiled at me because my legs and bottom were exquisite and his wife's were ugly. She and I did the firecracker ritual to be friends again. But I didn't trust her, so did the trick of Eight Characters. She went mad, was taken away to a walled building for mad people. I was glad."

"Grandmother! That's absolutely terrible!"

"Wasn't it!" Grandmother cackled with pleasure. "I tell it to you for guidance."

"Was her husband not sorrowful?"

"No. He too rejoiced." Ghost added coyly, "I not tell you who with! No sleep now, dozy girl."

Somebody knocked on the door. It was Charmian.

"Here's your water, KwayFay."

The filing clerk placed the plain glass in her hands, there being nowhere to put the drink down. KwayFay took a random file down from the shelves and rested the glass on it in her lap. She ought to have worn trousers today, slacks perhaps, had she money to buy any. She had the notes, of course, but whose were they? What if she spent some, and the threat-men from Kowloon who killed assassins and were cross when their knife got blood-stained, came back for the money, what then?

She told Charmian, "*Yao sam*. You have heart."

"Please, KwayFay." Charmian started to stammer. "If I can help you, I will. For teaching me that time."

KwayFay strove to remember the incident, but only had the vaguest memory of once having shown the woman how to clean a computer keyboard, and how to reassemble the wires and terminals if they became accidentally detached. Nothing else. She wondered at the strangeness of life, and concluded it must be the curious phase all Hong Kong was going through. It would all end soon, when the People's Republic of China came in with its Flower Flag and curiously bland currency notes and sullen street guards and bad manners, as all Hong Kong thought. Or perhaps it would all be sweetness, a permanent honeymoon with decorum everywhere?

"Not at all, Charmian."

She heard HC coming down the corridor. He barged in, almost sending her flying. Charmian fled.

"You found it yet?" he demanded.

"What, HC?"

"The file, the file!"

"File?" KwayFay removed her glass of water and offered him

the file she had taken to serve as a tray.

HC clasped it to his chest, eyes closed in rapture. "You sure?"

"That is it," she said firmly.

"Thank you, KwayFay. You won't lose from this!"

"What do I do now, HC?"

"Go back to work, KwayFay. Take the last hour off. You have done well."

"Thank you," she said, dazed.

"Come and explain it to me," HC said, beckoning with the door open.

"No," she said in fright. He stared. She babbled, "It will be unlucky for me. Page forty-seven."

"Forty-seven?" he repeated, gaping.

"That is correct." What was one fib more?

"Thank you, KwayFay."

"Not at all," she replied evenly, and went past him to sit at her console. She didn't even know if the file had a page forty-seven.

There was a sheaf of faxes and tiers of electronic e-mails but she did not mind. She seemed to have a job still, whatever the late afternoon might bring when HC discovered how meaningless the file actually was.

Chapter Eleven

The gambling in Macao's floating casinos were almost done for the night. Morning was slanting across the beige tables. The Fan Tan girls were sleepy at the East's most famous game of chance.

Old Man waited his opportunity out. He saw the baskets descend from the balconies where early – late! – diners sat to inspect the games below. He watched their place bets go in the baskets, to be lowered to the croupiers. Cards, roulette, Fan Tan, dice, they were all on the go, the croupiers slickly professional.

He liked to see the Fan Tan girls. They had a certain grace. A pile of white counters – pieces of pottery, as for the Japanese game of *Go* – was simply dumped into a heap. The Fan Tan girl would use her white wand to divide them on the green beige. Gamblers would wait as the girl used her wand to form the pieces into two piles. She would then sweep away – such feminine grace! – one mound off the table into a hanging pocket.

She might then stroll away to speak idly with other croupiers or maybe the casino boss, before returning to stand unsmiling by her Fan Tan table. No signals, no talking with the punters, no signs. Soon she would gracefully divide the mound into two, sweep away one of the heaps.

The game was this: would there be one piece finally left, or two? Would the last division be equal – two pieces – or one? Bets had to be paid before the end. Gamblers approach – no touching, or the harbour waters would be your only way home – and judge by peering to guess how the girl used her wand. The eternal question for the obsessed Fan Tan player was: did the pile contain an unequal number? Bets were bought and sold as the game progressed. Always the girl would wander, divide her remaining heap and stand gazing across the noisy place, before making her next discard.

Old Man knew it the most stupid game of all. He had seen fortunes lost on Fan Tan. Once he lost one of his best street men to it, when the fool had tried to bribe a Fan Tan croupier girl. Old Man had played once, and lost. He had never played again.

The Fan Tan table was surrounded by gamblers, all craning to see the girl move her white wand. A fool's enjoyment.

He also watched the dice, so popular since Americans flooded the world. Unlucky people, those Americans, because of their wealth. Money made fools of the moneyed, or so it was said.

Old Man had a great problem. He had seen it coming all his life. It had no solution.

He had to change his name, for so it had been foretold by his great-aunt from Fukien, that terrible place of famine, drought, wars, wars, wars. A visiting relative from Kwantung Province had prophesied the same the day he'd been born sixty years before. Had they conspired to guess that this name change would become necessary? No telling whether they had.

The lovely girls moved about the Floating Casino. One of them had tried for Jade Woman status among Triads in Hong Kong, and only just failed to make it. Still, she was wellnigh perfect. He had used her twice the previous year. She had been excellent.

Of the two Floating Casinos, he preferred the one in which he had shares. Extorted as percentages, of course, nothing written down for the Portuguese authorities to get their teeth into. Simply a product of combat in the waterfronts of Kennedy Town in Hong Kong Island and the bribery necessary to keep the opium divans off Stonecutters Island in Hong Kong's harbour.

His name.

It had seemed a problem that would never really arrive. Yet soon he would be sixty, and on that day it was ordained he had to change his name. They hadn't said to what. His sixtieth birthday seemed so far away. Now the new month was dawning over Macao, the sun stretching across the net-strewn harbour.

He was well known in Hong Kong, by the right people. His identity to others would not be a problem. If he said somebody had to go broke, die, or vanish, that fate simply happened and that was that. If on the other hand he decided that someone had to burgeon, succeed in some examination at Middle School, get honours at Hong Kong's *Dai-Hok* university then that too happened. He knew power. Yet this name change bothered him.

In life, only four reasons ever mattered.

One was "face", that elusive quality so valued in Chinese society. Youngsters still killed themselves when failing some examination and so losing face. The usual method was throwing themselves from a high building to splatter the pavement, tiresome to police and wretched for business. It was face. He hated the idea of suicide, but some things were imperative, *ne*?

Loss of face was easily dealt with: some things were designed for you. Evasion was out of the question. It had to be because it had to be. Simple! So face would be retained by changing his name. Everyone would understand.

No problems with face.

Second reason: money. Actually money always came first, but he worried about old things the older he became. Would he oblige his ancestors properly, now money was easy? Without doubt.

The new government from China had already passed word round Hong Kong that, the instant the English signed over their Crown Colony to the People's Republic, no folderol such as mysticism, ghosts or superstitions, would be allowed. Communist ideology was imperative. Yet a man of a certain age was bound to be secretly concerned. The Crown bowed quite easily to supernatural powers. When the soldier barracks in Central District, for instance, became haunted, why, the Crown Government – the Governor himself – had simply ordered exorcism. And paid through the nose, in accordance with ancient Chinese tradition. No problem.

The rituals had taken three whole days. The soldiers had gone elsewhere, waiting to return across the cricket ground, and things went on as normal. Bells sounded, the Taoist priests were paid, squeeze slipped here and there on the sly, the cellars were satisfactorily whitewashed and the ghosts laid for another three years. They would come back in three years, at a newly inflated fee, of course.

That was the old way, the best way; to compromise, consider what the ghosts wanted, find priests, pay money and get on. Job done, ghosts mollified, end of story. No problem with reason Number Three.

Except he was now in a dilemma, for whom did you consult

now Peking, that whore city where politicians ruled and mad philosophies thrived without no priests, no ghosts, and no spirits at all, sent orders about eliminating the Triads? No wonder the People's Republic of China was in such a mess. He felt nothing but scorn. Hong Kong had devalued its currency, and like a lapdog the mighty Peoples Republic of China had followed, devaluing penny for penny. Then Hong Kong had thought, here, hang on, we don't need to devalue our Hong Kong dollar, *and had revalued* a day later. Meekly, humbly, mighty China had revalued hers, following Hong Kong's financial gambado as a poodle follows its mistress through a whorehouse. How the whole international financial world had laughed!

Not only that, but the invincible United States of America had sent her money envoys begging Hong Kong to reduce its manufactures. Old Man felt nothing but contempt for the huge international superpowers. The posturing fools threatened each other and the world – yet who had to beg Hong Kong for handouts?

Now the world was changing, and with it Hong Kong. Here came Reason Number Four:

Reason Number Four was time.

Times were new. He was facing his change of name, foretold so long ago at his birth. But the old mystic ladies with their spells and incantations had failed him in one specific point. They had omitted to say what his name had to be changed *to*. How could one discover that? No time to linger, ask opinions, reflect. Also, if he started asking at the temples at this late stage, with the People's Republic of China and the Governor preparing the ceremony of Handover on Hong Kong's waterfront, what would the incoming Chinese authorities think? They might assume he was a political subversive, and simply vanish him and his Triad. The English had law, that plaything that the Orient could make as mysterious as it liked and get away with anything. But the People's Republic of China, who knew?

Reason Four was his problem. Time had run out.

What was his new name to be?

In the olden days, you could always blame luck and nobody would dare smirk.

He thought of the girl KwayFay, increasingly in his mind since that imbecile HC, too weak to control his gambling wife, had tumbled into ruinous debt.

Linda Ho was in the Floating Casino right now, making the silliest bets. She had a dozen infallible systems. Old Man had been watching her lose.

He signalled for a drink and was instantly served by the girl stationed nearby.

"What drink, sir?"

"Almond water and gin, equal amounts."

"Very well, sir."

He watched her move away. Such beauty in movement. Women mesmerised him. They always had. He loved women, could not comprehend how Ah Min, his gross lieutenant, could manage without at least one or two women.

He wished he did not need spectacles. Had he been anywhere else, he might have looked at himself in a mirror, but this was a gambling place. Mirrors brought calamitous luck. Spirits can only move in straight lines, like rays of the sun or shadows, so mirrors have to be avoided at all costs. So every mirror in the Floating Casinos had a trigram on it, assuring everyone that their reflection is deflected from a straight course.

Spectacles had been a matter of shame. He had killed a man – well, had him killed, not quite the same thing, no blame incurred – for having once jeered at him when he first got spectacles. He was sixteen. Now, he only felt irritation at those signifiers of advancing age.

Of course there were still merits. He could have any girl he wanted, sure, and anything he wanted. He could promote anyone, and influence any event, political or financial, in Hong Kong. And sooner or later he would obtain that marvellous source of salvation the fool HC was guarding in his storeroom. Of course the idiot would not know its importance but it was there, still safe.

Two birds with one stone? Get KwayFay, check her natural skill of foretelling the future, and use her? He loved challenges. The problems kept him alive. They killed others.

The Eurasian man arrived and stood in shadow. One of Old Man's men gave a signal imperceptible to any casual observer. Santiago obediently moved in, a new punter casually coming in, a confident half-smile showing easy familiarity with the place. Old Man knew the sequel: the Eurasian would move on Linda Ho, become her close friend, bed her before long, and the consequences were inevitable.

He accepted the drink from the girl.

"Basket," he said.

"Yes, sir. You want seat on the balcony?"

"No. Place my bet in the basket I shall indicate."

"Yes, sir."

Since he was on the ground floor, he obviously did not need to place his bet in a basket. They only rose to the balcony for gamblers who preferred to see the entire gaming rooms, believing in elevation as an attribute of luck.

"This bet must go in the next basket to descend."

"Yes, sir."

"With your right hand. And when it has come down to your shoulder, no lower."

The girl took the bundle of notes and went to stand by the basket used by HC's wife. Linda was chatting volubly to another woman, her atrocious luck was a source of eternal complaint.

Linda saw the old man send the bet to her basket. For a moment her eyes met his. He did not look away. She gazed after the bet with hunger as it arrived at the croupier's table, and saw it go onto the split line of four numbers.

The roulette wheel went round. The bet was lost. She was still looking down at him. He smiled, and pulled out another wad of red notes, transfixing her. Red, a hundred dollars each. He summoned a girl, asked for another drink.

"No gin, sir?"

"Almond water only."

He observed a man arrive and settle in to the next table, and nodded a return greeting. The man was a famed owner of ships and ocean liners in Indonesia, a regular. It was all working well for Old Man today, in this new month of name changing. An omen?

He accepted the drink, watching the ship magnate receive the house's list of all the roulette numbers called since midnight. The casino provided that service for heavy rollers, the serious players. Some stationed their own employees to take down every number, every final lie of Fan Tan, every card played in casino poker mistrusting the casino croupiers.

Old Man thought it all ridiculous. What was the purpose of games of chance? None. It was a substitute for life, not life itself. As *Tai-Tai* Ho would soon discover.

He beckoned and the girl was instantly at his side.

"I want the woman your friend gave me a week ago," he said.

"Yes, sir. When?"

"In one hour."

"Will you require a meal, sir?"

"Afterwards."

"Yes, sir. In which hotel?"

"The long place with the squeaky lifts, but not the suite on the same side as the temple by the waterfront. Find me a suite decorated in yellow."

"Yes, sir. Do you have messages, sir?"

"Yes. Tell the man who will telephone here in twenty minutes that I shall be in Macao at the ferry before eleven o'clock."

"Eleven o'clock today, sir?"

He told her sharply, "See to it!"

"I am sorry, sir. Yes, sir."

He dismissed her with a mandarin's gesture, knowing that Linda Ho would now be awed by his manner and the girl's submissive retreat. Santiago would soon be on hand to explain these events, impress the stupid woman. Purpose served.

Rising, he walked slowly away from the table. He would see this KwayFay soon and make a decision about his name after hearing what she had to say.

If she gave foolish advice, well one more girl would never be missed in Hong Kong. If she gave good advice, she would be favoured, until her good advice petered out.

Chapter Twelve

It was so early in the morning KwayFay was almost asleep on her feet. She actually staggered, rising in her improvised shack on Mount Davis.

Aware of the trouble ahead, unable to rest from being pestered by Ghost Grandmother, she was worn out before she'd even started the day. She got her things, made a brief toilet and descended into the maelstrom of Central District before even the Motorola lights across the harbour knew what to do with the remains of the night.

She wanted to sit on the steps near the Wanchai Ferry Pier concourse, but the buses were already starting up at Eagle Centre terminus. She tried to marshal thoughts of getting the sack over that queer file business. She would lose her squatter shack, go back to being a street girl begging, rummaging in the night streets.

There was only one quiet place, familiar from her Cockroach childhood. A no-family boy was tragic, but a no-family girl was doomed. She used to pretend to have a family – three sisters, two brothers, a mother and father, such joy. Sometimes she had actually believed it! Invariably the wisp of self-deceit would vanish, and she would be back to digging in the offal bins, stealing from delivery vans and market barrows. She was one of three hundred thousand Cockroach Children in the Colony.

Tiring – she should still have been asleep – she made the sports ground in Gloucester Road before dawn, and wormed in from the Hung Hing Road waterfront. English sailors from Admiralty had often fed her, when a child, but no sooner did she learn to recognise one and watch out for him he'd be gone on a ship to far away. One bought her a teddy bear, she remembered. She'd tried to eat it, taking an experimental chew of its arm, but it was only wool. She spat it out, enraged, and almost threw it away but soon saw the sailor's cunning. It was sought after by market people. She sold it to a Hokklo hawker for seven dollars, and ate in Ah Hau's Café of the Singing Birds in the Mologai for three days, real food in real bowls! Immediately she'd understood: the kind sailor knew that older children would steal her bear. He'd given her the inedible teddy bear . . . *which could be sold when it was safe!*

Thereafter, the cunning of the English seemed wholly admirable. They thought clever. She had been six or seven. That was before she even knew she had an age like everybody else. Ah Hau told her how old she was. She'd been so happy to learn that she was seven. Just like other children, she'd got her own age! A number! Later, Ah Hau explained she would become eight. She cried for two days at losing seven, which she'd thought would be her own for ever and ever, but learned it was called growing. Ever since, seven was her lucky number.

The stadium was empty. Early-early people ran round the grass perimeter. Nobody knew why; exercise folk came and went like weather, no reason or logic. Groundsmen also came with water hoses and knelt-walked the grass, peering at the green stubble. She'd tried to eat the grass when little and hungry, until a worker told her the head groundsman put poison down to make the grass grow better. She'd been so offended – why do such a thing? "The boss says so," she was told, and she withdrew with reverence. Another cunning trick. One day she might find the reason, become safe from poisons, hunger, getting caught. She did not eat sports fields after that.

A wan pallor showed in the East, the night not yet willing to go. She sat on a bench. A motor car approached, paused on Hung Hing Road, which was not allowed. A door slammed. Some early runner? No voices. Cool air enveloped her. She stayed motionless, the weight of her laptop computer cutting into her. Sometimes, she caught up with her work here, before the world began its cacophonous careering. She felt she was waiting for something to happen.

Day entered the arena. It came first as a mere night glow, slowly blotting the darkness, as if some secret child were shading the shadows with washes of different hues. In the gloaming, she heard two men walk by. She stayed still, to retain the feeling of magic, and they went on. Short cut to work?

Light stole in faster. Warmth came, and with it horrid high-heat humidity making her skin sticky. She heard voices at the gate nearby, a person wanting to come in and being told stay out. Maybe the groundsman with his grass poison? Soon, early runners and Shadow-Boxers would come with swarming day.

She saw movement on the empty field. Movement? Nobody could be there.

The daylight came almost with an audible rush out of the South China Sea. It was almost like hearing a gong's intensifying reverberation, a resonance of light. You could love it, if it didn't bring terrors of a job you couldn't afford to lose.

It was Old Man.

He wore the *cheong saam* garb of ancient China, high-necked and tubular, black down to his feet. He wore leather thonged sandals and was Shadow-Boxing. She watched him. It was quite beautiful. This was how a grandfather would be, had she one.

Slowly, befitting the most graceful of all rituals, he moved. It was a dance in the form of dedicated spectacle, but so personal and lovely it made her want to cry. He understood the meanings, she saw. He did them in order, as decided by the great Chang San-feng in his school at the Tigers Nest of Chung Nan Shan, the mountainous retreat where tigers roamed freely hundreds of years ago. Of course it was old long before.

Old Man understood all thirteen movements of the Great Ultimate Fist, *T'ai Chi Ch'uan*. Visiting foreigners always asked about it, especially Americans. They called it Tai Chi, but used the wrong tones so they were meaningless.

Old Man, though, knew all eight arm movements and the five essential leg movements. Wrinkled and thin, balding and skeletally old, but to him Shadow-Boxing was a way of life. KwayFay always told strangers no, she didn't know anything about Tai Chi, reluctant to encourage western delusions. Unless they came as disciples, to think and learn-learn, they would never understand the hidden bliss of Shadow-Boxing.

One movement made her smile. Old Man went gently into Return to Mountain Carrying Tiger, slowing his vital circular motion then rotating to a different point of the compass. So vital to know these. He lived every stance, entering the imagery so deeply she could see the actual scene, the bare mountain, the stratified clouds. She froze as he turned to a different compass point and descended to Find Needle in Sea Bed; she held her breath for him in case he ran out of air before he got back to the surface. She smiled at her folly, breathed more easily. He made it with balletic grace. She breathed again.

Had she been too silent when speaking to his guards, those young threatening assistants? They searched the stadium and grounds before Old Man Shadow-Boxed. They evicted street people, hitting them with brass knuckles, before admitting Old Man to do his silent ritual. He had spoken to her in Kowloon, that day they had taken her in a taxi. But the poor thing was their prisoner. She knew that much. What had he done?

The Japanese – her lip curled – stole Chinese Shadow-Boxing. They called bits they copied "Judo" and "Ju-jitsu", as if that made them originals. Purloined from China, of course, they then marketed them. Such silliness, when Shadow-Boxing was free in Hong Kong! Every park, every open space, filled with Shadow-Boxers doing their dawn *T'ai Chi Ch'uan*. Feeble copies in other nations were only for making kick-and-shoot movies. Here, she was watching pure heart-warming elegance straight from the Celestial Empire.

"Now east," she murmured.

Old Man slowly turned to the east, starting anew with such withdrawn reticence she wondered for a moment if he were about to begin the eighty-one leads-and-counters of the *Pa Kua* (as crude Mandarin northerners would call the Eight Trigrams; her nose wrinkled) of the Emperor Fu Hsi. No, for Old Man glided into a different sequence. Interesting! He must suffer a headache, coming to Shadow-Boxing as a cure – for which it was of course perfect.

One thing puzzled KwayFay. As light improved, she saw on the ground before Old Man a small bouquet. Irises, with their sword-like leaves? Her brow cleared. Of course! He was commemorating the Double Fifth, the fifth day of the fifth lunar month, when the mystic gift made to the Ghost Chu Yuan was, quite correctly, wrapped in iris leaves to symbolise spirit protection.

Other eastern countries, like the Japanese, knew no better. They gave swords to their little boys instead of lanceolate iris leaves, thinking only of killing. Like the English, barbarians.

Old Man must be fully relaxed now. She saw him enter a whole sequence. He became the *Golden Cock*, standing perfectly still on his left leg. He transformed into *Dragon-Swarm-Up-Pillar*. He became *Swallow Skims Pool*, then *Two Running Wheels*. He swooped so slowly she had difficulty seeing him move at all, as he changed into *Comet Chasing Moon*. She knew instantly, though, when he *Picked Moon Reflection From Water*, one of her favourites.

Tears dimmed her vision. He ended with a slow swirl, palms up and out as taught by the immortal Chang San-feng. He stood waiting. Two besuited threat-men walked to him. One picked up the bouquet. His warders were back.

KwayFay watched, afraid to move in case they hit her with their brass knuckles. They started towards the forbidden exit in Marsh Road.

The door opened as Old Man walked to it. His minions left first. Old Man paused as if hearing something, and gazed back in KwayFay's direction. She froze. He truly was the old grandfather man from that frightening interview in Kowloon, when she had learned she was to make two decisions, one choosing girls, one asking yes-no about some unknown man. Old Man moved away. He couldn't have seen her in the gloom.

She was alone. She waited until she heard the motor start and drive off. Only then did she get up and stretched. She carried her things and deposited them in the centre of the space, looking round. Such luxury! Such freedom!

In the stadium centre, she did the slow actions Old Man had left incomplete. She repeated *Return To Mountain Carrying Tiger* successfully without being bitten, when she sensed someone. Old Man was standing watching. She screamed and almost ran, but he was alone.

"Little Sister," he said slowly. "You add one Shadow-Boxing ritual to mine. Why?"

Her breath recovered. She felt ashamed in such drab clothes.

"Tiger is king of all land beasts, as dragon rules all sea beasts. They decide *Fhung Seui*."

"Tiger, *ne*? You saw me?"

"Yes, First Born. Your Tiger ritual was . . . beautiful, but not finished. I finish it for you before your warders took you back. Forgive me."

"Warders?" he asked.

"You should have gone on, First Born." She was appalled by her temerity and stammered, "Make *White Tiger*, as in side chapel in Pei Ti Temple on Cheung Chau. You would do it like original."

"An old man like me? Do ritual of a god general from the Yin Dynasty?"

"As *White Tiger Wong*. Why else does the tiger have four stripes on its forehead? Also means prince, *ne*?"

"Tiger Wong?"

"Yes, First Born. Tiger Wong." He seemed almost to smile. She was astonished: why did a prisoner smile? At what? She realised that his imprisonment had driven him mad.

"The tiger eats men, Little Sister, and so enslaves spirits as slaves for ever. You think I should be such a creature?"

"Of course, First Born!" She opened her handbag and pressed her foil pack of old rice into his hands. "You are too thin. Please eat today. Ask warders to heat it for you."

He stared at the kitchen wrapper. The girl might converse with spirits, but was clearly insane from her privations as a Cockroach Child.

She looked about. His guardians were nowhere to be seen. An idea took her.

"Run, First Born!" she urged with quiet desperation. "Run! They won't see you! I'll lead them in the opposite direction, as decoy!"

He looked at her, mystified. "Run? Where? Why?"

She saw how hopeless it was. He had given up all hope of escape. Had he no family, to bribe his guards? The poor, poor man!

"I go, *Sin-Sang*?"

He nodded, and watched her walk away and wriggle out of the

stadium under the wire. His question was answered. He had his new name: Tiger Wong. He would announce it to the whole Triad.

Chapter Thirteen

Linda Ho stared at the young man along the pillow. She was amazed at her fortune. Sunlight shafted across the hotel bedroom from Nathan Road, the traffic sounds below drumming through the hot afternoon. Air-conditioning whirred. She could hear people shouting, amahs and *fokis*, along the corridor as they moved from one room to another, calling for this number of new sheets, that pile of laundry, clattering distantly.

She'd never been worked like that in her whole life. It was a revelation. He had insulted her, beat her. She had cried out in ecstasy as he had thrust in. He made her gallop, twist, leap almost like a porpoise. He forced her to turn and mouth at him even as he had lashed with his open hand. He was an animal, bestial – she now knew how bestial – and made her bleed.

He was beautiful. Her skin was sore, for he'd shoved her along the bed. The words he'd made her come out with! She felt subjected, humbled, ashamed – except his shame proved the route to an emotional flight she had never experienced.

She wondered what his animal sign was. Would that girl know, the one whose genius with ghosts would bring in limitless wealth?

Tentatively, she touched his face. His eyes flickered open. He smiled – such a smile! She thought of her husband and felt only contempt. Had HC ever created such passionate soaring bliss? Never.

"Thinking, Linda darling?" Santiago said.

"My husband," she said simply. Best to be frank. "He is hopeless. I would have been a Los Angeles millionairess by now if it wasn't for him."

He lifted the sheet aside, exposing her breasts and body as far as her waist, eyeing the flesh, his gaze moving slowly over her skin until she almost began to feel, actually feel, his sight touching. It was a sight caress, an almost incendiary heat of a gaze. The stare slowed halted at her nipples. They tingled.

"Why? What did he do?"

"More what didn't he do!" she cried, wondering if it was time perhaps to stroke him. Or had he something different in mind?

"What didn't he do, Linda darling?"

This man loved women. His sympathy showed. She wished she had shaped herself more, kept in trim, show how splendid she could look given the right clothes, the correct amount of money.

"Tell me, bitch," he said lazily.

She was thrilled. There was that English film star Deborah Something, wasn't there, living with a movie director who, rumour told, ordered her about in terms of abuse. He called her "Cunt" even when they had company. "Come here, Cunt," he'd say, "Bring me a drink, Cunt!" And when Linda asked the reliable friend who'd reported this, "What on earth does she say? Isn't she offended?" The friend replied, "She loved it!" Linda understood. She now felt she belonged to someone who knew love from bestiality to romance. Were they the same thing, merely differing words for passion?

She decided to tell him, this lovely Santiago whose iron muscles and inflexible desire had shown her where she must go.

"I have a perfect betting system," she told him. There, it was out.

"What happened?" He licked his lips, eyes into hers. She shivered.

"HC won't listen."

"Doesn't he understand figures?"

She wouldn't have him making excuses for that dumbo.

"Understand figures?" she cried, shivering again as he licked her nipple. "Boss of an investment company? He's supposed to know figures!"

"Some people don't, Linda darling."

"I could make fortunes if only somebody would help me to reach out!"

"I knew you were a kindred spirit, Linda darling. You feel it too?"

There! she thought with triumph. He'd confessed to exactly the same feeling of togetherness. It was destiny.

"I knew it, Santiago."

"It's a pity your husband can't see your talent, Linda darling!

Can your scheme accept a partner, Linda darling?"

She raised her head from the pillow to see him better.

"I love a lady who has the courage of her convictions."

"You'd do that? For me?"

"I don't know how to say this, Linda darling," he said, averting his eyes. "But I've never felt like this before. You so attractive, and I'm just an idler who spends his inheritance on racecourses and idle living."

"Inheritance?" she said quickly.

"It's from land and farms in South America. I came here years ago and fell in love with the place. I learned Cantonese, private teachers of course, from Bonham Road."

That explained his idiomatic Cantonese. It had been one of her worries.

"I come six months of every year; the motor racing in Macao, the gambling. Nothing serious, a few hundred thousand here, a little there."

She swallowed at the sum. No wonder he was so casual at Happy Valley. As they'd shared a drink before they started to make love, he'd mentioned some cruise line his family owned.

"Doesn't your husband know the pleasure he might get from having a flutter?" And Santiago laughed with his perfect white teeth.

"He knows nothing."

"I love women," he sighed, admiring her. "Especially now I've found the one I want to be with."

"Do you mean it?" she asked in wonder.

He looked his amazement. "Of course! Look, Linda darling. I've made all the overtures. I begged you to meet me here, didn't I? I don't see any harm in it, Linda darling," he added seriously. "Do you?"

"Of course not."

"I was drawn to you the instant I saw you. Isn't he a gambler, a *lan-do-gwai*? Gambling's what investment people do, Linda darling."

There it was again, that faint frisson of worry at the unrelenting term of endearment. She shook the thought off, though it was unsettling. She would have to get used to worship.

"You would think so," she said, sullen with resentment, past grievances creeping in. She felt she could talk to Santiago, whereas she couldn't even confide in her friend Betty. One word to her and this would be all over Hong Kong in an instant.

"Maybe he has a gambling scheme of his own, Linda darling."

His hand had strayed, oh so casually, down her abdomen. She was still moist, but her thighs parted.

"How unlikely that is, Santiago!" she cried.

That name was a mouthful, with its unfamiliar slide in the middle. She supposed it was possibly Portuguese, Great Britain and that country having been friends for four centuries and always bonded across the Pearl River, Hong Kong and Macao being so close.

"Wouldn't he help you? It seems strange not to use a priceless woman to her maximum potential."

"You're so different, Santiago," she murmured. His hand was working, slowly but with a steady beat that drew her along, made her stir in synchrony.

"Don't tell me your scheme! Keep it to yourself, Linda darling."

His voice sank to a low huskiness. His eyes closed, his tongue flicking from side to side.

"I shan't," she said, breathless. "Unless you want to come in with me, Santiago."

"My love," he said in that lascivious gravelly voice she was coming to know. "My lovely darling Linda."

"What are you going to do?"

He simply threw her up so she suddenly found herself sprawling on all fours, his arms round her so tightly she could hardly breathe. His teeth sank into her shoulder with such force she cried out.

"I'm going to do what I want," he told her through clenched teeth. She felt blood flow down her shoulder and saw blood drip down from her breast. "We are one now, Linda darling."

"Darling!"

"Linda darling, it's your right, your privilege to win for a change."

"Yes!" she cried.

"Can you feel this?"

She knew what was coming, tried to open herself by thrusting back against him to lessen the ache of the first thrust in but only partly succeeded. He rode her back, feet raking on her calves as he reared on her, clasping and leaping.

This was her man for ever. They were one. Her life and her dreams were about to be fulfilled.

Chapter Fourteen

The dapper man was at the 5B bus stop. *Tai-Tai* Li had woken her, KwayFay bleary and resentful. Her superb priceless watch said six-ten a.m. Less noise for Sunday, but a man waited in a black *cheh* so hurry, hurry.

KwayFay was there in ten minutes after a skimpy wash and wearing her walk-to-work clothes with her office clothes in her plastic bag, the computer weighing her down.

"*Jo-san*, Little Sister."

She saw him extinguish his cigarette and slip something into his mouth. Mint, or those chlorophyll tablets.

"Good morning," she said back. Without explanation he drove her to the Central Harbour Services pier, the one she hated because she'd been caught there once, hiding under a barrow stall after stealing a paw-paw. She was seven and made frantic bleats, squealing she'd give the security man four-fold luck for his next Mahjong bet if he let her go. He'd released her. She never knew if he'd made any bet.

The driver booked her a ticket to Lamma Island. Twenty-three Hong Kong dollars, Deluxe Class. The ferry was a triple decker. Weekdays, the fare was only half that, and only HK$ 6.50 Ordinary Class on ferries with fewer decks, but today was Sunday. She hissed at the scandalous price. He gave her the ticket and a manila envelope. Duty pay, no red-envelope gift.

"Get off at Yung Shue Wan, Little Sister. Forty minutes."

"What is in Lamma Island?"

"Ferry sails at half-past seven. Have breakfast. *Joy-geen.*"

"Good bye," she said back, and embarked.

Even this early the ferry was fairly crowded. Her driver stayed on the pier observing the departure. He lit a cigarette as soon as the harbour waters churned. Did he never get bored? Was that what being calm meant?

The vessel docked on time.

Lamma Island, quite a size, had only a few thousand people. An enormous cement factory, a vast power station with twin chimneys you could see from Hong Kong and Lantau, still it was far less noisy than Hong Kong proper. The two villages were rural, Hong Kong people came here for seafood and walks. The crowd drifted along the one main street of Yung Shue Wan. An elderly woman wearing all black and plastic sandals approached. Her teeth had all but gone. She beckoned. KwayFay followed, turning right, away from the little public library and passing the post office.

It was little more than two hundred paces to the roadside temple. There, the old woman signed for KwayFay to sit, and entered a shack beside the Tin Hau Temple. Tin Hau was everybody's favourite, the world's most worshipped goddess, Queen of Heaven, and rightly so. KwayFay declined to wait, went inside to burn eight joss sticks, setting them upright in the brass earth-filled pot. Only then did she sit outside in the shade of the makeshift umbrella.

Soon a number of girls came in motor cars, from the direction of the only other village on Lamma. Sok Kwu Wan could be walked in an hour over the hilly centre of the wooded island, but people tended to be anxious on account of the prison there. It was harmless. KwayFay knew no prisoner would attempt escape from it until the end of the following year.

The seven girls who alighted were exquisitely dressed. KwayFay knew they were financed by societies she dared not wonder about. A suave, elegant chaperone accompanied them. KwayFay saw the girls enter the temple and observe the rituals, most of them careless and offhand. They emerged. One seemed not quite Cantonese – Singaporean? Malaysian? – and one was definitely Eurasian, though idiomatic in English and Cantonese. It was pleasant to see and hear them. KwayFay realised her envy when the girls burst out laughing at something one of them said. Sisters, how she wanted a family.

One girl asked the lady how long they would wait.

"One hour." She seemed to be their supervisor. Were they girls from some high-nose boarding school in the Colony?

One spoke in Japanese, then Mandarin Chinese. The others laughed. Two spoke in English, the other replying in what, Italian or German? More laughs. One girl, a lovely sylphic creature, said something inaudible and trotted inside the temple. She stood posturing before the two plain wooden tables serving as altars. Carrying poles were lashed to the sides of the tables. Women would carry the altars before the portable shrine on Tin Hau's feast day. The brass burner, with KwayFay's incense sticks still smouldering, stood on one among plates of fruit, sweets and toffees. Tin Hau's portable shrine – a simple wooden sedan chair structure with its pointed roof surmounted by a red silk ball – was behind the altars. It was a poor temple, but still belonged to the Queen of Heaven.

The girl swayed, dancing in the simple temple up to the crude shrine. She plumped herself down in the sedan chair with a shriek of laughter. Two of the girls withdrew in alarm, and one turning her face away in distress. The others laughed, applauding.

KwayFay gasped at the sacrilege. It was the grossest form of blasphemy. Tin Hau was the *Queen* of *Heaven*, no less, the great goddess who ruled storms and the oceans, everything from disasters at sea to the great *dai-fungs*, the great wind storms feared by all fisherfolk. If any goddess was Hong Kong's own greatest deity, Tin Hau was she: protectress of all who sailed, who control the very wrath of heaven itself. The girl had committed an unpardonable act of desecration, as had the others who had found her shameful act humourous. Only the three who expressed sadness were safe.

She wept silently from shame that she had not stopped them. The girls dispersed, talking and casually sitting on the wall in the shade of a giant bauhinia. They paid her no attention, except to make remarks about the shoddy girl behind their hands.

Without drawing attention to herself, KwayFay went round to the rear of the little makeshift temple and clapped her hands softly. The old woman appeared, eyes bright with vigilance.

"Have you rice-birds, *Tai-Tai*?"

"Yes. Two?"

"Please." She paid far more than was usual, two hundred Hong Kong dollars, for the two caged creatures. She touched the cage a moment, then handed them back. They would be released during the next service. This might go some way to repair the insult to the Queen of Heaven. She went back to waiting, not knowing what she had been sent here for. She was thirsty from the heat.

After an hour, the elderly woman who had been waiting all the while summoned the girls to leave. They assembled. Two cars appeared and parked on the road.

"Which three go first, Little Sister?" the elderly woman asked KwayFay outright. To the chorus of protest from the beauties, she said, "No, no! Quiet, all of you! Little Sister decides! You all want to be first into the car's air-conditioning!"

Without hesitation KwayFay indicated the three girls who had shown sadness at the others' antics in the temple. The remaining four pouted. The chaperone gestured to the selected three to head down the narrow path. The elderly lady stood until the car doors slammed, then turned to the four who stood waiting.

"You four can go," she said quietly. "Should you get jobs, pay half your salaries for ever to Hong Kong temples. Speak of what you have learned, you will live less than a single day."

She walked off and got into the second vehicle. The two cars drove away. A group of tourist walkers came plodding from the direction of Sok Kwu Wan. One played a mouth organ. One tourist whistled at the sight of the four lovely girls.

"Did she mean it?" one girl asked the others.

They talked together, looking sideways at KwayFay. One began to cry, dabbing her eyes with a lace handkerchief.

They came to ask KwayFay. "It is true?" and "Who are you?"

"I do not know what you mean." She felt flustered. This was none of her business. The old woman from the temple appeared from the shack and beckoned. KwayFay followed her down to the road without speaking. At the Tai Hing, a restaurant on the waterfront, the old woman pointed, grinning, and said, "*Sik fan.* Eat rice, Little Sister." She turned to retrace her steps.

Tourists were now strolling along the harbour front, examining gift stalls and bar menus. The prices seemed scandalous to KwayFay. She was no tourist! A youth emerged and beckoned her inside.

"No price, Little Sister," he assured her. "No price. Your ferry sails at one-thirty."

He showed her to a table. On the white cloth lay her return ticket, Deluxe Class on the triple decker ferry, Sunday price.

She could see the four abandoned girls standing forlorn at the temple of Tin Hau. As the old lady reached them, they crowded round demanding information. She ignored them, and went inside.

Old Man heard the result of KwayFay's choice in his house at the Peak with its perilously high view of Hong Kong's harbour. Ah Min was not often invited, but this occasion was exceptional.

"Did she give a reason?"

"No, First Born." Ah Min prayed he would not be criticised. If so, he would blame the chaperone; the woman supervisor should think of these things. Otherwise he himself would be to blame, an impossibility, *ne*?

"She definitely picked three, no hesitation?"

"Definite, Tiger *Sin-Sang*. The remaining four asked KwayFay what was going on. She said she did not know."

"Good, good! Wise girl." The old man thought on as Ah Min tried to guess the verdict. "How much have we spent on these four?"

"Languages, education, training, finance, learning, in all two million three hundred thousand, not counting support paid to families. More than usual."

Old Man sighed.

"Creating a Jade Woman used to cost only a hundred thousand. It still took years."

Ah Min remained silent. A Jade Woman, once chosen and trained, was the most valued of a Triad's assets. She would be light years ahead of any Japanese geisha, priceless for visiting politicians, bankers, conventions who wanted perfection. A Jade Woman – the term was as ancient as China – could converse in any major language, arrange any cuisine, join any conversation however rarified, and be conversant with stock exchanges the world over. They were perfection, brilliant in mind and exquisite in body. It grieved him to discard such a massive investment, even if they had not failed the final test of KwayFay's divination on

Lamma Island. He filled up at the terrible image of money squandered.

"Then," Old Man concluded slowly, "they will serve as whores in Gao Lung. Don't sell them to any lowly Triad. I won't have that. Put them under one of our brothel Mamas. Not in the New Territories. Somewhere along Nathan Road's east side. No drugs, nothing. Work them. Who recommended them?"

"Two came from the Philippines, that agency in Manila. Two came from the harbour agent place in Singapore."

"End their services," the old man said after deliberation.

"End . . .?" Ah Min was unsure.

"End. They have failed. Keep the agencies on, but the managers must end. Do it today."

"Yes, Tiger First Born. Dead today."

Ah Min took up his ledger and retired to make the necessary entries. A considerable loss such as this deserved more than just demoting four failed Jade Women to whores. His instincts were to have the girls finished there and then, but at least as street girls they would bring money in. It only showed the master's cleverness. Money in, instead of money out! He would use his best gold pen for the ledger entries. It was his favourite, only used when large sums were involved.

He made the sign for death against the two Philippino scouts, and the one from Singapore. He sighed with pleasure.

Chapter Fifteen

HC stared at the file. He had drunk too much in celebration, and it was too soon for his meal. The amahs were talkative, which annoyed him. Today he would examine this treasure that would at once redeem his fortunes. More money than anyone would ever believe, in an old file plucked from thousands, in that store-room he had guarded so faithfully at the Brilliant Miracle Success Investment Company.

His moment of triumph.

"Not now," he called angrily.

The amahs withdrew, whispering. He swelled with importance. His own talent would restore wealth, Linda's adoration, and humiliate his relatives. They were all swine, almost as bad as Kunmingese and their inedible eat-anything meals. By their cuisine you will know them, he thought contentedly. He hugged himself.

Soon he would bask in everybody's adoration, and be in a position to make them grovel. Knowing Linda *Tai-Tai* ruled in this No-Name house, they had exploited him. From now on, his staff wouldn't get the double pay necessary for saving face at New Year. Not they! He'd given it to them in the past, every single year, when he could ill afford it. Anything to keep face. Once he cashed in this marvellous boon, he would donate to the God of Wealth, if KwayFay said it was all right. If she said no, he wouldn't, and blame her if bad luck came his way. But Vitamin M, as Hong Kong called money, carried all religions before it.

He opened the file, feeling the tingle along his spine. He felt slightly tipsy. For a moment he didn't understand what he was staring at.

A traffic island. *Traffic island*?

Photographed from the air, cars caught in stasis swirling round, driving on the left of the road. He discarded the black-and-white grainy photograph. It was old, with fingerprints that had milked the dark greys to blotches. This couldn't be it. The treasure must be elsewhere, under the almost transparent flimsy papers.

He felt in the pouch. The file had Admiralty strings, those old fashioned shoelace ties. Nowadays they'd be rusted staples. No such improprieties years ago. He smiled, contentedly brought out a folded parchment sheet of calligraphy.

Musty, as with all old Hong Kong documents. Some of the Chinese characters were definitely not Cantonese colloquial. Was it Gwokyu Mandarin, the common speech of China? This seemed a double translation, first Mandarin, then Cantonese, virtually the same, in a scripted scrolled hand of great ornateness, so many flourishes he couldn't follow.

Then a small map. Again the traffic island. He recognised it. Once, that odd shape had held the Royal Hong Kong Yacht Club. It was called Kellett Island. He remembered it well, yachts and ocean-going pleasure boats there all through the Seventies, near the typhoon shelter where the junks waited in staid rows until storms abated. Then had come the enormous excavations of the Cross-Harbour Tunnel, driving everyone mad for months. Now the tunnel was finished the cars came churning from the mess called Kowloon, ruining the ambience of Hong Kong Island.

The trouble was, little Kellett Island was no more. It was now nothing more than a traffic island in the middle of a slow traffic jam. He stared, went back over the flimsies, the old photograph.

Surely there must be something more than this? He had ordered her to pick out the one that mattered. Hadn't he said that? The *one* that *mattered*, alone among the gunge in the storeroom. He'd told the stupid girl. She had betrayed him. She was a fraud.

He lay back in his chair, head resting on the wood and his eyes closed. No fortune, no king's ransom? She would have to be punished. He must sack her, show she had defaulted. Would that count with the Triads? He felt sweat trickle down his chin and itch under his arms. He might get away with it. By inflicting punishment on her, he could show the Triad he'd done as they commanded, sorted through all those thousands of incomprehensible documents. She had been *ordered* to bring out the one they wanted, the file filled with old shares now worth millions. Money with which they could bribe the incoming Chinese mainlanders, uncouth roughs whose politics masked nothing but avarice.

Sweat-drenched in his armchair, he imagining the horrendous consequences for himself. He would have to tell the Triad people when they sent their collectors for money. His debts moved like a creeping barrage across his mental landscape.

The amahs knocked. It was wide open. He stared at them in complete incomprehension.

"*See-Tau*," one said nervously. "*Tai-Tai* send message."

"What?"

"She get good luck from Kowloon."

Luck? Was there such a thing any longer? He'd never had any, not since that woman had become his wife. Perhaps there was a way of getting rid of her, clearing away all his bad luck in one brave blow?

"Ring Missie on mobile phone."

"*Ho-wer*," he said, wholly false. "Good, good."

They withdrew chatting quietly. He knew what they were saying: Something very wrong. Only he knew how wrong it was.

When he'd been given this investment company to run, a blunt message had come: protect the old files. Destroy none. Preserve. And go through them. Take your time. Select the most worthy, because the Triad needs it before the great Handover when the People's Republic of China takes over. He'd been so confident. Going through those files would be easy. Somewhere in there was rumoured to be a gold mine, something left by old people. It was his only interview with Triad people in Kowloon, to whom he had bragged about the rumour. Investments, money, possibly gold mines in Australia, South Africa shares in diamonds, some great companies who floated bonds at impossible Victorian rates, anything. But it was there. Triad people had chosen HC's company because it would never be suspected as their repository. They were stacked to the ceiling.

Find it, HC. It was in there. They did not know which. Six years, they'd told him as he took over in his grand new office, you have six years before the People's Republic of China marches in. Find the file, examine all in great detail, and explain to us what it means. Just do it.

Could it be six years ago? HC had worked the problem out. The number of files he'd need to check each day, to finish before the British ships sailed over the Kellett Bank and away, leaving Hong Kong to the People's Republic of China, was easy. Six thousand files meant 1,000 a year for six years. About 6,000, some with stuttering printing on tractor paper as the first computers had come in, others hand-written in admirable ancient calligraphy and so old they were frayed and yellowed. But somewhere among them was the treasure the Triads wanted. And that file was HC's rescue.

Rescue? The idle ignorant bitch KwayFay had ruined everything.

He sat up. Could it be that she was not in touch with spirits at all? That everything she'd done was nothing more than a trick, to save her useless job? Any girl could outdo KwayFay at computer work. He already knew that. They even made fun of her slowness and her endless day dreaming.

What if she was cheating him?

It was his way out! He wiped his face on the antimacassar, indispensable in the high humidity. This was salvation. Prove to the Triad's loan collectors she was a sham, that she had constructed an elaborate hoax. She'd simply pretended she was a necromancer. He would tell them he'd searched night and day, been through every single file. He'd tell them none made sense, even though he'd laboriously translated and burned the midnight oil and found nothing.

The first few days years ago when he'd assumed control of his company, swaggering about Princes Buildings, he'd worked hard. Maybe for two weeks, something like that. Then he'd thrown parties, gone with Linda to the races, lazed in the bath houses, used a girl or two on the side.

And postponed things.

After about a month, he'd reasoned that maybe eight files a day would do it. Reading, say, six files before noon, then do others in the afternoon when Threadneedle Street was going demented. That would do it. If he'd calculated correctly, there were 6,000 files with 15,000 subsidiary documents, wallets, folders, boxes. Menthol was the predominating scent, for first of every calendar month he'd had a *foki* replace the menthol balls against moths and insects.

Nine files a day would see it done.

He had imagined all sorts. He would savour that precious file, time and again, savour the delicious achievement. Then he would airily make a call, when he was alone in the office, and say in a commanding voice, "Tell the *bahsi* I've done as ordered. I've found the file. Okay?" And without waiting for an answer he would ring off and be there, swinging idly in his captain's chair when they came bursting excitedly into his office, full of praise for his brilliance.

They would reward him with millions, say a tenth, a third even? Not too much to ask for six long years of laborious perusing of documents he'd guarded with his life?

It had seemed so definite. Hadn't he a university degree in the bastard investment systems of Hong Kong? All he had to do was read through each of the files one by one. The one the Triads wanted would be so obvious it would seem lit up like a Boundary Street bar. He would send the staff away for a day, scatter old files round the office and bask in the Triad's praise.

He hadn't done any of it.

All those years ago he'd thought, why the hurry?

Then suddenly six months had passed, and he realised with a cold shock he'd done nothing. He couldn't even tell where he'd placed the first dozen or so files he'd looked at. He could only remember how boring they'd been, old rentals, leasehold deeds, development buildings in Mong Kok, none of importance. Back then he'd thought, well, for God's sake, I've years yet. Why not do, say, eleven a day? He'd easily make up the lost time.

Then, another six months had suddenly passed and he'd only five years remaining. He'd planned on tackling twelve, then thirteen a day. It would even out.

As time passed, he'd then begun to feel the first twinges of alarm. No, not alarm, for that was close to fear, and he was not afraid of a few old files. Yet it had definitely felt as if time was somehow running away. He begun to ignore the problem completely, for peace of mind. In fact, he'd stopped even going into the storeroom, preferring to send some clerks in for rubber bands or a box of pencils.

He forgot the problem.

Then KwayFay had come, when he was over five years in deficit. He became seriously frightened.

He needed KwayFay to go in there and divine which file was the one; which file was the miracle fortune file the Triad needed. With amazement, then utter joy, he had recognised KwayFay's extraordinarily strange moments of clairvoyance. Impossible to search through the files on his own. But her mystic powers would do it in a single flash of spiritual insight. And save his life and make him a millionaire.

Now she'd given him a file about a traffic island. The only way to save himself was accuse her of betrayal. He'd be in the clear, buy time that way, and promise the Triad he'd hire some economics graduates – his own expense – who would work under HC's close observation and discover the file. Solution and rescue combined! Naturally, he would offer to pay for the search, promise them a superb job.

KwayFay would die, or whatever they did to those who betrayed them. He, HC, would be thanked – who knew how? – for having identified the traitor and solved the problem KwayFay had caused. He knew he had found a safe way through the minefields. Speak to them sensibly, that was the way. For one crazy moment he thought of dashing back to the office and make a desperate lone search. But the People's Republic's army was already massing on the banks of the Shum Chun, with the terrible patience of certain seizure of the Colony. He'd no time left.

No, he would have to sacrifice the wretched girl, and that way save his skin. Well, she'd brought this on herself, betraying him with a worthless file.

He could see what she'd done. She'd been too idle, dozing about the place. Worthless cow.

Deciding against making a last desperate search, he poured himself a drink. Hopeless at this stage. He wondered what Linda was up to. Some trivial bet, he shouldn't wonder, on something worthless. She'd once phoned him in Macao when she'd won seventeen dollars at roulette. Was that the behaviour of a true supportive *loo-poh,* old woman who stood by her husband?

No, he'd already seen his salvation. He almost threw the wretched file aside. Better to keep it as evidence, show the Triad bosses what a stupid bitch KwayFay was to pass off rubbish to somebody with his brains. Proof.

The worse she looked to them, the better he would seem. The worse her fate, the safer he'd be. It was life.

Chapter Sixteen

"Never be Christian," Ghost Grandmother told Kway.

"Why, Grandmother?"

"Christians believe in love. They don't believe in madness. It limits them. Don't believe wrong things."

Where has this come from? KwayFay thought. Everything Ghost Grandmother told her lately was grievance or quibbles, like this Christian thing. Why not, when the Christians were western, and western owned every system in the world?

"They do not." Grandmother was angry at KwayFay's rebellious thought. "They think they own, but do not own."

"They have computers, administration systems," KwayFay said directly. If Grandmother heard her thoughts, she might as well come out with it.

"Death today, lazy girl," Grandmother said contentedly. She'd dealt with love.

KwayFay almost shrieked, "Death? Whose? Is it mine?"

"You no death today," Ghost said with contempt, as if death might be a performance beyond KwayFay's capabilities. "You in Singing Bird Café. Bet on smallest sing bird or I cross, ignorant girl."

KwayFay protested, "I do everything you tell me!" KwayFay cried in her sleep, weeping in fury.

"You disobedient granddaughter! Be silent to elder!"

"I must ask who, when you say death comes!"

"Mind own business!" Ghost cried sharply. "I tell-tell you!"

KwayFay had her own grievance, seeing she would have no job to go to. She had no money for bribery. Perhaps it would be different when the People's Republic of China came marching in with those drab suits and bicycles. Let the Chinese army try cycling up Nei Chung Gap, they'd soon see how useful their stupid bicycles were going to be, serve them right.

"They won't bring bicycles," Ghost said, still slyly eavesdropping.

"I won't ever get a job." KwayFay kept at it. "I soon starve."

"Job tomorrow, death today." Ghost cackled at the joke. "One piece space open after one piece space dead, *a*?"

"Yes, Grandmother."

"And don't be Christian."

"I won't, Grandmother."

"Remember: believe in madness."

"Yes, Grandmother."

That was the stupidest thing of all, KwayFay thought, covering her shoulders to keep warm. (How was it that shoulders always were coldest in bed in the morning, when feet were coldest in the evening?) And why did Ghost Grandmother talk sometimes in pidgin English, then ancient Cantonese straight from the fourteenth century or somewhere long ago, and other times in vernacular they'd pick up instantly in Kennedy Town or maybe even Stanley by the horrid Taoist temple where they still paraded some little girl on a great ornate palanquin? Mercifully, KwayFay could always understand whatever form of speech Ghost used.

Did Ghost mean a job for her, somewhere beyond the reach of HC's venom? Ghost did not often make predictions.

The other question was death. Whose death?

"Tomorrow learn Moon Cakes."

"You haven't taught me Moon Cakes!" KwayFay cried in alarm.

"You not listen!" Ghost shouted, grievances flying about the tiny shack so KwayFay couldn't even think straight.

Had she been given a lecture on Moon Cakes and forgotten, or was it one of Ghost's first talks when first she'd appeared to her?

"Grandmother!" KwayFay bleated in tears. "I good granddaughter!"

"Moon important women business. Then Amah Rock."

KwayFay knew Ghost had gone when she heard herself emit a faint snoring sound. She felt warm again. Whose death? Whose job? Maybe neither would be anything to do with her. She could sleep. No use getting up as if she had to go to work.

Worst thing an unemployed person – a girl, so she was worthless anyway – could do would be to lie abed, signifying to the world her uselessness for the foreseeable future, a maggot-in-rice female. Hong Kong people laughed at unemployed girls. They could not even become criminals, as the saying went.

✳✳✳

The man seated inside the door of KwayFay's shack was desperate to smoke. He had a small gold cigarette case, but smoking would wake the sleeping girl whose twitchings and moanings were almost sexual. She was being tormented by some ghost. He knew that. He made a mental bow to her small house god, with its red tinsel reflecting the feeble red glow. His gold case was made twenty years before, somebody said, in a shop in London where princesses went for rings and bangles. The trouble was, it clicked when he opened it for a Chesterfield, made in America where the best tobacco came from. The click would sound like a thunderclap in this confined space. The girl would wake up, maybe talk to Tiger Wong, as he was to be known from last week. Tiger Wong did not tell why his name changed. That meant some ghost had ruled it should be so. On account of this, the old man, Business Head of the great Triad, had ordered that this girl be protected from harm.

It would have been enough, the watching man thought, had new-name Tiger Wong ruled that one man must visit Mount Davis and tell the squatter camp to protect KwayFay. Then life would be easy: any harm to her, multiply by however much rage Tiger Wong felt if injury, harm, or bad luck befell her. Easy way, hard way. He shrugged mentally, watching KwayFay become more peaceable. The troubling ghost must have gone to wherever ghosts went for a rest.

He felt no animosity towards Tiger Wong, for the Triad master was there to give orders. Explanations were frivolous and not to be thought about. Easy way, hard way. They were all the same in the end, bearing no relationship to consequences. If the outcome of a given rule was success, good. If failure, then payment was due from whoever had been ordered to carry it out at the time of failure.

Easy way, hard way.

The watcher's name was Tang. He came from the harbour at Tai Po, over beyond Kowloon at Tolo Harbour. He almost chuckled at the memory of how as a boy he'd played the game of Giant Striding Earth in the market there. How they used to laugh! Giant Strides is what Tai Po's original name meant in the old language, folk said, so naturally it was right to stride with enormous steps, which is the proper way to avoid snakes and tigers who then can't keep up with you because they're easily tricked. They always think you're moving fast, when in fact you're not. Dumb fucking snakes, dumber fucking tigers. There must have been lots of wild animals about Tai Po back then before the trees were chopped down.

Not that his boss, now to be known as Tiger Wong, was simple, no. Tiger Wong could never be tricked. He said this girl was immediately to spend much of the money she had been given. And she had not yet spent a cent. Failure loomed ahead for somebody. Sanction would follow. He wondered nervously if it would be his.

This girl was a puzzle, or would have been if he had allowed his mind to wander into puzzlement, something he dared not do. She had a load of money, the exact amount specified by the boss, and hadn't even bought food for herself. She was hungry. Tang knew she'd had barely a mouthful the previous day, drinking water to allay the pangs the way everybody used to. If you were starving you ate grass back in Tai Po, until the amahs came out cutting grass for the horses before they raced. Here in Hong Kong Island, no chance of that. In any case, the spirit of some hillside might think, hey, what's that fucking thief doing stealing my fucking grass? Then you'd be for it.

He checked the money was still in her handbag. How stupid women were, thinking because there's a clip by the zip, it would be hard for a thief to steal the contents. Beyond belief. It wasn't stupidity, it was an invitation. He'd done his first robbery when four, bribing a cousin to run away from the tourist bus as if she had stolen the money and not he. Easy way, hard way. His cousin had gone like the wind, while he'd knuckled his eyes in his little plastic sandals in Tai Po Market where the tourist buses always pulled in by the old folks' home nobody was to admit was there because Chinese families didn't leave their old folks to rot. Tourists had said what a dreadful shame, that little girl stole money right from under the seats of the tourist bus. She'd been using her little friend to distract attention. Tang got the sense of the words though not understanding a single one. He'd cried and the tourist women had given him two American dollars, a lot back then before he'd earned enough to get a woman, and decide how to be treated.

Not a cent, this KwayFay had spent. The boss had decided that would be wrong. If the master said something was wrong and there really wasn't anything wrong at all, it was down to Tang to prove Tiger Wong right, that there really was something wrong but it was concealed, so proving the boss was right. Folk who assumed otherwise were simply too dim to get it. Therefore those others were traitors. Which was why Tiger Wong was Triad master and others were not.

Easy way, hard way.

Tang had three men hanging about down on the road. He'd told them to wait by the little café shop where the fat woman slept every night. What they did while down there where she slept was their own business. He'd told them that, but remember no noise. Too much silence on that road, so no disturbances. The road was in sight, darkness or no, of the Hong Kong Coast Guard station at Green Island, across Sulphur Channel. They had telescopes, spent their useless time staring into the dark. Who knew what they saw? They were Government, had uniforms to prove it, and could blank off the whole of Mount Davis in a minute, police swarming everywhere. So no noise. No blood, either. Fuck the fat woman or whatever, but in silence.

See Little Sister spends much money. Rule for the morning. A woman who didn't spend? Impossible!

He checked the time, one hour before dawn. He would have felt tired, even sleepy, if he'd have allowed himself. He thought with wry pleasure of the man who'd had to die down in that godown, Mister David the big shot. Tiger Wong, having changed his name on account of some spirit this girl knew about, hence all the fuss – Tiger Wong had visited, and spoken with the two men who'd killed the carpet shop man. Tang vaguely wondered what the man had done.

Up the hillside somebody coughed, hawked phlegm up from a bubbling chest. Pollution was what made folk cough so much in

Hong Kong, doctors said, but Tang thought doctors must be ignorant people, for everybody knew that Hong Kong people had cancers in the throat. In some it didn't grow, if you were lucky.

He hoped he hadn't got fast-growing cancer in his throat.

Morning must be here soon, for he heard more stirrings from the squatter shacks encrusting the hillside. He heard people clack down in their plastic sandals to the stand pipes, lazy bastards only going now instead of having gone the night before to bring water from the roadside. That would be a signal to his three men, who must be farting themselves awake and wanting something to eat. He wondered if they'd used the fat woman.

His problem was this girl. How to make her spend? He must report success to Business Head Tiger Wong. He considered the problem without the slightest anxiety. It would have to be so. Failure was out of the question.

Easy way, hard way.

KwayFay heard the first shiftings of life on the mountain, the squish of water and the sound of coughing and spitting, the rushing clatter of folk suddenly discovering they could successfully imagine they were late. She stirred, opened her eyes. The shack was dimly lit by the first daylight, just black shadows and slight pallor. She had worried for some reason during the night that Ghost Grandmother was going to ask her something tonight, but couldn't remember. She might remember later, with luck. She reached across and made a sign to the Kitchen God, seeing with relief that the little red light, one Hong Kong dollar for a battery that would last two months, still glowed protectively. Cheap.

She felt for her handbag, and found it exactly where she'd placed it under her pillow, exactly at the correct angle. If only she could use some of the money inside, how marvellous life would be! She was so hungry. She had eight dollars of her own left, enough for a bowl down Causeway Bay. She might walk to Sai Ying Pun and catch the tram, save a few cents, see if there was cheap rice on the stall outside the Singing Bird Café where the old men brought their cage birds to compete. She felt like going there today. They bet on which bird sang most beautifully. She might try a gamble, bet a dollar on which singing bird would win.

Her heart always over-ruled her common sense, though. She decided to back the tiniest bird, from sympathy. Invariably, they lost.

In half an hour she was up and out, dressed in what she hoped didn't look her only set of clothes, and was walking towards Sai Ying Pun.

Chapter Seventeen

Linda Ho waited until she saw KwayFay leave. The girl came walking down the mountain track plain as day, quite unashamed at having to catch a bus! Like any ordinary labourer!

Her lip curled. KwayFay was supposed to be unique, according to HC, able to manipulate the future. Could this really be so? *Tai-Tai* Ho examined the girl's moving figure with mistrust.

Foretelling events was an aspect of gambling that always troubled Linda. She watched the girl, thinking over the problem with anxiety. If KwayFay, she with the pretty curves and wearing the ugliest dress (surely the cheapest) in Hong Kong, repeat *if* she knew so much about the future, then why was she dressed in tatty scrubber's clothes? Superb talents should serve gambling, in which case the bitch should have gone straight to Happy Valley or the new racecourse at Sha-Tin Heights, maybe borrow a few dollars for the first race, then double and treble in compound growth . . .

She heard herself moan, not in envy at the pretty bitch in her shoddy attire, but at the thought of bookmakers' wealth funnelling into her own handbag. She worked it out with lightning speed: Lay, say, a bet of a hundred dollars to win at, say, eight-to-five against, then an any-back and American Twist on a nine-to-two non-favourite, a combo on the third . . .

The bus came. KwayFay climbed aboard. Linda watched the girl's figure tense her clothes and grudgingly scored her a decent seven out of ten. All right, then, eight. Her legs weren't the bulbous bowed calves you saw among Cantonese girls, now they had nothing to do except sit powdering their faces while they watched stocks and shares changing colours and numbers on a TV screen. They got paid far too much money for doing nothing.

The girl carried a laptop slung over her shoulder. Ha! So she was a thief, had stolen one of HC's computers! She must pay!

The bus pulled away. Linda was glad she could alight at last. She left the car, and started to climb the path towards the shacks. In only a few paces she was sweating and tired. The girl had seemed so brisk, but then of course the conniving bitch had been descending, not going up. Linda had no idea of direction, but the footpath did not branch until she reached the first shacks.

An old lady was swaying up the path ahead of her. Linda came slowly upon the figure, which was dressed in the black traditional garb of jacket and trousers with a cane hat. She carried a rough yoke made from an old broom handle, plastic water buckets hanging from each end. She wore plastic sandals, and foolishly carried her pattens of thick wooden blocks tied with their leather loops about her neck. Linda was amazed at the old woman's stupidity. Fine, to save a few dollars by declining to bribe for a stand pipe of her own on the hillside, but to carry her heavy pattens? It showed how foolish the poor really are, Linda reasoned. They made their own misery, doubtless to earn sympathy from money-eyed folk who'd done the decent thing, worked and saved to live a decent independent life instead of being wastrels. The poor slaved cunningly at being poor. Poverty was a trick to con the wealthy.

The old woman made to enter a shack made of corrugated tin. No doors, no windows, just a box pegged to the hillside by means of pieces of dowel round the edges, presumably to stop the hovel from slipping when torrential rains made the slope a ski-run of mud.

"Where is KwayFay's place?" Linda deliberately omitted courtesies.

The old woman stopped, slowly rotating her whole body, the yoke swinging the buckets so one container slopped.

"KwayFay gone."

"Where does she live?"

The old woman was Hakka, not Cantonese proper, a "guest family" person, one of those who had come to Hong Kong hundreds of years ago from the interior. They were still a race apart. Linda recognised this with distaste. The woman should be out working on the roads like all the other Hakka women, instead of idling on a hillside. No wonder she had nothing.

"She live ten places up."

Linda walked on, counting. The shacks were arranged as steeply as if on a staircase. Little children, mostly bare, came to stare. One or two women emerged to see her pass. She wished she cut a rather better figure, but the heat was already unbearable. Her heels were torment. She had deliberately selected shoes to enhance the smallness of her feet.

Ten? Had the old Hakka woman said ten?

There was only one hovel there, two steps to the right on a rough area of granite outcropping in front of a box of corrugated iron. Someone, presumably KwayFay, had reinforced the walls with pieces of wood, but the whole structure was already on the tilt. Marks in the powdered laterite showed where the makeshift hovel had moved under its own weight during the rains. One day it would simply slide down, accelerating until it struck the shacks below. That would be another tragedy enabling the *South China Morning Post* to invent yet more garish headlines. The Colony averaged five or six similar horrors every year, always attended with considerable loss of life.

Linda knocked to save face, for two women and several children were watching. She made a show of listening, and entered. The door was simply a fold of rusting tin pivoting on wire wound ineptly through two holes.

She stood as her eyes accustomed to the gloom. One window, with a piece of plastic fastened over the aperture. She looked through. She was unsure whether to let the girl know she had visited, but thought of the evident familiarity of the other people on the hillside. No doubt the old Hakka woman would tell the girl as soon as the bitch arrived back.

A House God, its red light barely alive, stood by the door. Linda acknowledged its presence to herself, which was all one needed to do to placate an Immortal, unless you were after a special deal. A truckle bed was folded against the tin wall. A bucket stood by, partly filled with water and covered with a small weighted piece of netting against flies, with two small bowls. There was a groove showing where the girl must stand to . . . to what? Linda stepped across and felt along the top ledge of the metal wall, but there was nothing. KwayFay must store something there. Nobody, not even the dreamy girl in her terrible wrecked shoes and awful shoddy dress, would have been so foolish, inviting thieves to reach in through the window during the night and steal whatever she kept on the smooth ledge.

So KwayFay was careful. Or merely cunning? Linda cast around, found nothing, then looked out. There stood a suited man, thin, wearing a cross-striped tie of many colours. He wore a trilby, as if from some old-fashioned film, the sort they always showed in Causeway Bay. People still flocked. Linda looked away from the thin man's flat gaze. She was disturbed, but not over-much, for her hired car was down on the road almost opposite Green Island and it would be noticed. Her visit was probably known to all the hundred thousand squatter people – that was how many lived here on the hillside. Another tenth of a million here or there was nothing to Hong Kong, carefully miscounted for every Colonial Government Annual Report, to satisfy the China Republic's arrogance.

The man had not changed position when she glanced a second time. She let him see her. Taking out her pen and notepad – no gambler was ever without those two essentials, she carefully made a note and tore the page out. She wanted a stone to weigh the paper down. He smoked his cigarette, motionless. She'd never seen anyone except a gambler stand so still, quite like a . . . well, a hunting bird, she'd have thought if she was of a fanciful turn of mind. Perhaps a money collector for the Triads who allowed the Government's stand-pipe water system to operate unhindered?

She folded the paper and slipped it into the corner join of the truckle bed. Another possibility was that he ran a franchise, purchased from the Triads, and was watching over the shacks of those who paid protection money of ten Hong Kong dollars a day. She was sure he hadn't been there when she'd arrived.

She had written, *KwayFay, I wish to meet you. You will learn something to your advantage.* No signature, but she gave her cell phone number. The old woman would provide KwayFay with her description. As long as the silly bitch didn't ring during supper, or when Linda was meeting the young handsome man, it would be fine. The slut of a girl wouldn't be able to resist the offer Mrs HC would make, for a little crystal gazing.

The hill proved difficult going down, with those elegant but inconvenient heels. She drove to the garage off Hennessy Road in Causeway Bay and returned the car, reclaiming her deposit. HC's plastic card did its wonder, and she was then free to find a taxi near where the trams turned in Wong Nai Chung Road.

In KwayFay's shack, the short suited man found the note, pocketed it, and left without trace.

Linda Ho told the taxi driver she wanted the money place off Granville Road in Kowloon. He almost hesitated, but she tapped the back of his seat angrily. Here was an imperious lady, and she was prepared to make a fuss if he declined.

Ten minutes later, and he dropped her off behind the Carnarvon Road branch of the Hang Seng Bank, giving her a quizzical look as she alighted and went down Cameron Lane. She entered the first narrow alley to her right. There stood the moneylender's Santiago had recommended.

One breath – she never showed fear at vitally important times, knowing all could be lost at the slightest trace of anxiety – and she entered the money house. No sign on the door, none above in garish neon light, just a small white card discreetly placed. As she went in the chill of air conditioning enveloped her, making her shiver at the delicious cool. It seared her lungs. She stood for a moment at the assault on her senses, of the red and gold room in which she found herself.

The red glow changed slowly in waves, gold flashes seeming to ignite the walls then recede into a dark scarlet. No furniture, everything stark and the colours violent all about. A door opposite stood ajar.

She crossed. An ordinary counter was there, a gentleman waiting politely for her to approach.

He greeted her with grace. An old man in formal but antiquated attire, his long slender robe was almost priest-like, the high collar loose about his thin neck. He wore spectacles and managed a few chin hairs. His fingernails were tidily cut, with the exception of those of his little fingers which were prodigiously long, quite a foot in length. A traditionalist, then, one for whom menial labour was anathema.

"*Tai-Tai*," he greeted her gravely.

"I want to borrow, if you please. I have my husband's card."

"No need, *Tai-Tai*." He smiled, his voice a thin reedy sound of a distant flute working against the wind. "You have honoured many previous loans in Hong Kong. We are still proud to serve you."

For just an instant, Linda felt a vague disquiet. *Still* proud? Suggesting a possible change in the offing? She almost bridled but kept control. There was no real cause for worry. Every loss she had suffered – almost all from unfair accidents, unfortunate weather or disastrously incompetent jockeys, unlucky rolls of dice or impossible sequences of cards – every single one had been honoured. She always told HC to pay on the nail, for an unpaid debt was death, literal death. She *would* be barred from every racecourse, every gaming casino, in all South-East Asia. That would be death.

"I was recommended to come here by a gentleman I . . ."

Was it correct to mention that she'd just met, bumped into, some punter at the horse races, and he, seeing her losses, had told her of this place? Would the old gentleman think her too forward, and refuse her loan?

"I understand, *Tai-Tai,*" the old man said. "We allow only the best terms, and are particularly generous when the honoured lady wishes to go on using her profit. There will be no complaint from us."

"How kind," she said. "*Yao sam.*"

"Thank you for saying we have heart. Many moneylenders, banks even, are cruel to the point of extortion when a fair-minded lady wishes to increase her capital." He smiled in silent appeal. "Is it not reasonable to borrow, to increase? To speculate in order to accrue? So great fortunes are won, *Tai-Tai*. I am only too pleased you have chosen our humble establishment."

"I was thinking of a small sum," she began.

He demurred, shaking his head.

"*Tai-Tai*. If I may, please accept more than you need. Would it not be unthinkable, were you to fail at the last hurdle because you underestimated the extent of your coming success?"

Those were the very words the young man Santiago had spoken! She remembered them exactly! "The sad thing," Santiago had said, pocketing his wadge of money, his winnings, "is underestimating your coming success. How many times," he'd added with a sigh, "have I made that mistake! Each time you fail to trust your instincts, you miss a fortune!" Then he had smiled quite like a film star, and went on, "I don't make that mistake any more!"

His very words, now burned into her brain. You fail to trust – *so you fail completely!* She saw it all so clearly. Lack of confidence had been her real adversary, trust in the life she could have, not merely pennies.

Look at it another way. Fail to trust your instincts, then you failed in life! If only she'd trusted her instincts, *she'd have won a fortune*. It was the gambler's loss, to win small and lose much. But to win a single giant bet was to reclaim all your previous losses! It was so logical! Her reasoning was beautiful in its accuracy.

"What limits do you set, *See-Tau*?" she asked, her throat dry.

He smiled, his cracked features almost shredding before her eyes.

"The limit is the *Tai-Tai*'s plan."

She began to feel heady. Power took hold. She had never before felt so gifted. She would win. She could touch heaven, the gambler's heaven, successes piling up in win after win after win. She had arranged to meet Santiago at the Golden Shamrock farther up Nathan Road on the left-hand side away from all those tiresome camera shops. He would be waiting for her.

"Please do not hurry. Take your time."

She swallowed, noted the hands on her watch.

Santiago had told her he would be there at ten-thirty. Quickly she reviewed her estimate of HC's worth. HC's credit was exactly the sum she could afford to lose. His job was secure. She had some depleted savings.

Her new inner strength empowered her. She had a woman's convictions, and the force that went with them. The old man's serenity became hers. Going to place her bets, she would walk on air. What an impression she would create among the other punters! She could afford to borrow the net worth of HC's firm.

The logic was inescapable. HC's money would earn for once. Think winning, instead of working.

Painstakingly she wrote on the old gentleman's pad – his fountain pen was heavy gold, she observed – HC's total worth, including his firm. It looked breathtakingly elegant written there, all those noughts trailing like stars after the comet of the first three numbers.

"As the lady pleases," the gentleman said calmly. "How does the lady require it? In thousand dollar notes? American currency?"

Of course, he probably dealt with large sums every hour, nothing taking him by surprise.

"Hong Kong thousand dollar notes, please."

"Very well." He pressed a button, and a hatch behind him slid open. He simply placed her signed paper in. It slid to. "One of our servants will carry it for you if you wish, *Tai-Tai*. Or a guard *foki* will accompany you."

"The guard *foki*, please. When I wish to return the loan, *See-Tau*, what arrangements do you make?"

"You can send or bring the capital sum yourself."

"And the interest?"

"Payable at the time of capital repayment, *Tai-Tai*. One per cent per day. It is normally twice that."

The situation was understood by both. Linda thought of Santiago. Their dawning affair was success waiting to happen. Why else would Santiago have shown such eagerness to talk? Why else had he asked to meet her, suggesting a time and place out of the way of her normal circuit? He was obviously attracted. Why else had he been so keen to back her judgement in this?

Everything came down to judgement. The money – this vast sum, an amount she had never before seen in one place – would soon be profit. An evens bet would make it all hers, minus the fraction for repayment of the interest. What was one per cent? Negligible!

She had discovered the perfect system, using moneylenders for profit! She was amazed she had never seen how foolproof it was.

"Thank you," she said, using the direct form of thanks for something given, not something merely done as a courtesy. "*Do-jeh.*"

"*Mmh sai*, no need," the old gentleman said politely. "The lady's money is waiting, and the *foki*. Whenever you are ready, *Tai-Tai*."

"I shall see you the day after tomorrow."

"Indeed, lady," he said, smiling. "Indeed."

HC was roused. The City Hall was noisier and more crowded than ever. HC had watched as a pathetically small Chinese dragon twitched its way along the tramlines, the feet of its carriers shuffling and flicking like so many inverted antennas. He must have dropped off, in the clashing noises, the drums and the squealing children.

The City Hall was thronged, and he noticed his drink – inevitably local San Miguel beer – was emptied. He glanced about, but security guards were herding the audience along. Always the shoving and hustling to get a view of what they could see almost any day, some celebratory Chinese dragon stopping the traffic and scaring children.

"No more," a man said.

He was in the next seat, facing the staircase. A plain man, and like HC taking no notice of the celebrations. Strangely, his attire could have been straight out of Hong Kong's waterfront – say, Kennedy Town near the tram terminus – from the streets of quarter of a century ago. He wore the long *cheong saam* and black shoes of the scholar, and was close to skeletal.

HC said to a waitress, "I'll have another San Lik *bey jao*."

His mouth felt dry. The mob decided they needed a seat. Outside, the Hong Kong Police Band pipers were having a go, the dragon crashing and thumping in its ancient rhythm.

The waitress ignored HC and simply vanished in the press of customers. HC almost called after her. He felt underneath himself, and retrieved his file. His evidence. He broke into a sweat of relief. Anyone could have taken it while he'd dozed. Very foolish risk to take, but he was so very tired. Worry tired you out.

"Glad you could come, HC," the man remarked.

"What?"

HC turned to inspect the man. One thing about older Cantonese gentlemen, they reached forty years of age then stayed exactly thus until death. Cantonese women were exquisite until they reached forty-five, when they became sallow crepe and stayed thus forever. Their morphology also aged, the female figure settling as if filled with fluid no longer held in shape.

This man was in his ageless phase. He smoked a cigarette. Nobody contested his transgression of the inflexible law against smoking in the City Hall.

"You brought it, I see."

The man flicked ash. A waitress ignored the old man, passed on into the crowd.

"Brought what?"

"My file."

"Your file?" HC's stomach constricted. He almost retched.

The man held out his hand with the cigarette stub. Somebody reached out with a silver platter. The old man simply let the stub fall, not even glancing to see where. HC felt his face prickle.

"Sir?" he said feebly. "I am to give it to – "

"Thank you, HC."

A hand took the file from HC's hands. The old man did not demur. The file had vanished in the crowd.

HC was suddenly breathless. He had been told to come here, wait in the City Hall in this phoney place made for rooking tourists, beer costing six times what they might pay elsewhere. At night the charges were even more insolent, atrocious squeeze being slipped onto the bills and receipts arbitrary. Surely after all his planning the Triad was not reduced to meeting here, where the world and his wife crammed to see some cheap dragon cavort on the waterfront?

"It was extremely hard, sir. Believe me, I worked night and day." He felt so sorry for himself and the lies he was about to tell. "It almost killed me."

"Really."

"Yes, sir. The girl KwayFay, the one with the special gift, she told me. I believed her. I gave her double wages."

"Then she would work all the harder?"

"Exactly!" HC was eager. The man was taking it all in. "She tries telling everyone who'll listen that she speaks to ghosts, has powers of divination. I paid her through the nose to find the right file."

"And?"

"You'll see what rubbish she finally came up with, sir."

HC tried a noble smile. The pipe band crashed and wailed. The presentation of medals by the Police Commissioner would soon begin. Much good those bits of tin would do when the drab Peoples Republic of China's army came marching in from Whampoa and down Nathan Road past the empty British barracks.

He wondered why the waitress had ignored his order for more beer. He also realised a space had cleared in the impossible mob around him and the old man.

"What did she?"

"Well, sir," HC said, staking everything, "she ignored my instructions."

"Ignored?"

"She gave me a defunct file, nothing to do with investments. She deceived me, sir. And . . ." Too dry altogether now. He managed a croak.

"What steps did you take?"

"I have told her to come see me."

"What will you do, HC?"

HC wished the man would stop calling him by his initials. It made even the most benign sentence menacing.

"Examine the file," HC said, sweat itching his armpits, "and see the worthless attempt she had made to cheat us – me and you."

"What will you do, HC?"

"I shall sack her. She already knows it's her fault."

"What will you do, HC?" The question kept coming.

"I shall see she never works in Hong Kong again."

HC found himself babbling. The space around them grew. The band outside halted as the cymbals stopped. The drums silenced. HC realised as heads turned that he was shouting.

"Will that be enough, HC?"

"No! No! She should be punished!"

"How, HC?"

The responsibility was too much. HC shifted in his seat. If Linda wasn't such a sorry drain on his income, he might have been able to escape. But what could a man do without a wife's support?

"How should she be punished?"

HC said miserably, "She should make restoration, or suffer death, sir."

The old man sighed.

"The trouble with power, HC." He almost smiled giving an oblique glance HC's way as if at some secret amusement. "Don't you find it so?"

"Find what so, sir?"

HC was shocked at how far he had been made to go. He'd never intended to make that suggestion. The girl was probably in difficulties worse than any he or his wife had.

"Knowing what punishment fits a betrayer's crime." Into HC's appalled silence the old gentleman said, "It must surely be so in business, no?"

"Well, yes." HC clutched at the mention of investments as at a straw. "Sir, might I say that if you ever need to invest in any stock, I should be only too pleased . . ."

The old man rose. The unseeing crowd simply parted and he left without another word. HC stood and made to follow. Inexplicably the mob became an impassable press. He tried edging along the line of seats and found he was trapped. Dismally, he stood while outside medals were presented to constables of the Hong Kong police force.

It was a full half-hour before he was able to leave, and then only through the enclosed garden next door, where he would be unable to get a taxi, and have to stand wearing a fake smile while two or three brides asked him to remain among their crowds of well-wishers, such being the customs of Hong Kong.

He would have to see KwayFay at the office and give her the sack. At least he could bully her, feel secure in chastisement.

That was a man's prerogative, and in a way his given duty when a clerk had made her boss's life a misery, forcing him into making statements he'd never intended. Serve her right.

Chapter Eighteen

Linda felt a strange misery. Sated, they lay together, just looking deeply into each other's eyes.

She found difficulty saying his name – such long names in foreign languages! Why not one syllable, or at the most two? Santiago was almost a whole sentence. Extraordinary, but already she loved him. He had done everything a man could do to a woman. She had only been partly alive until he had bruised her without mercy, made her whole.

This affair could not, must not, end. He slept. She cradled him.

Her investment in the new gambling scheme she had worked out would run the risk of ending their association. She knew Santiago for a supreme gambler. The tales he told! That Monte Carlo business! The London casinos begging him to return, offering him unlimited credit! His Las Vegas jaunts, where he and some woman (undeserving, worthless) had cleaned out Caesar's Palace with a triple sequence on roulette, blackjack, and finally the breathtaking, almost unplayable against-odds faro.

Unbelievable! He was the first truly major high-rolling international gambler she had ever met, and now he was her lover. Him so rich, so powerful! Why else would the international Formula One combines beg him to come to Hong Kong? Some incomprehensible deal to fix success for that nasty German driver and the Ferrari team. (Who on earth was interested in that?) Santiago knew them all by their nicknames, told how he'd attended their weddings.

She was only one person, not a huge industrial combine. He would soon go. Unless she could keep him. But how?

The next batch of races was due soon. She would gamble then, win hands down. Winning, he said to her, even as he'd entered her and set her working, winning is a bore when you can't lose. She'd challenged him on this afterwards. It stuck in her mind.

"The only risk worth taking, Linda darling," he'd answered, "is when the outcome is almost certain loss. Win then, you're a genuine gambler."

He teased her about it. He liked a woman with some age and

charm. That's what he said, "a deal of charm". He spoke all languages, conversed in Portuguese with the people in Macao on the Floating Casino where they played Fan Tan. He chatted in English, switched easily to Japanese when a group of tourists blundered onto their table in Macao. He was at home in Malay, she realised with a shock, and spoke Tagalog with the Pacific people. Spanish, of course, to the Philippino mobs with their floral designs and cheery faces. He was a superb horseman. He'd been a picador in the bull fights in Macao. It was a wonder she didn't know his face from photographs.

He had simply assumed he would become her lover, had chatted so matter-of-factly while instantly starting to undress her, his lips all over her skin as he discarded her clothes, talking animatedly of gambling, money, life, women . . . Besotted, she knew she'd do anything to keep him. When she was rich, after her coming gambling coup, she would compete with his life style. She was determined to multiply up, "ascend the dragon steps" as gamblers called that dangerous, risky gambling method.

That raised the question of the money from the Kowloon money-lenders, the exorbitant interest clicking inexorably. She'd told HC when he asked that she was going to work her own investment scheme, thank you, and wouldn't need his help. He had argued, expostulated, cried even.

She had the money. It would see daylight when it began its magic ascendancy, escalating to glorious quantities. Multi-millionairess! The word had a ring to it.

Meanwhile, she served her man, this lithe, successful, rich demon. They would dine in Macao, at the Jockey Club. He knew everyone, hobnobbed with those who mattered. He shook hands with a chief of police, and was at home in places she'd never imagined.

They made love that evening after dinner at the New Harbour View before a giant picture window, staring at the myriad multicoloured lights of Hong Kong even as they cried out and grunted in fulfilment.

The money was smouldering, waiting to ferment inestimable wealth for her.

She would meet KwayFay and obtain her spirit guidance on winning horses. Nothing must be left to chance. Gambling was life. All else was prelude.

Cradled in her arms, Santiago slept.

That same afternoon, a typed note was on KwayFay's stool in her pod. It read SUSPENDED UNTIL FURTHER NOTICE, in English and Chinese. She took her things and left without a word.

Chapter Nineteen

Walking to Tung Loi Street, KwayFay turned away from the harbour. She was aware of so many things, quite like they said happened to the mind when you faced death.

There was no sense of premonition. Grandmother had definitely predicted death. Spirits or ghosts could do what they liked within limits set for them by the Jade Emperor, the Supreme Spirit. Presumably Grandmother was being truthful?

She waited to cross. Hong Kong's traffic ran in stupid one-way systems she could never get the hang of. She had run wild in these very streets as a little girl, helping old people with their belongings, thieving, earning sums as little as the one-cent paper money, so beautifully printed (only made now for accountants worrying how to adjust their books with 0.0l of a Hong Kong dollar). Still, the lovely miniature notes had kept her alive more days than one. She had been lucky.

The streets were crowded. She realised this with astonishment. She had not thought how strange weekdays would be, out in the open, wandering about aimlessly. It had been a terrible decision not go in to be humiliated by HC and Alice and Beth and Felicity, and Tony, and Jimbo Yip who kept telling KwayFay he loved her. Yet he'd already done the thing to Alice in the stores cupboard, at least he boasted so. One day, Jimbo Yip told the world, he'd pull off a great seam in futures. He had it worked out in gold, copper, and coffee futures. His secret measures would hit the Brazilian, DAX, and the Nikkei. He'd use the Hang Seng, and do it in the exchange in Ice House Street. It would take him a single afternoon. Unlike Mister Nick, the English scammer who'd done for Barings Bank in Singapore to the tune of a billion American dollars, mighty Jimbo Yip wouldn't get caught. He said. KwayFay knew Jimbo Yip.

Dowdy, she felt today, dowdy and tired. She knew this was because she'd come on that morning. During her first day she became dispirited. All the other females looked so glamorous, and her feeling so shoddy. They seemed so colourful, their conversation doubly loud about night clubs, dancing with handsome spend-money sailors or share-brokers from Australia. This happened every month, never troubled other girls. She felt so tired, but couldn't remember if Ghost Grandmother had lectured her during the night. She felt the money in her handbag, twice had had to turn aside when some pickpocket had done his usual sidle to her left. It was easy switching the handbag to her other arm and lifting her jacket flap over the clasp. She did this mechanically several times a day among the office crowd. Office crowd! When would she belong again to an office crowd, able to chat with friends? Now they were remote from her life. They had never been friends.

No job now. Only doom.

Wing Lok Street West, with crazy traffic roaring into Central District. Just to make it difficult for pedestrians, the parallel Bonham Strand West traffic ran the other way, westward towards Kennedy Town. She paused, buffeted by hurrying people. Not a foreigner among the teeming schoolchildren in their uniforms – probably the Ying Wa Girls' school further uphill above Seymour Road, she thought enviously. How she'd have loved to have gone to a school where, she'd heard the others say at work, they sat in desks in rows of seven, the teacher walking along the aisles while the girls wrote their sums and words.

The crowds were thicker by the lanes near Hollywood Road, because tourists were unloading to enter the Cat Street Galleries, or to walk, complaining about the sapping heat, to the Man Mo Temple. She always felt off colour until the start of her third day, when the sense of oddity lessened and she could straighten. Odd how her shoulders drooped every time she came on. She'd looked for similar signs in other girls, but none seemed affected that way. It was her penance. The one day she could have done without this, when she'd lost her job and felt vulnerable, on she came. A sentence. She entered Possession Street, taking her life in her hands to cross the junction of Queens Road West and its Central run, the traffic maddened at the traffic-light pauses. Of course the narrow lane – it was no more than that – had become far steeper. She slowed, realising she hadn't had anything to eat since she'd got up. It was time she had something, but with what? She possessed a few dollars, no more. The notes in her handbag were a hateful embarrassment. Money you dared not spend? An insult.

The singing birds would be arriving about now. And Ah Hau would be serving tea. At least she could sit, get her breath, perhaps cool down. There'd be shade from the scalding sun. She made the last few steps to the corner, and there was the Café of the Singing Birds.

She saw Ah Hau's garish sign, still on its one nail, rusting against the wall. It had slumped there after one of the great *dai fung* winds, that struck Hong Kong the previous year. Ah Hau had never had it repaired, not caring if potential customers saw his sign. His custom was always the same. Come what may, old cage-bird fanciers came up from Sai Ying Pun to compete. Any minute.

KwayFay walked slowly up the two steps, avoiding the offal careless cooks had thrown on the pavement. Flies were much in evidence, but Ah Hau wouldn't care. The café inside was shady, no more than eight paces square, the tables rickety bamboo with rings of moisture. She brushed away the flies and said her good morning.

"*Jo san, Siu Jeh,*" Ah Hau replied.

Whatever the circumstances, Ah Hau always greeted her the same way, "Good morning, Little Sister," as countless times in the past. It did her good. He was a worn cripple of, what, thirty years, the jokey age he claimed, having made a birthday up for himself when she'd been about fourteen.

"How are you, Ah Hau. *Ney ho ma?*"

"*Cheng chor,*" he said, as if she was a valued customer. "Please sit down."

Ah Hau indicated a small stool. She perched on it, remembering the days when, a little girl, her feet swung high off the floor. What had she been, six, seven? Ah Hau fed her, kept her alive. She felt ashamed as she watched him limping behind his counter, preparing for the tribe of bird fanciers who would bring their cages ready for today's competition.

Many of the old men she recognised. Ah Hau was trusted for his responses to individuals. He never reproached her, as she believed relatives, especially mothers, did to offspring. Hear Alice Seng talk in the office, you'd think parents were nothing but trouble, vicious invigilators of behaviour who took perverse delight in shaming daughters: Where've you been? What were you doing? Do this, do that . . .

Alice explained how her mother – living in Yuen Long, New Territories – had given her solemn rules before going out with a boyfriend: "Now listen, Ah Ling," which was Alice's real name, "above here, is your own, understand?" And on *here*, Alice had graphically placed her open palms at her midriff, grinning at her listeners in the office. But the angry mother had gone on, "Below here," again the palms, "is mine, understand?" The account ended in gales of laughter, for by then Alice had already been working hard four months or more, to hear her tell, under a boy whose only wish was to become a famous DJ in Australia. Alice still spoke wistfully of Faz, a Eurasian Sino-Portuguese, her first, who'd broken her in one day after the Dragon Boats Festival at Little Hong Kong that tourists called Aberdeen Harbour facing Ap Li Chau.

KwayFay sat watching Ah Hau. He was lame from some childhood injury. A little girl cadging scraps to stay alive, she'd asked why he limped, he would reply, "I fell." That was that. He rolled rather than limped, from something high in his leg. She thought him handsome once, but hated his pigtail of sleek black hair he wore. Cantonese didn't do pony tail hair any more, seeing in it a remnant of the queue, from the past of Imperial history. Speaking of which, Ah Hau's Kitchen God was just the same as it always was. This testified to Ah Hau's superstition, something he denied. He saw her eyes go to the Kitchen God poster and said loudly, "I only keep it there as a joke. The real one's over there."

It was their old contest. Long since, Communist China took control of the printing offices throughout the entire Middle Kingdom. They hated anything to do with gods, spirits, old customs. They changed the very days and dates, would you believe, so that paradoxically only shreds of old traditions remained clinging to the China coast enclaves of Hong Kong, Portuguese Macao, and that strange business going on in Formosa, the island the Kuomintang government there now called Taiwan, Big Bay Country. So the only way you'd see ancient festivals was here in Hong Kong properly, for the Taiwanese were, according to Ghost Grandmother, unreliable and unable to think straight because they sang songs in the streets about owning Imperial China when they hadn't two copper cash to rub together and were running dogs of the USA.

Ah Hau's Kitchen God poster was the Communist one manu-factured half a century ago, would you believe. She felt her lip curl in contempt. What government is compelled to print what it does not wish? Despicable! Yet China had done this, to satisfy the farmers and peasants. She had, as a little girl, traced her fin-gers along the very foreheads of the two grossly coloured people represented in their garish yellows, reds and greens with their blotchy red cheeks. The man, the woman, were seated behind an altar with the customary five vessels in a hideous green with the two gods of Happiness and Longevity in front.

She'd always liked those two; small old men, one wearing blue, one red. She'd pretended to pull their beards, much to Ah Hau's amusement, when she'd waited here on the linoleum floor, idly catching cockroaches while she'd hoped for a little old spoiled rice. Ah Hau had never let her down, though some days she'd been too tired to come this far after carrying buckets of water from the standpipes on Ko Shing Street to the gate man at Sai Ying Pun Hospital during the droughts.

Those days, nights, she'd slept with other rat children in the market alcoves off Hollywood Road. She'd never shared Ah Hau, or his kindness, even though some of the other children, espe-cially the girls, ailed so badly they knew they would die before many moons came and went. She had been afraid for herself. Still was, and now she was here. And in her bag a wad of money, and a watch robbers would kill for.

Ah Hau's crack about the Communist version of the Kitchen God made her smile. It was faded now, its edges spotted with mould, insect droppings smudging the faces of the Eight Immortals, four each side, in their gaudy long attire. As an infant, she'd longed for coloured chalks and to draw those fabulous people (sorry, Immortals) – on virgin white paper this big. She'd often imagine coming in when Ah Hau was about to close at night, and she'd imagine that the poster was there without a single mark on it! Blank! And there beside the poster in her imagination would be a box of crayons, all colours you'd ever heard of, in rows, just like the English crayons you saw for sale in Whiteway's on the harbour road in Central! And how she'd take one, always red, unwrap it and then start to draw. And the Kitchen God would be proud to be done like that. And Ah Hau would say come and live in this lovely café where there was always food and have a box of new crayons every day and a stool of her own . . .

"The Stove Prince," came Ghost Grandmother's icy voice, querulous at having been roused by her errant granddaughter at this unconscionable time, "Ts'ao Chun, is the real Kitchen God, and don't you forget it!"

"Yes, Grandmother," KwayFay thought miserably in answer on her stool by the wall in Ah Hau's café while Ah Hau served the first old caged-bird man carrying his singing bird.

"Don't heed the rubbish they talk nowadays in the Middle Kingdom, either!"

"No, Grandmother."

"Thoughtless girl! Any mood comes along, your head turns."

"Yes, Grandmother."

"I was told by that whore from Cheung Sha Wan," Ghost Grandmother said, "who I won't name because she says she's our third cousin who used to sweep the ancient tomb at Lei Cheng Uk, where you should have gone a week ago to lay flowers and rice and red papers but you were too idle, lazy girl, to respect ancestors in the way that's proper – I was told by her who says she can read and always puts on airs, that there are words saying *Against America, Help Korea!* on it."

KwayFay said nothing, not wanting to help Ghost Grandmother, though she'd pay for it later.

"Is it there? Read it and tell me!"

The four characters were there on Ah Hau's poster. KwayFay knew them by heart. "Yes, Grandmother."

"And what else?"

"The poster also says, *Defend country, protect home.*"

"How have they written Country?"

"In the old way, Grandmother."

KwayFay heard Ghost Grandmother snort with derision. "Hah! See? They daren't even spell it their silly new way!"

The name for China had been given a different ideograph, a different character. The word Middle remained the same, but Country was now a mess of straight lines, unlike the old way with the mouth and spear in a box as KwayFay always thought it when Ah Hau had taught her to read. His first words for her had been Middle Kingdom, Chi-na, the two characters one above the other. He'd burnt a match, having no pen, and used the charred end to write characters on the linoleum floor. She'd drawn them beautifully, Ah Hau said, clapping in applause.

Spelling and characters were too absurd to argue about. Begging from university students along Babington Path – best place was just where it joined Lyttleton – she'd heard the strains of a violin, badly played, as university teachers tried to teach students the inflexions of English speech, up and down cadences everybody would catch instantly if only they'd listen. There was no other way for the sounds to go. It was so stupid.

"You do well to visit Ah Hau, lazy girl."

"Thank you, Grandmother."

"Death stays the far side of Hong Kong. Two in Philippines, one Singapore. Good, *a*?"

"Yes, Grandmother." KwayFay almost woke from relief. The deaths were accounted for!

"You should eat old rice when your period is bad, lazy girl. They sell it in Kennedy Market, by the last waterpipe. Never pay more than twelve cash a half-catty, you hear?"

"Yes, Grandmother."

The catty, the local weight of food, would be eliminated when the Chinese mainland marched in, KwayFay knew, but cash – Imperial China's copper coins with a square hole in the centre – had long since vanished except on barrows in Eastern Street for tourists to marvel at. KwayFay would have sulked, had she dared.

Three months before, Ghost Grandmother had made her learn the money tables, driving her mad, night after night the chant, "Nineteen cash make one old English penny; a thousand Imperial Chinese cash make one tael, four thousand five hundred and sixty Chinese cash make one English pound . . ."

Long gone before KwayFay had appeared out of nowhere, of course. She wondered if she herself would become a querulous crone making some poor mite lose sleep learning stupidities.

"Sixteen taels make one catty," KwayFay chanted inwardly, dozing against the wall in Ah Hau's café. "One-and-a-third English Imperial pounds weight to the Chinese Imperial Catty . . ."

Slowly she roused. The place was suddenly full of caged birds, every table occupied with bamboo cages, the birds excitedly calling and singing. All except two were minah birds, sparky black eyes alert and feathers shining.

Some old men had to unfold canvas seats to sit down. Ah Hau had a stock of discarded folding seats, rescued from the waste bins outside the antiques emporiums on Hollywood Road of a night. She had helped him stitch the torn green canvas with sailor thread got from the ship chandler in Sheung Wan where they collected the waste bins in the great barges during the dark hours. He had eighteen, he'd once told KwayFay with pride, as many as St Stephen's College! She didn't believe him, false praise being cheaper than truth and more rewarding.

This way, with the eight *dang-ji*, little bamboo stools he already had, he could seat most of the bird fanciers who came of a morning for tea and maybe a small amount of rice and green vegetables. Ah Hau also served locusts in bamboo and net cages, but this KwayFay hated because each of the cricket cages and locust containers meant something horrid would happen. She had to go. Her squeamishness always caused immense hilarity among the old men, who shouted advice after her, making jokes about women.

There was no way Ah Hau could delay it, though. The singing birds were fed by way of reward. Some old men kept to the ancient way of feeding their birds for having sung so beautifully, lifting out a particularly plump locust or cricket with their own chopsticks and placing it lovingly into their singing bird's open beak, there to be snapped and ingested. The other birds went silent with envy as the winning bird ate the live crickets and grasshoppers. No singing then, only jealousy.

She felt ill at the thought, though the old men had not even yet settled down. Some were outside under the Cola awnings while another arrival was still shouting his greetings through the window and finding a place to sit with his riotous black minah bird.

Ah Hau served her a glass of water. This was his trick, to show she was a genuine customer. He'd done this for years ever since she was little, and the old men knew it.

"You want anything else, Little Sister?" Ah Hau asked, quite as if she'd just finished breakfast.

"Nothing else, thank you, First Born," she said, and everybody relaxed. Honour was satisfied. Face intact.

"My bird did a double-trill with a paradiddle and a flam," claimed one old gentleman, adjusting his *cheong-saam*.

"Go on, then," another said, amid laughter. "Again!"

"It did, I promise."

"Then go *on*. We're waiting."

This one wore a suit with an oily tie and no shirt, and had managed to grow three or four long chin hairs quite as if he were a mandarin. He had toes as gnarled as walnuts, the nails piled on each toe as if trying to grow upward in ugly slabs.

There was a gust of laughter at this, the lot of them, inside the café and outside on the steps, swaying and laughing and coughing, some of them hardly managing to breathe from showing how ridiculous they thought the old man's claim.

"Minah birds can't do a paradiddle."

"Mine can! I heard it only last night."

"Make it sing it again then."

"And a flamadiddle? No bird's ever done that!"

"Mine does!"

The bird fanciers used the English words from the drum school out in the English soldiers' barracks, applying them to the birds' trills, mixing the terms they felt came nearest. This was how they went on each day, challenging the others to believe or to disprove their claims. If KwayFay ever came to love anyone it would be these old men with their fantastic claims to have the most marvellous singing birds on earth, and Ah Hau who ran this cockroach infested café with its shop-soiled Kitchen God poster.

The aroma of the food, rice and vegetables, made her almost faint from hunger. When had she last eaten? This was becoming serious. She drank the water, but even the first swallow felt so bulky inside her that she almost gagged. She felt the weight of the money in her handbag, wondered if she might at least borrow – only borrow, for heaven's sake – a little for a meal, but that was too perilous a step to take. She rose, with a single dollar.

"Please bet on the smallest bird," she said quietly to Ah Hau.

"Very well, Little Sister." He took the dollar.

"It will sing beautifully today." It looked a scrawny little thing, yellow feathers torn, evidently a refugee from the hungry kites circling the main harbour.

"Thank you, Little Sister."

"Good morning, First Born," she said back, and left the place. The old men approved, for they continued talking loudly over the exchange.

She set off down the slope towards Des Voeux Road. Down there, she might catch a tram down Connaught Road West, make Central District before noon, and get her final payment. It would be withheld, of course. HC was venomous to those who failed him. Maybe he would give her an insultingly trivial amount of money that would make the whole office smile. Nobody could give a smile like the Chinese, or hide it so successfully that the world would see, so doubling the disgrace. Shame was a pure industry in Hong Kong, the product of two great colliding empires. One empire would have been bad enough. Here, two had colluded, their beautiful rituals empowering their subjects to rise to the very height of social elegance. The dispensing of shame was its epitome.

Only a few steps, and she wished she hadn't stirred from Ah Hau's café. At least there she'd been in shade, with water.

A man was standing by the tram stop in Connaught Road when she got there. It was Tiger *Sin-Sang,* the old man. He wore the same ancient long *cheong-saam* as when she had last seen him in the Sports Stadium. Plainly still a captive hoping for escape. Two threat-men stood near him.

"*Jo san*, Little Sister."

"*Jo san*, First Born."

"You have not eaten, Little Sister."

"No. I am not hungry, First Born."

He considered this. A taxi slowed, honked its horn, then accelerated swiftly away with a screech of tyres. KwayFay noticed terror on the driver's face, his right elbow lodged on the window retracting instantly as he hunched down. She looked into the face of the old man with surprise. A taxi driver, afraid? Then she noticed the suited threat-men had moved to the kerb. His captors, never far away.

She said, "The taxi man was afraid, First Born."

He gauged her innocence and knew it for simplicity. "Was he really?"

"Yes. Why was that, First Born?"

"I will ask him if I meet him again." The old man's expression clouded. "You have not eaten. You entered the Café of the Singing-Bird near the Mologai, yet there too you did not eat. This is correct?"

"Yes, First Born. I will have something later."

She felt foolish and made as if to walk by, deciding to walk into Central. He pursed his lips. The threat-men's arms unfolded. She froze.

"Little Sister, this is not like starving yourself, as women do? I do not know the words for it. Staying hungry and making yourself ill?"

"Certainly not!" she said indignantly. "I am . . ."

She could not reveal her hunger, say how she'd almost keeled over from having had nothing. *I am poor* would not do, to this august old-*cheong-saam* gentleman ancient enough to be her . . . great-great-grandfather?

"It is religion?"

He waited. She noticed the pedestrians – always very few along Connaught Road West, never more than one or two every twenty paces or so, since they'd redesigned the waterfront – were avoiding the pavement. Several, even as they'd been talking, stepped into the road and crossed over, a perilous hazard in the new roadway, or entered a side street to climb inland to another level where there were no trams at all.

"Religion?" She had no knowledge of Catholics, but supposed he meant them. They had a weekday when they didn't eat, wasn't that so? And Mohammedans also, they were vague in her mind. "No, First Born. I am busy."

"Then you shall eat at the Peninsula Hotel, in Salisbury Road. You will be booked in. No need to give your name."

"I have . . ."

"The money in your handbag, Little Sister." His eyes bored into hers. She almost stepped back in alarm. How did he know she had money in her handbag? "It is a gift. It is yours. Please eat well. I am told you spend nothing. Now you shall spend many dollars on attire."

He was lost for words, evidently trying to work up to descriptions of dresses and shoes. His eyes pecked, like those of a bird, at her feet, her hem, her waist, arms, shoulders, as if choosing without knowledge.

"A gift?" She knew never to stammer. Ah Hau had said ladies did not stammer, for a woman who could not speak was ruined. "It cannot be."

"Cannot?" He frowned. She felt an ice on her cheeks. She lowered her voice to a whisper so the threat-men would not hear, and said, "Is it a message to someone?" He looked at her. "Yes," he said.

"Would it help you if I did as you say?"

"Yes."

She thought. Maybe the message was in the numbers on the money. "How much?"

"You must spend several thousand."

"Nobody can give so much, First Born. It is . . . it is thousands." She whispered, "The money in my handbag seems all red notes." At his continued silence she explained with reverence, "A red note is one hundred Hong Kong dollars."

"Is it?" A puzzled smile, but this time warm.

"There are two brown notes, and one yellow, First Born."

"Are there?" More amusement.

She was fearful of a sudden. What if it wasn't a gift after all? His concern had abated as soon as she mentioned the larger denomination notes.

"The brown notes are five hundred dollars, Little Sister," he said slowly. "The yellow is a one-thousand." Three men, in smart suits, did not move, just looking away. Why was this? She had supposed these watching people to be his warders, but now . . . "Have you not counted the money?"

"No, First Born."

"Why not?"

"It seemed . . . impolite."

"Always count the money you have, then you know exactly what you can do." He seemed curious. "After you have dressed in new clothes, after you have eaten, then you must return to your place of work. Understand?"

"First Born, I have no way of repaying it."

"Never repay a gift, Little Sister."

"I am afraid. My . . ." *Ghost* Grandmother would not approve? How could she say something like that? He would think her mad, like the women in those crazy movies from India they were always showing down in Wanchai, where hundreds of actors danced with their fingers gone wrong.

"Your who?" He looked over his shoulder. The men sprang into life and closed in. "Your who?" he asked again.

"I think of my old grandmother. She might not have approved, my taking money from your guards, for no reason."

"Where is your grandmother?" He spoke to the attentive trio in a voice cold enough to chill the air. "You reported she had no relatives."

"She has none, First Born," one said.

Old Man said directly to KwayFay, "You have no relatives."

"I mean, if my grandmother were still here, alive, she might not approve."

He smiled, nodding. "I like that. You think of your ancestors.

That is good. I am pleased."

The men faded, resumed their stances on the pavement, looking for all the world as if they were studying some distant view.

"Thank you, First Born." For what?

"Count the money, Little Sister. Eat dinner in the Peninsula, buy clothes. Then go to . . . to work." He almost smiled as he spoke his last word, but the smile did not quite reach and he moved away. "Here is your tram, Little Sister."

There was no tram in sight, but a large black limousine approached from the direction of Shek Tong Tsui and stopped.

The old man walked away. The driver was a youth who looked fourteen, grinned at her with a mouthful of gold teeth.

"Little Sister?"

"Me?" She looked around, but the old gentleman had vanished. Only one of the three suits remained there, watching her implacably, hands clasped, his trilby too large and his tie a flamboyant red. He was ugly, a tiny body under a wide face and eyes that looked dead.

She wondered if she ought to go to HC first, explain that she had had a sudden change in fortune, but the youth seemed suddenly to age as he scowled.

"Peninsula Hotel in ten minutes, Little Sister. Better get in."

"The gentleman said a tram . . ."

"He joking," the youth rasped out in English. "Tiger Wong all time joking."

He knew the old man? She entered the vast motor, as large as her shack. She seated herself, knees together. He signalled for her to put the safety belt across her shoulder. She managed it.

"All time joking," he said again, and added, "Except sometimes. Peninsula Hotel, ten minutes. And eat many bowls. Not for your health, Little Sister, for mine."

Tiger Wong asked the young suits guarding him, "Which bird won today at the Singing Bird?"

"The smallest."

"Did she bet?"

"Yes, master. And won."

He settled back. "It is she. Tell her to arrange funeral house."

"When for, master?"

"She will know when."

Chapter Twenty

The Peninsula, elegant folk said, had seen better days. It stood in the most prominent position by Hong Kong harbour, Kowloon side. Its fountain was a changing delight, enough to bring the Colony's typical exclamation *Waaaiii!* from a thousand voices. Its fame was perennial.

Servants in their elegant uniforms were the most pleasing anywhere. Rolls Royces, Bentleys, large American gas-guzzlers, adorned the front drive awaiting liners and aircraft, to bring yet more guests in time for faultless service. The Peninsula was the epicentre of all power in the Crown Colony, ceded New Territories and all. The true centre lay in the Governor's House, ending soon. Until the end came, the Peninsula Hotel ruled tourism's elite.

KwayFay was welcomed, five uniformed acolytes slickly competing to hand her out onto the steps. Doors opened as if by magic. Lights dazzled, floodlights on the façade and the windows gleaming. Astonishingly she felt only a little nervous, as if she had been there before. A Eurasian gentleman, dressed quite like some newsreel politician, greeted her. She'd seen his like when, a filthy child haunting Nathan Road of a night, she had free viewing as the main stores shut and Rediffusion came on, so many TV sets to each of the supermarket windows.

"*Siu-Jeh*, welcome! Will you have dinner first?"

She was starving, had almost keeled over in the car. The car! She didn't know whether to pay the driver or not. Would the old gentleman's warders be cross if she offered? And with what money?

"Dinner?" she asked humbly. "I don't want to be any bother." And how much would it be? A hundred paces away, she could get a bowl of hot rice for HK$ 2.50, with a scrap of green vegetable.

"Any you wish, Little Sister! I cannot tell you how honoured we are! Miss Brody, please!"

A half-coloured girl advanced, smiling. She had a glorious figure, and wore the Peninsula colours. Her hem was exquisitely cut, KwayFay noticed with envy. Her hair was coiffeured, and one of her rings would have kept four squatter shacks in luxury from one Moon Cake Festival to the next. What a delight to be so exalted, able to stroll about this elegant foyer among the rich!

"Your dinner first? Or will you have tea while we send for a selection of dresses and lingerie?"

The choice bemused KwayFay. She'd never heard of shops bringing clothes for you to choose. Had the girl got it right? And was it either-or, like in those logic questions she used to overhear in the Sai Ying Pun schools when, during inclement weather, she listened while crouching in the ventilator hoods. Dinner *or* clothes was it? Old Man had said she was to do both, for the message to work. He must be desperate. She had to get it right, for his sake, spend the money, as yet uncounted. What if they wanted it back? She became confused. Were threat-men watching in these palatial surroundings, reporting she was being disobedient? She felt tears start.

"Send?" was all she managed.

Miss Brody waited, not at all put out by her guest's evident poverty. Her own clothes would absorb all KwayFay's income for three years or more. She desperately wanted to know how the girl had got herself into such a giddy all-paid position. Sleeping with managers? Sucking off some Government civil servant, so often done down Wanchai and Causeway Bay? Or had this KwayFay learned even more heady skills scavenging among the bars? Was she from Gao Lung at all, or some squatter hovel on the Island? The plastic shopping bag was disgraceful.

"Perhaps a light tea first . . .?"

"Tea!" KwayFay blurted. Tea was a recognisable landmark.

She frantically felt for her handbag, terrified of losing the money and the Rolex. She was sick of the watch, beginning to wish she'd never seen it. Any cheap thief, any *chaak* prowling the waterfronts to rob unsuspecting tourists, might have it off her. It was a liability.

"Little Sister, your *sau-doi* will be safe," the girl said. "Nothing can be stolen in the Peninsula."

KwayFay stared in wonder. Nothing stolen here? She had never heard such a thing in all her nineteen years – if in fact that was her age. Could Ah Hau be wrong? He'd been strangling chickens for the meals he prepared for hawkers. They collected their hot food each night. (He made eighteen Hong Kong dollars a time from four hot-food hawkers every day after paying the squeeze on rent, supplies, and permission from the Triads. Not much, but not a bad deal.) She had asked, out of the blue, "How old am I?" and he'd said, coughing away, "Seven, Little Sister". Each year she'd added one to her number, as Ah Hau taught her. Her lucky number was seven. She looked about the hotel's luxurious interior for a seven, for comfort.

For the first time since entering through the double doors into this world of bliss and nectar-scented cool air, she really did look.

Orchestras seemed to be playing, like those she had listened to in the Mandarin Hotel in the Island when she was small, by the kitchens with five other children who let her join their thieving team. Here, ladies drifted by her in western attire, some seeming almost to float, their diamonds flashing. Amazingly shops were aligned along arcades stretching into infinity. Signs indicated restaurants, boutiques, hair-dressing emporiums, gift shops, windows crammed with jewellery, watches, clocks, paintings and even sports goods. It was a strange heaven.

"Tea, please," she said.

She hesitated, for Miss Brody was now posed in an attitude of mid-flight, nodding encouragement, get to the verb, Little Sister, and we'll do your bidding. KwayFay looked at the attentive faces. Was she suddenly so important that this creature, quite like an American doll in her superb clothes, would attend her whim? The question of money, that accursed wad she *had t*o spend or else, plagued her.

"Where, Little Sister?" Miss Brody asked, and explained, "Tea. Where would you like it served?"

KwayFay's vision blurred as tears came. She fumbled. Her hankie was gone. She panicked, rummaged in her handbag and found the money and watch still there.

The girl took her arm kindly yet with firmness. Two other similar girls appeared as if sprung out of the nearest pillar.

"Little Sister has decided to visit her suite first. Jessica? The lifts, please."

Three girls wafted KwayFay into an elevator and along a sumptuous corridor a whole hillside of squatters could inhabit. KwayFay sank, actually sank, into a carpet. They opened double doors, and KwayFay entered a sumptuous lounge.

Miss Brody summoned maids to run a bath – gold-plated taps, fittings, mirrors everywhere. Miss Brody fired off imperatives, clapping her hands, while KwayFay sat miserably in an ornate armchair.

"Miss KwayFay has decided to have tea in twenty minutes," the concierge carolled. "Hairdressers afterwards. I think Jakondio, or perhaps Wilhelmoso – alert both. *Allez! Allez!*"

The girl's hand-clapping worried KwayFay. There were no price lists. She was used to faded fly-dotted curling sheets taped to plaster walls saying how much a bowl of rice, how much green *sochoi* vegetables, and for the shredded *geung* ginger western tourists held in such awe. She was famished, desperate for some of the fruit that stood in a huge wicker-gilt basket on the marble table but was it real? Maybe it was only wax, real fruit being too expensive?

White and gold doors opened. Maids hurried with dressing gowns and towels. A bath was running. She wondered if it was near this vast room, hoping it was for her. Where would she put her own clothes? And what if the ones Miss Brody was bringing proved too costly? Would they hold her to ransom, clothes withheld until she could afford to pay? That happened in steamy bath-houses, the old trick for stealing a tourist's money while he was naked, his clothes locked away and the key on a string round his neck. After he'd had his rapture and was towelled by vigorous topless girls, he would find his belongings gone. The usual frantic phone calls to cruise ships or travel agents, the loans from relatives, were a mere endgame. His clothes would be given back.

She knew all the tricks. Money in her handbag, though, and the watch would cover whatever this cost. She waited until they seemed preoccupied, then nervously put her hand into her handbag and slowly counted the money unseen. Several thousand. Except, was the yellow note bigger or smaller than the brown?

"Little Sister." Miss Brody approached. "Do you want your personal safe activated? Or you can use the manager's?"

KwayFay eyed her with mistrust. This might be the start of the old wallet con. She had helped two bath-houses to work it when she'd been little, everybody trusting a child. Here, though, in the Peninsula?

"I'll keep it with me."

"Are you sure?"

"I must pay. My money . . ." Miss Brody seemed trustworthy, but didn't everyone?

"Little Sister, no payment is necessary. Your bath is ready."

No payment? KwayFay knew that old waterfront trick, too.

Two bath girls stood ready at the bathroom door. KwayFay pointedly clutched her handbag, ready to run for it if they made the slightest move. With the three maids, Miss Brody, and the two bath amahs, she was outnumbered, but she had escaped before.

"Will you still be here when I am washed?" she asked Miss Brody.

"If you wish, Little Sister. What do you require?"

"A price list."

The girl looked quite blank. "Price list for what, Little Sister?"

"I want it all written down, the cost."

The girl felt for her Motorola phone as if in serious doubt for the first time.

"Miss, there is no charge. It is already assigned."

"Assigned?"

KwayFay knew moneys were assigned, but debts? The term applied only to debt collectors, Triad threat-men, police squeeze-extortioners whose duty was to share illicit moneys leeched from shopkeepers and businessmen wanting to trade unhindered. It was all too familiar.

"Yes. There is no cost, Little Sister."

That old litany, reassurances before the filch! KwayFay's eyes narrowed. She wanted to show she was on to their game.

"Itemise the bill, Miss Brody," she said with what menace she could. "I want it here when I finish my bath, understand?"

"Very well, Little Sister."

It was either the good act of a superior con artist, or this Miss Brody with her half-idiomatic Cantonese, her obviously fluent Mandarin Chinese, and her impeccable English, was honest or an idiot.

"Yes, *lamah!*" KwayFay used the sharp ending. She would not change her mind.

She peered past the two bath amahs into the bathroom. It seemed huge, its ceiling vaulted like the English cathedral near the Peak Tram Terminus. Steam rose from a bath she could have swam in, though she had never swum. Other street children had wanted to teach her – a fish child scavenged more slickly than one unable to plunge into the harbour. She had been too frightened at the thought of not having solid earth beneath her feet. You could run away if your feet were on ground, but in water?

"No wash amahs, either," she said, clutching her handbag.

"Very well," Miss Brody said faintly. More imperious hand-clapping and terse instructions. No more doubts, though, and a good thing too.

They were all waiting. Slowly, before their eyes, she entered the bathroom, twice checking the lock to ensure she, and not they who watched in tableau, would have control. There was a con trick on businessmen, quite good, with an excellent financial return, that depended on locked bathrooms. Japanese and Indonesians responded best, understanding abduction as an art and even having official ransom rates payable, almost as if they were South Americans like in Columbia where the ransom rates were given in local newspapers before any kidnapping ever happened.

With a stare to show she was conscious of duplicity everywhere, KwayFay slowly closed the bathroom door.

Chapter Twenty-One

KwayFay soaked. The bath was so warm it seemed as if her skin was sucking sweetness from the pale blue water. All those bubbles! She tried to sing, because she'd once seen a movie in a Causeway Bay cinema where a pretty girl sang in her bath against a back-drop of mountains and snow. KwayFay's price ticket had been earned by giving an American sailor a quick grope, plus a clumsy maul of her breasts. The cinema's air-conditioning had saved her life, almost; she'd been so dehydrated she'd fainted all over Wanchai. Lucky, though, that discarded cartons from orange drinks were never quite finished. In the Ladies she drank the dregs of several cartons, and so kept going. Hydrated, she'd left the American sailor stranded and gone on her way.

Now, the pale pink of the bathroom ceiling lulled her. She felt so happy. Her handbag was safely within reach hanging on a gold tap. She started to doze, not really wanting to because of all the people out there who were going to charge her a mint for this luxury. She hoped she would get the money right. Old Man Tiger Wong depended on the hidden message getting through. Who among all these hotel people was his friend? Miss Brody didn't look quite up to it.

"Why?" Ghost Grandmother snapped, in a temper.

Just my luck, KwayFay would have thought if she hadn't been on her guard.

"Why what, Grandmother?"

"Why you deserve bath in gold water fountain? Are you Empress, greedy girl?"

"No, Grandmother."

"You sack from *See-Tau* Ho! Always smile and say nice thing when sack from work. You listen?"

"Listening! I am to smile and say something pleasant."

"No-Pay Girl, you!" Ghost Grandmother said yet with a hint of fondness that lifted KwayFay's hopes. Could this be a pleasant visit? Except, a No-Pay girl meant prostitute.

"I pay, Grandmother! With money from my handbag. A Triad gives it. They say I did well."

"Did well what?"

"I don't know," KwayFay confessed. "They sent me here in a *fo-cheh*."

"Big motor, *a*?" Grandmother laughed with scorn. KwayFay could have sworn Ghost Grandmother actually simpered as she said, "I once was a Mui Chai. You won't remember."

KwayFay was shocked. "*Mui Chai*? You, Grandmother?"

"Yes." Ghost chuckled. For once KwayFay did not groan at a coming harangue crammed full of useless old tales.

"Really?"

"I tell truth, disrespectful girl!" Ghost's silence extended. KwayFay put in a score of profound apologies for the incautious remark. This time, she wanted to hear Grandmother's tale. Ghost Grandmother, a sold slave sex-girl?

"I was bought by a Pocket-Mother from Chao-Chou in Kwantung Province. She was of course a Hoklo, spoke that dreadful dialect, worse even than the other Hoklos from the coast of Fukien. Nobody likes it. They talked Chang-Chou dialect, which is ugly."

"How old were you?"

"When sold to be *Mui Chai*? Eight, lucky age for buying slave girl."

"Slave!" KwayFay wailed. In English it sounded so much worse than in Cantonese.

"Don't feel bad, lazy girl," Ghost said comfortably. "I did really well. In Mandarin, they call us *Pei Nu*. Treated us vilely. I was sold with a cousin, MayTay, taller but ankles not pretty like mine. She'd be your . . ." Ghost gave up working it out. "She died of a thrashing for breaking a bowl. I still see her about, very little changed but with her hair quite pale. I told her only the other day I hate it. She never listens."

"Was it hard, Grandmother?" How had Grandmother survived terrible slavery in order to become her Grandmother two centuries ago?

"Hard-hard, Granddaughter." Oh, KwayFay thought, I'm granddaughter now am I? Not just lazy girl, or No-Pay Girl? "I worked every waking hour. Until I fourteen. Then I ousted First

Wife and took her place!"

"You took First Wife's place?" KwayFay squeaked in awe. "How?"

"Bad question!" Ghost cried angrily. "No ask bad question!"

KwayFay fell silent. Ghost calmed and went on, "I could have been sold into prostitution by the Hoklo woman. She was district regular Pocket-Mother, bought children each month to sell to Flower Boats on Pearl River and in Canton godowns. Did I tell you my cousin MayTay was also sold and died of a thrashing?"

"Yes, Grandmother."

"You no *Mui Chai*, hear me?"

"Yes, Grandmother."

"Speak to Old Man, Tiger Wong *Sin-Sang*. Tell him, Ghost say no. Save endless trouble."

"Ghost say no," KwayFay repeated carefully, anxious to get it right word for word.

"He from Sha-Tin. His family farmed in valley below Lion Rock. His ancestors not happy. Hong Kong change name of their land. Very cross people!"

"Not happy?" KwayFay stirred in alarm. Unhappy ghosts could do anything, change to spirits nobody even knew about. There was no telling with discontented ghosts. She shivered in her warm bubbles.

"I not write or read, Granddaughter," Grandmother said with the oblique pride of the handicapped. "His ancestors can. Old China people say Lion Rock is truly Tiger Head Hill, Hu-T'ou-Shan. Very bad to change name of mountain. What are dragons to do with *Fhung Seui* spoiled? They cross."

"Cross!" KwayFay moaned. "*Fhung Seui* spoiled!" Wind-water orientation, that westerners called Feng Shui, could never be overstated.

"That's why I told you, tell him change name!"

"Is that enough?" she wailed, not wanting Grandmother to leave her with half a tale.

"No, stupid Granddaughter!"

"Sorry, Grandmother."

Ghost's voice grew dreamy. "It was beautiful long house, the

Hakka families at Sha-Tin. Tseng Family house, with round end gables. Whoever heard of such a thing . . ."

Ghost rambled on about strange buildings, ponds, special green vegetables she used to like, the strange habits of the English who ate hard yellow slabs they made from cow milk by churning it in barrels, which was odd and unknown in old Hong Kong. She told of everyday things as if they were amazing, and amazements as if they were mundanities: "You remember seeing those two men flayed for their skins at the Execution Gate, near where . . .?" until KwayFay's mind gave up.

She came to. Grandmother was still talking, about how she'd almost been sold for a prostitute in Canton when she was bought by the Pocket Mother. She escaped this fate, though it would have been lucrative by pretending she could tell the future.

"Of course I could do no such thing! No such thing as good news!" Ghost cackled her sudden laugh. "I was kept, washing and cleaning all day long. They gave gifts, hoping I would promise good fortune! I just kept them guessing. With the money I bought myself free. I was eighteen, went home. All *Mui Chai* girls wanted to do same. That was when the man, official for Provincial Governor, took me back as Number One wife . . ."

Somebody knocked on the bathroom door, calling KwayFay.

"Can I go now, Grandmother?"

KwayFay couldn't help boasting a little. It wasn't the kind of thing you could do to a ghost, but this *was* her own grandmother; surely that must count? She took the risk. "I have never slept in a bath before, Grandmother, in a real bathroom. I want to remember it. I'll never have another chance."

A real bath was once-in-a-lifetime for a street girl. Even labouring Hakka women, in their black fronded wicker hats and black pantaloons and jackets, digging and shovelling roads, called Cantonese street urchins Cockroach Children, fond but disrespectful. See how she had got on!

"No sleeping when hair done," Ghost reminded. "Bad hairdressers take hair and use it to make spells."

"Am I to let them do my hair?" she asked in alarm. "They want to sell me clothes and jewels, and say I need not pay. It will lead to scandal."

"You no-account girl. How can no-account girl create scandal?" Grandmother spoke more peaceably, a sure sign a ghost was getting tired. "Tonight, lazy girl, I test you on three ceremonies and four rituals. I pick which, you tell which."

"I'm so tired. Too many new things . . ."

KwayFay came to some time later, the water cooling and people still knocking on the bathroom door calling was she all right because they heard voices.

Ghost had gone.

She stepped from the bath, careful not to slip, and stood for a moment regarding herself in the enormous gold-rimmed rococo mirror. For the first time, other than night reflections in Whiteway's waterfront windows, she had the chance to see herself in full.

The look she exchanged with her reflection, she realised with a start, was one of deadly complicity. Whatever opportunity was here had to be used, otherwise why had it come?

She covered herself with a large towel.

"I was merely singing," she called out as if irritated. "I am ready now."

The old woman from the gambling emporium in Kwun Tong was waiting for Old Man as he alighted at the Benevolence Bath House. He did not need to be told his slow progress across the pavement was safe. The fact he was not warned off by his threat-men was assurance enough.

Girls brought him to an upholstered gilt chair in the foyer.

"Tell."

"Little Sister bathe," the old woman said quietly. When young she had been a medium, but now had lost her gift. Useful still, but only for interpretation of what was overheard. "She does not want to buy clothes, jewels, food. She say it give scandal."

"Scandal?"

Old Man was startled. What was the matter with the girl? Something to do with prayers, maybe? Hong Kong's local Taoism was famously adaptable and could bend round any moral corner.

"*Chau-man*," the old woman confirmed. "Scandal. She said it. She asked the ghost about it. It speaks," she added, working things out, "Cantonese. It told about Lion Rock. The girl was puzzled by its new name."

"Good." So he had been right to change his name. "No more?"

"In bath, she spoke of your honoured ancestors by Lion Rock."

He thought for some time about this, then gestured for the old woman to continue.

"No more, First Born."

"See the girl spends money." He raised a finger slowly, to the terror of the bath girls, the old woman, and the four indoor guard-men watching his every move.

"Yes, First Born."

"And tell me every item."

The old woman faded. Tiger Wong nodded, and allowed himself to be taken into the bath house and undressed. He would have wanted to use one of the girls, but they lacked the enormous breasts he especially admired. Such decisions were unspeakably taxing. He felt drained.

The girls asked if they could. He told them yes. They flipped him naked onto the slab and slopped warm water over him. He hated this stage but it was the essential prelude to the flailing with hot towels he particularly liked so had to be endured.

"Different girls," he ordered irritably. He was peeved by the strange beliefs of Little Sister. Starving herself, and in virtual tatters? He was becoming annoyed. The two bath-house girls fled. Two others instantly took their places.

Worried about scandal, as if she was a great society lady instead of Cockroach Girl from the gutter? It was not right. She should exploit his generosity, take what she could grab. That he could understand. It was logical. It was what people did.

Yet she had delivered the strange old documents in the untraceable file about Kellett Island. You couldn't argue with that. It was a new and disturbing experience, to be in a quandary with no resolution. Also, and just as wrong, was the fact that she was a girl, not a man. If she'd been male, then even with strange powers he would have understood.

But a girl?

"Slow," he grumbled. "And no talk."

Wearily he submitted to their ministrations and the first heavy soapings. He was a martyr to everybody, including all these hangers-on he gave jobs, homes, food, protection, pensions, money, careers, while he suffered like a slave.

"No good," he groused, sulking. "Different girls."

They were replaced by two more. It was one thing after another, tribulations always heaped upon the Business Head, never on servants. Hard life for the master, easy for the hirelings. It was always so, hence the old Cantonese saying: A father's problems never end.

He sighed, filled with self-pity.

Chapter Twenty-Two

"The importance, Ah Min?"

"You own Kellett Island, First Born."

The old man considered this. Kellett Island was no longer an island. Once, it had been a small rocky, granite dot in Hong Kong's main harbour. A causeway ran to it, forming one arm of the mooring place. A typhoon shelter was there, where junks and all kinds of pleasure craft skulked when great *dai-fungs* came out of the South China Sea. The English made these safe places, but had committed the uttermost foolishness when they reclaimed land to engulf Kellett Island. No more Hong Kong Royal Yacht Club, just a small traffic island amid swirling screeching traffic. Now, cars wrecked the peace of the early morning *Tai Gik* people, who did the ancient ritual exercises in the parks and on high places. Where was serenity? It wasn't good enough. Kellett Island was the pearl in the mouths of Kowloon's Nine Dragons, the Gao Lung of Kowloon's name.

"I still do *Tai Gik*," he grumbled.

"Indeed, First Born."

"My new name!" the old man commanded sharply.

"Indeed, Tiger First Born."

"The English don't," Tiger Wong said, still in a sulk though the last pair of bath-house girls had given him rapturous sex. He should have been at ease, but could not rest.

He liked to do his early *Tai Gik* on the sports field, which he always had cleared to perform alone, in case enemies caught him by pretending to be exercise people. Lately, he'd had to hire a place in the Harbour Hotel or some such dump, as if he was a common tourist. Shameful, shameful. For a traffic island?

"Significance," he grumbled.

"A claim could be lodged."

About money, Ah Min always went word by word, unable to string a whole sentence together. An amah entered on a signal from Ah Min, placed a tray of tea and almond juice on the low wooden table. The old man liked her. She was beautiful, no black hairs on her chin, eyes downcast, shapely, not more than nineteen, good teeth. He felt inclined to use her, though she would be hard put to rouse him. Old age did not come alone, Chinese saying. Except one of these new amahs had been married aged sixteen; her husband had died in an accident. Another Chinese saying: *Never fuck widow; horse thrown rider!* He would make Ah Min check if she was a widow.

"The girl found the file, Tiger *Sin-Sang*. Kellett Island is yours. The deeds are yours."

"More. In full." He would never get to the next bath-house. He still felt dissatisfied, so the girls couldn't have done their sex work correctly, no matter how rapturous they had made him feel. They would have to go back to harlotry in the street. He felt hard done by.

"Kellett Island is yours. It never did belong to the Royal Yacht Club. They did not know this."

"It is mine?"

"It is yours. In perpetuity."

"This means I have a traffic island," Old Man Tiger Wong said drily. "The girl is fraudulent after all, *ne*?"

"Wong First Born," Ah Min said guardedly, choosing phrases with care as he sensed his master's testy mood. "The place is small, yes. But the existence of the Cross-Harbour Tunnel from beside Tsim Sha Tsui East Ferry Pier, underneath Salisbury Road, emerges in Hong Kong Island beside the Royal Hong Kong Yacht Club. Causeway Bay Typhoon Shelter is there, with the Hong Kong Police Officers' Club beside it."

"I wait."

"Business Head, you own access to all those places because you own Kellett Island. They never paid rent. They never bought it. English law confirmed Chinese Imperial law in the 1840s. The English conquerors said so. Sixteen decades."

The old man smoothed his *cheong saam*. His joints swelled these days. The last time he had used a lone bed-girl his knees became so painful he could hardly walk. His ankles were no better. Doctors were useless. He should have some traditional Chinese herbs. He deserved something, after all the years of dedicated service he had given to the Colony. His was dedication, total and generous. That was the duty of a father of business, ne? To give constantly, and receive nothing but ingratitude. He was not given enough respect. Only the mad girl KwayFay, who had once given him her last ounce of old rice wrapped in cooking foil, showed him respect. She was the granddaughter he lacked.

"What means this decades?"

"One-piece ten years, master. English law insists on Chinese rights," Ah Min went on, heart shaking at the excitement of the revelation he was about to make. "First Born will remember the Plover Cove Reclamation Scheme? Drought in the late Nineteen Sixties? The Colony decapitated mountains in the New Territories, on the Governor's command, and flooded the reservoir so created with clean water."

"I remember. I should have received millions in compensation, but Government paid the villagers instead. We only managed to milk a few paltry million pounds Sterling from that. A disgrace."

"Now is your time to reclaim your inheritance, Wong First Born. The Government must buy Kellett Island back from you. The fisher villages were paid a going price for their lands round Plover Cove, so must Government pay you. The laws of precedent say so!"

"Or what?"

"Or," Ah Min said, his beam radiant, "they must close the Cross-Harbour Tunnel from Tsim Sha Tsui."

"Close?" Now Old Man paid attention.

"Close, First Born. Instantly."

"Or pay me?"

"Correct, master. The money they owe is almost incalculable." He was shuddering, almost in orgasm. His Triad master watched with distaste.

"Can they refuse?"

"Only if they bequeath the debt to the People's Republic of China. An impossibility! Imagine how China would feel! To march in and be faced with the international disgrace of a massive debt left over from Imperial times, that Great Britain had failed to honour."

"The same argument over the costs of building the new airport on Lantau Island!"

"Indeed, Wong *Sin-Sang*! Neither could face it! Hong Kong Government will give you almost anything you demand! Can you imagine the Kowloon traffic blocked up all the way from Tsim Sha Tsui to the Shum Chun River? And all China's exports from Kwantung Province and the whole of South China halted?"

The old man thought a while.

"Fresh tea," he said quietly. An amah hurried in on Ah Min's gesture.

She was different, Old Man observed. He watched her figure move, and approved. It was time he went to a bath-house he did not own, in North Point perhaps, or even that terrible place in Quarry Bay. He might take his own bath girls. One of them did quite well when he was faced with a particularly difficult decision.

"I go to bath-house, six o'clock. Quarry Bay, or Shau Kei Wan. Choose six bath girls. I pick three. No Shanghainese or Fukien girls, though. Too harsh."

"Six o'clock, Wong *Sin-Sang*."

The old man leant forward to accept the tea bowl. Ah Min froze in fright, for the momentous statement to come.

"You have done well, Ah Min," Tiger Wong said gravely. "You remember those three cents?"

"Yes, Wong *Sin-Sang*?"

"They are forgotten."

Ah Min beamed, tears streaming down his face at the Triad master's magnanimity, and took a bowl of tea from the amah. The two men drank together, eyes on each other.

Chapter Twenty-Three

"Leave your brushes, combs, everything."

The hairdressers exchanging glances. "Leave them, dearie?" the so-elegant American exclaimed. "But my friend Elmore gave them to me. They're my presentation set."

"Leave them," KwayFay said again.

It was her way of testing the system. In any case, ordinary tortoiseshell could be replaced. If she was being honoured, or tricked, then he could charge a new set of implements up to the hotel.

"Elmore will be so upset!"

"Miss Brody."

"Yes, Little Sister?" The concierge signalled to Vane, the tall slender American hairdresser she'd finally selected for this young and august guest. She fixed Vane with an eye as she told KwayFay, "It shall be exactly as you say."

Vane was bustled out with his assistants, his lip trembling and his backward appealing stare ignored.

"Shall I have them cleaned, Little Sister?"

"No. I shall do it myself."

The mirror showed a different KwayFay now. Her hair was gorgeous. No lack of lustre in Hong Kong, not among the Cantonese anyhow, but this was exquisite.

She examined her features. How different she looked, from the bedraggled creature who'd stared back with such belligerence from the bathroom's mirror! If she were not dressed in a bathrobe, she might appear even . . .

"Clothes, now, please. Give prices."

Miss Brody murmured, worried, "You will not be billed for anything. I have orders."

"Price items!"

The parade began ten minutes after she had tea. English biscuits, crumpets, toasted tea cakes, jam and a small pot of marmalade. She had said marmalade because she'd once heard of it. The word had stuck with her as a mantra, mar-ma-*lade*, since she was eleven. Two English ladies had been having tea in the

Gloucester Tea-Rooms on the Island, where KwayFay begged at the door. One lady, wafting suavely out, had given her two fifty-cent pieces saying, "Sorry about the marmalade, chuckie."

KwayFay remembered scrutinising the coins, staring at the Queen's head with grave suspicion. She bit the edges, rubbed them to test if they shone (always the best test, because of cunning Shanghainese unworthies practically taking over Quarry Bay to counterfeit coinages, having nothing worthwhile of their own).

One coin had been sticky. During the biting test, she'd been astonished to discover an amazing new taste. It was bitter, then spread sweetly over her tongue. Ever after she'd passed the Gloucester Tea-Rooms with a kind of reverence, seeing it as a place of special affluence, a great tall palatial building at least as grand as the nearby General Post Office but able to create selective tastes surely only royalty were used to.

When the Gloucester Tea-Rooms closed, the sight of the rebuilding work broke her heart. She'd known then she would never again taste that fabulous mar-ma-*lade*. From the euphony, she wondered if the sweet tang was actually made from horses: Big Horse Road in Cantonese was *Dai-mar-lo*, where once the English governors rode their great horses along the harbour waterfront.

Now, a whole pot! It looked strange, a sticky spoon all its own. Once she licked the spoon the memory came flooding back. Her vision blurred. She had made it to marmalade! And her own jar! Not much in it, but perhaps the Peninsula Hotel with its gold taps and priceless arrays of jewellery had secret special-price deals with some hawkers? She drew breath. It must be the costliest food on earth.

Models paraded through the suite.

"Leave this one."

KwayFay was reclining on a chaise longue, remembering that USA actress, famous from the scene where a real live lion sprawled over her as she (the actress, not the lion) snarled and roared. Except the actress lay like the sphinx, forearms out parallel before her, and that would have been inelegant. Different for a movie star, everything permitted. Read the newspapers blowing along the waterfront, and anybody'd know it was true.

The girls paraded at intervals of one minute, ladies from the boutiques on the ground floor and the other shopping malls listing things KwayFay wanted to see again. She had done the lingerie – such shameless shapes! Why, one slip even left a breast showing! She blushed and felt exposed, though it was these thin girls strolling, and even dancing, through the suite to music, displaying colours and styles. She picked three pairs of knickers, two petticoats, a camisole.

"Is that all, Miss KwayFay?" one lady, desperately trying to seem French though she was from the Philippines, begged in alarm. "Our superior styles are – "

KwayFay said firmly, "I do not exploit!"

Three times Miss Brody, now quite harrowed, explained there would be no charge. The Peninsula's only wish was to prove what excellent choices they showed their august visitor. KwayFay was getting used to authority and quickly learned to speak sharply. They even approved of a stern corrective, the models particularly appearing smiley when she made a definite choice.

"Only one full set of lingerie, though . . ."

"Now dresses."

She stood firm, insisting they leave her old clothes with her cracked old shoes. Miss Brody wanted to send them for cleaning.

"No," KwayFay ruled. "Leave here, please."

"But why?" Miss Brody's helpless gesture said it all: KwayFay's attire was rubbish. The hotel was eager to replace every stitch by the best, most expensive garments that fashion could offer. It was all free.

"If you take them," KwayFay told her, "I might never see them again. What will I wear then?"

"These new clothes!" Miss Brody wailed.

Miss Brody understood that Miss KwayFay wanted to burn every single strand of her hair trapped in the combs, brushes, on the carpet, but there were *fokis* to do just that. The Peninsula's famous Domestic Division was renowned.

KwayFay had them bring matches, ash-trays, towels, and a small incinerator device, and burned the implements and her entangled strands of hair. Miss Brody swayed with distress. KwayFay sympathised. She too had felt hunger, but the lady's worry was only caused by thoughts of the hairdresser. In any case, the American hairdresser's friend Elmore would leave him for another friend before the week was out – they were already ensconced in a Kyoto hotel making private arrangements. Where was the problem? The amahs and assistants twittered.

The dresses proved difficult. So many! Eastern, western, Indian, Indonesian, saris and sarongs, evening wear and cocktail dresses. Materials were problematic. Some textiles were so heavy! Others were gossamer. The couturiers leant towards impact rather than shape, fashion as opposed to detail. KwayFay had a hard time. Finally she selected an elegant silk day suit, the skirt exquisitely cut, the jacket with its false lapels showing a two-tone effect perfectly. Two day dresses were quickly chosen because she was getting tired. She still had to go to HC's as ordered, but why?

"Now shoes."

Exotic creatures of indeterminate gender rushed in with tiers of boxes of shoes. Extra mirrors were brought. Brogues, stubby toes she knew were coming back into fashion, and the anklet-hangs were definitely out. She finally selected two pairs of Italian and a slight pair of London design.

She stood while they dressed her.

"Box up all clothes, please, and shoes," she told them. "In case."

"In case of what, Miss KwayFay?" cried Miss Brody, now woefully distressed.

"In case I want them."

Had she still enough money to buy a dinner? She asked to see the itemised bill. She stared when it came, didn't believe the amount. So many noughts?

She told them to leave her alone as she counted the money in her handbag. To her relief it just covered the cost of one outfit. If she left most, she would still have some money over, six hundred

Hong Kong dollars. Would it buy a meal in the Peninsula? She doubted it. If she dressed back in her old clothes and left by the rear entrance, she might escape without arrest and buy a two-dollar bowl with a wisp of green vegetables behind Connaught Road. The Star Ferry was the cheapest way back to the Island, leave this madhouse and Kowloon behind. The Tiger Wong had said spend. She had spent.

Quickly she ate the rest of the biscuits and a piece of cake, which she saw on the bill, but her stomach rebelled at such richness. She poured a cup of cold tea, glancing surreptitiously towards the double doors, and drank it before summoning them.

"Who will pay?" she asked.

"It is already paid, Miss KwayFay."

"Let me see."

They showed her the bill. It was cancelled. KwayFay knew this trick, one bill seeming the same as another, then the miscreant was arrested on the way out of the hotel and it was prison on Lamma Island among hoods and robbers. Unlike other thieves, she would have no contacts in the Triads or Hongs or police to get her off a trial. She had helped to work the trick several times, before she'd become respectable employee in HC's Company.

"I pay."

"Miss, please . . ."

Miss Brody was taken away in tears. A second concierge, grand and old, quite forty or maybe even more, appeared and listened in silence while KwayFay counted out the impossible sum of money onto the rosewood table. The new woman simply agreed with whatever KwayFay said, concurred with her selections, then smiled.

"You only wish to pay for the clothes you are wearing?"

"Yes. I shall not have the others."

That would leave her enough for a good meal every day for a month. She was no fool. And she'd destroyed all her strands of hair, as Ghost Grandmother said.

"Little Sister, it is a pleasure to do business with you. May I extend the hospitality of the hotel before you leave? We have excellent international cuisine and – "

"No. I go to work now."

"And your purchases? The other ones?"

"Leave them," KwayFay said cunningly. "Maybe I collect them later from your front door, bringing more money."

"A hotel limousine to your destination, perhaps?"

"No. I go on Star Ferry. Thank you."

"Thank you, Miss KwayFay. May I accompany you down to the entrance?"

The elderly concierge chatted all the way, pointing out the beautiful jewellery in the hotel shops as she went. KwayFay found difficulty in walking on such costly shoes, and she hated the thought of her expensive skirt being crumpled. It was the unaccustomed susurrus of her silk underclothes, and the impossible shoes causing her to tread as if her feet were old, like those of tourists.

KwayFay could not resist pausing to gaze at the galaxy of brooches, pendants, rings, earrings. Some she had not even seen before, though she had spent year after year night-staring into the windows of the late shops in Nathan Road of an evening. One stone in particular caught her eye, a most deep violet blue.

The elderly concierge recognised her guest's craving and said, "Tanzanite, Miss KwayFay. It is a stone only known for fifty years, from Tanzania. They call it African Sapphire, but it is different."

"It is exquisite."

"Isn't it?" She could tell KwayFay loved the pendant. "They say a famous film star, the one who always buys the most expensive jewels, has the only perfect necklet. Five flawless large tanzanites!"

They went to the main door. Uniformed porters leapt to allow her through.

"Miss KwayFay, your suite will be kept here, by order."

"What suite?"

"Simply call the hotel and you will be conveyed here from anywhere in Hong Kong, at any time."

She dismissed the concierge's words as yet more trickery. Also, how much would a suite cost? KwayFay said painstaking thanks and left, carrying her old handbag, laptop over her shoulder, and the plastic shopping bag holding her old clothes and shoes. The concierge watched her go. Tourists and pedestrians paused to see.

The concierge smiled. She went to telephone the head of the Triad, earning her retainer.

Chapter Twenty-Four

The journey to work seemed arduous, quite as if she was now becoming a tourist. Except, she thought as she caught the Star Ferry, she had no *home*. Did Ah Hau's Café of the Singing Birds off Ladder Street in the Mologai count? She sat in the unaccustomed luxury of the upper deck of the Star Ferry, avoiding the window seats because of her hair. She kept catching glimpses of herself – an amazing creature! So elegant! – in the windows of the place called MacDonalds and the waterfront camera shops. Schoolchildren were already out in their bright uniforms, this homework, that task set by too-strict mistresses.

Tourist, though. KwayFay shouldn't feel like a tourist. They had homes. She had none, not even here.

Yet the concierge said she now had a suite in the Peninsula. Had she meant it? And for what exactly? Everything was trade. Transactions, more than stars in the sky or thoughts in mankind, waited to be enacted. Pay your money at the turnstile and the Star Ferry carried you to Hong Kong Island from Kowloon. Pay your HK$ 16.00 at the Government Pier in Central District, and the Hoverferry takes you to Cheung Chau, 9.00am start, there in 35 minutes. All was the rule of money. It happened as night followed day. And why? Because you'd paid, *ne*?

Three men in suits boarded and sat close.

She saw their reflections. One talked into a cell phone. The others were the sort who ought to look bored because they were parted from their investment tracker charts. Usually, young suits couldn't leave off analysing numbers all the way home, and were still checking when they arrived next morning.

These three were already in their job. She felt them looking round the upper deck as the *Evening Star*, just like the Star Ferry vessels in green and cream, churned slowly out of the jetty.

They didn't look at her. They examined everybody else. The young man snapped his cell phone shut. She heard him mutter something but couldn't make it out. Among themselves, threatmen used slang full of puns, even rhymes and homophones. This was traditional. In ancient China, ladies of the Imperial Court wrote to each other using a secret set of ideographs, inventing characters for a written language only they understood.

What were these threat-men telling somebody about her for?

She thought of that wheezing man who'd interrogated her, to no purpose, in Kowloon that time, and suddenly believed she'd guessed it was he. He must be a Triad Head, who was cruel to his prisoner the poor old man from the Sports Field, who did the *Tai Gik* in the ancient way.

Suddenly it all came flooding in, and she realised.

They were keeping the old man as a business hostage! He was being held for ransom, which was why he refused always to try to escape. Not a prisoner, but someone held to force his family's complicity.

This explained his weariness, his need of her help. He was stolen from his family! How terrible! She felt almost sick. At least she had her freedom, whereas that poor old man was imprisoned against his will. What for, some merger? The only exercise he was ever permitted was when the Sports Field at Causeway Bay was vacant. She'd seen him taken out for exercise. How cruel people were! She almost wept at the image of the poor old gentleman. Would he never be freed?

Now she fully understood that meeting near the Western Market. The threat-men were obviously making sure he didn't pass on some coded message, the sort of thing a desperate hostage would do. She simply hadn't understood. And his words about money clearly had some double meaning she hadn't taken in. What a fool she was! How broken-hearted he must be. His poor family, possibly children, grandchildren, all weeping for their poor old grandfather. She hadn't helped him at all.

These young hoods might be the same ones from the Sports Field. They suspected a rescue attempt, which explained their vigilance, their aggression.

Such a helpless old man. And stupidly she told him he should name himself Tiger! He must have thought she was mocking his imprisonment.

There was only one way out. She would do a deal with these awful men. Some Triad had abducted Old Man, and had chosen her – young, poor, an ex-urchin without connections, dispensable – to be the one who carried the message for the ransom money! She knew well how it was done. Didn't Hong Kong's newspapers report ransom demands two or three times every single week, sometimes every day? It was the Colony's horrid game.

She was a no-name person. Even her name was something Ah Hau, the cripple of the Café of the Singing Birds in the Mologai, made up to call her when she came begging.

The poor man must be got free. He must not be allowed to suffer. Ghost Grandmother would be proud of her. And if her decision proved disastrous and they killed her, then at least she would be well received. Who knew what help she might get from the Jade Emperor, Lord of All, if she helped the old gentleman to freedom? While it was still safe and nobody was sitting next to her, she slowly opened her handbag and withdrew the remainder of the money.

She waited until the *Evening Star* docked and the crowd disembarked. The three followed her up the ramps. She could hear one grumbling, something about the time taken crossing on the Star Ferry, instead of driving. One laughed, the other took no notice. She started to walk towards Princes Building. At the end of the concourse she halted and turned suddenly. The men paused. The traffic lights were twenty paces off.

"I have money," she told them. "Take it."

She thrust the notes at the one face she recognised, the driver man the others called Tang. He looked startled, stared at the money in his hands.

"Leave the old gentleman alone. Please let him go. I know he won't tell if you set him free."

"What?" one man said.

She knew what he was up to. She'd used the surprise trick on tourists from the cruise ships, and once at a furriers in Wanchai. It sometimes worked, but less as she'd become a teenager.

"Please don't hurt him. He's an old man."

"Old man?" It was quite a good act, she recorded with a twinge of envy, but they must be trained in this kind of thing.

"It's no time for games," she said, emboldened. "The money

the threat-men gave me I've spent, like they said. That's what is left. If you want the clothes back, you can get them from the Peninsula Hotel. I still have my old clothes. Please don't hurt Old Man. He means no harm."

"What?" the man said stupidly. They looked at each other. She lost patience.

"I can let you have my computer. It's very expensive. I know where you can sell it. It's still modern, nearly."

"Computer?" The fool Tang kept staring at the money in his hands.

"You know where I am," she said evenly. People passing were starting to glance at her, standing talking to three young men who had arrayed themselves in a line before her across the pavement.

"Where you are?"

The man was a dolt, she saw, now fully committed. What could they do to her? She knew she wasn't worth even killing, only forgetting.

"The Brilliant Miracle Success Investment Company," she said scornfully. "Princes Building. You know where I mean."

"Princes Building," the idiot repeated. He glanced at the taller of the others, making her wonder if she'd addressed the wrong one, a *foki* instead of the *bahsi*. She stepped back to include them all.

"That's where I am going now. I can sometimes guess investments. I'll try to do it for you, if you let Old Man go. Please tell them. Promise?"

"Promise, Little Sister," the tallest one said. He must be the leader because he took over. "I promise."

"Very well." She told them the telephone number of HC's firm, and how she could be got on a direct line if they wanted to ask about investments. "I have nothing else to give you. Please treat him kindly. Do you give him enough to eat?"

"Yes, Little Sister."

The tallest threat-man seemed amused at her attempted belligerence. The other two were still acting bemused. She wasn't taken in.

"Are you sure? He is thin."

"Yes, we are sure, Little Sister."

"Please remember he is old enough to be your great-grandfather."

"I shall, Little Sister," the tall one said gravely.

"He can stay in my hut, if you let him go, if he has no family to take him. I promise he won't tell the police, just help me carry the water to other squatters."

"Right, Little Sister."

"Very well, then."

She turned on her heel and left them, making for the side entrance of Princes Building. The computer was cutting the shoulder of the new dress, but she'd made her decision and knew it was the right one. Sure, she would have nothing left. And she might even lose her shack if they made her pay her wages to free Old Man. It was the only time in her life she'd been in any position to help anyone. She felt really proud.

Saving lives brought terrible responsibility. A person who rescued another was responsible for him for ever. Had to support him against all adversities, in fact, through famines and riot. That was the Chinese way.

In olden times, desperate people would throw themselves into fast-running rivers like the Yangtse or the Pearl, in hopes of rescue – thus making the rescuer their Rice-Bowl-and-Roof for the rest of their lives. Innocent English, newcomers in olden days to the Shanghai Bund or Canton godowns, were often duped into saving a poor "drowning" soul, only later realising their profound obligation to the supposed victim and having to fund the indolent leech for ever. The Chinese, wiser in traditions and smiling behind their hands, would watch from the passing boat while the man simply drowned, in the absence of some dupe.

That was the obligation. This, she knew, was a real case of kidnapping for ransom. She almost wept for Old Man. Tiger? More like a lamb. If she rescued him, she could have him as her own private family and keep him for ever. She would transform him into her very own grandfather! She had never done anything like this before, but would try. He could be her family!

She wondered if he had his own teeth. He looked clean. Maybe she could have him mind two or three of the nearby squatter shacks, perhaps earn water money looking after babies while mothers worked in Kennedy Town Market?

There was risk in it, she already knew. She once tried to save a puppy's life by stealing scraps for it, but some lads from the Yau Tong squatter shelters stole the puppy and sold it to be cooked for rich people who needed belly heat, for which puppy stew was best. They'd made a dollar apiece, the five of them. She'd wept. Tragedy was everywhere when living things got stolen, but what could you do?

The entire office of the Brilliant Miracle Success Investment Company was sombre and quiet. A few telephones rang on low switch. Tony was talking but listlessly as if his Futures scheme was going nowhere. Alice looked up, quickly bent down to concentrate, not even a false greeting this time, though she stared at KwayFay's clothes and hairdo and shoes.

KwayFay's desk was littered with spare notes, scraps of yellow stickers with telephone numbers, Stocks and Shares pages. One or two extinct print-outs from several different FTSE and Dow Jones reports, American most of them with London latests. So much, she thought bitterly, for loyalty. They'd all assumed she was gone, and had used her terminal, console, even her desk drawer, for rubbish.

Deliberately she took her time. Let HC come sweating and call her in. The SUSPENDED sticker was still there, now curled at the edges. She was past caring. For the first time in her life she felt committed to another living person. Old Man – *her* Old Man – was hostaged. Her duty was to extricate him. She would preserve him and the learning his early *Tai Gik* and old age represented.

The desk rubbish she simply scrapped, screwing up the bits of paper and notelets and discarding them. She accepted a drink of water from Charmian the *foki* servant, and smiled.

"You look beautiful, Little Sister!" the *foki* said admiringly.

"Thank you."

"I missed you, Little Sister." Then, "No work here," Charmian
covered her face as she helped KwayFay to get rid of the rubbish.
"Why?"
"Business Head angry all days."
More than likely, KwayFay thought. She sat down to the console. She was heartily sick of tap-screens. You were forever making sure you didn't split the wretched things, which gave under
the push of your finger in the creepiest way. What was wrong
with a resolute key? HC again, moving with the times.

She sipped the water, carefully not letting her lipstick smear
the glass. The water was always super-chlorinated, foul to the
taste and horrid to the skin, but it was free, and she had a second
person to think of. This was how pride felt. Different from a
mere job.

The stupid Cook Bounty Island Pacific currency was now
ignored on the main currency exchanges, she saw. None of the
major currencies or banks had taken it up, except for five or six
who'd got their fingers burned. Serve them right. She almost
choked to see that HC, in despair, had finally succumbed and
taken out loans using a Bahamian international and some
Commerce Bank outfit in Hannover. He'd lost the firm's
monthly take, a gross folly. Considering the warning she'd given
him, it could only have been a psychic bid of despair.

The investments were in a terrific back-log. She got down to
clearing them. The office finished in two hours, but by the time
the clock jumped on and the buzzers sounded for closure, she
was through a good half. People began shutting down and
stretching and calling their bits of news, the usual nonsense, all
trying to sound as if they'd set up some monumental buy order.
She wasn't deceived.

Alice called a tentative goodnight as she passed. KwayFay, con-
centrating on her screen, gave a distant nod. Tony bellowed and
did his dance, creating an impression. Franny the new stats girl, a
Hong Kong University graduate who claimed to have investments of her own – a fiction, supposed to bring the boys flock-
ing – gave her a guarded smile, but only after checking HC was
on the phone. Franny was a plain girl whose uncle was a political

man among the godowns in Shek Tong Tsui. She bragged about him on every day except the Double Tenth when the Nationalists put their stupid flags out and talked of moving to Taipei where they could "live in freedom" among the Komintang. The Red Guard factions called Taiwan (still "Formosa" to old English people) The Island of Looters.

Only Charmian the servant remained, sweeping up and humming a melody from the famous *White-Haired Girl* opera. HC struck, seeing KwayFay.

This was it. Resigned, she left her screen.

"I am a forgiving person," HC said straight out, standing shaking his keys and twitching his shoulders.

"Yes, Business Head."

"I am keeping you on for a few days, see how you go."

"Thank you."

"You did not warn me about the Cook Bounty Island Pacific Republican currency."

"I did. It is in the records."

"Don't contradict!" he bellowed. "You did not warn me! I lose money!"

"Sorry, sir."

"I review your job in three days."

He turned then and saw her for the first time in her new clothes. He started, sweat already speckling his forehead. He had lost weight. He regarded her, his eyes travelling up and down, studying her hair as if across a graph of London percentage-earning ratios. He almost shook his head – no, couldn't be true; wasn't this a slut from squatter shacks?

She left when he said nothing more.

"Say again."

Ah Min seated himself to hear. He had previously been standing, impatient to have done with her. Now he had to absorb it slowly. It was after all about money. He had only recently escaped censure by the forgiveness of Tiger Wong. He looked at the fistful of money the man Tang held.

"Little Sister would not take it all."

"She did not spend as instructed?"

"No, First Born."

Ah Min closed his eyes. Yet more impossibilities. Useless to ask "Why not?" as if there were reasons for such irrationality. The girl was bone poor. So whose pay was she in? The sudden hope that she was betraying the Triad because of a better deal rose to comfort him.

"She gave this money back."

"She . . ." Ah Min dared not open his eyes. Money was food, air, survival in a malevolent world. She discarded money, for death? The room swung.

"She said to say, First Born . . ."

"Say it." This new phenomenon had to be exterminated before its canker spread and destroyed the universe.

"She will buy Tiger Wong back, and set him free."

This was better. The girl was mad! Ah Min opened his eyes and studied the man awaiting orders. The dolt was starting to guess that his life was forfeit for concocting such a hopeless fantasy. Buy back the head of the Triad? A person who could fund investments, new currencies from newly-independent Pacific republics with barely a thought, and make mints from an afternoon's whim? Who could call out hundreds of adherents to change destinies of whole industries, even countries? The girl clearly was insane.

Relief swept through him. He would escape the consequences now quite easily. The gods were with him. Accountability was restored.

"Tell more." Comfortable now.

"She seems to think Business Head is hostage."

"And?"

"She says she will look after him once he is freed." Tang hesitated then rushed on in a gabble, "She said Tiger *Sin-Sang* can live with her, and he can carry water from the stand pipes and mind squatter babies."

The girl, a street urchin with nothing – with *no thing*, nothing except some hutch she'd built from fragments of corrugation and cardboard on some hill where she had *no thing* of her own – was offering to buy the Triad head? Such delusion was more than crazy, it was gigantic in its madness. He beckoned for the wad.

The threat-man riffled the notes to show nothing was concealed. Ah Min watched his face and saw only simple concentration there. He had not done this before. Ah Min signed again. The man put the money on the table.

Perhaps he had been too hasty to think of having the man killed?

"Tell me again what she said."

Ashen, eyes staring with effort, the man began to repeat the story. "We followed. She would not take the limousine. She turned as we neared Statue Square . . ."

Chapter Twenty-Five

Ghost Grandmother was annoyed. KwayFay thought this so unfair. She'd learned everything Ghost commanded. There seemed no plan to Grandmother's bullying, no system. Ghosts ought to be fair, relatives or not.

"Did you learn it?"

"Learn what, Grandmother?"

"Typical! Just typical!" Ghost screeched like ghosts did, as if being strangled, then instantly reverting to a normal querulous voice. "What of this funeral house you buy? When," Grandmother said pointedly in scorn, "Ching Ming festival already gone!"

"I have not been told of a funeral house, Grandmother."

"Buy in Kowloon," Ghost instructed testily. "No Wanchai rubbish. First go to Lion Rock, give green vegetable on noodles and mushrooms for the Old Man's ancestors."

"Which ones, Grandmother?"

"His male ancestors, stupid girl!" Ghost cackled a derisory laugh. "You think to honour his female ancestors, silly child? That would diminish luck for male ancestors! Only Wuhan idiots do that! And make sure the food is hot."

"I have no money for hot food!" KwayFay wailed.

"Do without your own meal," Ghost ordered comfortably. "Then you have money. Now tell me. How will you make sure honoured ancestor has finished eating his fill?"

Miserably, KwayFay gave the right answer; anything to shut Ghost Grandmother up.

"Toss two coins. If one heads, one tails, then honoured ancestor's spirit is still eating. When two heads or two tails, then finished."

"Good. You go today to Lion Rock. His great grandfather was very angry man. That trouble over the Hoklo girl wasn't his fault. She was a bitch, always putting on airs. I shall tell her so, too, the cow, next time I see her."

"You didn't say where at Lion Rock, Grandmother," KwayFay reminded, but Ghost had gone.

She got up at the right time and the thin suited man Tang sat beside her on the bus.

"Little Sister, remember this number." He leant close and muttered. She nodded. "It is instead of paying. You understand?"

"Yes. I buy funeral house today."

He looked at her, frowning. "Who told you?"

"I go to Lion Rock. Then funeral house."

That seemed to throw him. He shook his head. "I know nothing of Lion Rock, or any funeral house."

"Please can I have a lift?"

She paid with the last of her money for noodles in a foil-covered polystyrene bowl, with fresh vegetables and mushrooms, and held them in her lap in the limousine all the way to Lion Rock. It was the best she could do to keep the food warm. She was hungry but didn't dare to contravene Ghost Grandmother's instructions. She felt close to tears, everybody giving her orders, do this, do that, and she not knowing the consequences of any of them.

The instant they were in sight of Lion Rock near Tsz Wan Shan she had the man stop. She alighted, walked into the new country park until it felt right, then sat on a stone and undid the foil. Nobody was in sight. She placed her chopsticks on the bowl's rim, balanced the bowl and waited, making a mental apology to Old Man Tiger Wong's ancestors for the poor meal she had brought.

Knowing it would be rude to invite Old Man's ancestor's spirit to dine, she kept silent. Spirits had rights just like everyone else. It was only fair. The driver man stood some distance off checking the time, but his bosses were no concern of hers. She was doing as she was told.

Ten full minutes she stayed immobile, then apologetically brought out two coins. She begged the spirit's pardon, not to give offence, and spun them. One heads, one tails. She said a polite apology and put them away. It was vulgar to ask too often if a spirit had finished his meal, so she waited a similar period before spinning the coins again. Two heads; the spirit had finished. She said her thanks that Honoured Ancestor had accepted the meal, took her chopsticks and walked back to the path.

The driver was speaking into his cell phone.

"Why Lion Rock, Little Sister?" he asked, phone held out at arm's length.

"It is the right place." She was impatient to be in Kowloon buying the funeral house. She'd had nothing to eat all day. The food she had left on the stone was no longer food, for its goodness had been eaten by ghosts of ancestors. It had to be left there.

The motor was a hundred paces off, but easy walking. The driver followed, muttering into his cell phone. She wished he would stop. He was so annoying.

"Little Sister? Who told you about a funeral house?"

"I'm not telling you." She was so annoyed. All these tasks, no time of her own, starving to death.

He was still growling into his phone when she was sitting in the motor. He clicked it shut and slid into the driver's seat.

"Kowloon, Jordan Road."

He paused before turning the ignition. "Not Wanchai?"

"Hurry, please." She now knew which paper shop was necessary. She would easily find it, and only hoped the proprietors – five workers in the family, not counting eleven women and girl children, the boys naturally at a fee-paying school – would not recognise her as the street-stealer child who once purloined regularly from their premises. "Take quickest route, please."

She knew paper shops. Choosing one now was difficult. None felt right. She'd not been down this street since she'd thieved here.

One she particularly liked. She used to filch fragments of coloured paper, her favourite. Her pattern was well established by the age of ten. She sold the paper to young thugs from North Point, fifty cents for twenty scraps, as long as the edges were not torn.

Alighting at the corner, she stared in dismay. The shop had gone! In its place stood a quick-sell shop crammed with phoney-logo jeans, anoraks, hooded jackets of fake leather and sham alpacas.

She wandered down the road examining the remaining paper shops. Each was typical, but would any suffice? The threat-man Tang had told her a secret no-pay number. It was a command, get the order right. How? What order, exactly? For whom?

Then she saw it, the one from which she'd stolen. It had simply moved round the corner! The last time had been four years ago, when she'd graduated to being a pickpocket at City Hall, the Star Ferry concourses and the Lantern Market. She'd had to pay squeeze for permission to thieve. The Stanley bus – Number Six from Central, to Stanley Village – was the most favoured pickpocket route. For a place on the No. 6 she had to surrender four-fifths of every stolen item. Robbery! She was good on the No. 6.

So relieved, to see her favourite paper shop.

Hesitant in case the proprietor recognised her, she dawdled and peered in at the funeral papers. Responsibility weighed heavily. How many of the Hundred Deities, to which everybody had to sacrifice at New Year, would one offend, if you got funeral rites wrong? She felt close to tears. Tears were happening a lot lately, since this all began.

Resolute, she made herself stand in the doorway. The shop had shrunk to less than a third of its size. It still looked the best. Dazzling colours, not a single deity forgotten, everything a dead ancestor might want in the Hereafter.

As in all paper shops, huge candles of red wax, with golden dragons swarming vigorously up them, hung in bunches from the ceiling on red twine, quite like drying vegetables. These were always necessary for funeral rites. Incense sticks were also customary. She did not favour the stout fragrant incenses, for they burned with great slowness and she wanted incense to burn properly, or it would waste money. (She had never actually bought incense, only stolen it; the fat three-inch-diameter incense sticks were too difficult to steal, being impossible for a little girl to conceal while running away; the thin ones were a disgraceful insult to ancestors, who might take terrible ghostly retribution; the intermediate size, quarter of an inch in diameter, were best.)

Pigeon-holes along the shop wall held Hell banknotes printed, with cavalier disregard of solemnity, in the jauntiest shade of lucky red. They were all in fantastically high denominations, bundles of them.

"Yes, Little Sister?"

A middle-aged man appeared, making her jump, smoking his crumpled fag and wiping his hands as he came from the back room. He did not scream for the police. She remained aloof, as if she had a family and had come to buy goods for ancestors in the Afterlife.

"I want to place an order."

"Certainly. For . . .?"

"Make me a funeral house."

"A death! I am sorry, Little Sister." The man's expression did not change. Sympathy was transient. You couldn't sell sympathy. His interest in the value of her order for his wares, however, was immediate, permanent and total. "How much?"

"Money." She reflected, wavered. The command had not said.

"What limit for your honoured relative?"

"None," she said, calling to mind Ghost Grandmother's abjurations. Ghosts had to be treated with respect, or they might punish the living severely. They would brook no excuse if they were short-changed. Nothing cheap.

"No limit."

The man leant back to eye her, incredulous. For an instant his brow cleared – was it recognition, the street urchin racing from his back door with paper streamers flying from her hand as she scampered into the warren east of Nathan Road? Then his natural shopkeeper's instincts took hold, and they were off, for this was money.

"No limit," KwayFay repeated. "I want fast order. Concubines – eight – in paper house, with gardens, trees, eight Rolls Royces and a Bentley, all gold. Three storeys, eight bedrooms, gold bathrooms on every floor."

"Garden!" He was impressed. "Yes, Little Sister! How soon?"

"Make from new," she commanded, now in the swing. "Fastest. All clothes, many greys and blues, no green dresses for concubines."

"Naturally, Little Sister. Green colour for foolish, right?"

"Shoes, *cheong saams*, suits, kitchen and dining rooms with feasting everywhere. Bed clothes, linen, very best beds, every possible thing. And many Hell Bank notes and ingots."

"The payment . . ." He was respectful. A money-money order.

"This number." She dictated the sequence she'd memorised and saw him literally tremble as he repeated the numbers.

"You sure, Little Sister?"

"Telephone any Hong Kong number at eight o'clock tonight to check." That was the instruction. Finished with.

"No need!" he chirruped anxiously. "That no-limit number! How soon, Little Sister?"

"Soon. Tonight, at darkness."

He said anxiously, "Real tonight?"

"Nine o'clock exactly. Not sooner, not later."

"Can!" he cried, understanding immediately: this Little Sister's ancestors were partial to nine o'clock. Nine it had to be.

"You want me to sign?"

"No need! No-limit number!"

She left, her task done. She prayed she'd ordered exactly what the threat-men wanted. If it was wrong, she would have no excuse; she had to have guessed right.

That night she worked late. The office closed, except for Charmian, the foki cleaner who slept, KwayFay thought, somewhere in the building by arrangement with the night security men who were bossed by two Sikhs with shotguns, the usual guardians in Hong Kong.

At eight o'clock she shut her console down, took up her laptop and left. She caught the Star Ferry to Kowloon and walked to Jordan Road. The paper shops were busy, clusters of people looking in at the wares. Outside the shop, standing in the gutter, was a structure made entirely of iron, with holes for carrying poles. It was almost exactly the size and shape of an ancient sedan chair, in which *fokis* used to carry ladies up Hong Kong Peak in the olden days before the Peak Tram came. This iron sedan was a Government edict. In it, KwayFay's funeral paper house would burn safely, and not cause a wholesale spreading conflagration, as so often funeral ceremonies had in the past.

She went to stand on the pavement and saw her paper house being carried out exactly ten minutes before nine. It took four men. Amahs would have been as careful, but women were cheaper than men, and Immortals, not to mention ancestors who were to receive this expensive sacrifice, would be offended if they suspected she had ordered on the cheap.

"*Waaaiiii!*" went the crowd, clustering closer, impressed by the lavish paper house. KwayFay was pushed back. Not tall, she had difficulty seeing the lovely structure close.

It was somewhat taller than a doll's house and entirely made of coloured paper. Lit from within by cool amber light; she couldn't see how but that didn't matter. All its doors were ajar, elegant rooms inside the tall storeys. Every room was complete with paper furniture of Chinese Imperial design. She managed to eel her way closer, and was particularly pleased with the miniature bedrooms. In the master bedroom, a grand paper bed was already made with pillows, the bedclothes turned back. On the bed lay paper dressing gowns, with white Cloud-Striding Shoes and slippers by the foot of the bed. Everything paper, so tiny and intricate she inhaled with pleasure.

Along the path of the paper garden, eight miniature paper concubines wandered in elegant court dress. Eight superb small Rolls Royces and a grand stately paper Bentley glowed in gold paper, ready for Honoured Ancestor to drive about the skies. Trees, ornamental shrubs of exquisite design were distributed about the lovely walks and ponds. The garden walls were even more ornate than those of the China Centre on Hong Kong Island.

Downstairs, paper tables were laid for sumptuous feasting, paper food and cutlery, with paper carpets of superb design, and armchairs awaited ghost guests. Upstairs in other rooms, wardrobes stood open revealing suits of western and traditional Chinese cut. The paper curtains, looking as if made of pure velvet and silk, were drawn back to display the artistry. Pictures and paper mirrors adorned the walls, and paper windows were cunningly coloured to show vistas of natural splendour and cloud-forming heavenly countryside of moving beauty.

Tears really did flow now. The shop man emerged, still in his grubby tee-shirt, floppy pants and plastic sandals, a crumpled cigarette drooping from his wrinkled mouth. He sidled up.

"Good-not-good, *a*?"

She said, "The Hell Money. I want to see it."

He shouted, and his men came at a trot carrying bundles of the Hell Money she'd see in the pigeon-holes earlier. She examined each denomination, the gathering crowd withdrawing respectfully, giving her space, wanting to see if the girl approved.

No denomination was less than 500,000. Some bundles consisted of denominations of one to eight millions. The ancestor would know the currency, which required no specification, for what if Hell Money were specified in some international currency – dollars, pounds, yen – that suddenly fell just as the Hell Money burned and flew to Heaven? The shame would haunt a family for ever, and insult spirits.

The important thing was for the denominations to be impossibly high. Most were labelled HELL BANK NOTE, complete with serial numbers. Eight bundles, each of eight blocks. Gold and silver ingots shone on paper trays. The paper-shop man had included paper money-printing blocks simulated in paper, in case Honoured Ancestor wanted to print yet more Hell Money up in the skies.

Everything was paper, from the walls of the house to the concubines, cars, trees, windows, beds, money, ingots. It was as exquisite as anything she'd ever seen. She had been coming to steal from these shops for as long as she could remember, but had seen nothing to equal this feat of artistry.

"Good-not-good, *a*?" the man asked anxiously.

"Replace the silver ingots with gold."

People murmured, nodding and talking of funeral houses they had known. He shouted, and the ingots were swapped for new gold-paper ingots.

"Good-not-good, *a*?" He was beside himself. The cluster of pedestrians waited for her reply, speculating loudly.

"Good," she said finally, into a chorus of exclamations from those watching. A tourist lady across the road smilingly took out her camera, only to be foiled by two young men in suits who approached her. They took the camera from her, producing some badge or other.

"You light it for Honoured Ancestor, Little Sister?"

KwayFay pondered a moment. "No," she said. "Honoured person light it," and edged her way through the crowd.

At the corner of the road, where it turned between Canton Road and Battery Street, she paused an instant, sensing the beautiful sacrifice-house's moment had come.

In the gloaming she saw a stooping, old man emerge from the paper shop and stand before the iron chair. She saw a match flare, gilding his features for a moment. He touched the match to the paper house and stepped back. The whole lovely building with its furnishings, paper clothes, paper gardens, ponds, concubines, Hell Money and all, went up with a whoosh of flame.

Old Man stood silhouetted between two threat-men, one of them swinging the tourist woman's camera from his wrist. The paper, fragments still burning, swirled up into the night sky. The house was gone in seconds. She walked away, without tears.

Chapter Twenty-Six

"This is beyond description, Witherspoon."

The Deputy Governor of Hong Kong was more civil servant than political appointee. He saw the two terms as synonymous. The Governor, a lifelong politician, was a cynic who fancied his chances at Cantonese. Consequently he was taken for a ride by every hawker who paused, grinning like an ape, to applaud the silvery haired git as he strolled, sweat-stained and scrawny from dehydration, through the street markets in his crumpled suit. A failed political nerk for Governor of practically the last Crown Colony. Ugh!

He could not say such things to his Head of Protocol, who had headaches enough and wouldn't thank him for criticisms, implied or overtly stated, until the Handover was done with. Witherspoon had more mistresses than the parson preached about, but most of the people in Government here had the tact, and others the subservience, to ignore the obvious. Hong Kong's way.

"I know, sir. It does seem unlikely."

The Deputy Governor cut through the crap.

"Have we proof?"

Witherspoon sighed heavily, shaking his head, his mannerism to show acceptance of the impossible. He wasn't chewing gum today, *Deo gratias*.

"More than enough. The fucking idiots in Whitehall have turned something up. You knew the moron in Great Smith Street, I think?"

"Don't tell me it's Frobisher."

"You were with him in that Rhodesia business, with some cret from Immigrants and Demographics. The passport scam that time?"

"Don't remind me."

The Deputy Governor stood at the window of the building next to The Four Seasons restaurant near the bottom terminus of the Peak Tram. It was all terribly secret, supposedly belonging to the next-door American Embassy, whose windows were never opened. Of course it didn't, as everybody knew and pretended otherwise. It was still Crown property, thank God, and would be until the People's Republic came shuffling in with their red stars and russet drabs, new shams for old. Empire was all a parade of shams. Wait until Hong Kong was an autonomous region of China; then you'd see fur fly.

"Is he here, the claimant?"

"Downstairs with the Legal Service jokers, sir."

The Deputy Governor would have sighed, had he been that demonstrative. The weather in Hong Kong seemed somehow to pervade indoor sanctuaries, even working its evil humidity through walls. God knows how they managed in ancient China. That's a point, he thought.

"How did his documents survive this long? The relative humidity, I mean." He explained when the other looked blank, "Think, Witherspoon. Where the west-bound trams do that shifty dog-leg. The street market there, right?"

"Left, sir."

"I know it's left. Right would run the fucking trams into the harbour before they got anywhere near Western Market. There. The book stalls."

"Sir?"

"Have you ever seen any old books, calligraphics or not and however valuable, that wasn't rotted to hell by the humidity, and covered in mould?"

"Come to think of it . . ."

"Neither have I." The Deputy Governor added with feeling, "My fucking amah puts my shoes out into the sun to crack them. Does it deliberately, the cow. Saves them from going mouldy, sure, but she sells them once they're cracked. I found my best fucking patent leathers in the Snake Market at Shau Kei Wan. Bitch."

"The documents should have rotted, sir."

Master of the bleeding obvious, the Deputy Governor thought. The standard of civil servants had gone downhill ever since the new lot got in by a landslide, general elections back. Grumpy at the depressing news of the old Cantonese man's find about Kellett Island, he stared out at Cotton Tree Drive.

"I wish they'd built these Government Offices higher up. What's wrong with Magazine Gap Road?" It was all irrelevant now, so near the Handover, clock ticking, the end of the China Lease from Nanking *et seq.*

"Possibly too high up in the old days, sir."

"I didn't mean it literally, Witherspoon, for Christ's sake."

"Sorry, sir."

"Let Gresham handle it. He can talk to the old man."

"Any instructions, sir?"

"Yes. Tell him to bat out time if he can."

"Or what, sir?"

"Or we're in the clag even more than we imagine, Witherspoon."

Gresham welcomed the old gentleman between two legal eagles from the Supreme Court. That only meant the young lawyers had retainers keeping a locker somewhere on the premises so the addresses would sound right to strangers. Hong Kong was not deceived. Gresham, though, was a career diplomat with useful connections Home and Oversea, meaning watch your gossip when he was around.

He was an able man for all that and looked the part. His assistants Jane Kelvedon and William Barr worked with him and had done well so far. Only trivial matters, but law was law and principles remained inflexible whatever the worth of the issue. Jane, the brighter of the two, lived with a younger sister who "taught the flute to sailors", as the *South China Morning Post* once blithely reported, ha-ha, so unless she stopped all that would have to go. Money didn't matter much; law did. These two knew this. It held the key to defining criteria for what decisions remained.

"Mr Min," Gresham said, smiling, shaking the beaming man's hand. "And Mr Wong! So good to see you!"

"Kind of you to receive us at such short notice, Sir Robert."

Trust Hong Kong, Gresham thought with pleasure. Other nations could never get the hang of titles, but even Hong Kong beggars and hawkers got them right every time. He'd been called

Sir Gresham, Lord Gresh, anything in the Middle East, bloody Yanks the worst and most uncomprehending of the lot. Good old Hong Kong. He began the joust immediately.

"We have perused the documents, Mr Min. There are a few points that puzzle us."

Ah Min spread his palms. "And we too!"

His beam was inflexible. Gresham guessed it stood for astonishment and dismay as well as a how-de-do. He would have to work it out, light on his toes with this man. Was he too a lawyer? Gresham glanced at Jane who smiled, getting the query and nodding yes, she'd looked him up. He guessed the man had a degree in law from Peking. He'd have heard if it was Sun Yat Sen University in Canton.

"What points puzzle you, Mr Min?"

The old man who called himself Wong did not smile. Features with the skin of an ochre-coloured prune, he simply listened. Could he speak English well? At all? Gresham had had no warning. He glanced at William who shook his head. No data on this man. Oh dear, Gresham thought, it was one of those, was it; no information, so the man could be anyone and up to anything. Was he at least registered in Hong Kong as a citizen, with a Hong Kong identity card under any name at all?

William shook his head. Was that a no, or a dunno? William irritated Gresham. William Barr supported Liberal Democrats back home. Liberal Democrats were wet wallpaper trying to be Rembrandts, and their leader, that sandy git from Fife, was an itch hoping for a scratch. British politics were the pits.

"How could the documents have remained in storage so long without decay, Sir Robert?" Mr Min said, beaming still.

"The same thought occurred to us. To me," Gresham amended immediately. Careless.

Mr Min took up the litany. "One only has to see books and calligraphics on the street markets – where the trams turn, what, left is it? Before they reach Western Market, I mean – to see how Hong Kong's vile humidity treats documents stored without air-conditioning!"

"Indeed," Gresham said, feeling slightly sickened. "What else puzzles you, Mr Min?"

"The significance of Kellett Island, Sir Robert."

"Significance," Gresham stated, leaning back in his chair and wishing the office were better appointed.

You could be too spartan in colonial circumstances, but that was the effect of this Governor. Ridiculous of the man to clean his family's own shoes of an evening, stupid bastard. Didn't he know he was letting the side down? As bad as washing your own car. A dreadful appointment, quite dreadful. What on earth the Prime Minster thought he was up to putting the silly sod into this slot, God alone knew. Okay, losing his seat at the general election in sacrifice to the Conservative Party was one thing, but the common sense and practicalities ruling this last-remaining colony imposed dictates of their own. This Governor would blubber like a tart at the Handover ceremony, he guessed. Government staff were already taking odds of 3-1 that he'd do exactly that. "I too wondered about significance," he said, ball in their court.

"The size of it, for one thing," he went on when neither spoke. "The fact that the Royal Hong Kong Yacht Club has owned it for so long. And the proximity of the Admiralty, the Police Officers' Club, the Typhoon Shelter at Causeway Bay . . ."

Mr Min's beam was inflexible, like a neon lamp irritatingly left burning during a fuel shortage. Maddening but unavoidable.

The old man said nothing sitting there in his *cheong saam*, the material draped across his knees and his leather shoes black and dulled. Gresham wondered what he wore underneath. Quite like a priest's cassock.

"The Harbour Tunnel from underneath Salisbury Road in Kowloon," Gresham said, thinking, cut to the fucking chase, man, for Christ's sake, or we'll be here all day.

"Ah, yes. That too. It seems the area to be considered is far larger than the present extent of Kellett Island would suggest, Sir Robert."

"Does it, Mr Min?"

"I am as uncertain as your good self, Sir Robert. The implications are difficult to define."

"But if they were precisely delineated, Mr Min, I should hope for an effective compromise, or at least the start of negotiations."

"That too seems possible, Sir Robert. Or would be, in different circumstances."

Here we go, Gresham thought miserably. We've already lost and the swine is still playing catchee-mousee. He was heartily sick of this job. His brother was retired in Stourbridge learning watercolour painting Tuesdays and Thursdays, had a fine handsome woman on the sly for afters. Guess who'd live longer.

"Different circumstances, Mr Min?" he put in, more to complete the taped recording than any hope of deflecting this beaming bastard's next move.

The palms spread again. "The Lease expires soon, when Hong Kong will return to the sovereignty of the People's Republic of China. So little time left! Negotiations often proceed at snail's pace, far too slow for the issue to be resolved in session after session."

"Do you have a suggestion, Mr Min?"

The old man's silence was getting on Gresham's nerves. Very soon he would commit the unforgivable and speak to him outright. The thought made him almost redden with embarrassment, but mercifully he'd eliminated that silly tendency in his first month as a diplomat. Twenty years on, it was a non-starter.

"I was hoping that perhaps you, Sir Robert, might make some proposal leading to a solution, of a kind. Without wanting to prejudice your case, of course."

The two smiled benignly at each other, the issue settled. Gresham tried to match the visitor's radiant beam but couldn't come anywhere near. They rose together and shook hands.

The visitors left immediately and without another word.

***

An hour later, Gresham was ushered in to see the Deputy Governor. He flung his file down on the mahogany desk and dropped into the leather armchair.

"Well?" the Deputy Governor growled.

"The transcording's in your outer office being put to type, sir.

The buggers won't move. They know the implications. If we don't deal immediately, they'll let the cat out of the bag. China's probably already got wind of it. The consequences. . ."

"I know the consequences, Bob. Don't give me consequences. What will they settle for?"

"Par value, plus rental from somewhere near 1844, give or take. They'd be mad to take less. They probably know what Great Smith Street's found."

"Hmph." The Deputy Governor stared at his desk. "Better get down to nuts and bolts, then. Make a show, cut them in on the costs as a rental allocation. You know how to make do. The usual American dollar accounts elsewhere. Is it knighthood time?"

"No, sir. That would be a stigma, seeing who's going to come marching down Waterloo Road."

"Right, right."

They went to tea to discuss the least they could get away with.

Chapter Twenty-Seven

She tried reading the financial news from Japan and the United States, but politics got everywhere. Instead, she spent her break at the Peak Tram Terminus, Western tourists and sight-seers from mainland China thronging the sloping queue. She looked enviously on. One day, she would ride it to the Peak, and there have a wondrous supper among flowers and music in the cool. She had seen an advert for the restaurant there, while waiting for yet another re-run of *The Great Waltz* in the original 1938 scratchy-voice version Hong Kong could never get enough of.

The heat enveloped her. She listened to a chanting crocodile of Glenealy School children coming from some celebration at St John's Cathedral opposite. It melted her heart to hear the little ones singing. How she'd wanted to be one of them! She felt like weeping for no reason. She leant back against the pedestrian rails. She was sitting on the top step of the concrete flight leading down to the gardens. Here, brides and their grooms came to be photographed in their finery. Their favourite places were the Tea Museum and the doorway of St John's Cathedral. Sometimes a cascade of several brides, all in bridal gowns and folderols, were visible above the carp pools in the steep vegetation, a lovely sight. She dozed, and in spite of only having half-an-hour that nagging voice screeched in her ear.

"What choosing?" Grandmother sounded fretful, but when wasn't she? KwayFay was in no mood to listen. She wished, not for the first time, that she could dream like English folk, and wake up knowing it was nothing to be concerned about. Instead, Chinese knew that dreams were fact, ignore them at your peril. No wonder English people were so calm. Americans were calm because they were all millionaires, the English because they ignored dreams.

"Calm?" Ghost screamed with laughter. "They are so busy being Hero-Country folk – *Ying-wok* people – they have no time left for real dreaming. It isn't sensible, silly granddaughter!"

"No, Grandmother," KwayFay whimpered.

"Tell now: what choosing?"

"I don't know yet, Grandmother. I thought I had already done it at Lamma Island. Remember? I told you."

"Easy!" Grandmother said with derision. Then, full of tricks, said casually, "Did you learn the Festival of the Hungry Ghosts, in full?"

"Yes, Grandmother."

"Oh." Ghost was disappointed! "And Hakka funeral ceremony?"

"Yes, Grandmother." KwayFay said it with pride, wishing she could have spoken the English command for dismissal; she had heard it once. A visiting London dealer had said, "Put that in your pipe and smoke it, Jim!" A brilliant remark, full of power. She had wanted to say it to somebody ever since.

"In full?" More dejection! KwayFay was even more pleased.

"In full, Grandmother." The time she had spent in the Hong Kong Library at City Hall excavating the myriad details! She had been exhausted for two days afterwards. That was ghosts for you.

"This choosing. Tell."

"I think it is choosing girls for something."

Grandmother shrieked a laugh.

"Then you must pretend it is Moon Festival. Go to Amah Rock tonight."

KwayFay wailed, "I shall be frightened, up there alone, Grandmother!"

Two passersby saw the dozing girl twitching and tutted, guessing she was yet another young person drugged in broad daylight.

A car honked and KwayFay woke, startled to find herself near Cotton Tree Drive, looking across at the Peak Tram Terminus. She saw the time, and got up and ran to work.

Soon after five – the day hell, with Business Head ranting and, Alice said, "going into one" – KwayFay caught a taxi. It was only a phrase she had picked up from her disastrous brother, meaning a fit of weeping or berserk distress. KwayFay never believed Alice's tales; her friend was death on Futures and With-holds. Alice's help was always trouble.

On the way, she glimpsed a horrendous accident. A heavy

Mercedes Benz motor crushed a small child against the wall of a narrow street. The contour roads above Central District were notoriously meandering, the edges being simply stone walls in some places. The child had been standing on a skate-board, and was rubbed, simply rubbed slowly against the stones by the huge car. His arm hung in a mess of blood from his shoulder. The driver of the splendid motor got out and harangued the mother, then angrily drove away. He made no attempt to give money, or telephone for help.

"Did you see that?" KwayFay exclaimed to the taxi driver. "We should stop and help!"

"He is a Business Head, and a diplomat."

"The man is Chinese!"

"So?" The taxi driver shrugged, and would not stop, simply drove on along Bowen Road. "He can't be touched. Diplomats can do anything." He lit a cigarette one-handed. "You think they pay parking fines? Or debts? Or get themselves arrested when they batter prostitutes in Causeway Bay and Nathan Road?"

"Yes!" she cried, because she did. Police arrested people. They'd arrested her when a child for stealing three plums from a hawker's barrow.

"You're wrong. He will already have forgotten it happened."

Dismayed, she heard out the taxi driver's litany of complaints against wanton diplomats, and alighted in a mood of dejection. She tried to put the incident out of her mind, but it kept recurring. She wondered if Old Man's captors had the power to punish the man in the big motor, who had shown more concern for his car's radiator than the unconscious child.

The hillside was steeper than she remembered. She was tempted to stay with the taxi and return to Central, but she had come too far. And what would she tell Grandmother?

The taxi meant more expense and less food. She started the climb towards Wang Nai Chung Gap, site of the Amah Rock. Once before, she had come with some other street children, for one of them had been ill with blood-spitting disease and they went to ask Amah Rock to make her well, but their little accomplice had sunk into torpor and was taken away. Her name was Ah

Geen. She too had been eight, the age KwayFay guessed for herself. One day, she might try to find out if the Rutonjee Sanatorium had given spindly little Ah Geen charity medicine and made her better. She might have got to America and married one of the Warner Brothers! It did happen, in movies.

The climb was two-and-a-half miles, but she was too frightened of the consequences to turn back. The taxi man had wanted paying off, and she'd not had enough money to tell him to wait, so she was on her own. She had the necessary provinder, to pretend Ghost's silliness about the Moon Festival, so far away in the year it was ludicrous to be doing this. She took off her valuable shoes and walked in her bare feet.

The path ran from the back of what was once the Military Hospital but was now Island School, with bits let off to charities and other daftnesses, and ascended the central peak of Hong Kong. She struck over a small bridge across the deep ravine, unnerved at being so far from anyone. You were never farther than, say, three paces from a hundred folk. Now, here she was climbing away from civilisation among the lantana bushes she loved – always there, always trying to flower with their yellows, orange, pinks, reds, and their green leaves. So loyal, she felt they sometimes might deserve a god of their own. She halted for breath, worrying that the lantana bushes might actually have such a thing, and mentally apologised in case some god was already frowning at her impertinence.

The water below formed a lovely waterfall. She gazed, not going on until she felt it had been shown the right degree of respect, for she had heard its sound was full of music. She tried listening, but no music came, only the delicious sound of splashing clean water. Maybe that was the music? She smiled at the fantastic idea and walked on.

Eventually the track narrowed, becoming nothing more than a slender path, ever steeper, until she could only progress by clutching the overhanging foliage. Disturbed clouds of butterflies rose, mostly little yellowish creatures. Why was none of them down in Pedder Street or Sai Ying Pun, where free colour was needed? The ground became slippery and craggy as if the powdered laterite was trying to revert to the hard stone outcrops from which it originated. She was breathing hard by the time she came to a huge stony crag, surmounted by a hunched stone figure. It looked quite like one of those English guardsmen the London poster showed in Kai Tak Airport, but as she approached it she could tell it was a woman, a baby on her back.

This was Amah Rock.

She climbed the steps and sank with relief onto the stone seat. It was worn by former visitors, traditionally young lovers swearing fidelity in betrothal. The rock, so like a young fisherwoman carrying her babe slung in a binding cloth, was famed throughout the Colony.

Its story was that the woman's husband, a fisherman centuries before the English came with their Raj, had been lost at sea. As days passed, fearing for his safety, she climbed this sacred place to keep watch for his vessel. It did not come. Fiercely loyal, she remained there, kept by her devotion until she turned to stone. The Immortals pitied her, for they knew he had been lost in a *Dai-Fung* on the ocean. They lifted her soul and that of her baby into the heavens, where she was reunited with her drowned husband, to live among the Immortals for ever. KwayFay's eyes filled with tears as she gazed at the stone, imagining how the fisherwife's soul had been encouraged from her dead form, and how the baby's soul too had been teased carefully out of the granite by the Immortals to fly into the stars to eternal joy. No wonder Amah Rock was the place for the Wedding Walk, the stroll of Hong Kong's betrothed.

She sat in the shelter of the rock slanting above her stone seat. Three cracked earthenware bowls held the stumps of many burned incense sticks and scraps of Spirit Flags – paper bearing pious characters wishing for fidelity and progeny in generations to come.

From the gathering dusk she guessed it was eight o'clock. She decided to make her preparations first, then rest until it was time to do her ritual, which would give her the answer to the Triad people. For a moment she wondered why she never had any doubt this would happen just as Grandmother said, but she quickly put the thought from her. There could be no doubt. Doubt was for people, certainty for ghosts.

Perhaps this was tonight's lesson, the realisation that people had lost the art of sorrow, in their rush to gratification? Living was an art, as Grandmother seemed to understand. All the folk KwayFay knew craved instant satisfaction. Tired, she began to prepare for the Harvest Moon.

Properly, the moon was at its brightest on the fifteenth night of the Eighth month, the fabled dazzling apogee. This was the time for celebration of harvest, village, the tribe, safety, existence, life, celebrated only in China as it should be, for all other peoples were barbarians and would not know such things.

She had bought several *heung*, incense sticks, and placed them upright ready to light. A polystyrene cup of jasmine tea, which Heng O, the Lady in the Moon, would naturally love, was beside her.

"How foolish the English are!" Grandmother squeaked loudly in her ear, making her jump in fright. "They see the face of a man in the moon! Can you imagine?"

"No, Grandmother."

"It is clearly a toad, and always has been. At least, ever since that Heng O stole her husband's potion for prolonging life, and got herself chased from Earth – though you can't really blame her – so she had to dodge into the Moon and now hides there. I never knew her." Grandmother sniffed in disapproval. "Did you bring the water caltrops? And make sure they are correctly bat-shaped?"

"Yes, Grandmother." Did Grandmother think she was stupid, not to check water chestnuts? Each one had to retain its horns so that, bat-like, they would bring good fortune.

"I heard you think that, rude girl!"

"I try to remind Ah Poh how careful I was, doing as you told me at the last Moon Festival!" KwayFay almost started to cry, but put a stop to that. She would not be cowed, not in this. Her survival might depend on it.

"So I did!" Ghost cooed. "I taught you how to choose vegetables! Good, good. Did you bring something red and something green, lazy girl?"

KwayFay swallowed her pride and said she had. Two scraps of expensive silk, one of each colour. She had had to steal them from the silk merchant shops in Wanchai, no big deal.

"And a lantern?"

"Only an oil lamp, Grandmother. I had no more money. It is open clay, with a little oil in a shoe-polish tin, and string for a wick."

"It's not much, is it? Not a decent lantern."

"I sorry, Grandmother."

"Did you bring a moon cake?"

"Yes, Grandmother."

She had begged Alice for one, who had three left over in her fridge at home. They kept, at least that was in their favour. She had brought it wrapped in a tissue. It felt heavy, as all Moon Cakes did, and was probably stiff with almond nuts and mashed millet seed, pork and fat, and sugar to make it absurdly sweet.

"Did you learn a poem of Li Tai-Po?"

"No, Grandmother!" KwayFay wailed. "You didn't tell me to."

"He composed poems to the moon, always the moon. You know he loved Heng O so much that he drowned trying to embrace her reflection?"

"You told me, Grandmother."

"If you didn't learn his poem, then you can only wait. People pass here at midnight. They tell answer."

"What if nobody comes?" Then she would be left here until morning, and have to go to work worn out.

"Distrustful granddaughter!" Grandmother shrieked, and gave her what for, abusing her laziness, shiftlessness, ingratitude, when she should be grateful to a caring ancestor whose talents were renowned throughout . . . throughout . . .

KwayFay slept.

She woke, and saw from the harbour glow in the night sky and the positions of the stars it was almost midnight. She thought a thank-you to Ghost for rousing her, and lit her incense sticks. She made sure the cup of jasmine tea, now stone cold, was in position, and laid the unwrapped moon cake beside it. She had no paper crown to wear, as was proper, which was just bad luck. The two coloured silks she put beside her on the stone seat. She was stiff, wondering how much colder it would get. If it really had been the Fifteenth of the Eighth Moon, it would have been hot and sticky with Hong Kong's enduring humidity. Now, she shivered in the cold and stayed quiet.

She must have dozed, for the stars had moved on when she heard voices. She thought in panic, voices? Miles from anywhere on the high mountain?

They were speaking English, and wore heavy boots. One was whistling, another calling for silence. A flashlight washed pallor across the stones and foliage on the steep hill. Soldiers came by, two of them Ghurkas. They were from the garrison, and each held a flashlight. The leading man carried a map. He stopped.

"Miss?" he said uncertainly. "Are you all right?"

"Yes, thank you," she said back in English.

"What are you doing here?"

There was nothing for it. "I am praying."

The soldier behind him muttered something. They were all only young, just twenty perhaps. They carried many pouches.

"Yes, okay," the leader said irritably in reply to his next soldier. "Do you want some water?" He saw her hesitation and said, "It's a gift, love. Tide you over."

"Thank you for your kindness." She accepted the plastic bottle, saying "*Doh jeh*," in thanks for something given.

"*Mh sai*," the soldier said in quite the wrong tones, but trying. They went on their way, pleased.

As they left, she distinctly heard one of them say to a Ghurka behind him, "Third, then, Subardar Sahib."

The Ghurka laughed and said something she could not catch. They went on in single file, chuckling and making remarks about returning to the meeting point.

Third! He definitely said third. Third what? It hardly mattered. Third of whatever she was told to choose from, was the answer.

"Thank you, Grandmother," she told the night sky, now pale about Amah Rock. She asked the spirit if it had finished with the

Moon Cake, picked it up, had a drink from the soldier's bottled water, and went carefully downhill, eating the cake as she went. This was ever Hong Kong's method: simple, but exhausting.

Chapter Twenty-Eight

"Why Bonham Strand?" KwayFay asked the driver.

He was Tang, the same driver who always wanted to smoke but was afraid to, in case he gave offence.

"It is here, Little Sister."

"It is near many hospitals."

"It is here." The same calm inflexibility. He was male, and would never be called, as any girl sooner or later heard herself called, maggot-in-the-rice, a problem, taking up valuable assets that should rightly be spent on males. She envied him so.

The Tung Wah Hospital was one level up, with the Prince Philip Dental Hospital, the Tsan Yuk Hospital, the Sai Ying Pun Hospital . . . She shivered. Hospitals were bad luck, yet so many were given felicitous names as if they were not. Why, except for disguise?

She alighted when the man opened the door. The driver muttered to a man on the pavement in a voice of fear. KwayFay was astounded. The fear was hers, *ne*?

The new man was young, bit his nails to the quick and wore gold bracelets, gold rings, a gold watch the size of a clock and smiled with gold teeth. His hair was slicked down. His suit shone, lumpy with felling stitches testifying to its expense. His shoes were handmade.

"It is in here, Little Sister. Please follow."

The driver was ignored, his mutterings unanswered.

Inside, a meagre hallway smelling of decaying food was littered with plastic bags and unswept debris including shards of glass crunching underfoot. One shard pricked through her shoes and hurt her foot so she cried out, then apologised profusely as the suited youth turned quickly, drawing a bulging black lump so swiftly from his sleeve she did not even see his arm move. It vanished when he saw there was no visible threat.

"I am sorry. Broken glass hurt my foot."

He paled, licked his lips. They entered a lift, the gate clashing to. It rode to the third floor and she was ushered onto a landing. There was one door. Two others had been blocked off with planks screwed against the door jambs. The place was filthy. A stink of stale urine hung in the air. Dead flies dotted the one opaque glass window. The landing was lit by a single bulb. She was shown into a bare room.

"Please, Little Sister."

A screen made of carved redwood was erected at the far end. She could scent its aroma, not bad. Three windows were blocked, two light bulbs giving poor light. The man led her round the reverse of the screen and invited her to sit on a stool beside a ricketty card-table on which lay a slender file.

"This is your place, Little Sister. There is water and a note pad."

"Write what?"

He looked flustered, as when she had exclaimed about the broken glass.

"I do not know. I was told."

The man paused as if for instructions, then left. She waited in silence, wondering what to do. She afraid to open the file. It was a beige colour, as you got from near Central Market for Middle School. Should she open it? But what if she was not allowed? She knew the Hongs could knife people in the street with impunity – she had seen it. She sipped water. The heat was unbearable.

Quarter of an hour she sat there, in quiet only broken by the dull roar of traffic, the distant shouts of vendors and the clashing of lift doors. She felt tired and drowsy, wanting to keep awake.

Tony spoke of a singing act he used to do with his brother. Alice said she was hoping to win a calligraphy competition, but that art was impossible for females as everybody knew. Calligraphy was for males, since calligraphers had been men since the dawn of time. Benny Weng, who had joined as a computer expert three weeks before, said he was going to set up some website scheme Americans were sure to go mad for, and had gone about the office asking people for investors. He claimed he had a friend in Manhattan who knew the Rockefellers.

"Good evening."

She jolted from slumber, almost crying out in alarm. She glimpsed a figure through the minute fenestrations in the carved wood. Somebody must have come in as she dozed. It was a girl's voice. She noticed the girl remained standing a few paces away. KwayFay leant forward and put her eye closer to the screen.

Beautiful, alert, young, exquisitely dressed in a costly outfit. She was at ease, confident in her beauty and knowing her allure could only serve to please. She was one of the girls at Lamma Island.

The girl could see nothing of KwayFay. The screen, KwayFay knew instinctively, was old, cunningly made perhaps for this purpose. Was this girl the first of the ones she must choose among?

Perhaps the file held details of the girl's name, her origin, her talents.

"Yes?" she said tamely, ashamed that no question came to mind.

"Thank you," the girl began easily. "I am Cantonese, born in Jahore Baru. I am seventeen, and know eight languages. I excel in investment economics, history, art, am capable in computer science, clothing design in western and oriental traditions. I am able in several sports, and have directed five student films, three of which won international awards." The girl smiled a lovely smile, waited a moment before giving herself a nod to carry on. "I am learning Hindi and Arabic – though the pronunciation of the Maghreb dialects I find unpleasing."

"Yes?" KwayFay said in the next pause. What was the girl telling her all this for?

"My family has no connections that would make difficulties to the Triad master. I understand the implications of being promoted Jade Woman, and would serve with all my skill and endeavour. I am virgin, and harbour no problematic religious or political convictions. My family support this move, if the Triad masters would give me the honour of this advancement."

"Go now, please."

"Thank you for your kindness," the girl said, brightening the room with a smile, turned on her heel and walked to the door. She left, closing the door gently.

KwayFay pondered. Jade Women? She had seen one once, in the Yau Ma Tei street market. She had been twelve, stealing from a street barrow belonging to a hawker called Chun, who used to thrash her if he caught her. The wretched man whipped her with a knotted rope if he caught her or any of the street urchins stealing rotted fruit long since thrown away. Chun was not kind.

The day KwayFay saw the Jade Woman, she was hiding between two barrows. She became aware of cries of adulation. She had looked up thinking perhaps the Governor himself was passing, only to see the most beautiful of women. The lady was in silks, not young, and went among the stalls as if royalty. Vendors pressed wares on the lady. She sailed through with serenity, but did not stop. Henchmen went ahead to clear a way through the crowd. KwayFay wanted so much to be her, pausing whenever she wanted, looking at anything while Triad men guarded her progress like some warrior maiden, maybe even the exalted White-Haired Girl of legend who was universally adored and saved all who loved her. She cried herself to sleep that night under the shrine in the bus station in Kennedy Town, where the leper hospital used to be.

"Good evening," a new voice said in the room beyond the screen. "I am instructed to enter and explain myself. I thank you for your kindness in honouring me with this interview."

KwayFay said nothing. Another girl.

"If I may begin?" The girl politely allowed a moment then started with assurance, "I am the only Cantonese-speaking girl left from among the seven hundred and eighty-nine who applied from the Philippines and Indonesia, representing over four thousand finalists from different regions of South-East Asia. I hope for promotion to Jade Woman. I have eleven languages including Tagalog and the major western languages, Punjabi, Urdu, Hindi and Mandarin. I . . ."

KwayFay was lulled by the girl's voice. She took a look, eye pressed to the fragrant screen. The girl was nineteen, expert in perfumes, commerce, engineering and pharmacy, and had a degree in the history of art. She could dance in every known style, and her Russian was exemplary . . .

She waited another ten minutes, during which the girl gave her instances of her inordinate skills, beliefs, talents.

"Leave now."

With elegant expressions of thanks, the girl left. KwayFay wondered what happened to the girls who were rejected.

"They become Flower Girls," Ghost said in her ear, full of scorn for a granddaughter who did not know obvious facts, "but of the highest order. To be a nearly Jade Woman is honour, *ne?*"

"On the Flower Boats near the godowns?" KwayFay asked. "You told me about the ones along the Canton godowns, and the Shanghai Bund where the foreign devils used to assemble."

"That's stupid!" Grandmother cried. "Flower Boats were for Chinese and sometimes for opium smokers, not for foreign devils, foolish girl!" Grandmother cackled a laugh and confided, "Have you been in the opium divans in the lighters moored near Stonecutters Island off Sham Shui Po here, west of Kowloon?"

"No, Grandmother!" KwayFay was shocked.

"Don't you get high and mighty with me, girl!" Grandmother screeched. "Putting on airs, just because I was once a *Mui Chai*. Being a slave sex-girl takes skill. I should know!"

"Yes, Grandmother."

"The next one will wear a pearly pendant. You will like it."

"The third one, Grandmother?" KwayFay said with meaning, remembering the soldier's remarks at Amah Rock.

"I rather liked the first one, didn't you? She was slender. I loved being slender. I was exquisitely slender. Everybody looked at you."

"They were both beautiful."

"Call that beauty?" Grandmother sneered. "They would have been laughed at when I was girl."

"The one chosen will become a Jade Woman?"

"Yes." Ghost's voice grew dreamy. "They will be multi-million-airesses. Their families will bask in money. They will be hired out by the Hongs to visiting princes, businesses, arrange functions for world leaders and entertain kings. They are educated to speak with the world's greatest minds, and know everything. They never know hunger or want. They are the most perfect women on earth. Idiots think they are the same as geishas. Japanese trollops! Can you imagine?"

"Ridiculous, Grandmother."

"The next girl's pearl pendant is a baroque. She has common sense. She is from the Tai Pu Sea, that used to be called the Mei-Chu Pool during the Five Dynasties. You won't remember. You call it Tai Po, near the Lei Yue Mun Channel leading to Hong Kong main harbour. That's because you copy the barbarian English, who don't know any better."

"I sorry, Grandmother."

"It's where best pearls came from," Ghost said wistfully. "The conches were huge in the old days, much bigger than you get now. All China wanted Hong Kong's pearls and incense. The Emperor Liu Ch'ang of the Nan Han – I only just missed seeing him go by during last year's Ching Ming Festival – loved pearls so much he sent nine thousand men to work our pearl fisheries. That was in the sixth year of Ta-pao, a thousand years ago."

"How lovely, Grandmother." KwayFay wanted the third girl to hurry, so she could go home.

"That's why the Great Pearl Legend persists, of the Pearl Nullah, a great underwater cavern. All Nan Han pearls were stored in a water channel. Thousands and thousands of the choicest specimens. I never saw it. Divers all along the coast of the Celestial Empire still seek it!" Ghost cackled, setting herself coughing again and coming to only when she calmed down. "What fools people are!"

"Are they fools, Grandmother?" KwayFay knew she had fallen quite asleep, because she could no longer hear the traffic and the room was darker. She felt comfortable and no longer so hot that she was almost dripping with sweat.

"Of course, silly girl! They say Hong Kong's name comes from that horrid woman pirate Hsiang-Hu – the written characters of her name look like Fragrant Harbour, see? Or from that waterfall – you know the one crossing Pokfulam Road near Dairy Farm? Stupid, stupid!"

"What is it from, Grandmother?" KwayFay had heard it all before but as long as she was allowed to doze undisturbed. She was so tired.

"Incense!" Ghost screeched triumphantly. "It's from *kuan-*

hsiang, incense. Hong Kong is the incense port, the Fragrant Harbour!"

"I see, Grandmother!" KwayFay tried to hide her yawn. There was a brief period of quiet. "*Kuan-hsiang* was the name of the incense?"

"Yes, in olden days," a girl's voice interrupted. KwayFay shot awake. There was a new girl standing before the screen. "Properly called *Aquilaria sinensis.* The best was grown in Sha-Tin, where the new racecourse now is. And at Sha-Lo-Wan on Lantau Island. How sad the new airport will cover the old incense grounds!"

"What a rude bitch!" Ghost Grandmother bawled. "Interrupting like that!" She whispered spitefully in KwayFay's ear, "Ask this know-it-all which was the best Hong Kong incense."

"The best?" The girl answered immediately, quite as if she heard Ghost Grandmother. "The best was Daughter Incense, called so from being used for temple worship. But that was before the Ch'ings moved all coastal folk inland. There was no more incense growing after that."

"Horrid cow!" Ghost spat, and left in a temper.

KwayFay stared at the wooden screen in wonderment.

"I am sorry if I gave offence," the same girl's voice said from out in the room. "I thought you asked me."

"No need sorry."

She leant close and looked through. A girl stood there, quite as lovely as the two who preceded her. She was wearing a pendant of a single baroque pearl, and plainer clothes. She was the last of the three exquisite girls, the one who had been most upset at the blasphemy in the Queen of Heaven's temple on Lamma Island that day.

"You were born by the Tai Pu Sea, in the place now called Tai Po," KwayFay said.

"Yes, Little Sister."

Same place, KwayFay thought, different name. This was the one, the third.

"Leave now."

"Thank you." The girl left, closing the door softly. KwayFay was shaken by the encounter, never having met anyone else who heard Ghost before.

She sat waiting. Were there more? She heard the door open, and Ah Min's slow steps come across the room. She saw his vast shadow, and heard other footfalls by the door.

"You have chosen, Little Sister?" his voice whined. She did not look at him. He hated her, and she him.

"Yes. The last one."

A prolonged silence, then, "How did you know she was from Tai Po? You did not consult the file you were given."

"She is the one."

"Why?"

"She is the one."

"You understand what she is chosen for?"

"Jade Woman."

"Did you ever meet her before?"

"No."

"Was the pearl some signal?"

"No. She wears it in honour of an ancestor, a long-ago grandfather in the Tai Po harbour, that used to be called the Pearl Pool. He was a Tanka pearl fisher many hundreds of years ago, and died swimming."

"Your choice is acknowledged, Little Sister," Ah Min said. "Is there any gift you need in return?"

"Not to me, though I thank you for your courtesy." She thought. "I would ask a favour, if I may."

"Ask."

"A man in a large silver motor hurt a boy of six in Bowen Road as I went to Amah Rock in a taxi. Can I ask for the boy to be made rich, and the rich man made poor?"

Ah Min's reply took a moment coming. KwayFay knew he was waiting for signalled approval of some other.

"Given," he said. "Please buy more new clothes, Little Sister, and wear them in future. Also," he added drily, "wear shoes on your feet, then broken glass will not harm you. Eat. Spend."

"Thank you," she said.

She heard them leave. Eventually the no-fingernails threat-man came and showed her out into the street.

Chapter Twenty-Nine

Dawn. Santiago was on fine form.

He had been unable to resist taking Linda across to Macao on the jumbo-sized jet catamaran from the Shun Tak Centre on Connaught Road. Thank God the Portuguese still owned Macao! They had enough gambling centres to satisfy anybody who wanted a flutter. There he played Fan Tan, with the stately croupier girls wafting their wands to separate the mysterious white counters. His mystic touch and led Linda to three successive wins! After that their luck changed, they withdrew, had supper on the balconies and lowered occasional bets down in baskets.

Linda loved showing her young man off, with his obvious wealth and Eurasian features. Let HC worry himself sick in his wrong-floor Investment Company. She was the one making the running. She decided she would let HC go once she got her winnings. That was how she thought of it now, a letting go, as derelict junks had been let go in outlying New Territories islands, there to burn for months on end, fleet after fleet. Rejects! HC was a reject person.

Her new man adored her. He said so, and used her body as a lover ought. His power over and in her was total. She pitied other women who openly admired Santiago at gaming tables. What hope had they, when he loved her? Life was radiant. She would soon be wealthy beyond dreams.

"The races!" she whispered to him as they wakened that morning. "We have little time!"

They were in the most expensive hotel in Macao.

"I have the return tickets," he said, smiling. She had the impression he had been awake for ages. "Transport to Hong Kong is often booked up. My darling Linda mustn't miss her special day!"

They made leisurely love until breakfast, even more satisfying than usual. Linda was beside herself at the thought of the races. She spread newspapers all over the dining-room table.

Horses, jockeys, the possibility of defaults, everything had to be discussed. Twice she telephoned friends asking for rumours of sickness among the horses, weight changes – not always unlikely – and about the jockeys down to ride.

"Darling Linda," Santiago said, smiling with those brilliant teeth. "Haven't you already identified this girl, the one who knows winners?"

"I'm making certain!"

"Certain of what?" His smile melted her. "If we know the winners, why study others?"

"It's so clear in my mind, darling! We double, with a staggered American twist, three-fold – "

He laughed. "Don't let plans take over, Linda darling. Just do it!"

"Let's!" she breathed, shaking with desire of a different kind.

By coincidence they were on the same jet catamaran, the same seats, as when they had crossed to Macao. The luckiest of omens. Santiago jubilantly gave away all his Portuguese *patacas* to begging children near the ferry concourse.

"We could have gone to the horse-racing on Macao's Taipa Island," she reminded him. "There's racing today. The stands there are air-conditioned. Have a warm-up bet!" She smiled mischievously, knowing how he liked to be cool when they lay together. "Build up our stake!"

"You'll be suggesting the dog-racing next! The horses will provide all we need, Linda darling. Let's go!"

Laughing, they boarded the huge jumbocat. Linda dropped her last *pataca* coin overboard for luck. As if she needed any!

His eyes met those of the elderly concierge. She no longer wore her Peninsula Hotel attire and remained standing in Old Man's presence. Below, the early lights of Hong Kong were dowsing slowly, as day arrived.

"She declined money," Tiger Wong repeated.

"She left most of the clothes and goods she purchased."

"She declined money."

This was the strangest thing imaginable. Ah Min was listening in grief. He held the money KwayFay had returned via Tang the threat-man in a manila envelope, a reproach.

Tiger Wong pondered, seeing Ah Min's distress. Yet she had unerringly chosen everything exactly as he had wished at the Paper Shop to placate his innumerable ancestors, especially his father. Now this.

He had a headache. Could it be that the girl was simply honest? His throbbing temples stabbed pain at his eyes at the thought of honesty. What was honesty for? Not even ancient Chinese philosophy could answer that.

"She did not return to her reserved suite?"

"That is correct, Business Head. And went by the Star Ferry."

Ah Min hissed in outrage. Could Tiger Wong not see the girl was causing disrespect?

"Who *is* she?" Old Man asked. "Tell me everything again."

Both began to speak together. The woman fell silent. Ah Min explained she had no family, was a street urchin with no name. It was a familiar litany. Old Man Tiger Wong knew it by heart.

"Ah Hau is a crippled Cantonese, Hong Kong born. Runs the Café of the Singing Birds near Sai Ying Pun. She scavenged there, a no-family Cockroach Child. He fed her occasionally. He invented her name. She stole. The usual."

"Her name?"

"Ah Hau says he made it up. He has forgotten how, and why. He guessed her age, invented a birthday for her. He mentioned her gift of clairvoyance to one of our retired threat-men, an elderly Cantonese who lives near Ladder Street and who has a singing minah bird. The man reported it to his old banner-man."

"And?"

"I thought she should have a job in HC Ho's Brilliant Miracle Success Investment Company. She is a clerk."

"Continue."

"She is in her squatter shack on Mount Davis. She carries her old clothes in a bag."

To Ah Min it seemed an impasse, unless that bitch Linda Ho won a fortune at the horse racing today.

"More."

Ah Min's fat fingers plucked nervously at his garment. Once

the subject left his only topic, money, he was lost. This girl showed no righteousness, impervious to the exquisite ideals money represented. How could such a person live? For a moment he dwelt on the notion of her possible death with fondness. Could such a thing be arranged without the knowledge of the Triad master Tiger Wong?

"Has Ho defaulted?"

Money! Ah Min's beam regained its old conviction.

"Yes. HC Ho borrowed a further sum – listed in my dawn report, First Born – and will default tonight. He invested in a new currency. The girl – " he almost said the mad girl " – warned against it, but HC guessed for himself and has lost over six-eighths of the borrowed sum in less than a week."

"He borrowed from us?"

"A money-lender's in Hung Hom. You own it. You wish to sanction the proprietor?"

"No. This wife?"

"*Tai-Tai* Ho? Calls herself Linda, sleeps with the Eurasian Santiago. Lovers. She has borrowed largely to bet on horses. They return from Macao for the racing. They intend to make the girl tell them which horses win."

"Which racing?"

"The old race course at Happy Valley. They gambled two days in Macao at Fan Tan and blackjack, a few times at roulette. You wish to hear their talk?"

"No."

Ah Min waited, his mind edging close to terror. This was the most detailed interrogation he had ever had to endure. So many details! It was not natural. It was all the mad girl's fault. Her death looked more inviting.

"You let them win?"

"Only a little! Three times at Fan Tan, and once – "

Tiger Wong waved him to silence and beckoned the concierge to come closer.

"Why does a girl who is so poor refuse gifts of money, clothes, jewellery, things all females like?"

"I have never seen it before, First Born," the woman said. She too was badly frightened, searching for anything the Old Man might blame her for.

"Why?"

She dithered. "She wants to help you."

He stared from the concierge to Ah Min. "Help *me*?"

"She believes you are being oppressed by family or business rivals."

This matched his early information. The girl had given him a spoonful of rice and greens in kitchen foil. He still kept it, sometimes looking, always wondering. Ah Min saw the old man's face crinkle. A faint sound as of a distant nullah caught his attention and he looked querulously at the concierge. She too looked puzzled. The old man shook slightly, his *cheong saam* quivering.

Old Man Tiger Wong was laughing. Ah Min stared, never having seen such a thing. He gestured to the concierge, gathered up his two ledgers and followed on tiptoe, as one might leave a place of sickness.

They were by the 6B stop at the junction of Mount Davis Road and Victoria as KwayFay stepped down the mountain track to the metalled surface. Linda Ho waved.

"We shall give you a lift, Little Sister! Save you the bus."

"*Tai-Tai* Ho! Are you sure?"

The girl looked wonderful in new clothes. She now had a clever hairdo and wore lovely imported shoes. Her laptop as ever was slung over her back, with that ridiculous plastic shopping bag in her hand. Despite that, she was quite like a flower. Such style! Linda wanted to rumple the bitch's look.

"Get in!" she commanded.

Santiago was driving. Their plan was working well. He made conversation – where KwayFay lived, what she did at Ho's firm – then chatted about her ambitions for when China moved in at the Handover.

She was monosyllabic, which did not worry him. He had his plans to follow. Astonishing KwayFay, he drove up Wang Nai Chung Gap Road towards the reservoir.

"Excuse me, sir," KwayFay said timidly. "I must go to work.

Central District."

"This journey first, Little Sister."

"HC's orders," Linda said reassuringly.

At the reservoir Santiago stopped the car and alighted, holding the door open for KwayFay. She shook her head, frightened.

"I must go to work, sir."

"Linda, please."

Linda got out and walked off, as if a tourist inspecting the stupendously wide view across the harbour, the falling valley and the mountains to the right, the ships and crammed city below. Santiago leaned in.

"Can I see your computer, please?" When she did not move to comply he explained, "You have no choice, Little Sister."

He whisked the slender laptop box from her and clicked it open. She sat, mortified, watching as he took out a small penknife, prising the base up. It swung, revealing an old abacus. The ancient system, thirteen slender stalks each bearing a five-and-two set of beads in a wooden frame. He examined the whole thing minutely, to the extent of closing the computer base and starting it up.

The screen filled with mundane data, investments, records from Ho's firm. Nothing new or unexpected, except the ancient abacus. Its frame was dried and warped, the beads cracked. Frail. The irony did not escape him, this antique abacus hidden in modern technology.

"There is nothing secret in it, except this?"

"No, sir."

"I want the winners of the races today. They begin at seven o'clock, until eleven o'clock. Do you go?"

"No."

"Tell me the bets Hong Kong Club calls the Double Quintella or the Six-up. Either will do. Can you do that?"

She thought. Was he simply asking to discover which horses won? What was the point, except for gambling? And where was the merit in betting?

"I don't know."

Linda turned just then. He gave a shake of his head, not yet, admire that view.

"Tell me what you can."

"There is no merit betting on a mare," she told him, looking up against the early sun. Luckily, the day's heat had not yet struck so high up the mountain. The sun would thump directly on the whole Colony soon and be intolerable. "Gambling is not good."

"Mare?" he picked up, his voice quiet, this just between them. "Did you say mare?"

"The one we passed on the way." She indicated the Happy Valley racecourse below. It was just visible in the smog haze.

"I didn't notice it." But he would have. "What colours did the rider wear?"

"Red. A pale dot in the middle of the rider's back. Striped cap, yellow."

"And the others? You saw them?" They had passed no horses.

"Yes." She described the jockeys' silks, pleased she remembered some of the horses' numbers. "Only six, though."

"Did you not see any more? I thought we passed a whole string."

"I'm sorry. Only those six. So tall and pretty. Do you think they give them enough to eat? Some looked thin!"

"Yes, Little Sister," he said kindly, but badly shaken. "I'm sure they are properly fed. Weren't they handsome!" He returned her laptop. "Thank you for letting me see your abacus. I've never seen one so ancient. Where did you buy it?"

"I've had it since I was little. It was one of the first the old scholar ever wrote about."

"Scholar?" he echoed. He had orders to discover any connections she might have among local criminals. Scholar, though?

"Yes. Dao Nan Tsang." She smiled shyly. "He had a monkey on his table. It mixed his ink! The book he was writing was *Cease Farming Sketch Book*. He gave me a sweet plum and the abacus, so it is mine." She added anxiously, "I didn't steal it."

"Of course you didn't! And you kept it all this time?"

"Yes. I hid the beads so friends wouldn't steal it, and only put them back on when I was learning to count. That was when I became nine years old."

He said evenly, "Thank you, Little Sister. It has been a pleasure for me to make your acquaintance."

"And for me yours, sir," she replied in English, settling her laptop on her shoulder.

He called Linda and they drove back to Central, where she was only half an hour late. HC did not fine her.

Santiago made excuses once they were free of the girl. He had to draw out enough cash to play sensibly when Happy Valley opened. Tourists would flock in mobs arranged by the Tourist Agency, $350 fee including dinner and entrance to the special Members' Enclosure of the Royal Hong Kong Jockey Club. It was cheaper to go alone, a mere $50, but you received no meal and no special treatment.

"The pity is," he laughed as he explained his temporary disappearance to Linda, "I only had time to ask her for the Double Quintella and the Six-Up. She gave me both!"

They discussed the options, Linda thrilled beyond expectations. The Double Quintella – the first two horses home in any two races on the same day – and the impossible Six-Up, where you had to select the winner or the second, in all six races, well, she'd never had enough luck or money for either of those. Santiago had stories about winning the Six-Up in successive weeks.

"Was she definite?" she breathed.

"Absolutely certain, Linda darling! She described the jockeys' colours, numbers and everything!"

"Was it a vision?" Linda was breathless. The girl was a goldmine. Linda could own the world, buy noble houses in every capital city in the world, purchase firms outright in London, New York, estates in California, mansions in Hollywood.

"Yes. She actually *saw* the horses in a string as we came through Happy Valley. We hadn't passed any! Her second sight. We are in heaven, Linda darling."

He went to return the hire car and book a room in the Shangri-La for later that evening. He was sick of Linda and her clinging. It would soon be over.

Once this was finished he would ask Business Head Tiger Wong's permission for a night off. He planned to use a bath-house girl he was fond of. She at least knew how to conduct herself in company, unlike Linda, and had a measure of politeness in her. And Linda was proving as sexually enthralling as a plastic doll. He'd had enough of the damned woman.

He went to report.

Chapter Thirty

"She said Dao Nan Tsang?"

Santiago told Ah Min the name of the book. Ah Min's hand shook. He signalled for rice wine and sipped it, eyes closed. Santiago watched. Ah Min's fingers never ceased caressing the leather cover of his ledger. It lay before him on the café table.

The whole place had been emptied of customers. Outside, traffic in Nullah Road tried to block cars coming down Tung Choi Street. Drivers were out of their vehicles, yelling abuse in a score of Chinese dialects. Ah Min came to, and spoke softly to the Eurasian.

"You know Dao Nan Tsang?"

"No, First Born."

"Indeed not. He lived centuries ago, Yuan Dynasty. He wrote a book on the mathematics of the abacus."

Santiago had the world's best memory and important facilities with women, but wasn't the brightest button on the Triad's quilt.

"It can't be, First Born." He added, as proof, "She remembered him distinctly. Dao Nan Tsang gave her a sweet plum and the old abacus with the cracked beads. She recalled Dao's little monkey on his writing table. She liked to watch it mix his ink."

Ah Min's headache returned, almost whimpering as it struck his forehead. Ancient scribes in the days of the Emperors truly did train monkeys, it being their conceit to have a pet to mix ink neatly for their writings. They kept them on their desks. The monkeys were highly valued. Ah Min knew that the rarest species of this precious monkey had died out altogether – except that, a few months since, two pairs of these rare primates had been rediscovered in the Chinese interior. Dao Nan Tsang was the second-greatest ever exponent of the flowing style of Chinese calligraphy, the exquisite "grass-character" writing, in 7,000 years of history. Miserably, he acknowledged that Tiger Wong must be told.

He opened his eyes to see Santiago's smug face. How could this idiot, with his impossibly narrow understanding of anything, coerce women to do the Triad's bidding with such success?

"You must be right. Say nothing of this." Ah Min signed for *fokis* to open some windows and let in the traffic din. Noise flooded the place, almost making speech inaudible.

"Further orders, First Born?"

"Go racing in Happy Valley. She must lose."

Santiago left the café. He looked back for a brief second and saw Ah Min with his head in his hands. Why did so powerful a man, second in the entire Triad, not live in splendour without noise, far from the wretched stew of Hong Kong? And, he thought, mystified, if literally millions in Sterling, American dollars, every known currency under the sun, passed through the man's hands every week, why did he always hold court in a tacky café in a Kowloon street? It was beyond him. But he had a job on.

He went racing in Happy Valley.

KwayFay was disturbed to find her desk had been cannibalised by Tony, who was back to his usual chirpiness about Futures. Alice was hunched and depressed. Jenny Lan had sunk into despond, was tapping feeble guesses into her terminal. A.K. Sau, a girl of august lineage and impressive figure, who'd taken the name Elise, came over almost in tears and told KwayFay she felt unwell. KwayFay listened, trying to set up her terminal on the pod ledge, now the only free spare place. Elise's problems involved some youth in the Land Refill Unit. KwayFay's mind glimpsed him in a brief flash, swaggering in Des Voeux Road West from his job at the Bonham Hotel where he had a wife working in Reception. Bad luck, Elise.

Francis Moy, the oldest employee at thirty-five, moved across. He was innumerate and lowly, because the firm was natually submerged in numbers. He had prematurely greying hair, and helped out some Christian folly at a church. He spoke Portuguese, a hindrance to anyone, and lived from day to day with dull resignation.

"HC is weeping, KwayFay," he said. "I think today we go bust."

"No-job day?" KwayFay did not guess ahead. There was a time and place for that.

"For everyone."

He spoke with no satisfaction. It had simply come for him, as he'd known. The others, Moy understood, were younger, could decipher screens filled with integers. KwayFay knew Moy saw the world as an admix of feelings and words, where numbers were simply beyond comprehension. A cripple, but a kind one who normally kept out of the way and did not gossip. She remembered Grandmother's instruction never to become Christian, for they were incapable of believing in madness.

She did not feel tired, despite having been frightened by that film-star man, so tall and distinguished yet looking false. He was going to kill *Tai-Tai* Ho today in some manner, but there was no saving the woman. KwayFay felt slightly put out, for Ghost Grandmother had given no warning of this. Linda Ho wanted to possess the oily Eurasian, but never could for she was drugged on gambling. Just like any opium addict smoking his resin along Hollywood Road or lying stuporose in opium-divans on the lighters floating off Stonecutters Island. Linda Ho would kill to avoid being saved. It was the destiny she craved. She would not risk rescue.

KwayFay went to see Alice. She seemed morbid, almost haggard. KwayFay prevented a host of images from crowding into her mind. "Alice. Did you block my data access?" Her console would not function.

"Yes. HC said to."

KwayFay looked around. Nobody would meet her eyes, except Elise Sau who only wanted somebody to moan to, about her double-crossing young man.

"If you're not using yours, can I?"

"HC said no."

"*Mh gan-yiu,*" KwayFay said as casually as she could. "Not important."

She plugged her laptop anywhere, resting it on two waste baskets, one above the next. She set to. The FTSE was roller-coasting along behind the Dow Jones, the Hang Seng Index was being bothered by some corporate failure in America. Nothing seemed stable. She almost laughed. It would even out by mid-afternoon and everybody would be wondering what the fuss was about. The

Almighty Dollar would go off a whole point, Sterling would rise and Europe trail after. She glimpsed a troubling vision of some European men – a bottle-blonde woman drove their Fiat van, wrong side of the road, so it must be Europe – counterfeiting the impending Euro, which made her smile. So far, they were only prototypes, but soon that mischief would rock national economies. The forgers would not be discovered until tomorrow, when Italian police . . .

She realised HC Ho was standing before her.

"What are you doing?"

His face was so pale it was almost green. She felt his waves of distress. He should never have gambled on the new currency. Stains on his jacket seemed to be food. His shirt was soiled, the cuffs sweat-clinging to his wrists. He spectacles were dotted with grime; this was the man forever polishing his glasses and holding them up to the light. The great thinker.

"Working, First Born."

"Stop now."

He went to the water-cooler. It was only ever filled with plain tap water. From here important announcements were made at bonus times. He clapped his hands for attention. The place stilled. It had come, what they were waiting for. Some stood.

"We close now," he said, trying to smile. "Only for today. Maybe a take-over. Or a merger! Work no more today!"

"We come tomorrow?" somebody asked nervously.

"Of course! There is always tomorrow!" He gave a hearty laugh, and went round shaking hands. "The Brilliant Miracle Success Investment Company will join an important exchange company."

"We shut down?"

"Temporarily!" HC boomed, reaching for hands to shake. The employees seemed reluctant and drifted to their desks. "Only temporary, until the merger is signed! Definitely."

Alice was in tears. Elise looked drawn. Charmian was searching faces for hope, quite lost. She caught KwayFay's eye but quickly searched on. She'd seen HC speak to her.

"Now we have rest day!" HC was exclaiming, trying to grab

hands, a politician working a vanished constituency.

Telephones were ringing. No one answered.

People began to take things from their desks. HC was having a hard time finding hands now. He ignored KwayFay, still seated at her improvised work station.

"There will be no job losses!" he cried. "I promise! We work better than ever!"

A few paused, the rest gathered up their drink flasks, always a bad sign.

The office emptied as HC returned beyond the glass door. KwayFay worked on amid ringing telephones as people left. Charmian, bemused into reflex, got out the vacuum cleaner and began to hoover the carpet as if at the end of a long day. KwayFay closed down her laptop and told Charmian the *bahsi* had decided to shut the office.

"What will I do, Little Sister?"

"I shall try to see you get a job somewhere else."

"You have mirror eye, Little Sister. I starve?"

"No. You will not."

The woman put away her cleaning implements. KwayFay watched her leave, hearing the wobbling lifts crash and whine their way down to the ground floor. KwayFay looked round. She heard a door close along the corridor. The next set of rooms was a laboratory, the Health Victory Eternal laboratory, always on the go, wafting gusts of heat onto the staircase, the staff grabbing all the elevators at midday. For a moment she thought of going there to ask for a job but she knew nothing about medicine, and diseases frightened her. She went towards the office. Perhaps HC had some influence with the cruel fat man who had trapped the frail Tiger Wong.

HC, she saw, was standing by the windows looking out. No jingling of money, no nervy humming or tapping fingers on the glass. She drew breath.

"Ho *Sin-Sang*?"

He did not even turn. "Little Sister. I told you to leave."

"The old gentleman. Please can't you help him?"

Now he did look round, astonishment making his features

almost recover to normal.

"Me? Help him? You mean . . .?"

"Yes." A sense of disorder took her, images and miniature visions cascading across her mind in a torrent, sights so fleeting she could not find any sense in them. "Please."

He barked a laugh, so incongruous she stepped back in alarm. "For all your mirror sight, KwayFay, you are a stupid bitch."

"I will see money dreams for the cruel fat man," she offered. She had nothing else. Even suggesting this she was in the wrong and would catch it from Ghost Grandmother, but what could she do? "I offer to guess his money in . . ."

In what? She didn't know in what, or how to see ahead for somebody else. In fact, she didn't know how to see ahead for herself, let alone hostage-takers. "In dollar stocks," she proffered lamely.

"Go home." He went back to staring out of the window. "This building is tall, isn't it?"

"It is tall," she answered, wondering.

Was he going to effect the merger, then bid for rooms on the eighth floor, the luckiest place in Princes Building? It had lucky *Fhung Seui*, wind and water combined to please the flying dragons who, destined to seek sea water daily, you dared not impede. She hoped so, though he would need monks to exorcise the place before such a move, at a cost of at least HK$ 8,000, doubled if he wanted good priests, because some were unlucky.

"Go home, KwayFay."

"*Joy geen*, goodbye." She retreated enveloped in a curious sadness.

She stopped in the Ladies to wash one last time. It was halfway down the office. She was quiet in there. She heard voices outside. They were already well into abuse when she finally emerged and stood wondering at the feeling of menace.

The fat man Ah Min's bulk shadowed HC's doorway, his back towards her. She moved to see into the room. Two of the threatmen stood by, one of them the tall man she'd given the money. She saw the colour of the room as if newly painted, a kind of horrid magenta and orange combined, sickly and necrotic. She detected a stench. The place seemed to be rotting, worse even than anything in Central Market after the night abattoirs had been working. She wanted to run.

" . . . intolerable losses," the fat man was saying in his beam-sieved whine. "You can repay, a?"

"It is difficult." HC had to swallow to get words out.

"For me, difficult! For you . . .?"

"I shall know, when my wife . . ."

"Your wife?" the fat man prompted. "She has the money you borrowed?" He chuckled. He already knew.

"She will win money tonight in Happy Valley. She will bring home a fortune."

"What money does she gamble with?"

"She borrowed on my firm."

The fat man did not wait for HC's answer. "Your wife will win nothing. You repay our money."

"No. Tonight . . ."

"Tonight nothing."

KwayFay could no longer stand the terrible odour and colours. Her senses were overwhelmed. She turned away, frightened lest they punish her too. It was death, the hues and stink of death. She had to leave. She had made promises, so many promises. How now to save Old Man Tiger Wong?

The whole office was empty. She tiptoed to the lifts. Oddly, the laboratory section outside, beyond the fronded plants and the poinsettias, was also silent. The lights were off, the doors locked. Had everyone gone from here too? Beyond, the two chairs for patients were vacant. She became even more frightened. It was as if the whole building was empty except for HC's horrid mis-coloured office. Even the lifts had stopped working.

"Little Sister," a voice said, so close she almost leapt.

Old Man was seated there in his *cheong saam* and leather sandals.

Outside, she could hear traffic still faintly roaring, the Happy Valley and Shau Kei Wan trams clanging and whirring. Yet it was as if the whole world was more wary than before, complicitors everywhere, while she remained in ignorance. What was coming.

"*Sin-Sang!*"

"The answer, Little Sister?"

"Answer to what?"

"Is the one I asked you about to be trusted? Promoted?"

"For now, yes. But not later." The words were out before she thought. It did not seem to be her voice.

Despite the terror he induced, the fat man in there facing HC was to be trusted, but only for a while. His actions were predictable, she meant to say, and would have said more but Old Man raised a hand to stay her words.

He seemed tired. "Tell me one thing more, KwayFay. Are you she?"

"She? Who she?" She almost bridled at the question. She was herself. She was KwayFay, nobody else. "I am only KwayFay."

"Are you she?"

"No, First Born." She measured the distance to the fire exit, the stairwell. "Can you run? We could make it to the street, though the lifts have stopped working. They are arguing with HC."

"Run?" He seemed mystified. "Why should I run?"

"To escape! I could get you to Sai Ying Pun. I have a friend, an old man nearly thirty-seven years old. He has the Café of the Singing Birds. He can hide you. They won't think of looking!"

"They won't?" He waited. "Who won't?"

"The threat-men!" She ran to him and tried to make him stand up. He stood looking at her. "I could take word to your family."

"Why do you know some things yet not others?" He explained, "The lifts, KwayFay. I said they are not to work. The laboratory, three businesses on other floors, I stopped them also."

She drew back. "You?" This frail old prisoner did all that?

"The fat man is the one I ask about. You say he is loyal now but will not be later. He is my man, as are the others."

"Others who?" This was shaming. "You mean the hotel?"

"I use hotels for my purpose." He sat down. "They do as I say. The money was my gift of thanks. There is already more in your shack, in appreciation for the funeral pyre, choosing the right paper house for my ancestors. When I saw it, I knew you were she."

She felt angry with him for deceiving her. "She who? And the Eurasian man who stole me today and asked questions?"

"Everything, Little Sister. Everyone. They all obey me."

She realised she somehow had suddenly far less to fear, though the feelings still would not balance. "I am cross with you, *Sin-Sang*. I was very frightened. Please ask them not to hurt HC. He is weak. And I apologise."

"For what?"

"I . . . I offered to buy you, keep you in my shack to carry water."

He was amused. "You offered six hundred Hong Kong dollars to buy me – plus of course an out-of-date laptop, and guesses about investments!"

"I am ashamed."

"Do not be. It was everything you had."

He went solemn, but she knew he was smiling within. "Are you she?"

"Who?"

"The Clear-Eyed One."

"No. I am only KwayFay. I was Cockroach Girl, street child in the Mologai. No family, no ancestors. Now I have no job."

The Clear-Eyed Girl was famed throughout China's history, and was one of the puppet-theatre fables. Ming Yen appeared in incarnations down the ages, to advise the Pa Kua, the most powerful of secret societies. Seances ruled by the Girl guided all decisions after her revelations began at the end of the Ming Dynasty.

"The Clear-Eyed Girl also had no ancestors, no family. Are you she?"

KwayFay felt giddy. The accusation was a new burden intolerable to someone who had nothing. Now she was to blame for everything?

"Neither have any of the street people, First Born." She felt such misery. "We are all without ancestors. Can I please go?"

"You work for me."

"And do what?"

"Answer questions. That is all."

"What questions?" And asked hopefully, "Investments? I might guess numbers for you. Except, sometimes I am wrong."

"I have people for numbers."

He spoke a few words as if casually reflecting on some idea, and the elevators started up immediately. She looked but saw nobody who could hear.

"From today, Little Sister, go to any hotel, any place in Hong Kong. You pay nothing. You remember your no-pay number?"

"Yes."

"Tell that. It will buy you anything, give you any suite, any service. You will be my girl with clear eyes."

"I am frightened, master."

"Your squatter shack life is finished, child." He smiled with, she thought, not a little sorrow. "You have family now. I am your family, and you are mine."

The lift doors crashed open. She stepped in. The doors closed on him and carried her to the ground floor, where Hong Kong seemed busy and back to normal.

Chapter Thirty-One

Nothing could thrill like the start of the racing in Happy Valley. Or anywhere. Watching on screens when the Derby ran in far-off England, the Grand National horses parading at Aintree, crowds shouting "They're off!" at Newmarket, it was life. And lately, the Melbourne races in Australia – in fact, anything with her money riding on the winner. Linda was exhilarated. Her day had come.

The prospect of winning was a constant. The weight of the money was not.

"Six-Up," she told Santiago. It was her decision. His eyes were for her alone, but she had to concentrate on the issue. He was desperate to maul her, then straddle her compliant flesh . . .

"Wait, darling," she said, rejoicing.

Today she would soar into a dazzling new life. She would leave this humdrum existence. Age gap? No such thing! Life was hers to use. When her new fortune was banked in that tiresome new Hang Seng Bank, they would grovel when they saw the size of her cache of American dollars. Then she would be free.

The first thing would be to repay loans – a mere residue – to the Kowloon money-lenders. She would love to see their faces when she strolled in with her handsome young Santiago, give them a glimpse of her new life.

"Sure, Linda darling?"

"Six-Up. The colours, the numbers."

She'd seen the paper on which he'd written the girl's visions. Obsessively she had added form, trainers, owners . . . They had paraded exactly as on Santiago's list.

"And a Quintella. That's it."

"No savers, Linda darling? No single each-ways in case? We mustn't be too trusting!" he said, his sobriety making her laugh.

"Milk the bookies," was all she said.

Betting being regulated by the Royal Hong Kong Jockey Club, you had to be careful. On the way they stopped off in To Kwa Wan before crossing the harbour – for the last time! The notion of finality thrilled her. She placed bets in four illegal off-course betting shops. That was to allay any suspicions when they did their on-course spreads. The money would grow anyway. Odds for two of KwayFay's vision horses had begun to narrow, showing other punters were getting wind of heavy bets. Gamblers sensed big money, which suggested insider knowledge. Most unfair, when she wanted huge odds for maximum gain. Even at relatively low odds, the money would multiply as first one winning horse came romping home followed by another winner in the next race . . . Was it even greater than sex? She kept her expression formal as Betty, her best friend, walked by, then paused to stare. Linda deliberately ignored the bitch.

The first race was called. Santiago gave her a quick smile, then bent over his race card. Linda had the eyes of a lover for her mount. It would work. It was beautiful, stylish and frisky, aching to run and leave the others standing. The exquisite beast would make her existence utter bliss.

KwayFay sat in the Café of the Singing Birds with a glass of water. Was it all over now?

Ah Hau was at his soiled counter. He had seen off the noon rush and was serving bowls of rice to a few street children. Fifty cents. KwayFay watched him, hunch-backed and limping. He had to swing his whole body to get any length of stride. He was the butt of scorn, as with all deformities.

Remorseful, she remembered how she had taunted him with the thoughtlessness of a child, giving him nicknames that surely must have hurt. Yet he was unwilling to let street-children starve, plague him how they might. KwayFay's little gang of marauding Cockroach Children stole and hawked between Sheung Wan and Sai Ying Pun down the narrow streets. Even with only a few grains of rice left, still the man showed generosity of spirit. She wondered if he was the reincarnation of some saintly courtier or heavenly general. It happened.

People clattered up and down Ladder Street and Possession Street, their pattens making the perennial rattle of Hong Kong. All were shouting, and giving messages. Ah Hau never looked up, busy, just gave her a glass of water and got on.

What would she have done without him? Died, that's what.

Succumbed to hunger and illness. Twice when she'd been ill, Ah Hau bought herbs for her from the herbalists in Kennedy Town and letting her sleep on his cockroach-ridden linoleum floor with its flecks of offal and that pale pink scent of decay. He fed and rescued. Even now, when she was grown, he gave her water when she was faint from the heat. No pay at the Café of the Singing Birds run by Ah Hau. For her. She never asked after her friends, the gang of infant thieves. Had Ah Hau been a street child when small? Who knew what happened to folk?

He didn't look a saint. Maybe real saints never did?

"This your sanctuary, Little Sister?"

Ah Min sat on a stool beside her. She looked, but suddenly Ah Hau had gone. She was alone with this bulbous beaming threatener. She recognised his hatred of her. In life there was no sanctuary from such people.

"Ah Hau is my friend."

"I know." Ah Min's beam was no different. She wondered what he would look like if it were removed. Would he vanish? "He is your good friend, *ne*?"

"I am his good friend," she corrected, wanting it clarified.

"He named you."

"I am in his debt for more than a name."

"So you say, Little Sister." The fat man signalled to a trio of threat-men outside. They melted away, only one remaining to lean on the door jamb. "You recommended me to the master Tiger Wong. Whom," he added pointedly, "you named in turn."

"I did as I was told."

He was discomfited and shifted on the stool. She sensed that women made him want to punish, the simplest way of riddance. This was a partial man, far lamer than Ah Hau or any other cripple, all women would do well to fear.

"Was your recommendation unqualified, Little Sister?" His beam hardened. "When Tiger Wong asked was I trustworthy or not. Or did you add a caution?"

"I said as I was told."

"By whom?"

"I do not know."

He nodded slowly, then stood. For the first time she saw how tall he was. No midget, just rotund and tall. Massive, yet a fraction of a man.

"I shall tolerate you, Little Sister. But only for the moment. It is Tiger Wong's fancy to indulge your fantasies. As long as you are useful to the Triad, I shall say nothing about your fraudulence. I understand his sensitivities."

"I understand." She was no longer afraid. Resigned, yes.

"The instant you are no longer essential, Little Sister, it will end. Do you follow?"

"Yes, First Born."

"We understand each other!" He spoke as if agreeably surprised by an easy victory. "Report everything to me daily. I shall convey it to Tiger Wong. Henceforth, you do not speak to him. Do you understand?"

"Yes, First Born, but no." She rose and went to the door. "I obey ancestors. I refuse you." Let him argue with that.

In disbelief he watched her walk away. Surely she couldn't be going back to her squatter hut among the rubbish people? For a moment he was tempted to send his threat-men to bring her back, knock some sense into the ignorant bitch. Then he recalled Tiger Wong's ruling.

He said to the nearest threat-man, "Finish Ho."

She hired a taxi on Connaught Road West, and told him to drop her in Statue Square. She could walk back, not far.

The crowds were mostly gone. It was late, the banks and taller buildings only showing lights because of guards. Late tourists were docking at Queen's Pier, and further west Blake Pier, always a centre of shops even this late, swarmed with tourists disgorged from late runs to outlying islands of the New Territories. The gambling ship was already in at Queen's, a trad jazz band giving their all. She recognised the tune, but it hadn't been in a famous movie, so it was useless.

Astonished by her changed fortune, she realised she could now see any film she wanted, even the most recent! And sleep anywhere. Fantastic! She hitched her computer over her shoulder, and was conscious of two grinning youths blocking her path.

"Hello, Little Sister!" She tried to get past, but one moved to obstruct. "You got computer? How much you pay me to keep it?"

Two men in suits stepped from the shadow of the shopping mall. The youths looked at them, at KwayFay, then simply walked away, heads down. The threat-men lit cigarettes and stood talking. The incident had simply not occurred. KwayFay's heart thudded. She did not know whether to thank them or not. Was it proper to give them a tip? What should one do? And how had they known the youths would try to mug her here, exactly here?

"Thank you," she told them.

They looked at her with surprise, as if noticing her for the first time.

"*Mrh gan-yiu*, Little Sister." Not important. Therefore routine?

"Can I go now, please?"

They were mystified. One gave her an uncertain nod.

Nervously she walked to the rear of Princes Building. The entrances were shut by the ubiquitous grilles. She went round to the front, trying not to look into doorways to see if more of her protectors lurked there. How many people in Hong Kong obeyed Tiger Wong? Could she go anywhere with impunity? And the way she had spoken to Ah Min! She began to regret her manner. She would apologise to him when, if, she ever met him again. Then again, perhaps not. She understood that immense sumo-fat partial man, as he understood her. Enough.

Distantly, she could hear crowds roaring at the last race in Happy Valley. Only Hong Kong's lessening traffic permitted the rare luxury of hearing distant sounds. They would all be pouring back into Central soon, happy or sad, flushed with money or broke and sullen. A tram whirred by. Road menders had made a large hole, leaving warning lights and trestles. She stepped into the road to avoid the workings.

And above her came a loud crack. She looked up, and saw silhouetted against the night sky a figure splayed as if trying to assume the form of a cross. Shards of glass glittered up there in the darkness. She ducked away, running quickly along the road to avoid whatever was about to fall. A few pedestrians did the same. Somebody screamed and stood gaping.

She was almost at the corner when the body slammed with a splashing sound on the kerb. It did not remain still, just rocked slightly for a moment. She wondered in awe, Do they always do that, rock from side to side once they hit the ground, or is it because he is a somewhat stout businessman . . .? Falling glass rattled and cracked in a shower, with a sound of rattling gunfire. Fragments disintegrated into a bright shower that was almost beautiful, like the artificial Christmas rain stores did in mid-winter.

It was HC, her boss.

She remain crouched against the wall. Suicides were common in Hong Kong. People leapt from high buildings from business failure; women did it from marital shame, school-children did it from mortification after examinations.

And HC. She felt to blame. Sirens started. The main police centre was only a matter of yards away. She was careful to make certain the raining debris had ceased before she went to look at HC.

Tears ran down her cheeks. Bystanders were exclaiming in awe: "I was just going to cross the road when I heard . . ." I, I, I, always the first person at calamities. She wept for the folly that had led to this.

Somebody touched her arm. "Little Sister?" The young driver, who had taken her to the Peninsula Hotel. "Your motor."

He indicated a long blue car parked illegally across the road. It obstructed the tram lines. A tram waited patiently. Yet trams had right of way. English laws said so, from the days of the King long ago, when trams came.

"Where must I go?" she asked.

HC's spectacles were broken, his teeth grinning askew out of the side of his face. An eye lay on his cheek, dislodged from its socket as if it wanted to look under his chin. His legs were awry, one rotated so the foot toed the pavement, the other at an absurd angle. Blood oozed from three ribs protruding whitely from his waistcoat. His fob watch – he was always proud of that – still jerked its second hand round the dial. She saw the time was ten minutes past eleven.

"Wherever you say, Little Sister, and whatever you want."

She looked at Tang. He too was calm, with the calm of all threat-men. It was what conferred respect. To him, servant of the Triad master, everything was predictable in its dullness. This was Hong Kong, and she was the Clear-Eyed Girl, so where was the problem? For the first time, KwayFay saw herself through the threat-man's eyes.

In the morning, she would walk to the Café of the Singing Birds in Sai Ying Pun. She would sit on the stool Ah Hau would proffer, and accept the glass of water he would provide, so saving her shame at not having a dollar to pay for the smallest bowl of two-day rice. Then she would leave a tip, whatever she was allowed, to the cripple who had kept her alive for so long for no reward.

"How much money can I have tomorrow morning?" she asked.

"Whatever you say, Little Sister."

"A hundred? A thousand?"

"Yes, Little Sister."

"Ten thousand?" She felt giddy. "In a red envelope?"

"What time, Little Sister?"

"Seven o'clock tomorrow morning."

"*Ho*, Little Sister. Good." His calm was undisturbed. She saw this with wonder.

"The squatter shacks in Mount Davis, please." Her home.

He went ahead to open the door and stood waiting. She entered. He reminded her to buckle in, started the car, and they drove away. The tram clanked past the dead man as police and ambulances arrived.

This could not happen, Linda told herself.

The bets went down, one after another. She was alone. Santiago somehow vanished as the racing began dead on seven o'clock. Frantic, as successive horses failed her beautiful scheme, she ran about almost screaming. She had gone twice to see if Santiago was at the betting windows. She'd even asked a gentleman to look in the loos for him.

The horses lost. The Quintella went down, the horse she backed coming nowhere.

She hurried from one vantage point to another. This had to be some terrible mistake. Had she somehow got the wrong list? She looked down from the photographer's perch, the TV commentators' windows. No Santiago. She wanted to know what to do. The remains of her scheme had to be changed, and quickly. She had to claw back her money.

Another horse lost. Money gushed away, tens of thousands of dollars with each race.

Another horse failed, the fifth. One last race remained. Her mind spun. She wept, desperate, wanting to change the bet. But to what? Could she make a switch? If only she could find Santiago . . . He had the RHKJC tickets, even the dockets from the illegal bookmakers' shops across the harbour. The girl KwayFay must have misled them in some evil plan.

The last horse came nowhere. No Santiago.

All around people were shouting, some cheering and jubilant, others cursing. She tried to think as the Happy Valley floodlights clicked off and the illumination in the stands faded.

She glimpsed Santiago with a Chinese woman among the crowds drifting to the exits. He was offering the woman a cigarette from his gold case, making his open-handed gesture. It was not the image of a loser. In the throng Linda saw him tear two betting slips and discard the pieces.

She ran after, got close near the taxi ranks. She forced her way through and caught his arm. Departing punters saw her. Some laughed aloud at her evident misfortune. She must look haggard.

"Santiago! We . . ."

"Lost, Linda darling?" He flicked ash. "It happens! If you can't lose, don't choose."

He strolled on in the mob, signalling for a taxi. The woman with him gave her a mischievous smile and went with him. Linda heard his patter begin, "Once, I was really lucky, got the Six-Up

– just luck, no planning involved . . ."

She stood weeping as the crowd thinned. Trams clanged. Hawkers trundled barrows and pedalled their bikes, all selling done. She waved a taxi down, told him Princes Buildings in Central.

Her inner self had gone. She felt hollow, no mind to think with, nothing to gamble. No chance of new bets to restore her fortunes. Santiago was heartbreak, but the loss of gambling was more, much more.

The lights of Hong Kong glided past the taxi windows.

HC would be working still. He'd told her when he'd rung her cell phone earlier. Midnight, he had told her, come by the office as soon as the races end. There was something he wanted to say. She'd replied, with such gaiety, "And I'll have something to tell you!" Cruelly, she had taunted him by telling him where she was, at the races. She had intended to tell him how much she'd won, then say goodbye for ever.

Her bitterness focussed and held. How foolish she had been. Duped by that charlatan Santiago into believing she had sufficient money to perfect her gambling scheme! She saw quite clearly where she'd made the crucial mistake. If she'd gone it alone, she'd have won. Shortage of money had caused this. If only she'd had enough, the balance would come right.

There would be racing on Wednesday at Sha-Tin Heights. And Macao's casinos functioned for ever. All it took was one small bet. By doubling, you could recoup enough to make a flying start for really big winnings. She'd been so close. If it hadn't been for that treacherous girl who'd cheated her by telling Santiago the wrong horses . . . Or, cruellest thought, had Santiago concealed KwayFay's revelations for himself, and deliberately misled her with false information? She moaned in pain.

The driver's eyes stared knowingly in the rear-view mirror. She was his eighteenth loser this week. He wondered how long she would last before madness took over. He knew madness.

By the time they reached Central, Linda had gathered herself. Betting odds were what counted, not the motives. HC would surely have enough for her to make a new beginning. HC could always raise a loan. She would not ask much. Maybe a few hundred dollars. Okay, then, a couple of thousand, certainly not more. A new jockey was due in next week from England. Rumour said he'd ridden winners at Ascot, Newmarket. She had to be there. It was essential. How else could she win enough to pay back the money-lenders? HC would see the plight she was in, and arrange what, three thousand, maybe four? Very well, a round figure, say five thousand, a decent starting bet.

"Police ahead," the driver said. The taxi neared the end of Queensway.

Louts mugging tourists no doubt, Linda thought irritably. She told him to set her down by the Hong Kong and Shanghai Bank corner and flung him her last few dollars. Quickly she crossed the road into Statue Square. Penniless. The quicker she reached HC, the quicker she could start afresh. Even for HC she knew she must look confident, a winner. Few gamblers knew how to turn losing into winning, but she did.

The prospect ahead was filled with golden opportunities. Any gambler could see that.

She approached the building. Police and ambulances were just arriving, quickly blocking off crowds. A large blue limousine parked opposite started up and pulled away. For one mad moment she imagined she saw KwayFay's pale face in the rear window as the vehicle accelerated westwards, but that could only have been fancy. Linda resolved to have the bitch sacked.

She pushed to the front among the chattering spectators and stood staring at the scene, the scattered glass, the flashing police lights, the disordered corpse on the pavement, and looked up to identify the office from which the fool, doubtless another pathetic failure, had taken the final step of shame. What fools some people were, she thought.